SEA OF STARS

image

JASON AARON
DENNIS HALLUM
WRITERS

STEPHEN GREEN
ARTIST

RICO RENZI
COLORIST

JARED K. FLETCHER
LETTERS + DESIGN

WILL DENNIS
EDITOR

image

SEA OF STARS™, VOL. 2. First printing. December 2021. Published by Image Comics, Inc. Office of publication: PO BOX 14457, Portland, OR 97293. Copyright © 2021 Golgonooza, Inc., Dennis Hallum, and Stephen Green. All rights reserved. Contains material originally published in single magazine form as SEA OF STARS™ #6-11. SEA OF STARS™, the Sea of Stars™ logos, and the likenesses of all characters herein or hereon are trademarks of Golgonooza, Inc., Dennis Hallum, and Stephen Green, unless expressly indicated. IMAGE and the Image Comics logos are registered trademarks of Image Comics, Inc. No part of this publication may be reproduced or transmitted in any form or by any means (except for short excerpts for journalistic or review purposes), without the express written permission of Golgonooza, Inc., Dennis Hallum, Stephen Green, or Image Comics, Inc. All names, characters, events, and places herein are entirely fictional. Any resemblance to actual persons (living or dead), events, or places, without satiric intent, is coincidental. Printed in the USA. Representation: Law Offices of Harris M. Miller II, P.C. **rights.inquiries@gmail.com** ISBN: 978-1-5343-1834-2

IMAGE COMICS, INC • Todd McFarlane: President • Jim Valentino: Vice President • Marc Silvestri: Chief Executive Officer • Erik Larsen: Chief Financial Officer • Robert Kirkman: Chief Operating Officer • Eric Stephenson: Publisher / Chief Creative Officer • Nicole Lapalme: Controller • Leanna Caunter: Accounting Analyst • Sue Korpela: Accounting & HR Manager • Marla Eizik: Talent Liaison • Jeff Boison: Director of Sales & Publishing Planning • Dirk Wood: Director of International Sales & Licensing • Alex Cox: Director of Direct Market Sales • Chloe Ramos: Book Market & Library Sales Manager • Emilio Bautista: Digital Sales Coordinator • Jon Schlaffman: Specialty Sales Coordinator • Kat Salazar: Director of PR & Marketing • Drew Fitzgerald: Marketing Content Associate • Heather Doornink: Production Director • Drew Gill: Art Director • Hilary DiLoreto: Print Manager • Tricia Ramos: Traffic Manager • Melissa Gifford: Content Manager • Erika Schnatz: Senior Production Artist • Ryan Brewer: Production Artist • Deanna Phelps: Production Artist • IMAGECOMICS.COM

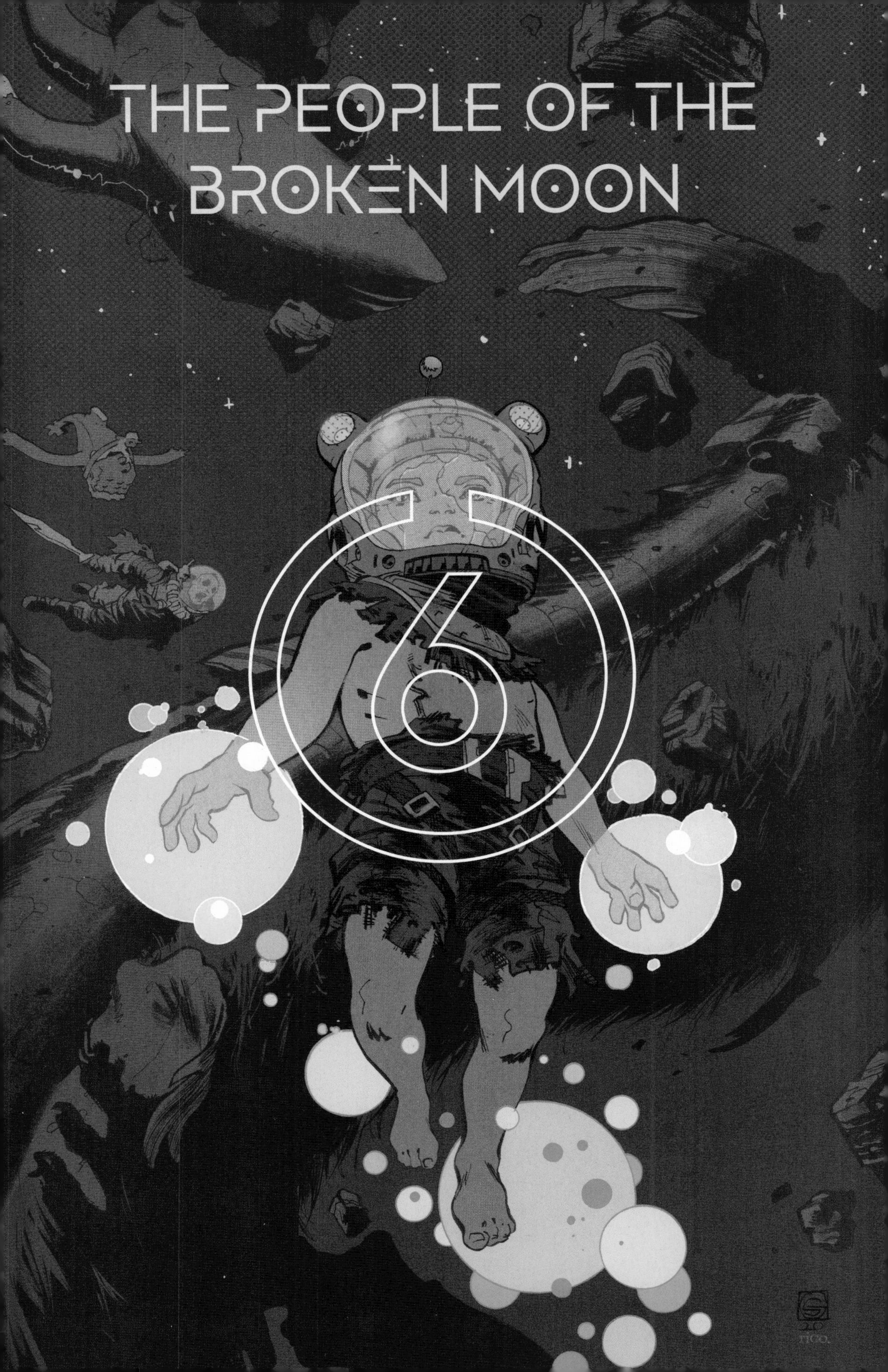
THE PEOPLE OF THE BROKEN MOON
6

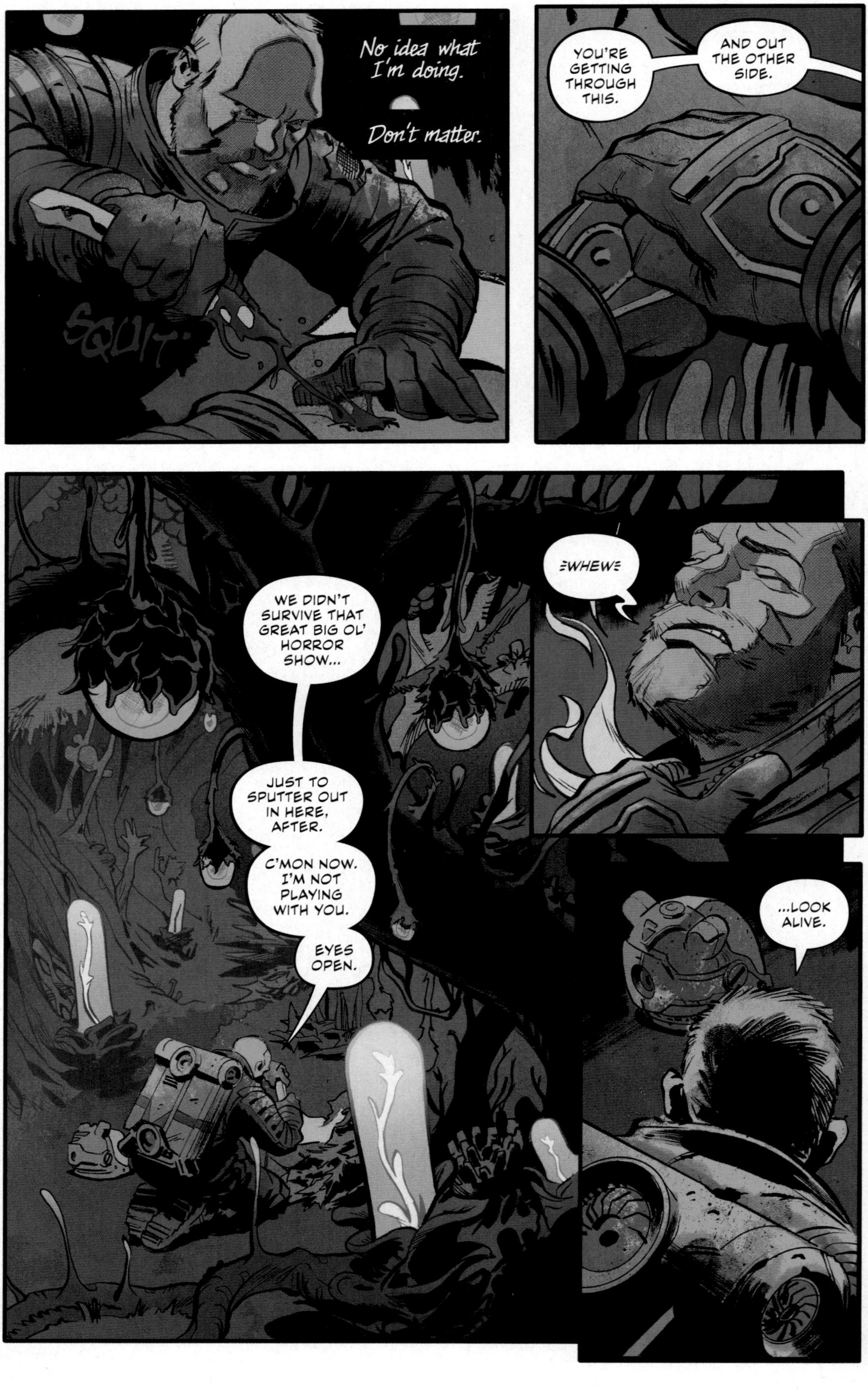
No idea what I'm doing.
Don't matter.
SQUIT
YOU'RE GETTING THROUGH THIS.
AND OUT THE OTHER SIDE.
WE DIDN'T SURVIVE THAT GREAT BIG OL' HORROR SHOW...
JUST TO SPUTTER OUT IN HERE, AFTER.
C'MON NOW. I'M NOT PLAYING WITH YOU.
EYES OPEN.
WHEW
...LOOK ALIVE.

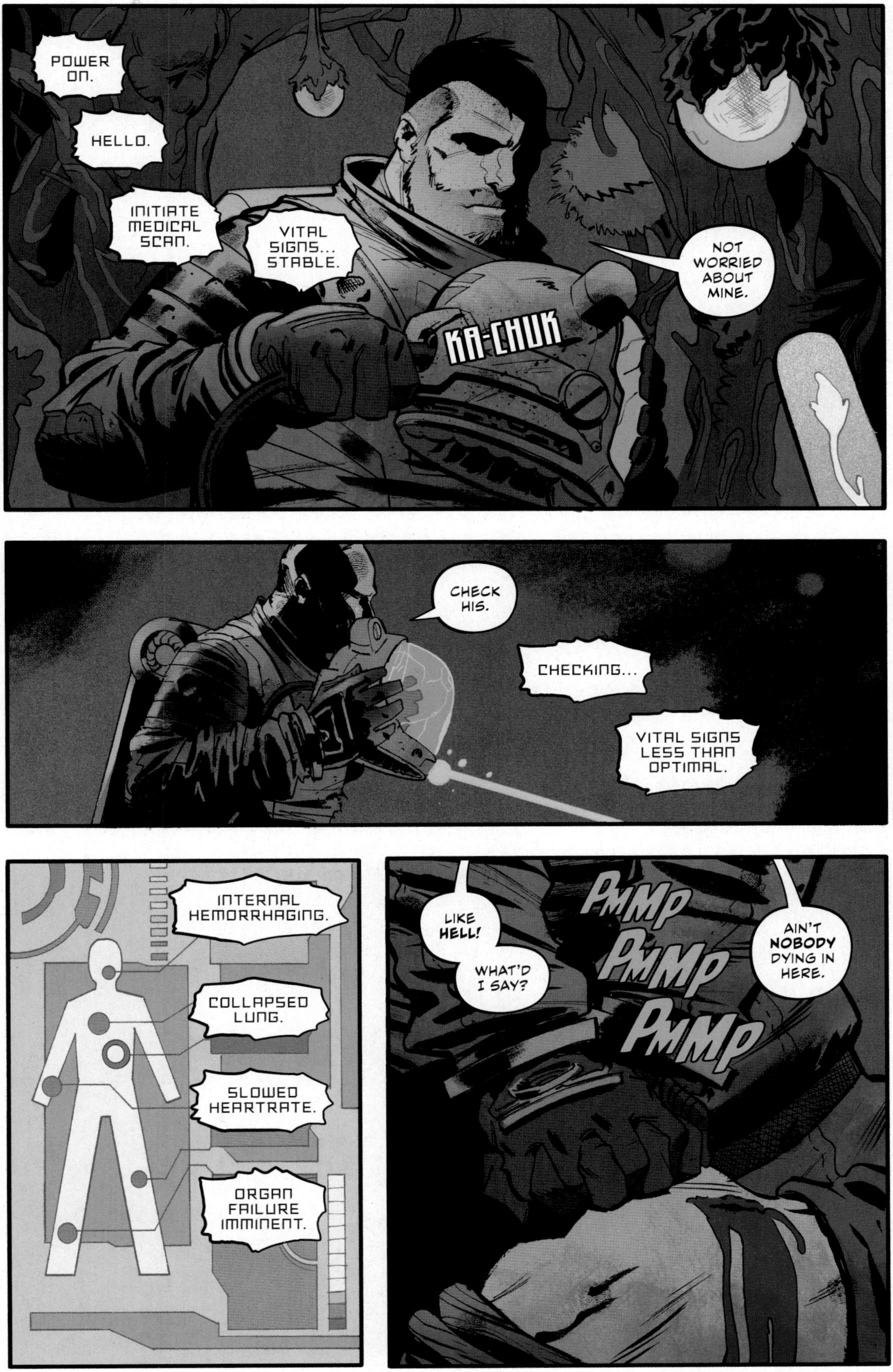
POWER ON.
HELLO.
INITIATE MEDICAL SCAN.
VITAL SIGNS... STABLE.
NOT WORRIED ABOUT MINE.
KA-CHUK
CHECK HIS.
CHECKING...
VITAL SIGNS LESS THAN OPTIMAL.
INTERNAL HEMORRHAGING.
COLLAPSED LUNG.
SLOWED HEARTRATE.
ORGAN FAILURE IMMINENT.
LIKE **HELL!**
WHAT'D I SAY?
PMMP
PMMP
PMMP
AIN'T **NOBODY** DYING IN HERE.

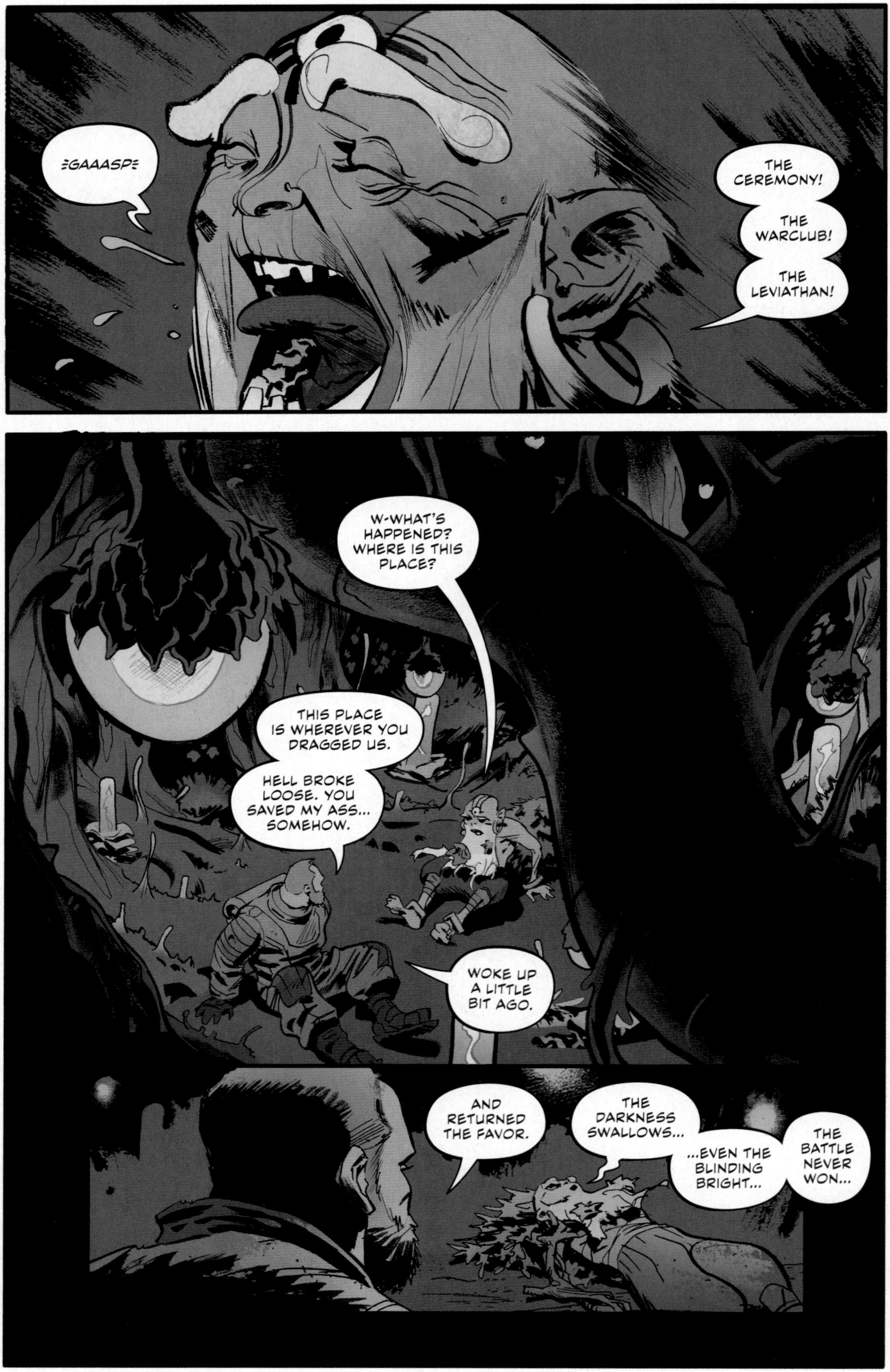

=GAAASP=
THE CEREMONY!
THE WARCLUB!
THE LEVIATHAN!
W-WHAT'S HAPPENED? WHERE IS THIS PLACE?
THIS PLACE IS WHEREVER YOU DRAGGED US.
HELL BROKE LOOSE. YOU SAVED MY ASS... SOMEHOW.
WOKE UP A LITTLE BIT AGO.
AND RETURNED THE FAVOR.
THE DARKNESS SWALLOWS...
...EVEN THE BLINDING BRIGHT...
THE BATTLE NEVER WON...

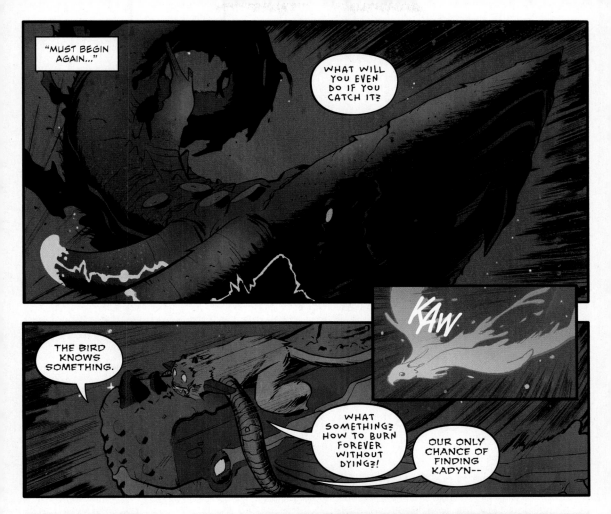

"MUST BEGIN AGAIN..."

WHAT WILL YOU EVEN DO IF YOU CATCH IT?

KAW

THE BIRD KNOWS SOMETHING.

WHAT SOMETHING? HOW TO BURN FOREVER WITHOUT DYING?!

OUR ONLY CHANCE OF FINDING KADYN--

IS A ZZAZTEK WAR SQUAL?! DO YOU HEAR YOURSELF?!

THAT THING CHOKES OUT WORDS LIKE IT'S GAGGING! WHAT COULD IT TELL US?

YOU HAVE A BETTER IDEA?

YES!

DON'T DIE SPLAYED OPEN ON AN ICE-TEROID WITH OUR SIZZLING GUTS PECKED OUT--

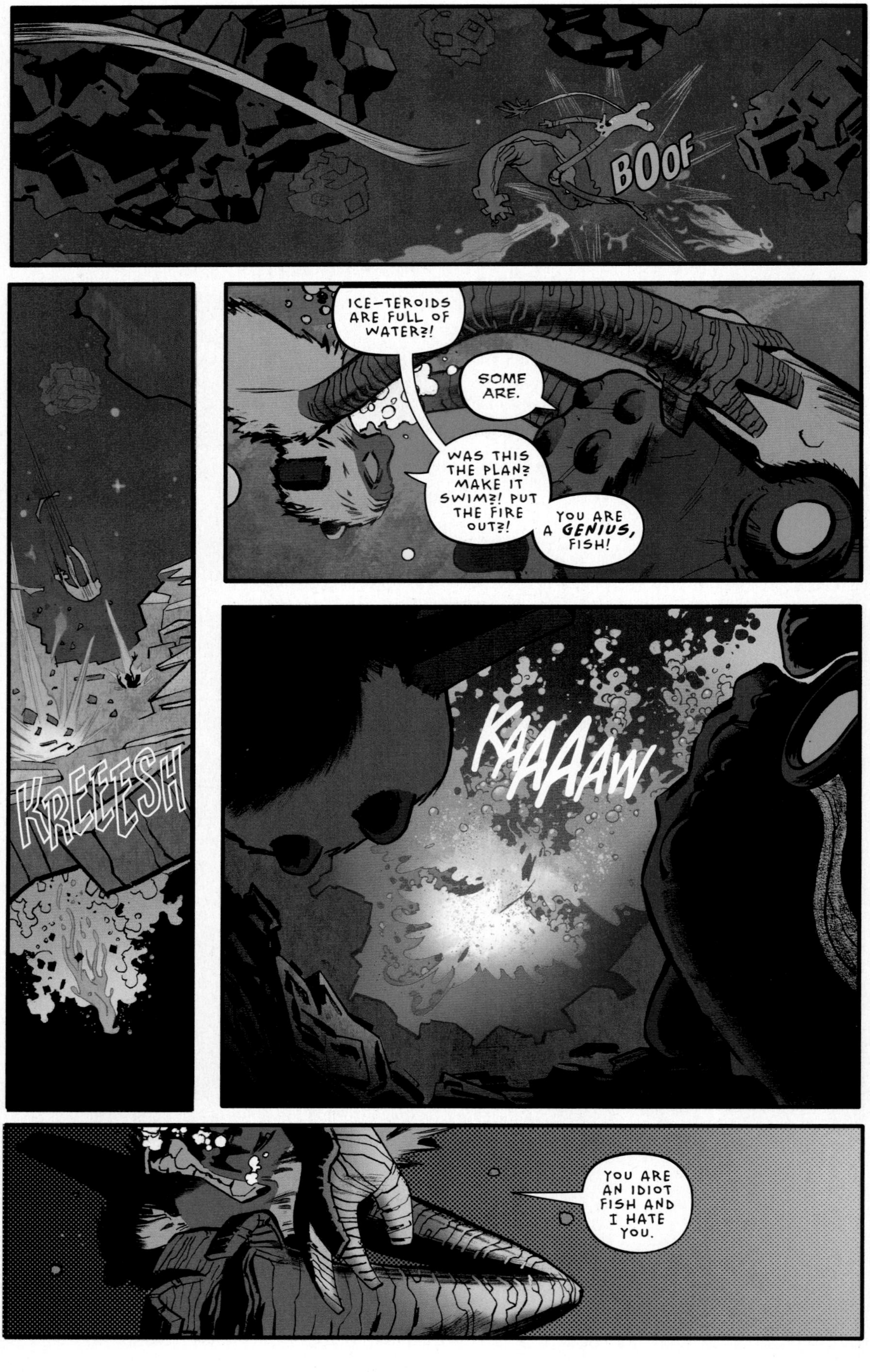
BOOF
KREEESH
ICE-TEROIDS ARE FULL OF WATER?!
SOME ARE.
WAS THIS THE PLAN? MAKE IT SWIM?! PUT THE FIRE OUT?!
YOU ARE A *GENIUS,* FISH!
KAAAAAW
YOU ARE AN IDIOT FISH AND I HATE YOU.

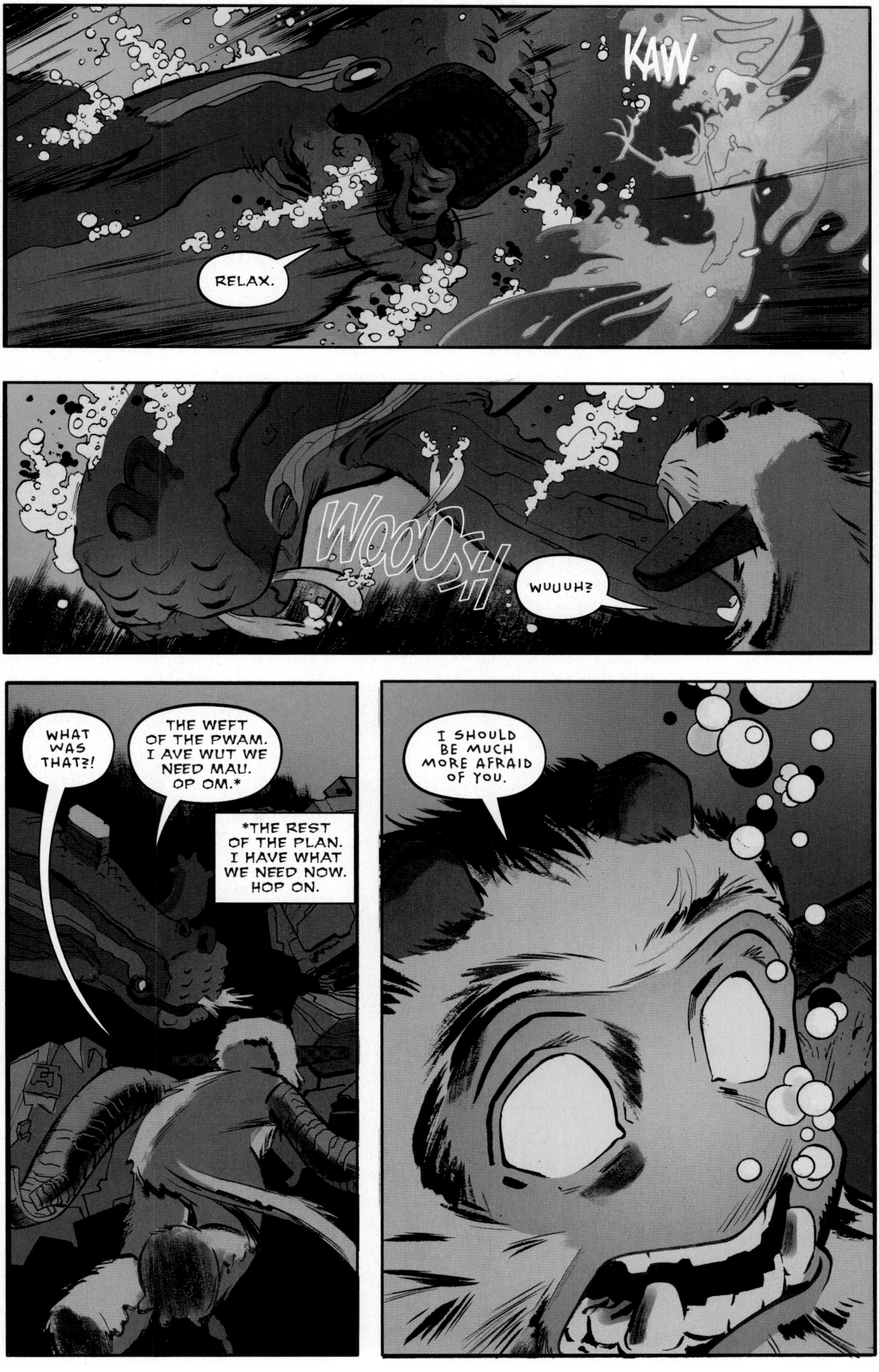
KAW
RELAX.
WOOOSH
WUUUH?
WHAT WAS THAT?!
THE WEFT OF THE PWAM. I AVE WUT WE NEED MAU. OP OM.*
*THE REST OF THE PLAN. I HAVE WHAT WE NEED NOW. HOP ON.
I SHOULD BE MUCH MORE AFRAID OF YOU.

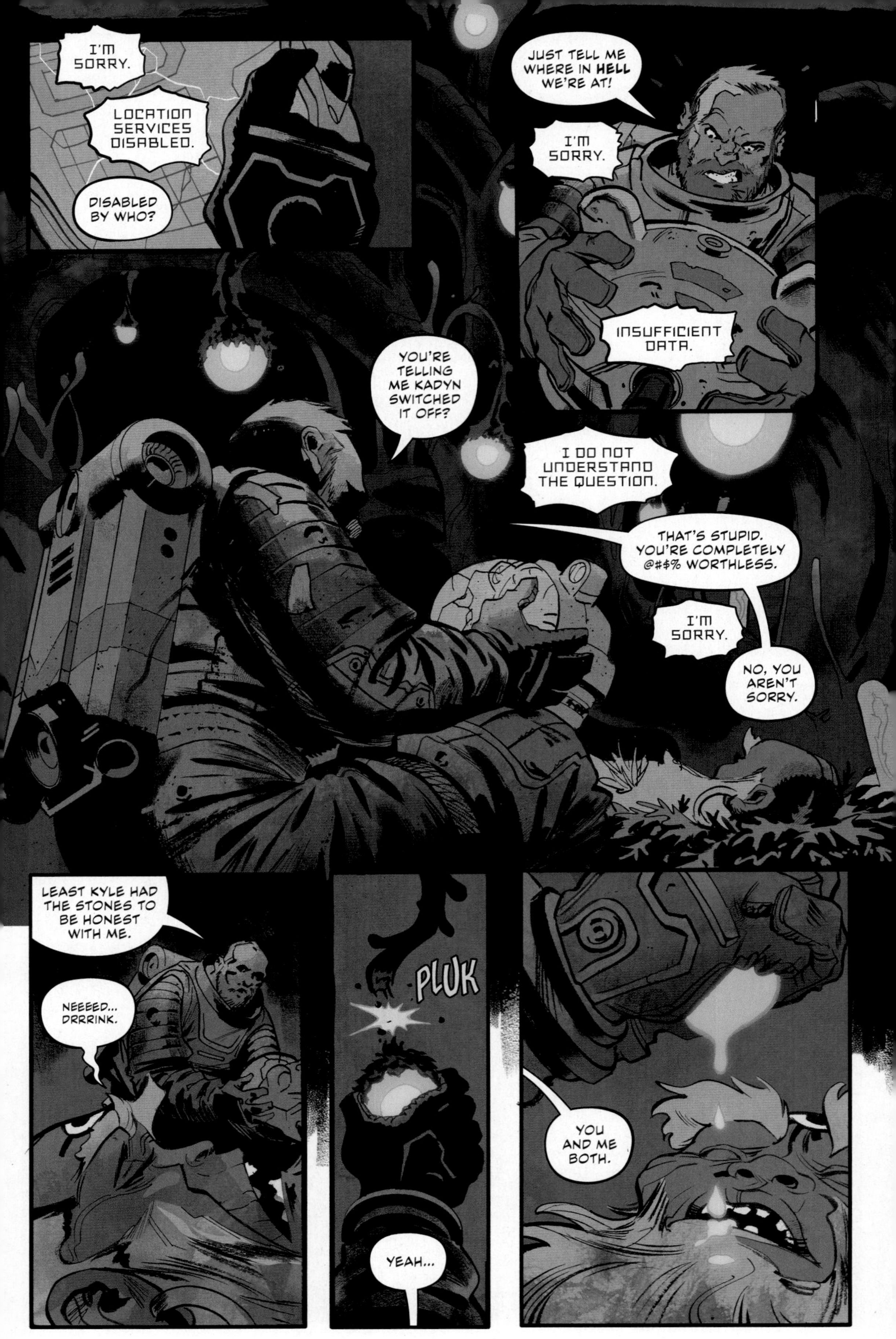
I'M SORRY.
LOCATION SERVICES DISABLED.
DISABLED BY WHO?
JUST TELL ME WHERE IN HELL WE'RE AT!
I'M SORRY.
INSUFFICIENT DATA.
YOU'RE TELLING ME KADYN SWITCHED IT OFF?
I DO NOT UNDERSTAND THE QUESTION.
THAT'S STUPID. YOU'RE COMPLETELY @#$% WORTHLESS.
I'M SORRY.
NO, YOU AREN'T SORRY.
LEAST KYLE HAD THE STONES TO BE HONEST WITH ME.
NEEEED... DRRRINK.
PLUK
YEAH...
YOU AND ME BOTH.

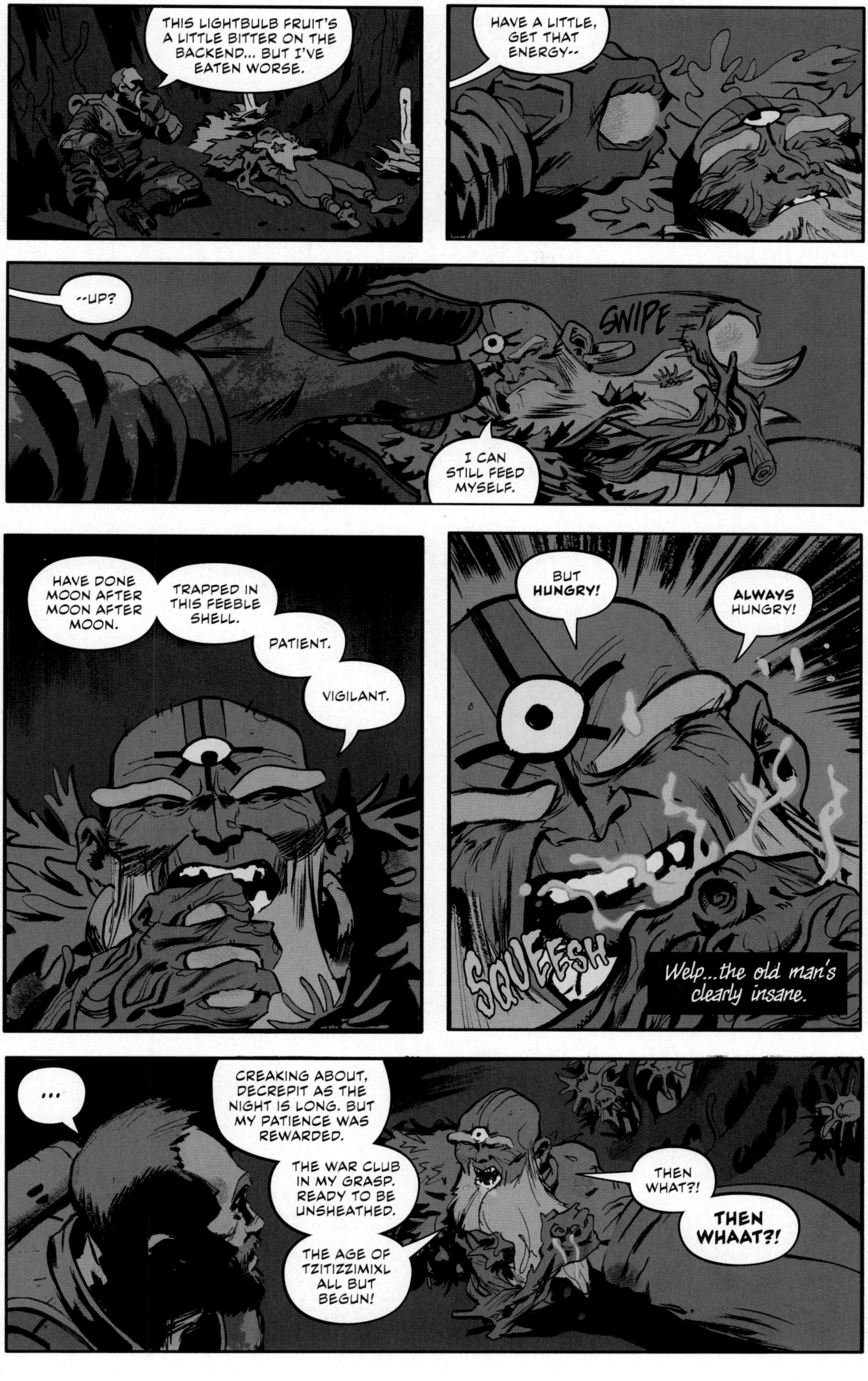
THIS LIGHTBULB FRUIT'S A LITTLE BITTER ON THE BACKEND... BUT I'VE EATEN WORSE.
HAVE A LITTLE, GET THAT ENERGY--
--UP?
SWIPE
I CAN STILL FEED MYSELF.
HAVE DONE MOON AFTER MOON AFTER MOON.
TRAPPED IN THIS FEEBLE SHELL.
PATIENT.
VIGILANT.
BUT HUNGRY!
ALWAYS HUNGRY!
SQUEESH
Welp...the old man's clearly insane.
...
CREAKING ABOUT, DECREPIT AS THE NIGHT IS LONG. BUT MY PATIENCE WAS REWARDED.
THE WAR CLUB IN MY GRASP. READY TO BE UNSHEATHED.
THE AGE OF TZITIZZIMIXL ALL BUT BEGUN!
THEN WHAT?!
THEN WHAAT?!

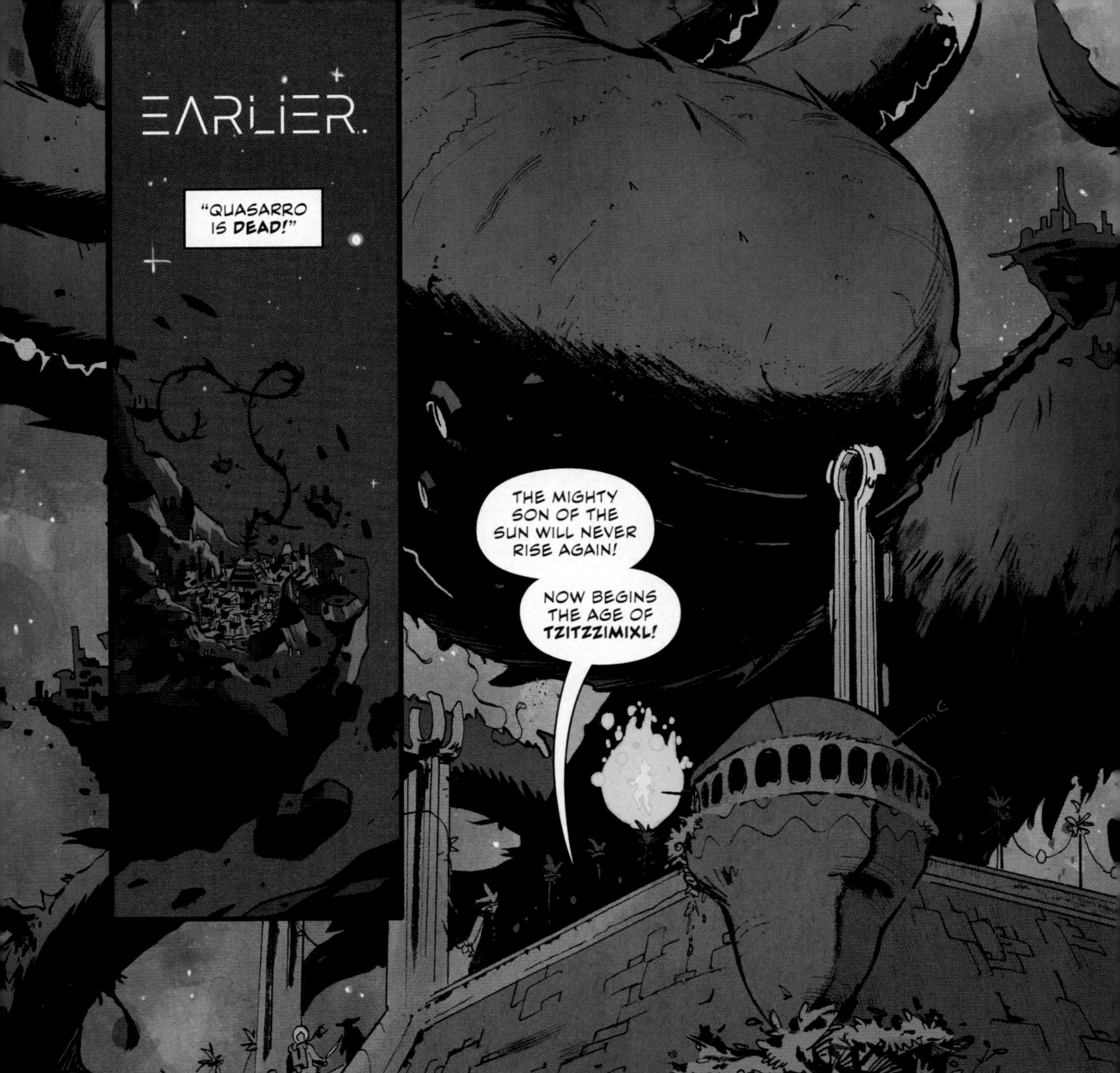
EARLIER.
"QUASARRO IS DEAD!"
THE MIGHTY SON OF THE SUN WILL NEVER RISE AGAIN!
NOW BEGINS THE AGE OF TZITZZIMIXL!

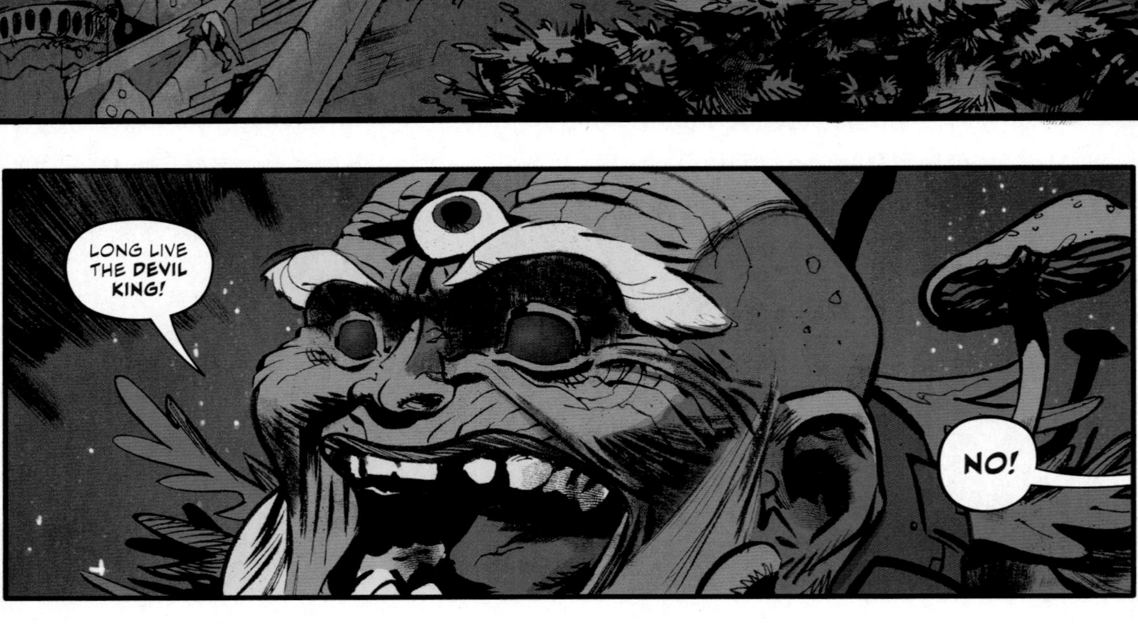
LONG LIVE THE DEVIL KING!
NO!

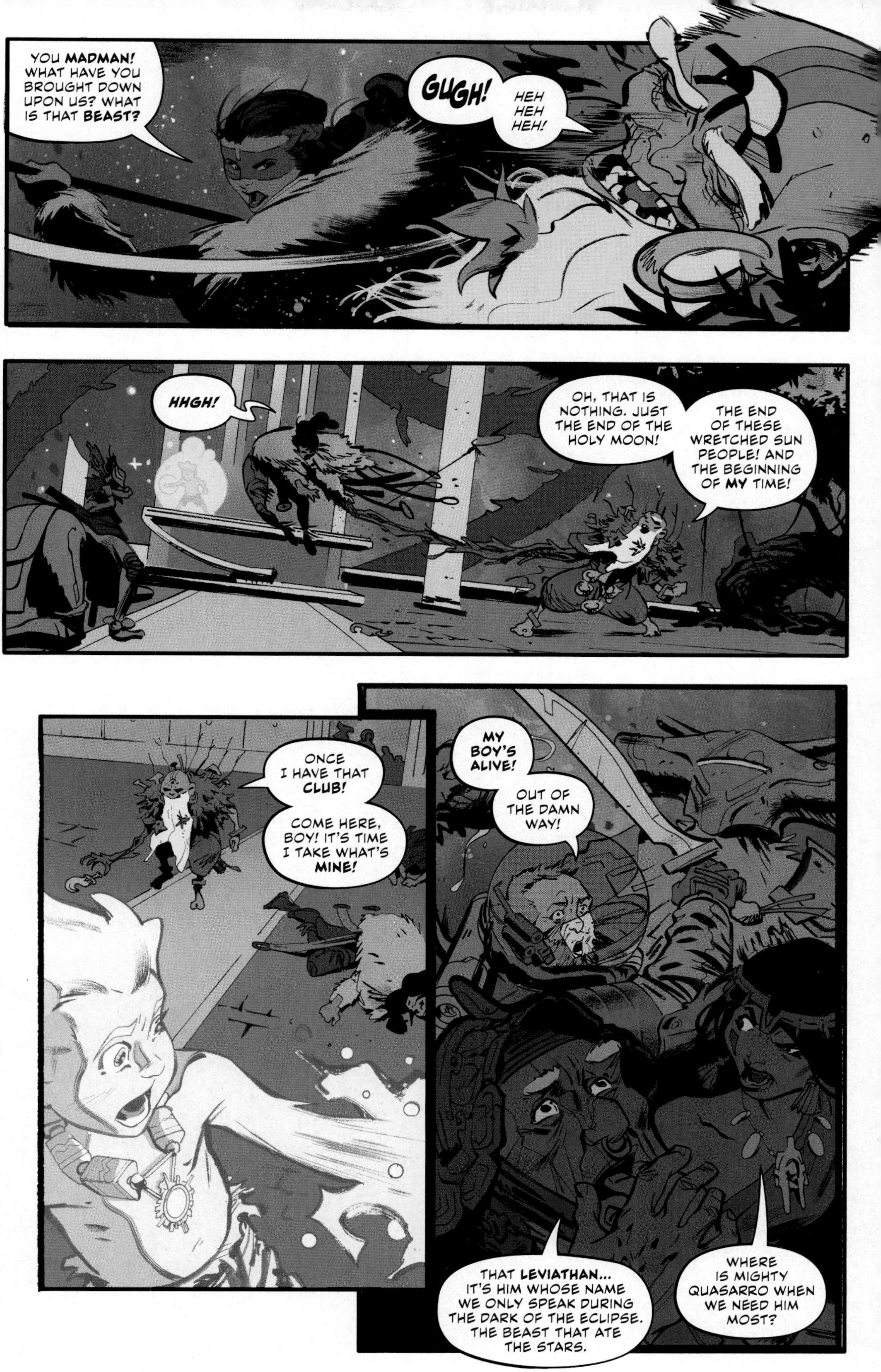
YOU MADMAN! WHAT HAVE YOU BROUGHT DOWN UPON US? WHAT IS THAT BEAST?
GUGH!
HEH HEH HEH!
HHGH!
OH, THAT IS NOTHING. JUST THE END OF THE HOLY MOON!
THE END OF THESE WRETCHED SUN PEOPLE! AND THE BEGINNING OF MY TIME!
ONCE I HAVE THAT CLUB!
COME HERE, BOY! IT'S TIME I TAKE WHAT'S MINE!
MY BOY'S ALIVE!
OUT OF THE DAMN WAY!
THAT LEVIATHAN... IT'S HIM WHOSE NAME WE ONLY SPEAK DURING THE DARK OF THE ECLIPSE. THE BEAST THAT ATE THE STARS.
WHERE IS MIGHTY QUASARRO WHEN WE NEED HIM MOST?

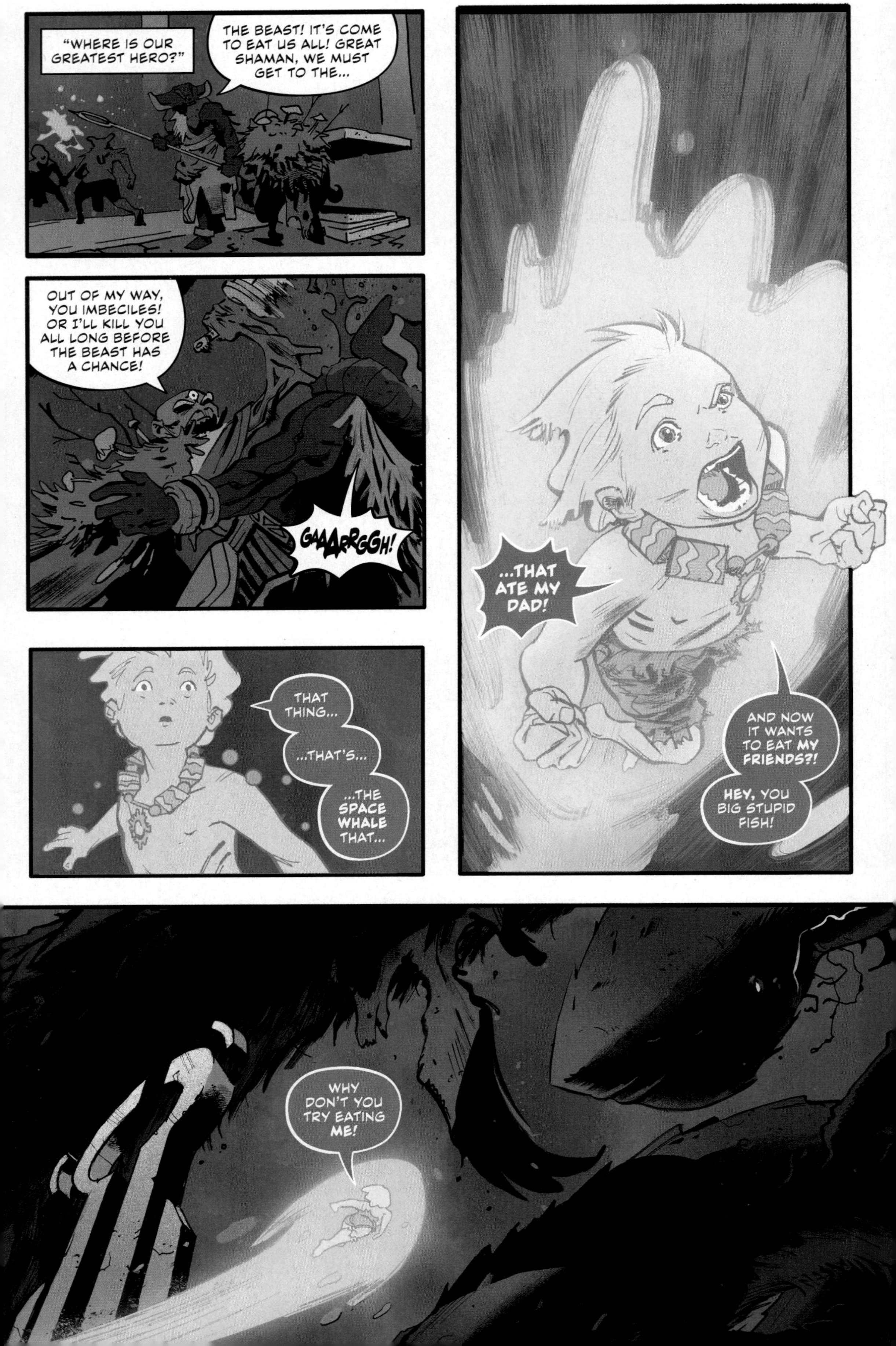
"WHERE IS OUR GREATEST HERO?"
THE BEAST! IT'S COME TO EAT US ALL! GREAT SHAMAN, WE MUST GET TO THE...
OUT OF MY WAY, YOU IMBECILES! OR I'LL KILL YOU ALL LONG BEFORE THE BEAST HAS A CHANCE!
GAAARRGGH!
THAT THING...
...THAT'S...
...THE SPACE WHALE THAT...
...THAT ATE MY DAD!
AND NOW IT WANTS TO EAT MY FRIENDS?!
HEY, YOU BIG STUPID FISH!
WHY DON'T YOU TRY EATING ME!

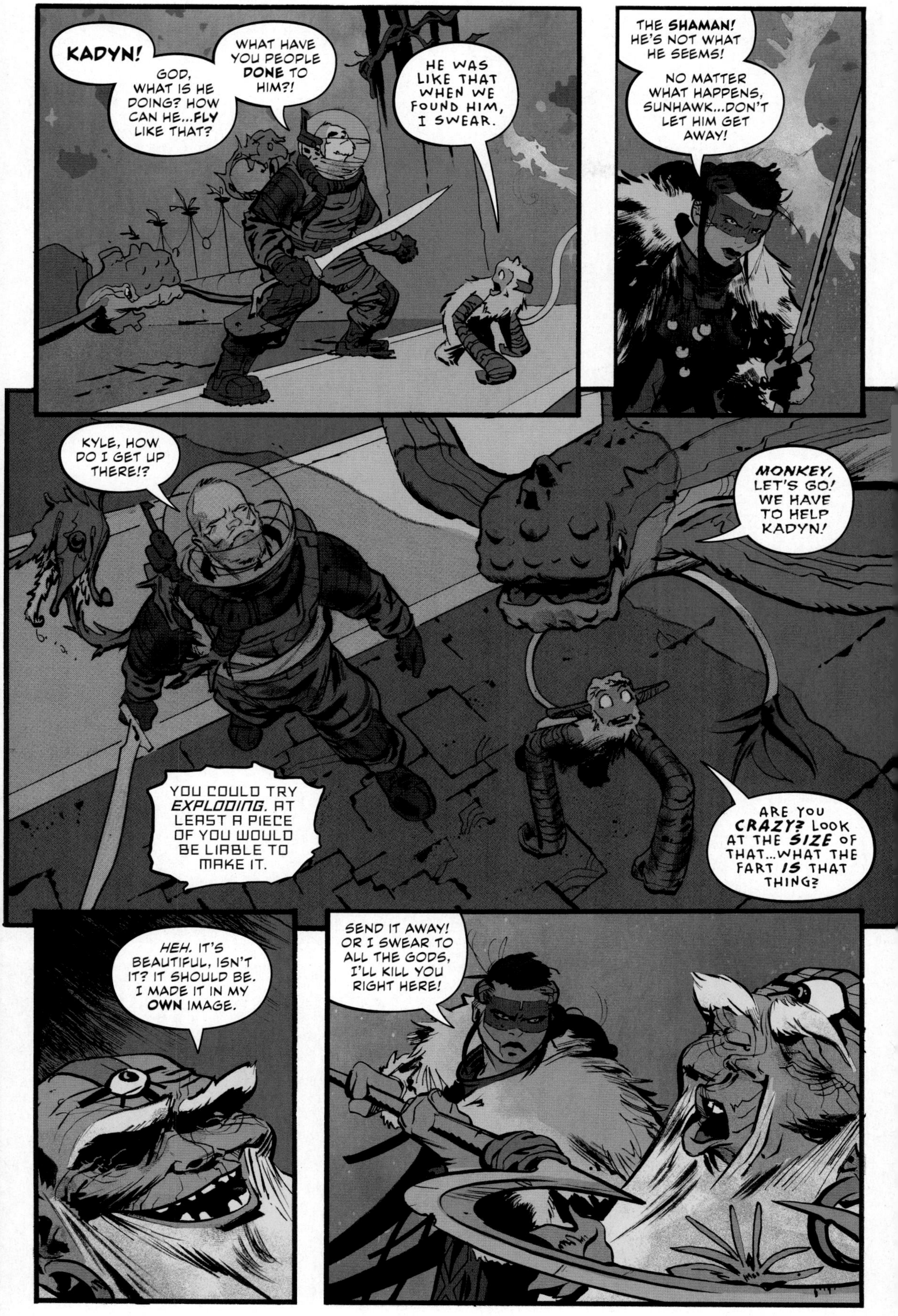
KADYN!
GOD, WHAT IS HE DOING? HOW CAN HE...FLY LIKE THAT?
WHAT HAVE YOU PEOPLE DONE TO HIM?!
HE WAS LIKE THAT WHEN WE FOUND HIM, I SWEAR.
THE SHAMAN! HE'S NOT WHAT HE SEEMS!
NO MATTER WHAT HAPPENS, SUNHAWK...DON'T LET HIM GET AWAY!
KYLE, HOW DO I GET UP THERE!?
MONKEY, LET'S GO! WE HAVE TO HELP KADYN!
YOU COULD TRY EXPLODING. AT LEAST A PIECE OF YOU WOULD BE LIABLE TO MAKE IT.
ARE YOU CRAZY? LOOK AT THE SIZE OF THAT...WHAT THE FART IS THAT THING?
HEH. IT'S BEAUTIFUL, ISN'T IT? IT SHOULD BE. I MADE IT IN MY OWN IMAGE.
SEND IT AWAY! OR I SWEAR TO ALL THE GODS, I'LL KILL YOU RIGHT HERE!

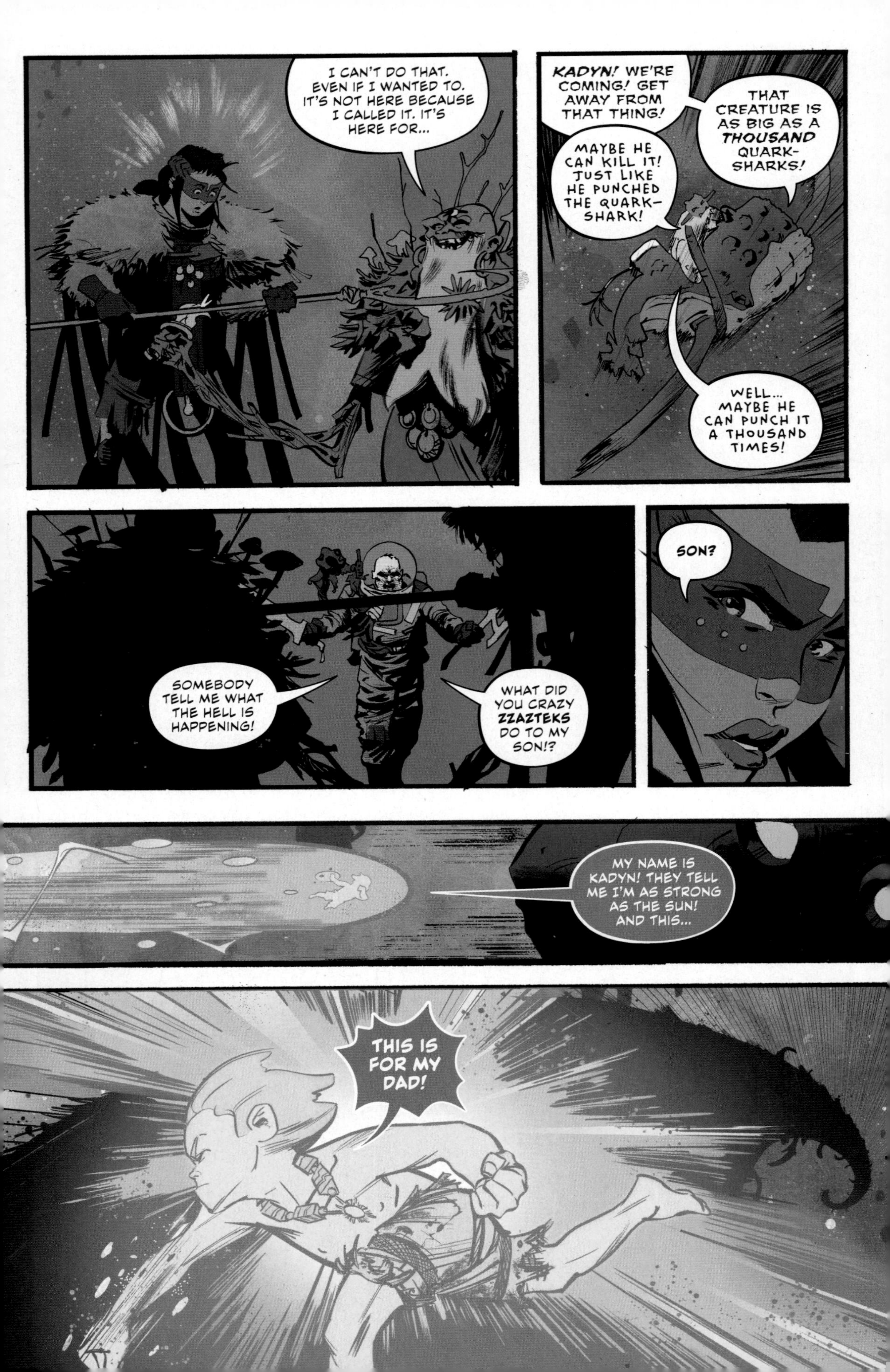
I CAN'T DO THAT. EVEN IF I WANTED TO. IT'S NOT HERE BECAUSE I CALLED IT. IT'S HERE FOR...
KADYN! WE'RE COMING! GET AWAY FROM THAT THING!
THAT CREATURE IS AS BIG AS A THOUSAND QUARK-SHARKS!
MAYBE HE CAN KILL IT! JUST LIKE HE PUNCHED THE QUARK-SHARK!
WELL... MAYBE HE CAN PUNCH IT A THOUSAND TIMES!
SOMEBODY TELL ME WHAT THE HELL IS HAPPENING!
WHAT DID YOU CRAZY ZZAZTEKS DO TO MY SON!?
SON?
MY NAME IS KADYN! THEY TELL ME I'M AS STRONG AS THE SUN! AND THIS...
THIS IS FOR MY DAD!

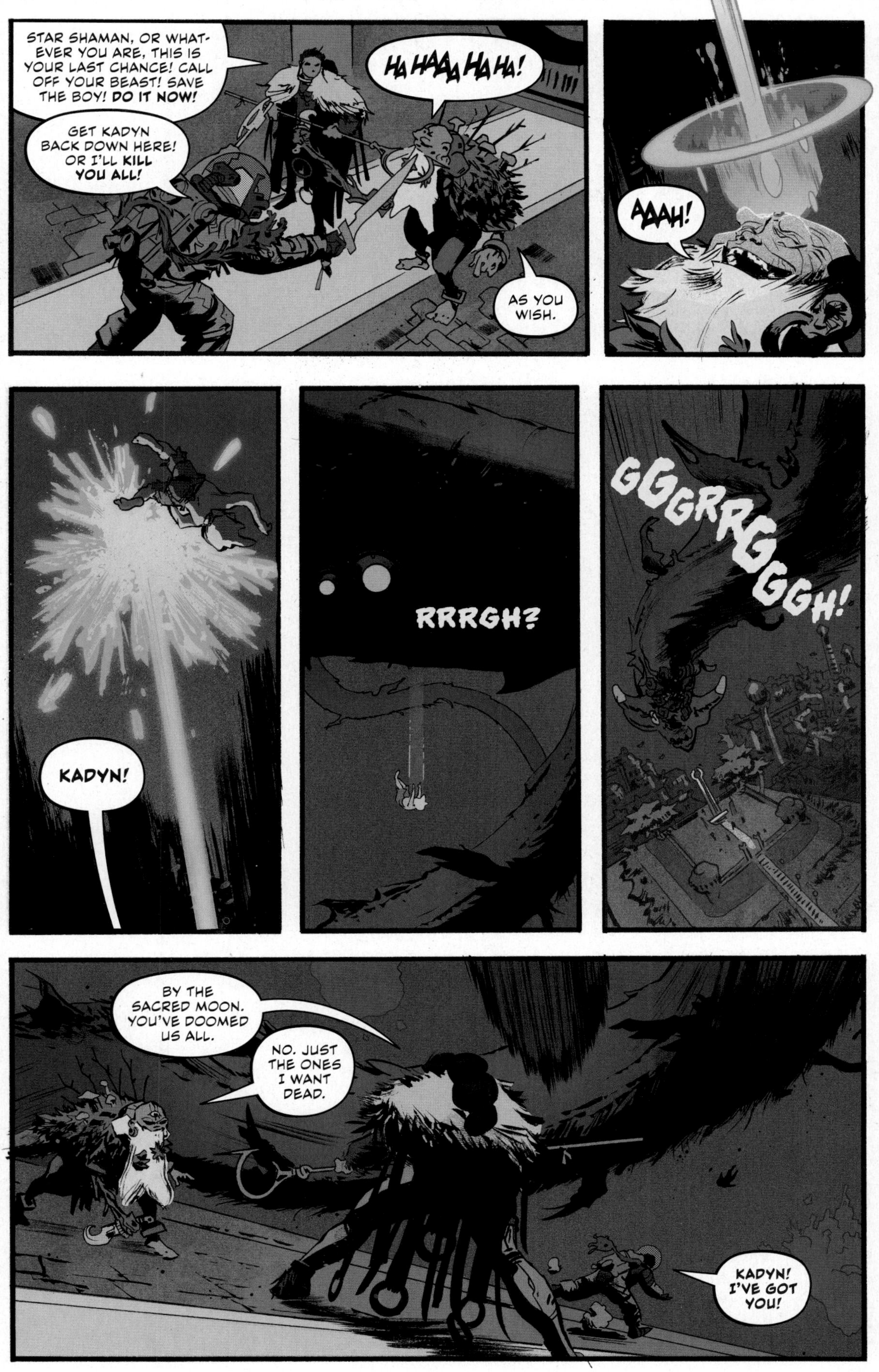
STAR SHAMAN, OR WHATEVER YOU ARE, THIS IS YOUR LAST CHANCE! CALL OFF YOUR BEAST! SAVE THE BOY! DO IT NOW!
GET KADYN BACK DOWN HERE! OR I'LL KILL YOU ALL!
HA HAAAA HA HA!
AS YOU WISH.
AAAH!
KADYN!
RRRGH?
GGGRRRGGGH!
BY THE SACRED MOON. YOU'VE DOOMED US ALL.
NO. JUST THE ONES I WANT DEAD.
KADYN! I'VE GOT YOU!

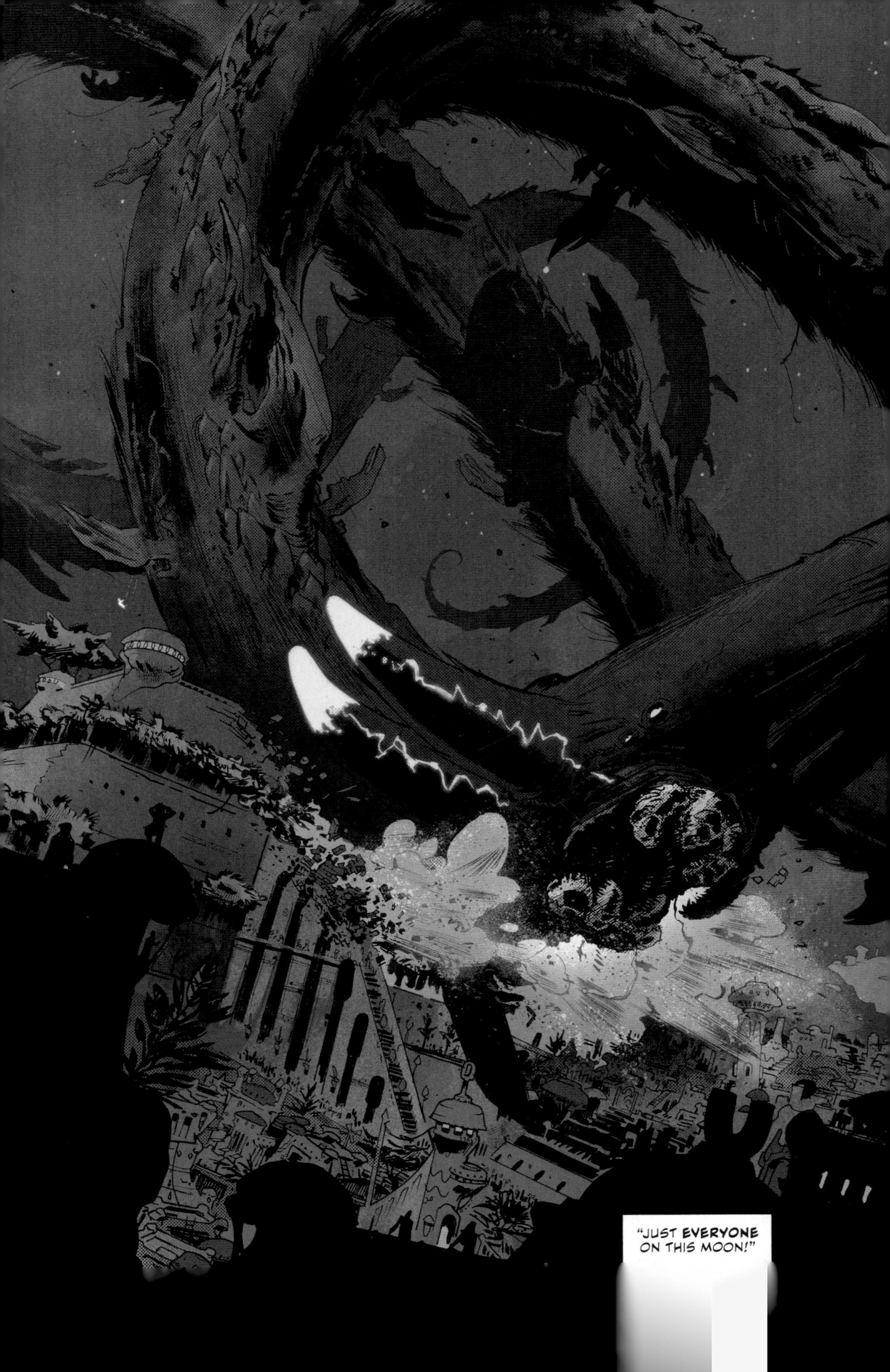
"JUST EVERYONE ON THIS MOON!"

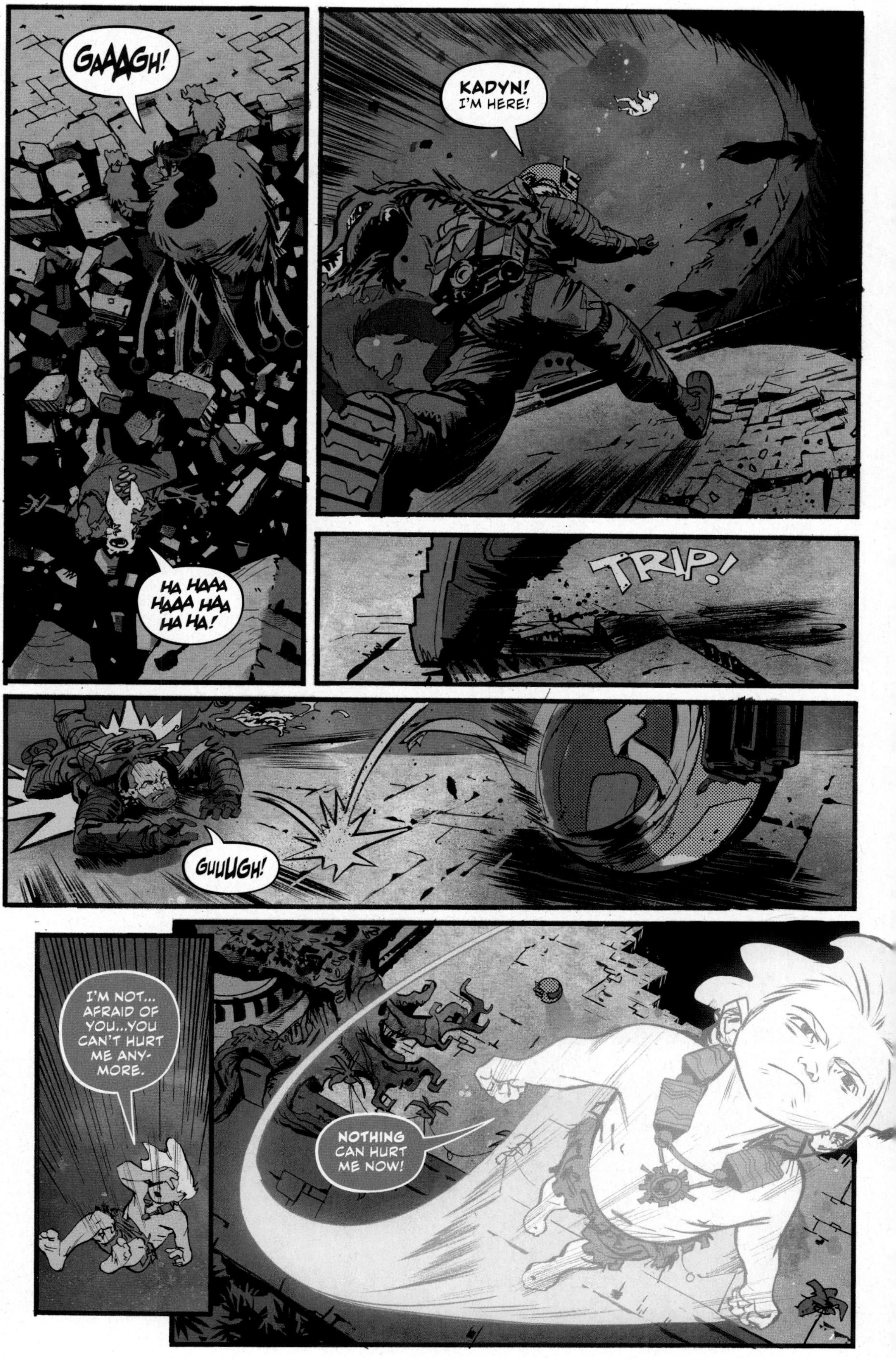
GAAAGH!
HA HAAA HAAA HAA HA HA!
KADYN! I'M HERE!
TRIP!
GUUUGH!
I'M NOT... AFRAID OF YOU...YOU CAN'T HURT ME ANY-MORE.
NOTHING CAN HURT ME NOW!

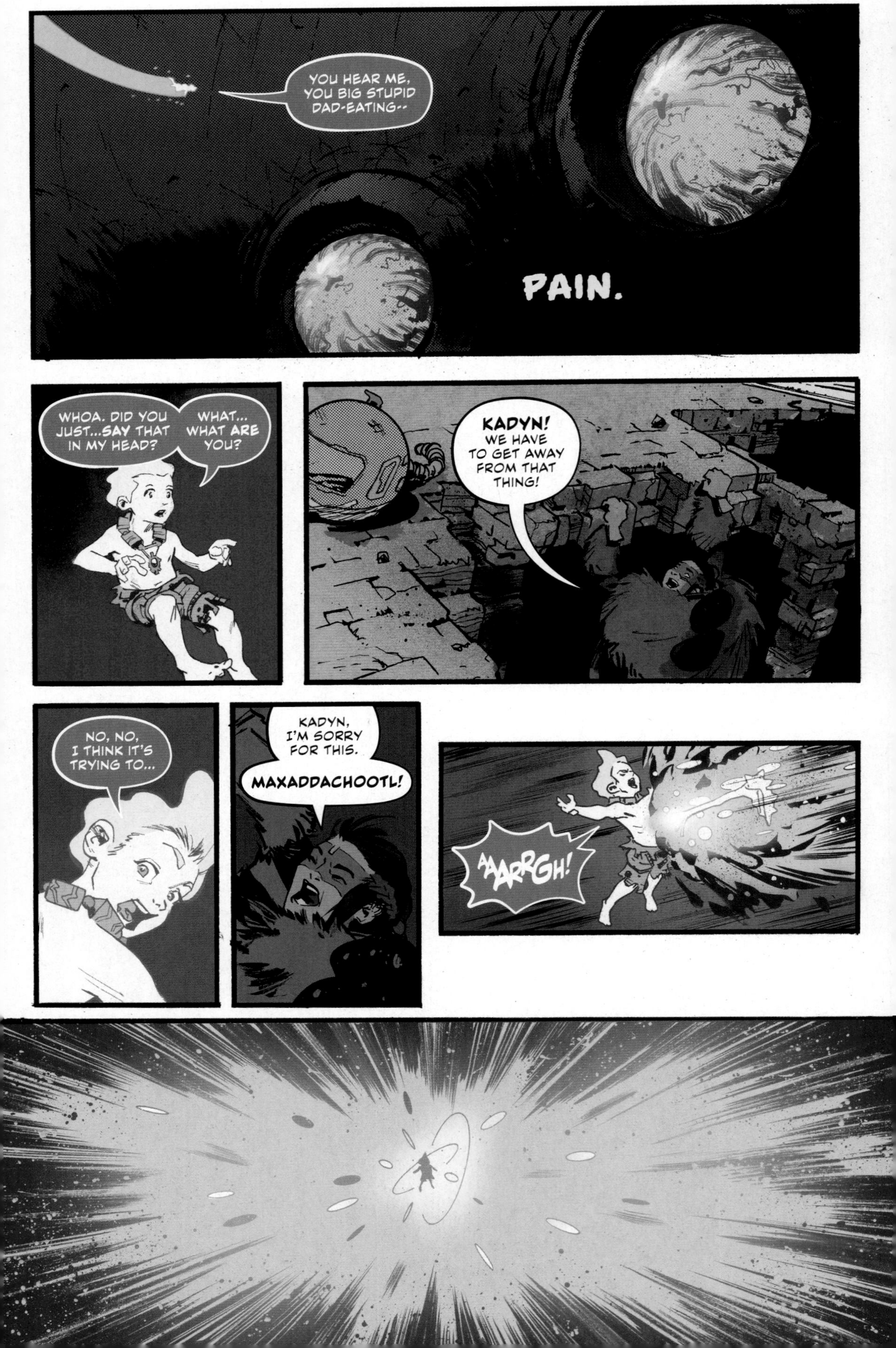
YOU HEAR ME, YOU BIG STUPID DAD-EATING--
PAIN.
WHOA. DID YOU JUST...SAY THAT IN MY HEAD?
WHAT... WHAT ARE YOU?
KADYN! WE HAVE TO GET AWAY FROM THAT THING!
NO, NO, I THINK IT'S TRYING TO...
KADYN, I'M SORRY FOR THIS.
MAXADDACHOOTL!
AAARRGH!

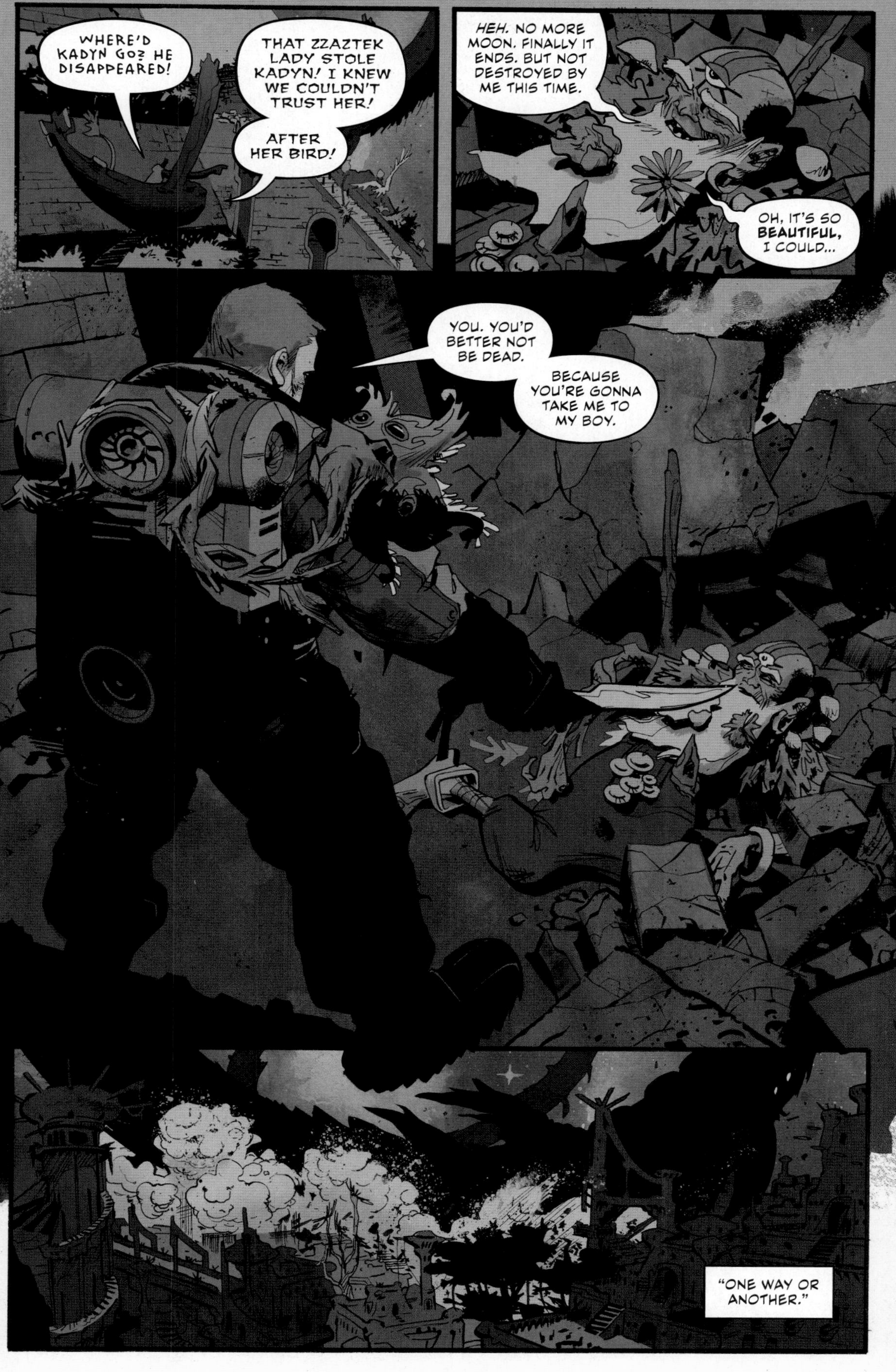

WHERE'D KADYN GO? HE DISAPPEARED!
THAT ZZAZTEK LADY STOLE KADYN! I KNEW WE COULDN'T TRUST HER!
AFTER HER BIRD!
HEH. NO MORE MOON. FINALLY IT ENDS. BUT NOT DESTROYED BY ME THIS TIME.
OH, IT'S SO BEAUTIFUL, I COULD...
YOU. YOU'D BETTER NOT BE DEAD.
BECAUSE YOU'RE GONNA TAKE ME TO MY BOY.
"ONE WAY OR ANOTHER."

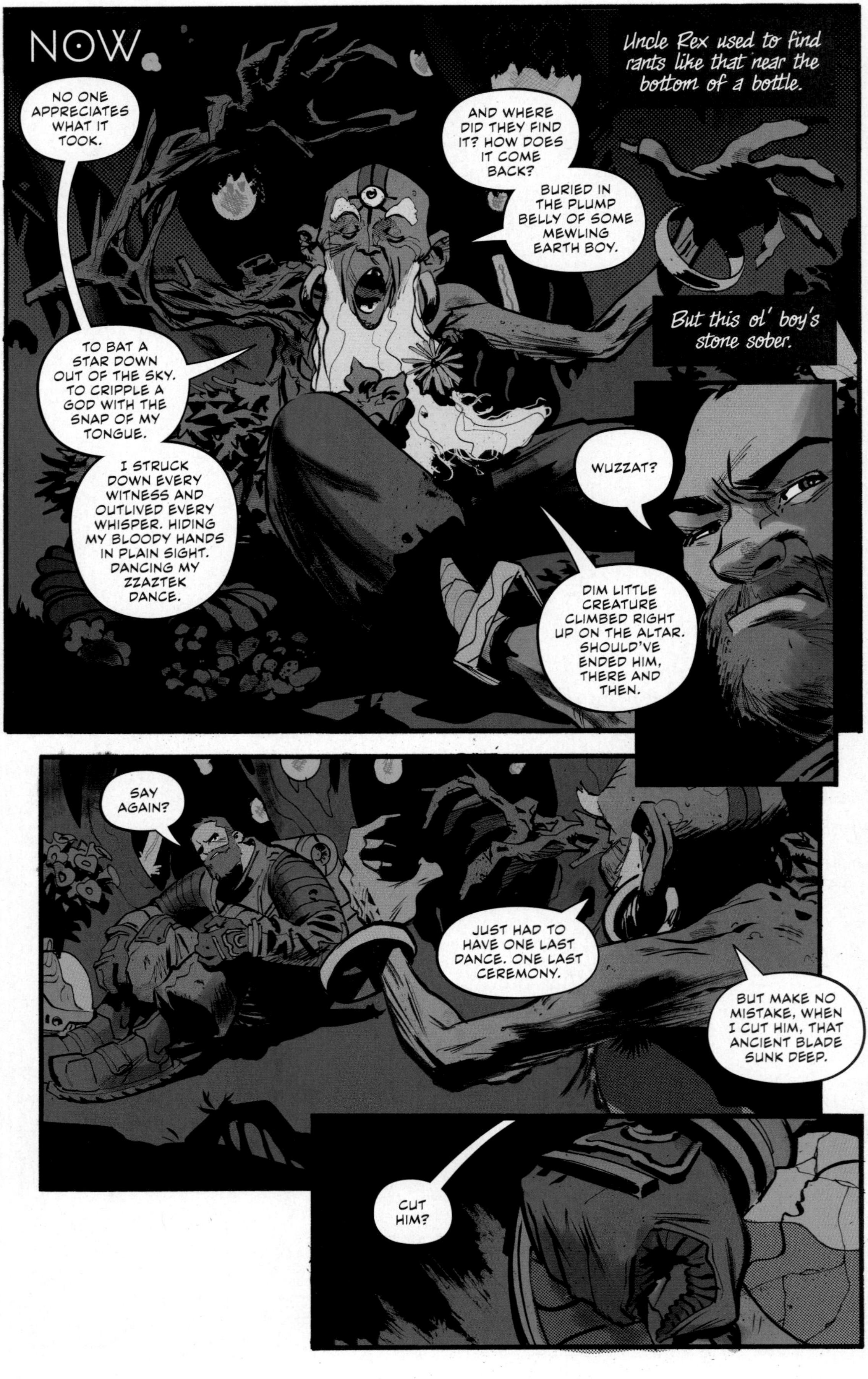
NOW
Uncle Rex used to find rants like that near the bottom of a bottle.
NO ONE APPRECIATES WHAT IT TOOK.
AND WHERE DID THEY FIND IT? HOW DOES IT COME BACK?
BURIED IN THE PLUMP BELLY OF SOME MEWLING EARTH BOY.
But this ol' boy's stone sober.
TO BAT A STAR DOWN OUT OF THE SKY. TO CRIPPLE A GOD WITH THE SNAP OF MY TONGUE.
I STRUCK DOWN EVERY WITNESS AND OUTLIVED EVERY WHISPER. HIDING MY BLOODY HANDS IN PLAIN SIGHT. DANCING MY ZZAZTEK DANCE.
WUZZAT?
DIM LITTLE CREATURE CLIMBED RIGHT UP ON THE ALTAR. SHOULD'VE ENDED HIM, THERE AND THEN.
SAY AGAIN?
JUST HAD TO HAVE ONE LAST DANCE. ONE LAST CEREMONY.
BUT MAKE NO MISTAKE, WHEN I CUT HIM, THAT ANCIENT BLADE SUNK DEEP.
CUT HIM?

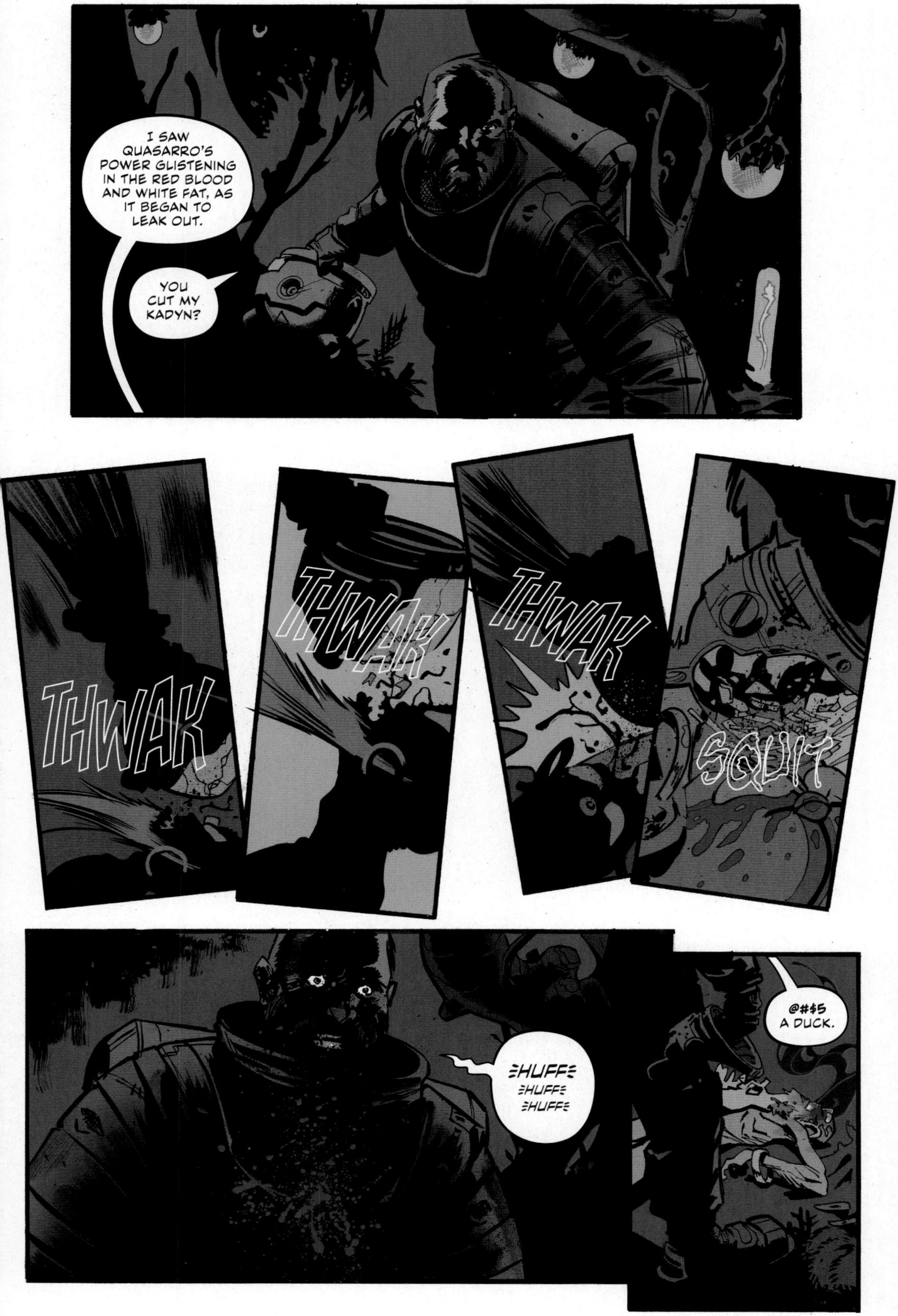
I SAW QUASARRO'S POWER GLISTENING IN THE RED BLOOD AND WHITE FAT, AS IT BEGAN TO LEAK OUT.
YOU CUT MY KADYN?
THWAK
THWAK
THWAK
SQUIT
HUFF HUFF HUFF
@#$5 A DUCK.

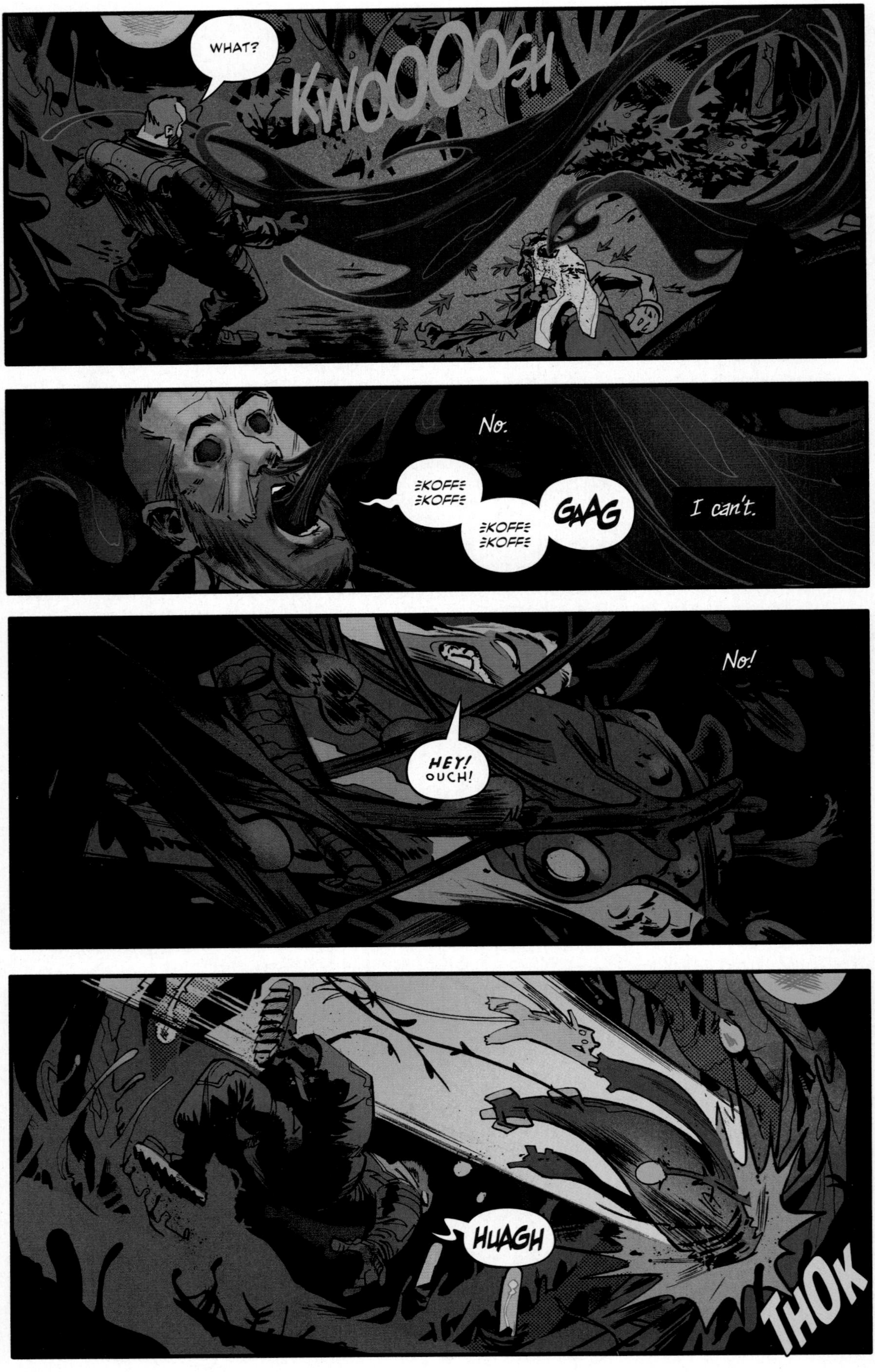
WHAT?
KWOOOOSH
No.
KOFF KOFF
KOFF KOFF
GAAG
I can't.
No!
HEY! OUCH!
HUAGH
THOK

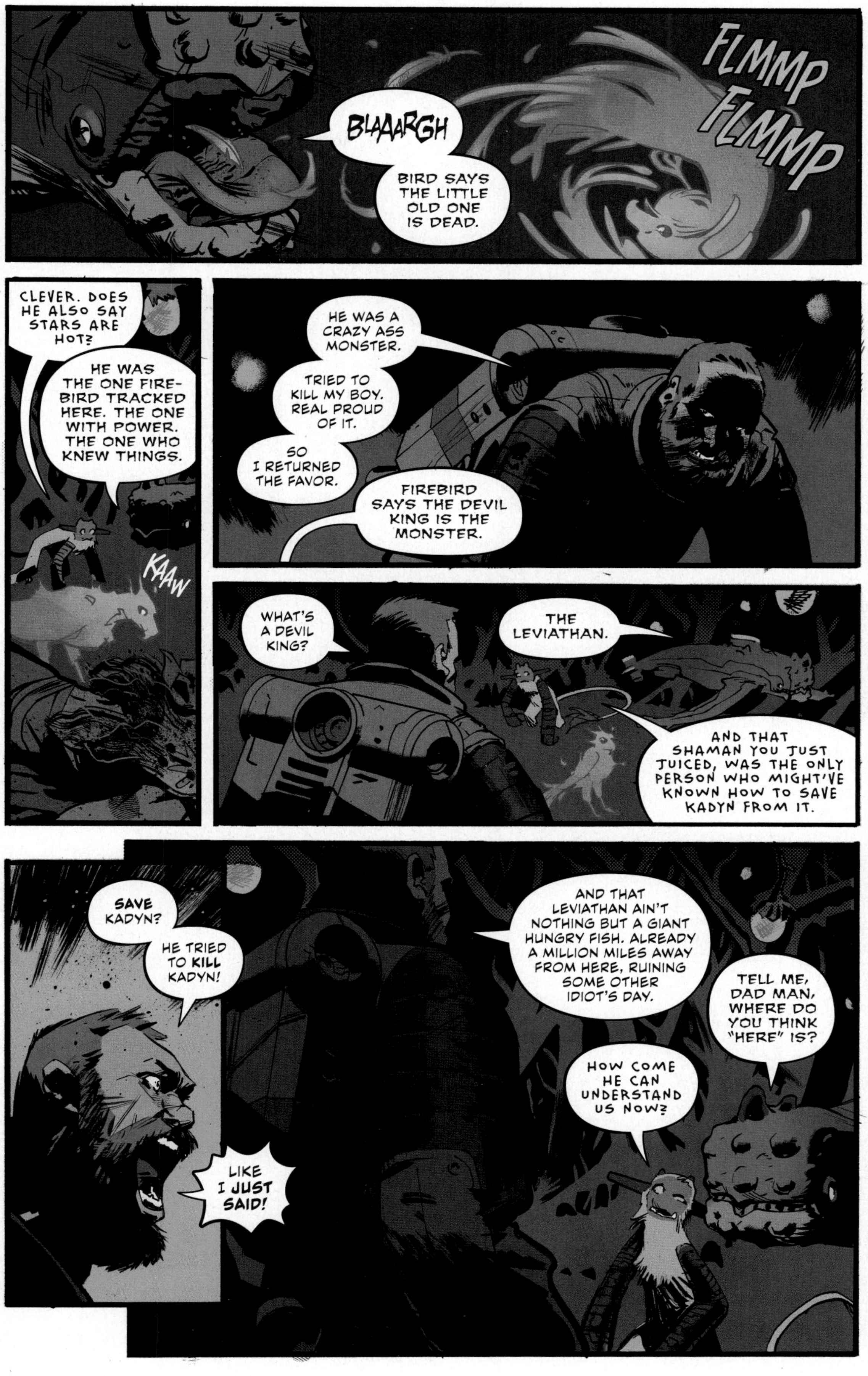
FLMMP FLMMP
BLAAARGH
BIRD SAYS THE LITTLE OLD ONE IS DEAD.
CLEVER. DOES HE ALSO SAY STARS ARE HOT?
HE WAS THE ONE FIRE-BIRD TRACKED HERE. THE ONE WITH POWER. THE ONE WHO KNEW THINGS.
KAAW
HE WAS A CRAZY ASS MONSTER.
TRIED TO KILL MY BOY. REAL PROUD OF IT.
SO I RETURNED THE FAVOR.
FIREBIRD SAYS THE DEVIL KING IS THE MONSTER.
WHAT'S A DEVIL KING?
THE LEVIATHAN.
AND THAT SHAMAN YOU JUST JUICED, WAS THE ONLY PERSON WHO MIGHT'VE KNOWN HOW TO SAVE KADYN FROM IT.
SAVE KADYN?
HE TRIED TO KILL KADYN!
LIKE I JUST SAID!
AND THAT LEVIATHAN AIN'T NOTHING BUT A GIANT HUNGRY FISH. ALREADY A MILLION MILES AWAY FROM HERE, RUINING SOME OTHER IDIOT'S DAY.
TELL ME, DAD MAN, WHERE DO YOU THINK "HERE" IS?
HOW COME HE CAN UNDERSTAND US NOW?

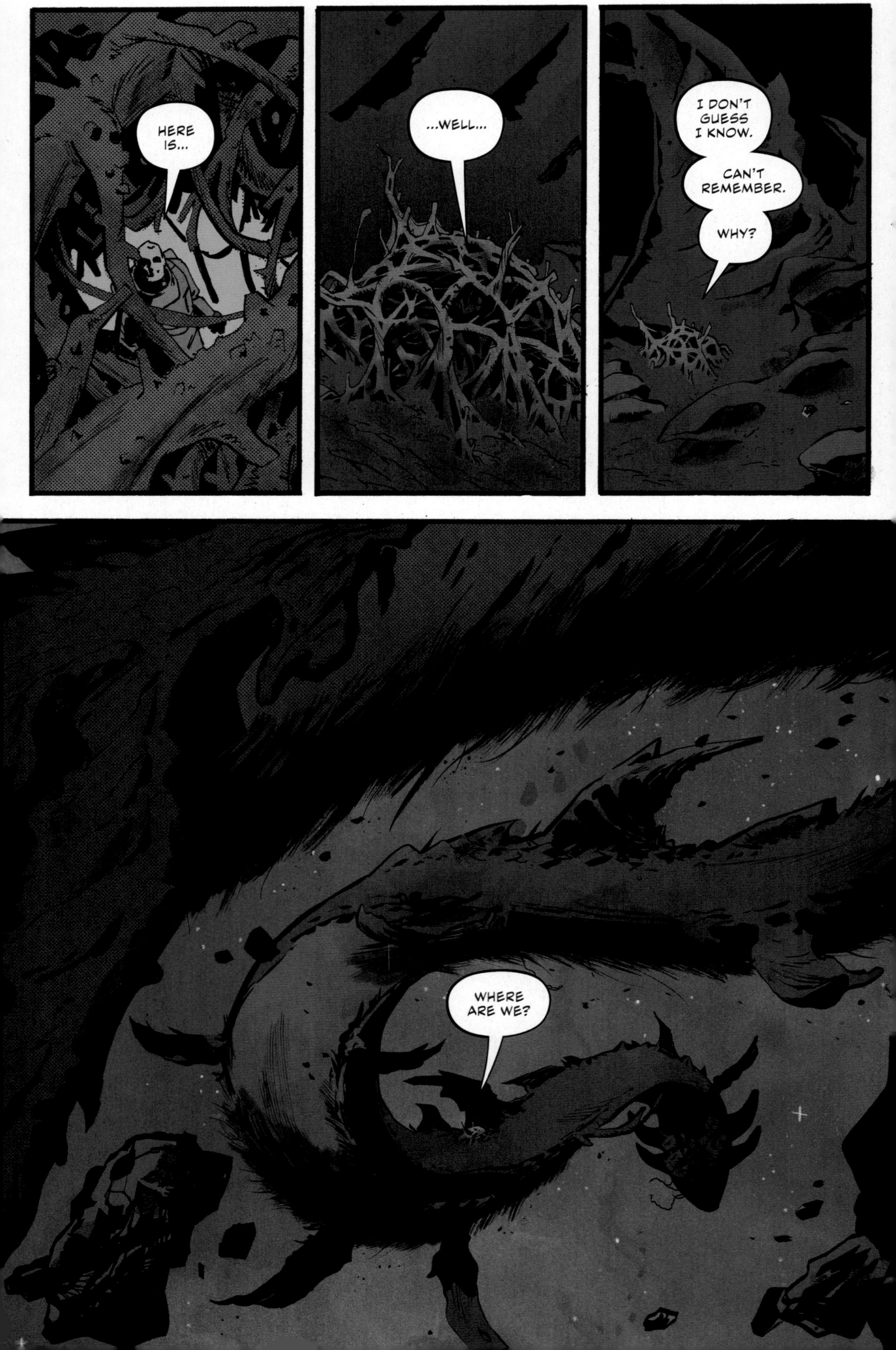
HERE IS...
...WELL...
I DON'T GUESS I KNOW.
CAN'T REMEMBER.
WHY?
WHERE ARE WE?

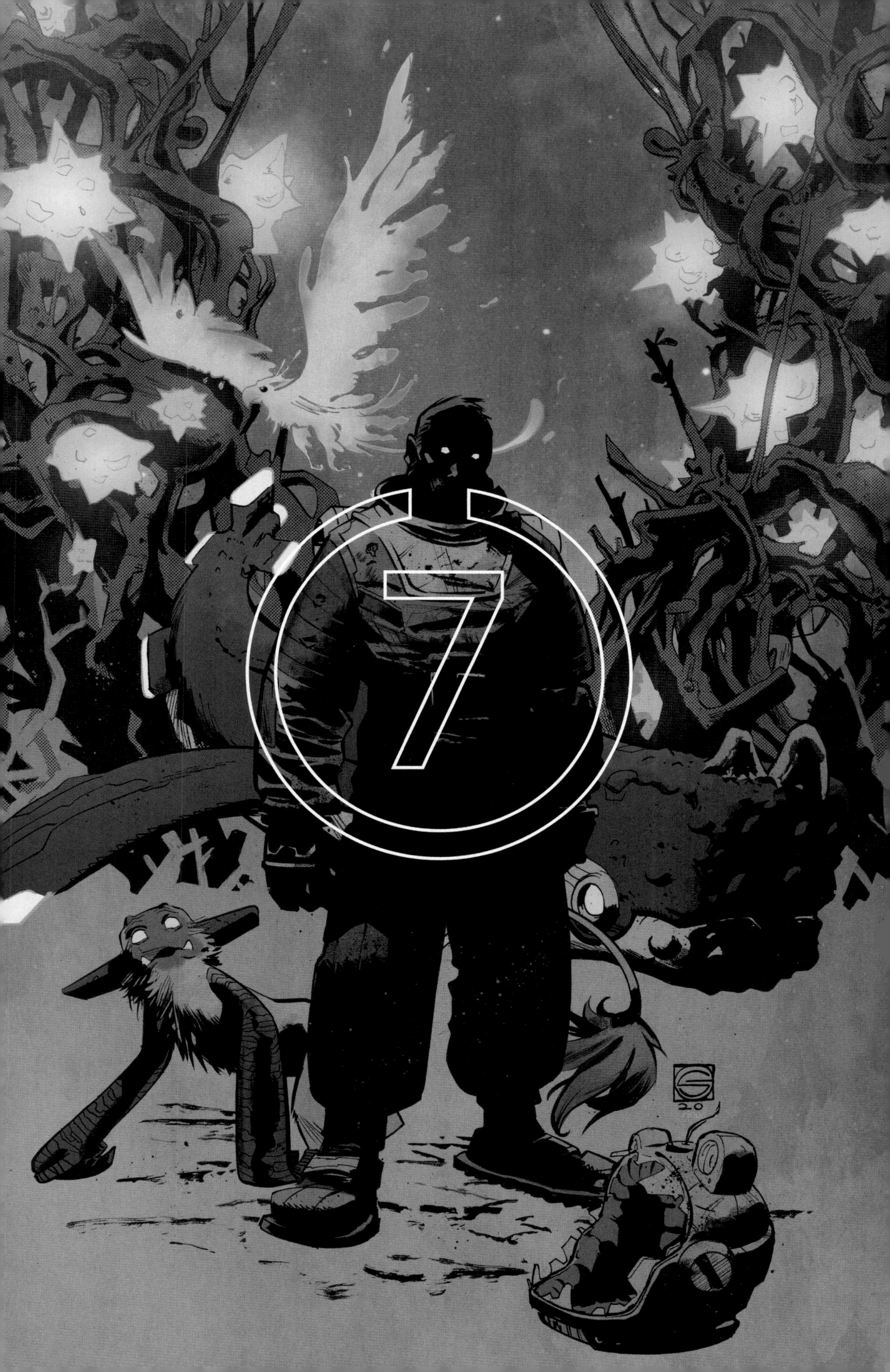
7

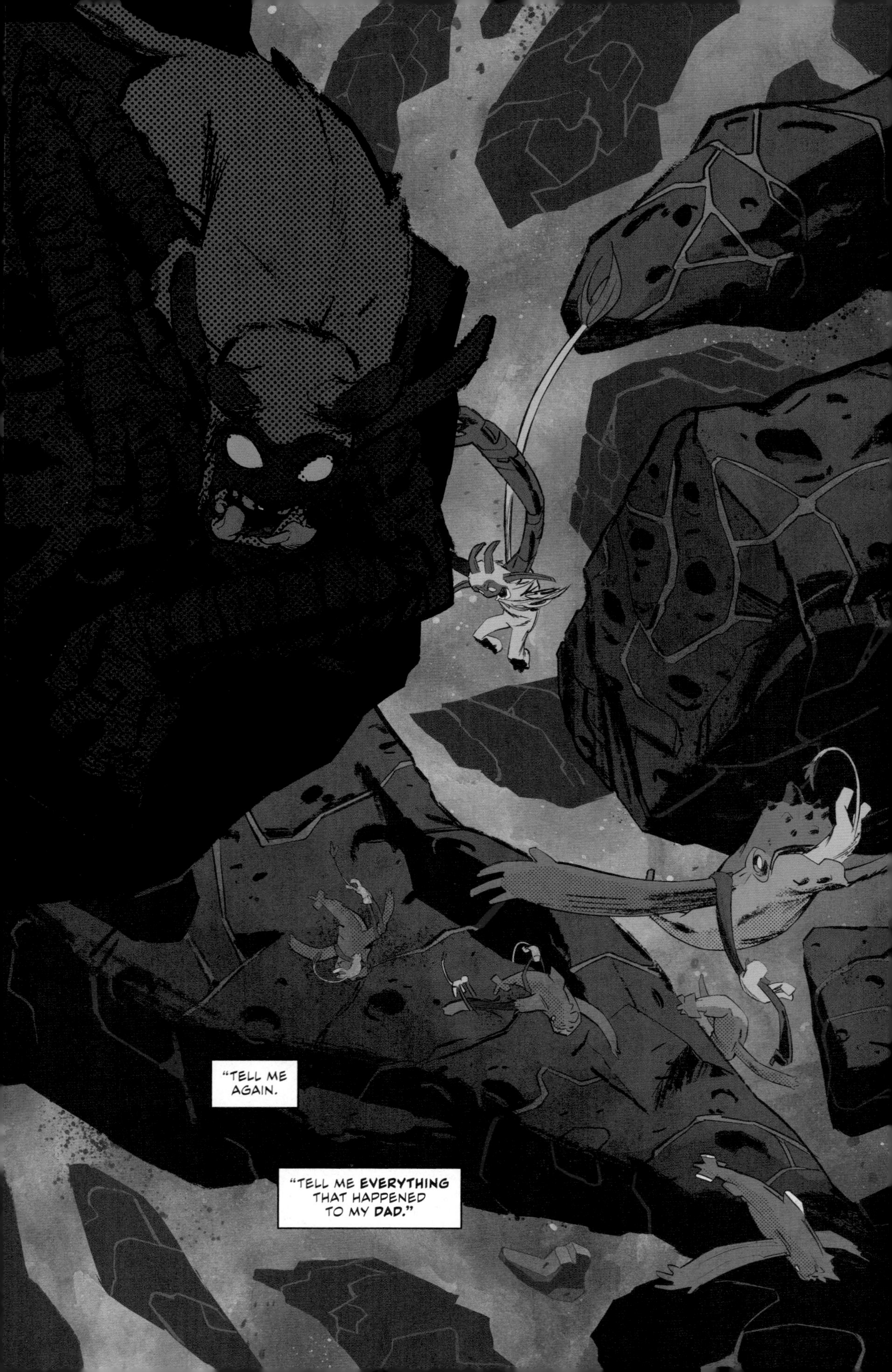
"TELL ME AGAIN.
"TELL ME EVERYTHING THAT HAPPENED TO MY DAD."

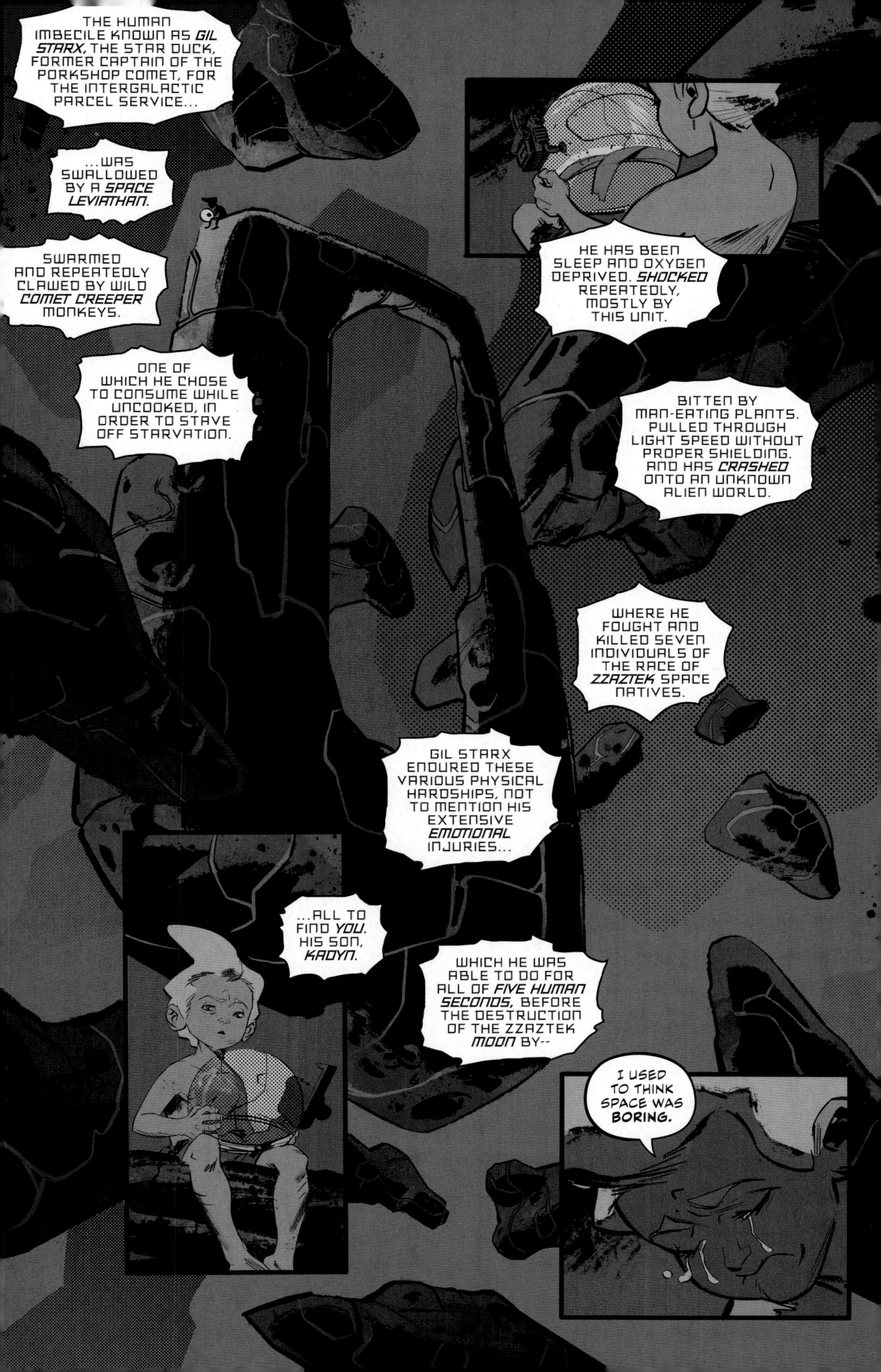
THE HUMAN IMBECILE KNOWN AS GIL STARX, THE STAR DUCK, FORMER CAPTAIN OF THE PORKSHOP COMET, FOR THE INTERGALACTIC PARCEL SERVICE...
...WAS SWALLOWED BY A SPACE LEVIATHAN.
SWARMED AND REPEATEDLY CLAWED BY WILD COMET CREEPER MONKEYS.
ONE OF WHICH HE CHOSE TO CONSUME WHILE UNCOOKED, IN ORDER TO STAVE OFF STARVATION.
HE HAS BEEN SLEEP AND OXYGEN DEPRIVED. SHOCKED REPEATEDLY, MOSTLY BY THIS UNIT.
BITTEN BY MAN-EATING PLANTS. PULLED THROUGH LIGHT SPEED WITHOUT PROPER SHIELDING. AND HAS CRASHED ONTO AN UNKNOWN ALIEN WORLD.
WHERE HE FOUGHT AND KILLED SEVEN INDIVIDUALS OF THE RACE OF ZZAZTEK SPACE NATIVES.
GIL STARX ENDURED THESE VARIOUS PHYSICAL HARDSHIPS, NOT TO MENTION HIS EXTENSIVE EMOTIONAL INJURIES...
...ALL TO FIND YOU. HIS SON, KADYN.
WHICH HE WAS ABLE TO DO FOR ALL OF FIVE HUMAN SECONDS, BEFORE THE DESTRUCTION OF THE ZZAZTEK MOON BY--
I USED TO THINK SPACE WAS BORING.

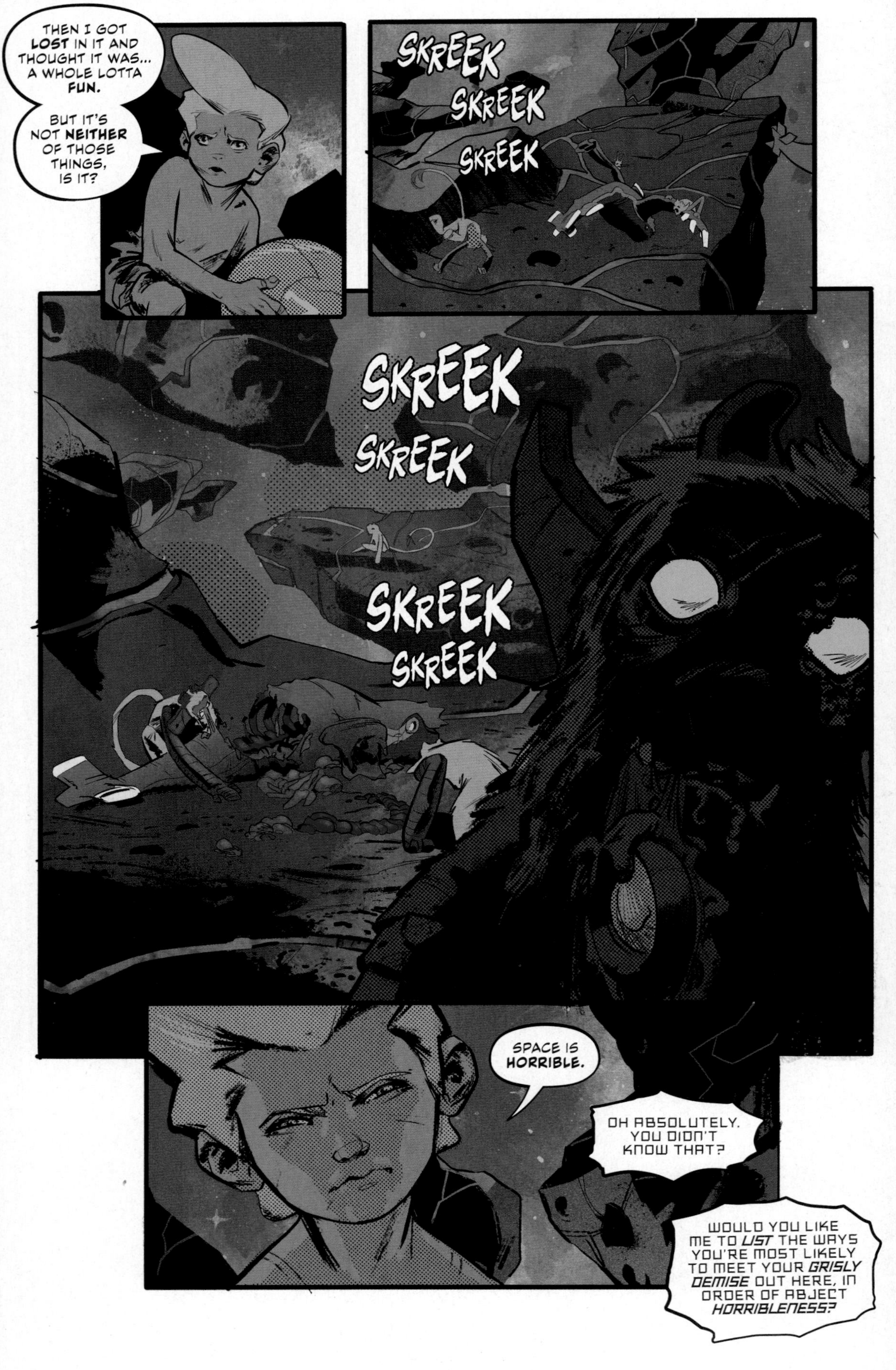
THEN I GOT LOST IN IT AND THOUGHT IT WAS... A WHOLE LOTTA FUN.
BUT IT'S NOT NEITHER OF THOSE THINGS, IS IT?
SKREEK
SKREEK
SKREEK
SKREEK
SKREEK
SKREEK
SKREEK
SPACE IS HORRIBLE.
OH ABSOLUTELY. YOU DIDN'T KNOW THAT?
WOULD YOU LIKE ME TO LIST THE WAYS YOU'RE MOST LIKELY TO MEET YOUR GRISLY DEMISE OUT HERE, IN ORDER OF ABJECT HORRIBLENESS?

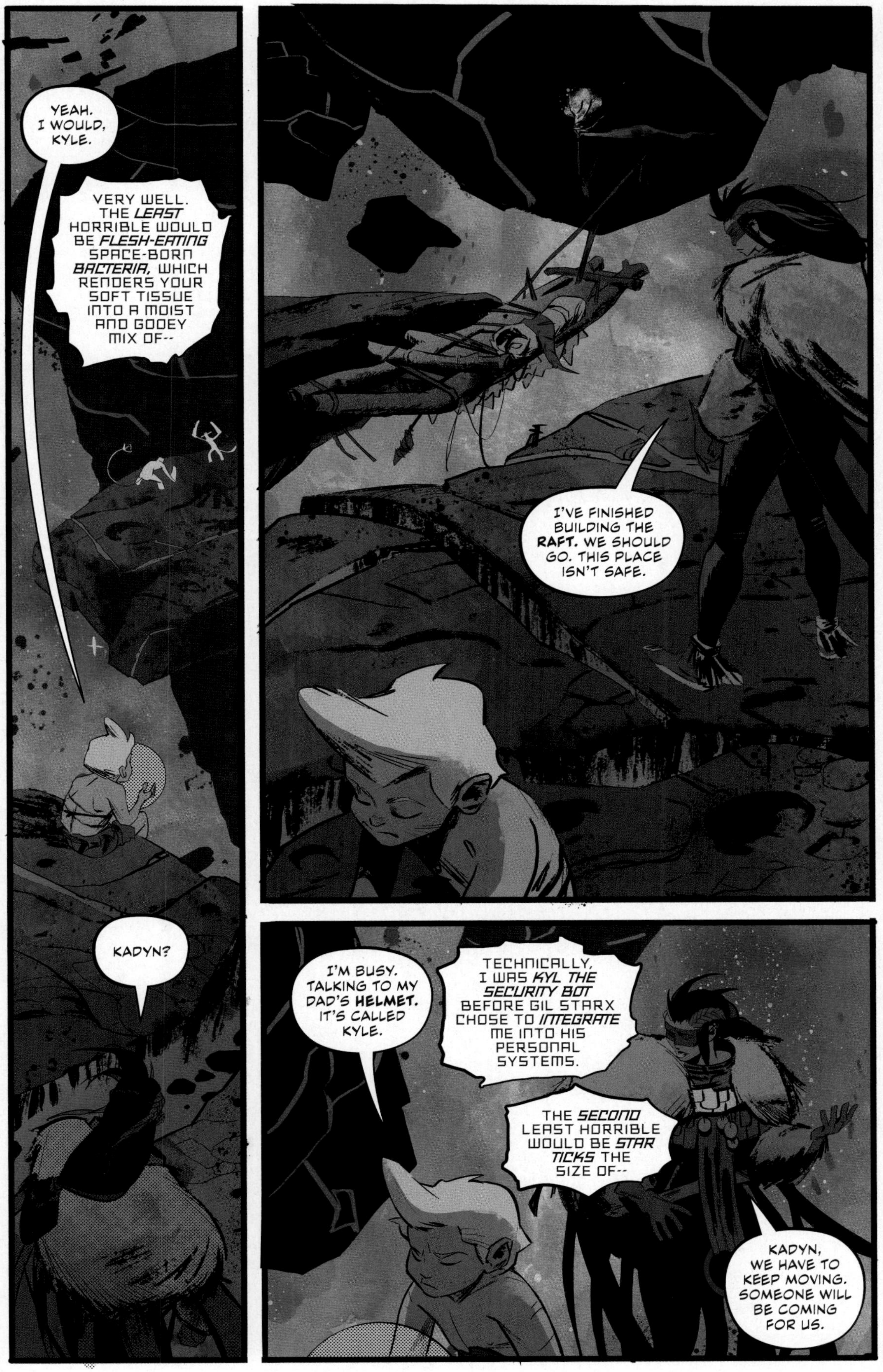
YEAH. I WOULD, KYLE.
VERY WELL. THE LEAST HORRIBLE WOULD BE FLESH-EATING SPACE-BORN BACTERIA, WHICH RENDERS YOUR SOFT TISSUE INTO A MOIST AND GOOEY MIX OF--
I'VE FINISHED BUILDING THE RAFT. WE SHOULD GO. THIS PLACE ISN'T SAFE.
KADYN?
I'M BUSY. TALKING TO MY DAD'S HELMET. IT'S CALLED KYLE.
TECHNICALLY, I WAS KYL THE SECURITY BOT BEFORE GIL STARX CHOSE TO INTEGRATE ME INTO HIS PERSONAL SYSTEMS.
THE SECOND LEAST HORRIBLE WOULD BE STAR TICKS THE SIZE OF--
KADYN, WE HAVE TO KEEP MOVING. SOMEONE WILL BE COMING FOR US.

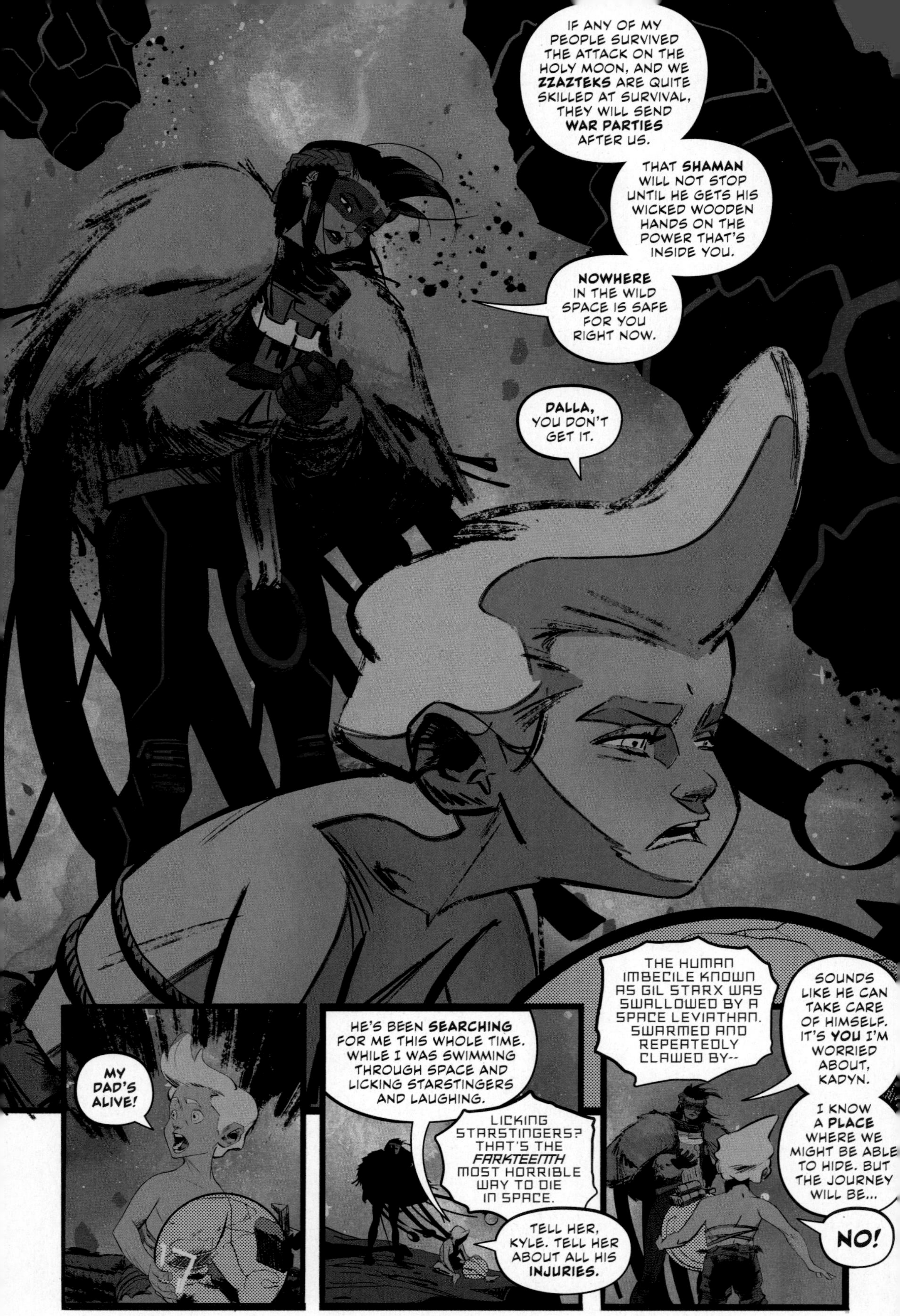
IF ANY OF MY PEOPLE SURVIVED THE ATTACK ON THE HOLY MOON, AND WE ZZAZTEKS ARE QUITE SKILLED AT SURVIVAL, THEY WILL SEND WAR PARTIES AFTER US.
THAT SHAMAN WILL NOT STOP UNTIL HE GETS HIS WICKED WOODEN HANDS ON THE POWER THAT'S INSIDE YOU.
NOWHERE IN THE WILD SPACE IS SAFE FOR YOU RIGHT NOW.
DALLA, YOU DON'T GET IT.
MY DAD'S ALIVE!
HE'S BEEN SEARCHING FOR ME THIS WHOLE TIME. WHILE I WAS SWIMMING THROUGH SPACE AND LICKING STARSTINGERS AND LAUGHING.
LICKING STARSTINGERS? THAT'S THE FARKTEENTH MOST HORRIBLE WAY TO DIE IN SPACE.
TELL HER, KYLE. TELL HER ABOUT ALL HIS INJURIES.
THE HUMAN IMBECILE KNOWN AS GIL STARX WAS SWALLOWED BY A SPACE LEVIATHAN. SWARMED AND REPEATEDLY CLAWED BY--
SOUNDS LIKE HE CAN TAKE CARE OF HIMSELF. IT'S YOU I'M WORRIED ABOUT, KADYN.
I KNOW A PLACE WHERE WE MIGHT BE ABLE TO HIDE. BUT THE JOURNEY WILL BE...
NO!

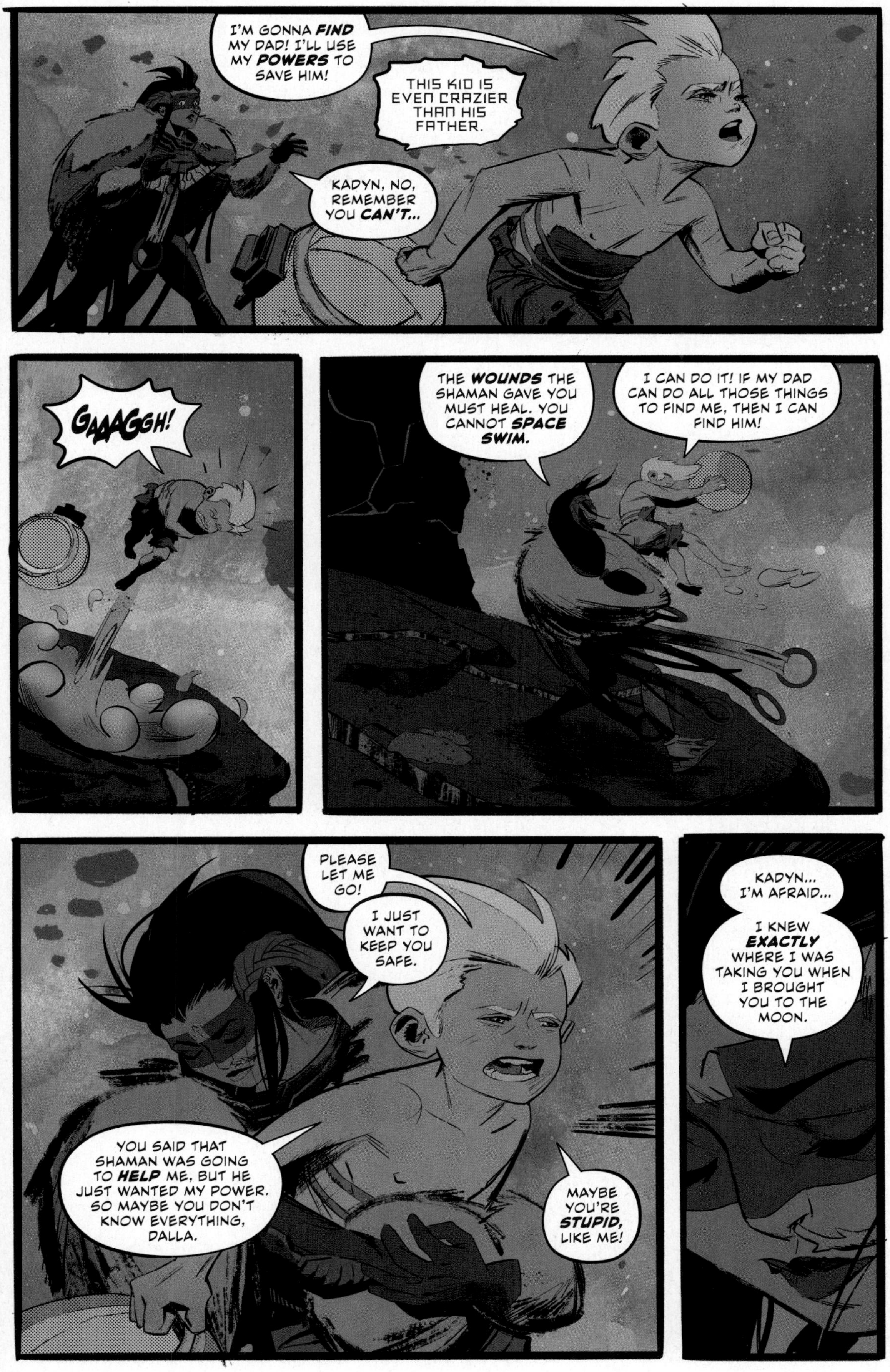
I'M GONNA FIND MY DAD! I'LL USE MY POWERS TO SAVE HIM!
THIS KID IS EVEN CRAZIER THAN HIS FATHER.
KADYN, NO, REMEMBER YOU CAN'T...
GAAAGGH!
THE WOUNDS THE SHAMAN GAVE YOU MUST HEAL. YOU CANNOT SPACE SWIM.
I CAN DO IT! IF MY DAD CAN DO ALL THOSE THINGS TO FIND ME, THEN I CAN FIND HIM!
PLEASE LET ME GO!
I JUST WANT TO KEEP YOU SAFE.
YOU SAID THAT SHAMAN WAS GOING TO HELP ME, BUT HE JUST WANTED MY POWER. SO MAYBE YOU DON'T KNOW EVERYTHING, DALLA.
MAYBE YOU'RE STUPID, LIKE ME!
KADYN... I'M AFRAID...
I KNEW EXACTLY WHERE I WAS TAKING YOU WHEN I BROUGHT YOU TO THE MOON.

WHAT DOES THAT MEAN?

NEVER TRUST A ZZAZTEK. EVEN *BOTS* KNOW THAT.

I KNEW, BUT I COULDN'T LET THEM DO IT. AND THE SHAMAN IS FULL OF *LIES.* HE'S NOT WHAT HE EVER SEEMED TO BE. HE'S...

YOU KNEW THEY WANTED TO *HURT* ME?!

YES.

YOU *LIED* TO ME.

I WAS BANISHED FROM EVERYONE I'VE EVER LOVED, KADYN. I THOUGHT I WAS WILLING TO DO *ANYTHING* TO EARN MY WAY BACK... BUT I WASN'T.

I HELPED YOU THEN, AND I WANT TO HELP YOU NOW. TO *MAKE UP* FOR THE...

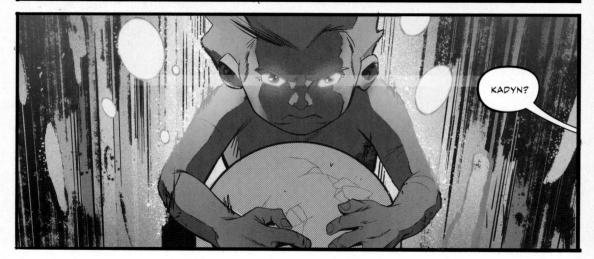

KADYN?

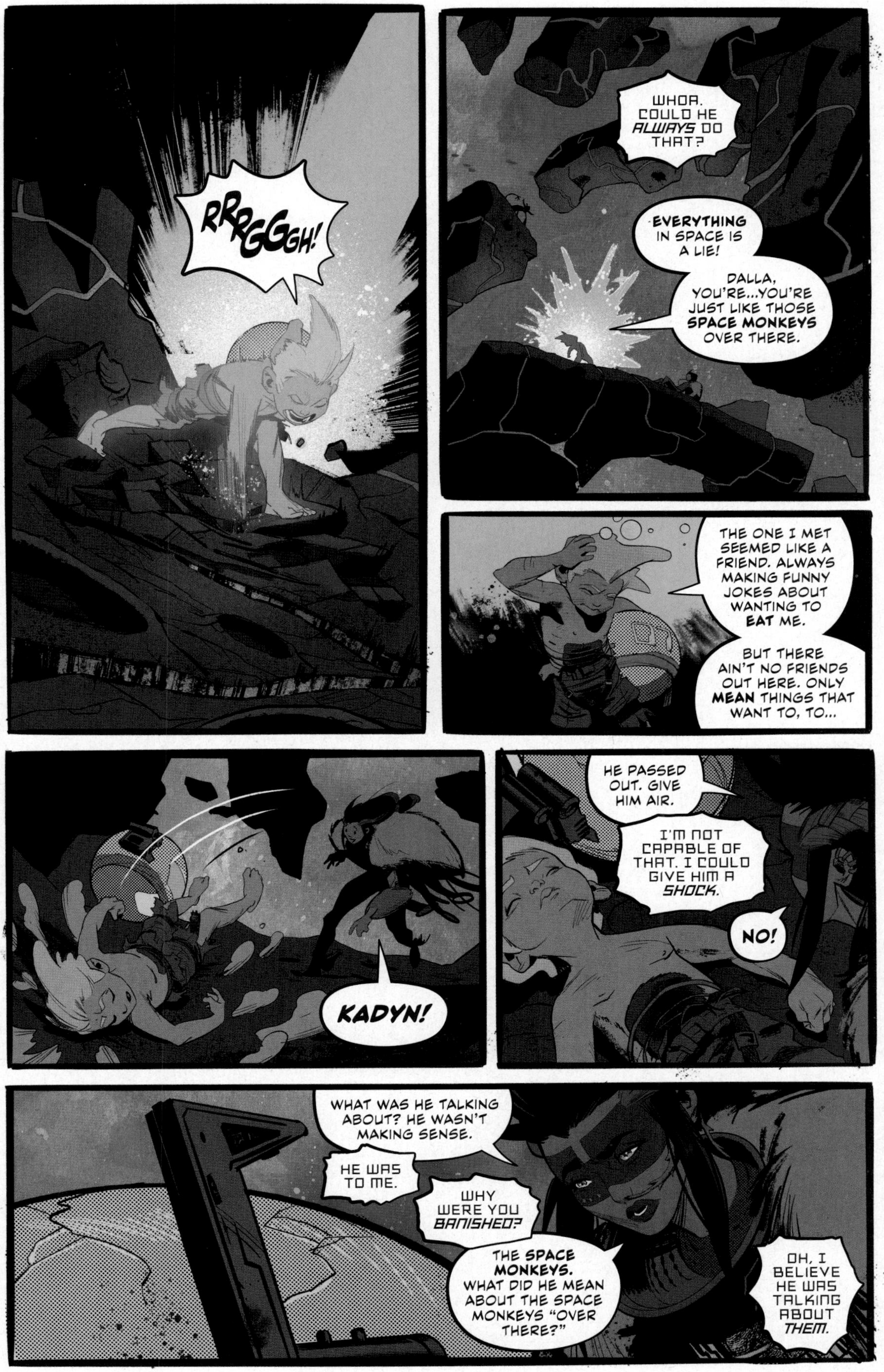
RRRGGGGH!
WHOA. COULD HE ALWAYS DO THAT?
EVERYTHING IN SPACE IS A LIE!
DALLA, YOU'RE...YOU'RE JUST LIKE THOSE SPACE MONKEYS OVER THERE.
THE ONE I MET SEEMED LIKE A FRIEND. ALWAYS MAKING FUNNY JOKES ABOUT WANTING TO EAT ME.
BUT THERE AIN'T NO FRIENDS OUT HERE. ONLY MEAN THINGS THAT WANT TO, TO...
KADYN!
HE PASSED OUT. GIVE HIM AIR.
I'M NOT CAPABLE OF THAT. I COULD GIVE HIM A SHOCK.
NO!
WHAT WAS HE TALKING ABOUT? HE WASN'T MAKING SENSE.
HE WAS TO ME.
WHY WERE YOU BANISHED?
THE SPACE MONKEYS. WHAT DID HE MEAN ABOUT THE SPACE MONKEYS "OVER THERE?"
OH, I BELIEVE HE WAS TALKING ABOUT THEM.

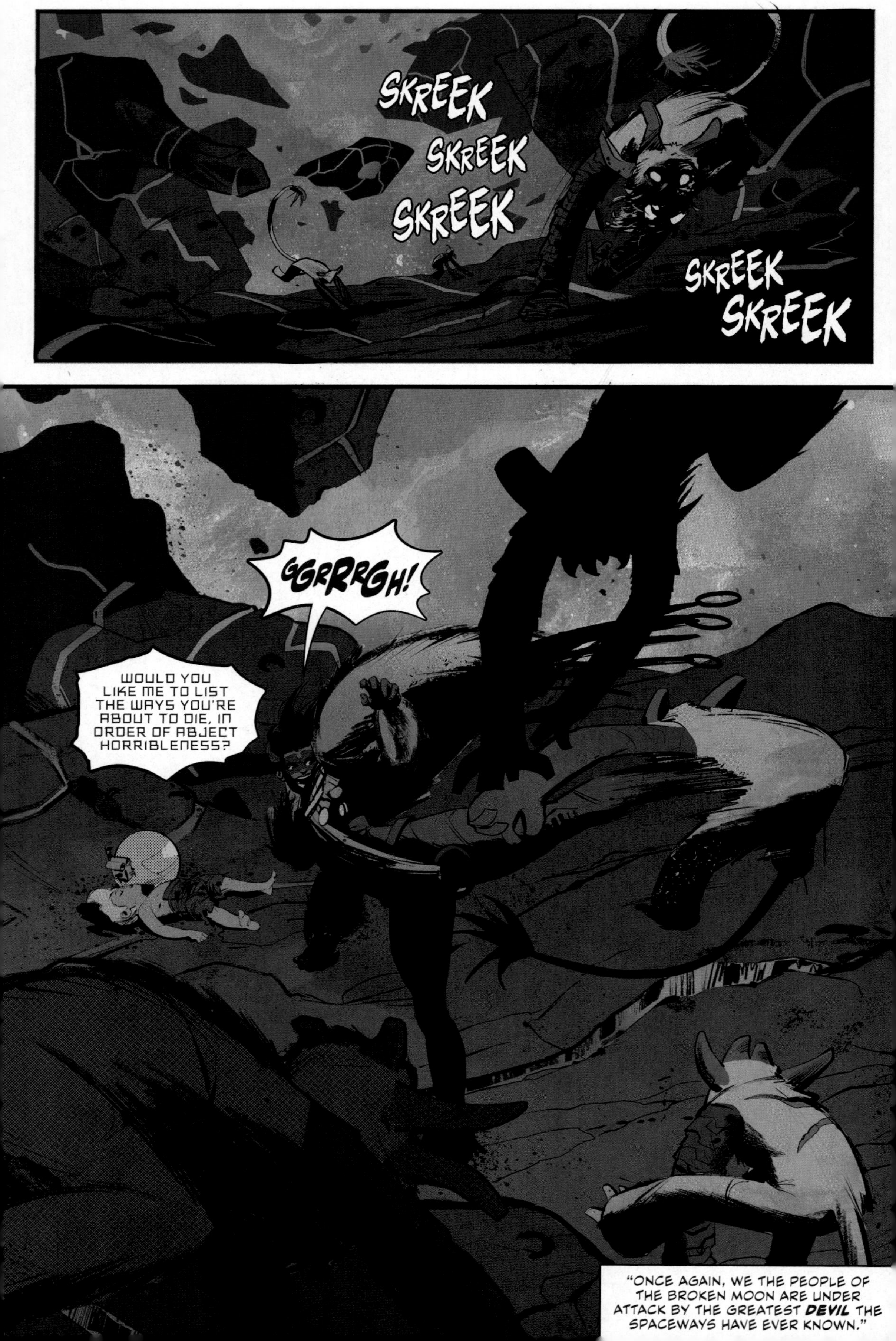
SKREEK
SKREEK
SKREEK
SKREEK
SKREEK
GGRRRGH!
WOULD YOU LIKE ME TO LIST THE WAYS YOU'RE ABOUT TO DIE, IN ORDER OF ABJECT HORRIBLENESS?
"ONCE AGAIN, WE THE PEOPLE OF THE BROKEN MOON ARE UNDER ATTACK BY THE GREATEST DEVIL THE SPACEWAYS HAVE EVER KNOWN."

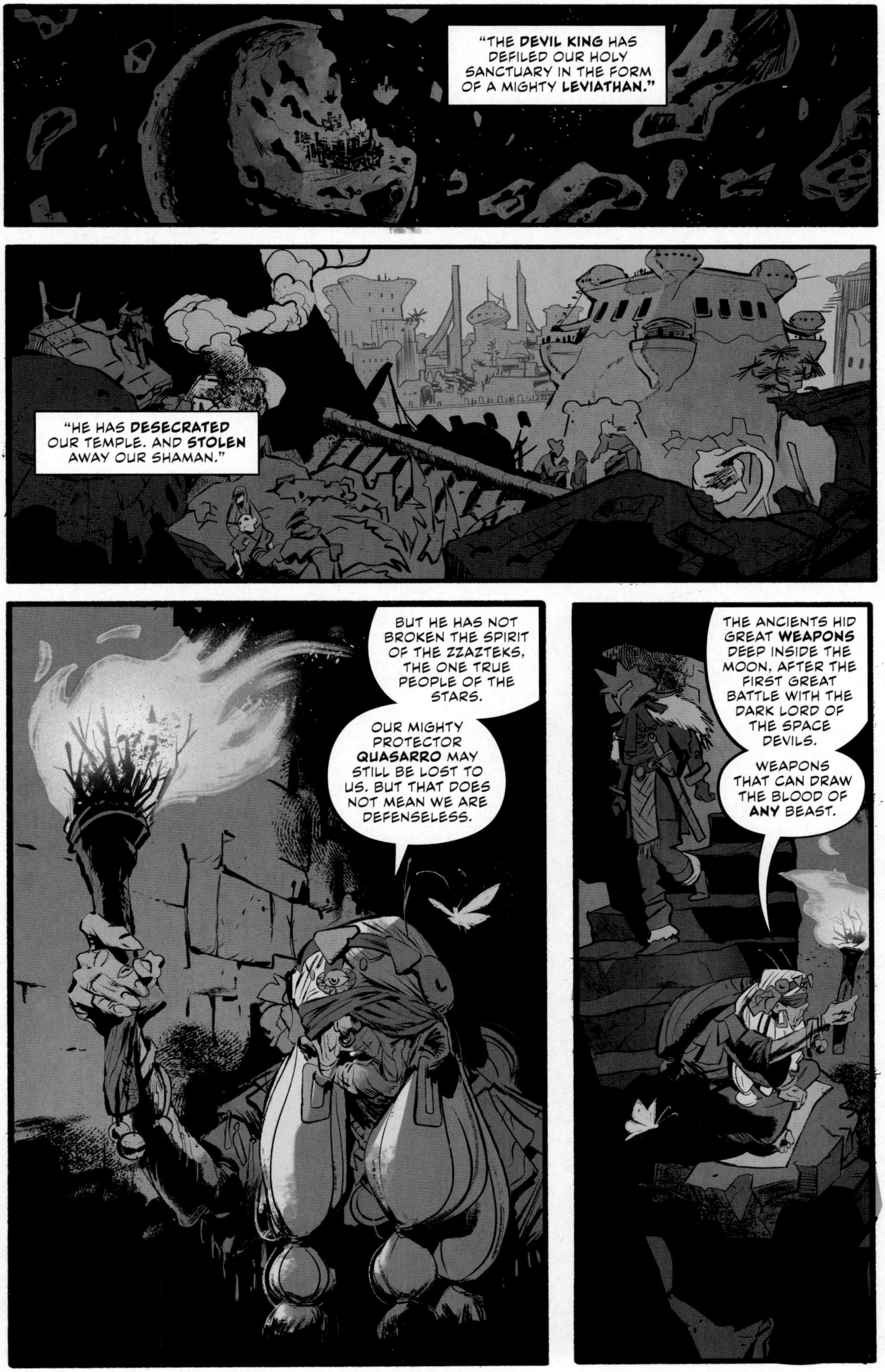
"THE DEVIL KING HAS DEFILED OUR HOLY SANCTUARY IN THE FORM OF A MIGHTY LEVIATHAN."
"HE HAS DESECRATED OUR TEMPLE. AND STOLEN AWAY OUR SHAMAN."
BUT HE HAS NOT BROKEN THE SPIRIT OF THE ZZAZTEKS, THE ONE TRUE PEOPLE OF THE STARS.
OUR MIGHTY PROTECTOR QUASARRO MAY STILL BE LOST TO US. BUT THAT DOES NOT MEAN WE ARE DEFENSELESS.
THE ANCIENTS HID GREAT WEAPONS DEEP INSIDE THE MOON, AFTER THE FIRST GREAT BATTLE WITH THE DARK LORD OF THE SPACE DEVILS.
WEAPONS THAT CAN DRAW THE BLOOD OF ANY BEAST.

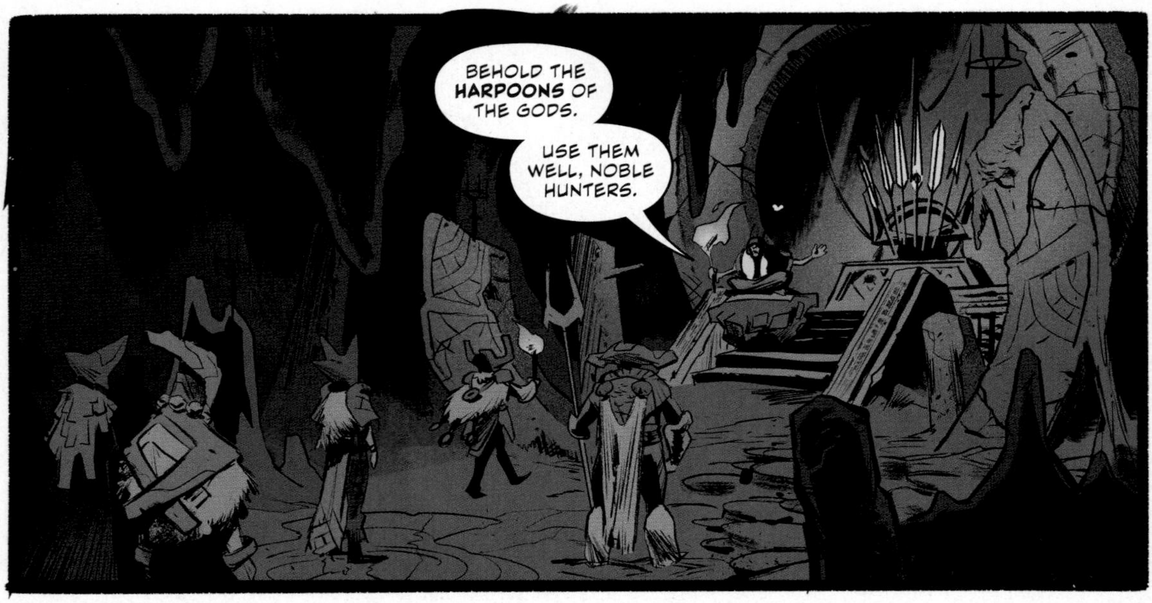
BEHOLD THE HARPOONS OF THE GODS.
USE THEM WELL, NOBLE HUNTERS.

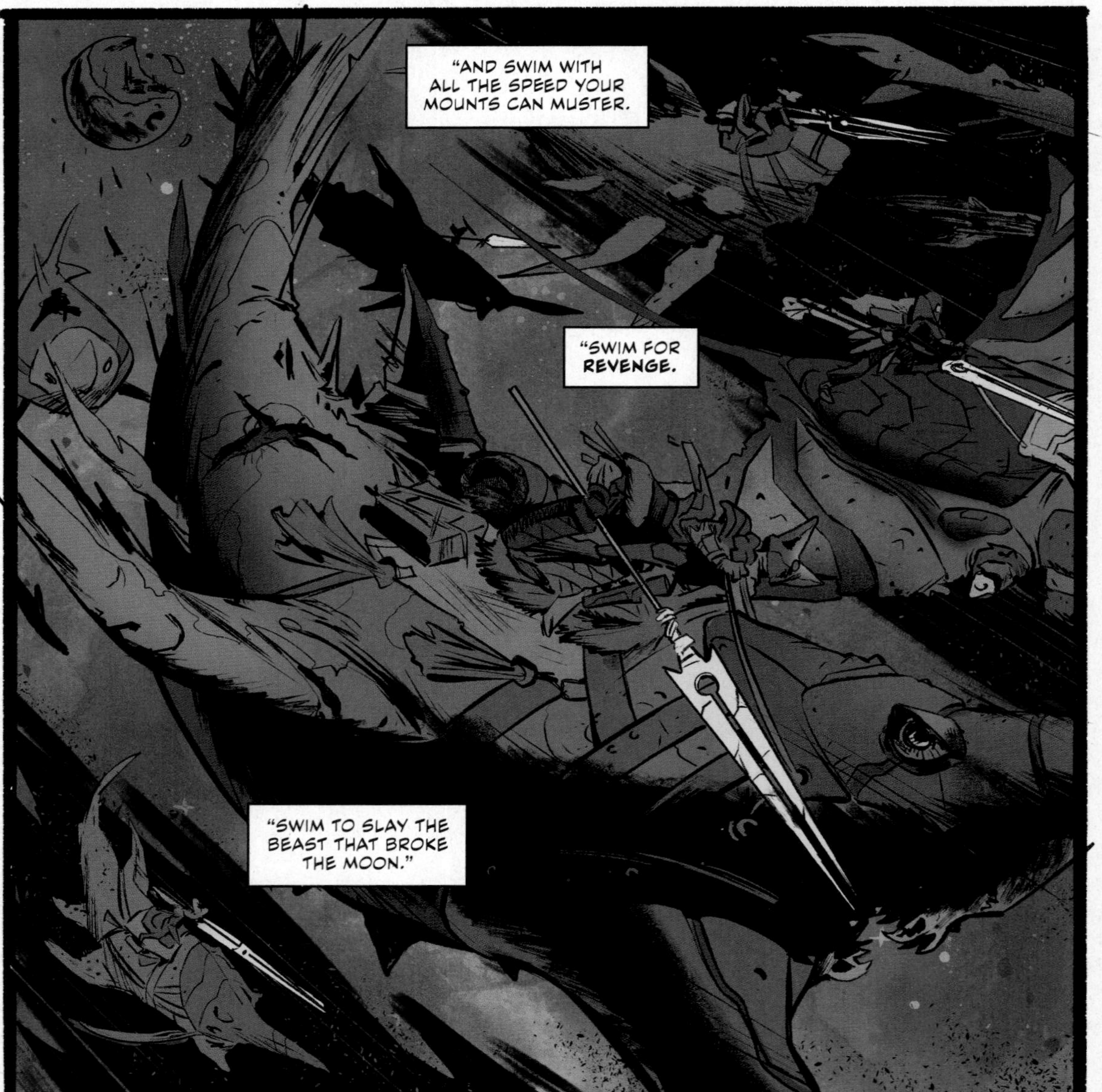
"AND SWIM WITH ALL THE SPEED YOUR MOUNTS CAN MUSTER.
"SWIM FOR REVENGE.
"SWIM TO SLAY THE BEAST THAT BROKE THE MOON."

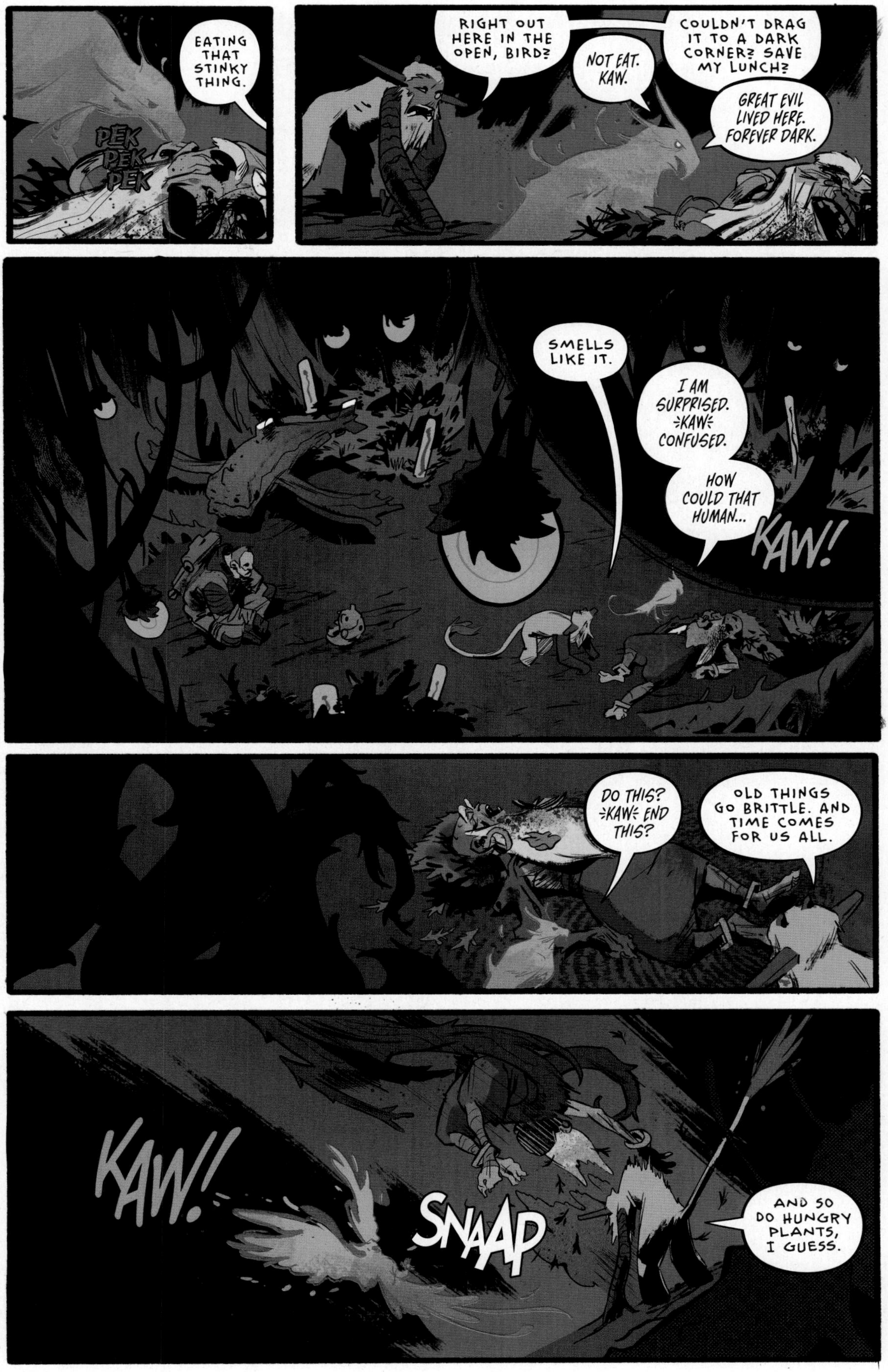
EATING THAT STINKY THING.
PEK PEK PEK
RIGHT OUT HERE IN THE OPEN, BIRD?
COULDN'T DRAG IT TO A DARK CORNER? SAVE MY LUNCH?
NOT EAT. KAW.
GREAT EVIL LIVED HERE. FOREVER DARK.
SMELLS LIKE IT.
I AM SURPRISED. *KAW* CONFUSED.
HOW COULD THAT HUMAN...
KAW!
DO THIS? *KAW* END THIS?
OLD THINGS GO BRITTLE. AND TIME COMES FOR US ALL.
KAW!!
SNAAP
AND SO DO HUNGRY PLANTS, I GUESS.

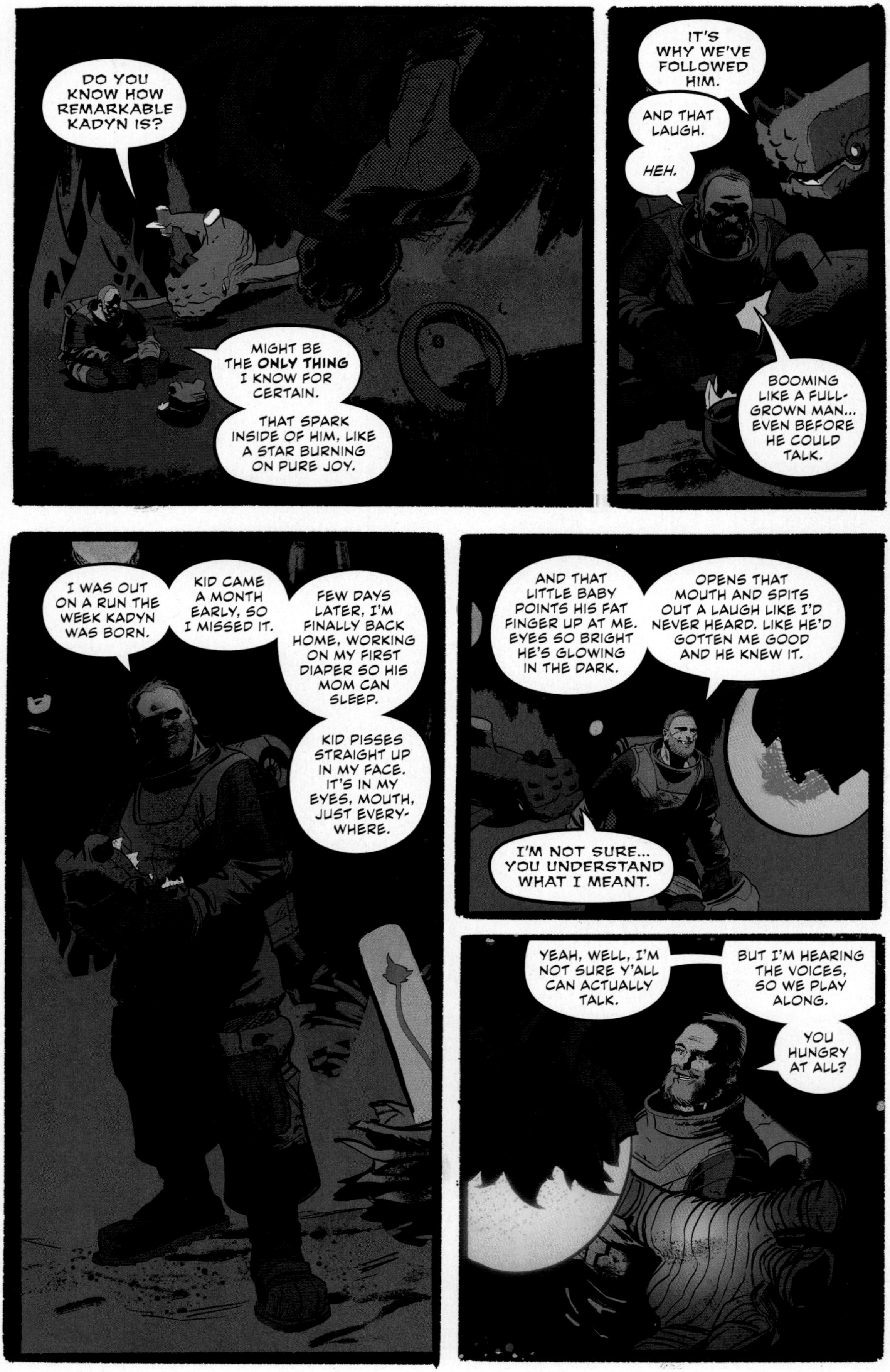
DO YOU KNOW HOW REMARKABLE KADYN IS?
MIGHT BE THE **ONLY THING** I KNOW FOR CERTAIN.
THAT SPARK INSIDE OF HIM, LIKE A STAR BURNING ON PURE JOY.
IT'S WHY WE'VE FOLLOWED HIM.
AND THAT LAUGH.
HEH.
BOOMING LIKE A FULL-GROWN MAN... EVEN BEFORE HE COULD TALK.
I WAS OUT ON A RUN THE WEEK KADYN WAS BORN.
KID CAME A MONTH EARLY, SO I MISSED IT.
FEW DAYS LATER, I'M FINALLY BACK HOME, WORKING ON MY FIRST DIAPER SO HIS MOM CAN SLEEP.
KID PISSES STRAIGHT UP IN MY FACE. IT'S IN MY EYES, MOUTH, JUST EVERY-WHERE.
AND THAT LITTLE BABY POINTS HIS FAT FINGER UP AT ME. EYES SO BRIGHT HE'S GLOWING IN THE DARK.
OPENS THAT MOUTH AND SPITS OUT A LAUGH LIKE I'D NEVER HEARD. LIKE HE'D GOTTEN ME GOOD AND HE KNEW IT.
I'M NOT SURE... YOU UNDERSTAND WHAT I MEANT.
YEAH, WELL, I'M NOT SURE Y'ALL CAN ACTUALLY TALK.
BUT I'M HEARING THE VOICES, SO WE PLAY ALONG.
YOU HUNGRY AT ALL?

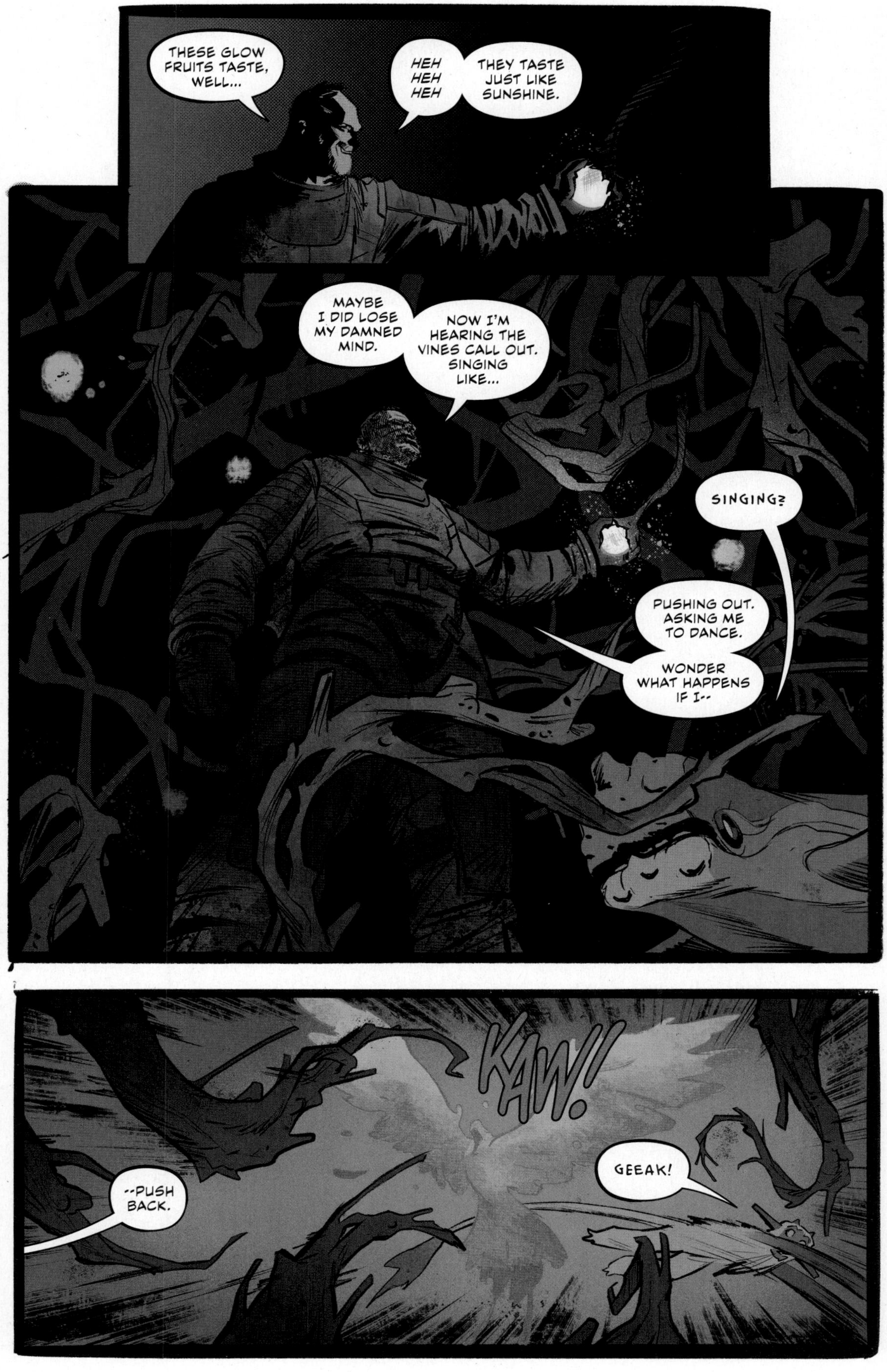
THESE GLOW FRUITS TASTE, WELL...
HEH HEH HEH
THEY TASTE JUST LIKE SUNSHINE.
MAYBE I DID LOSE MY DAMNED MIND.
NOW I'M HEARING THE VINES CALL OUT. SINGING LIKE...
SINGING?
PUSHING OUT. ASKING ME TO DANCE.
WONDER WHAT HAPPENS IF I--
KAW!
--PUSH BACK.
GEEAK!

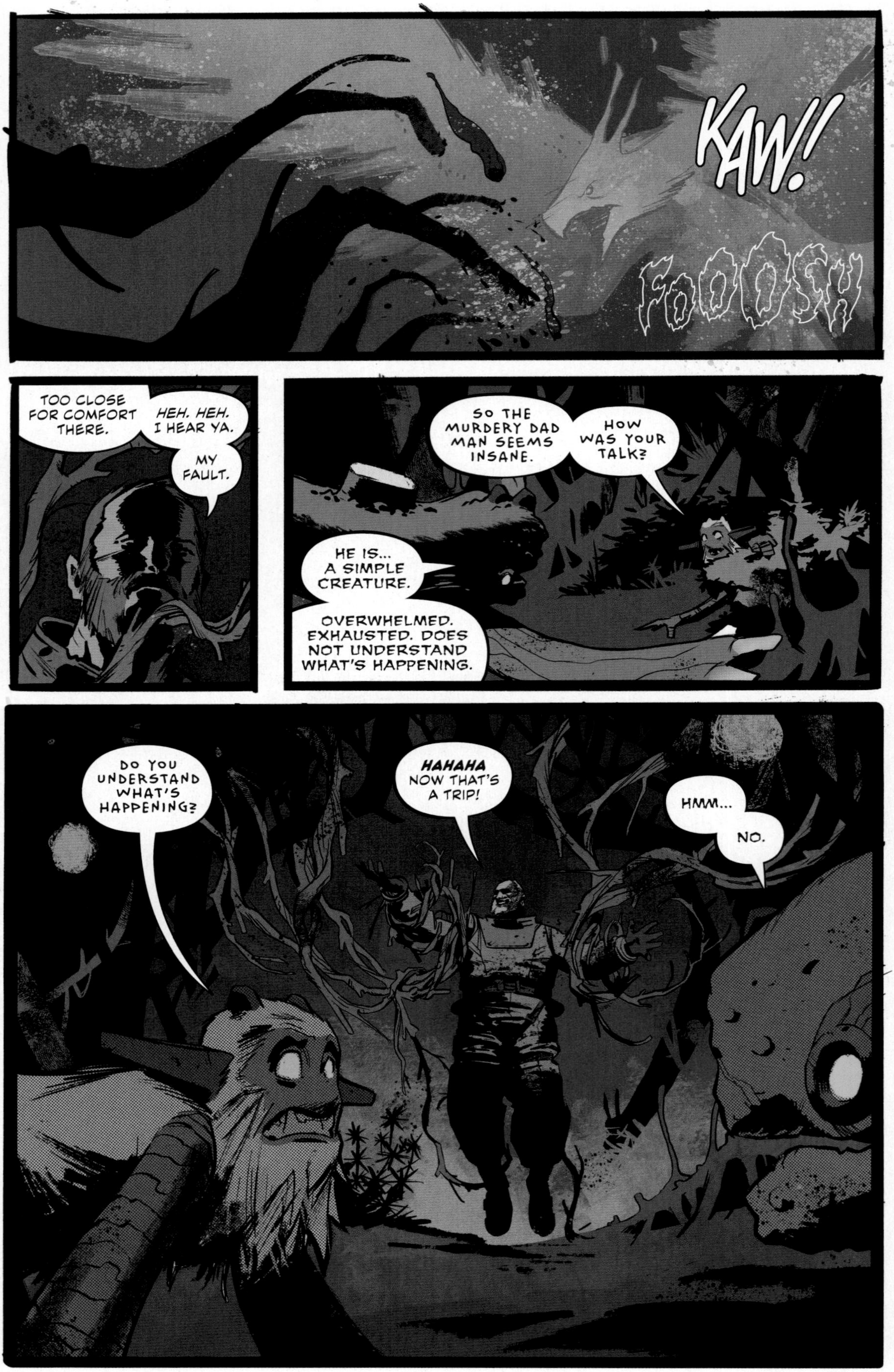
KAW!!
FOOOSH
TOO CLOSE FOR COMFORT THERE.
HEH. HEH. I HEAR YA.
MY FAULT.
SO THE MURDERY DAD MAN SEEMS INSANE.
HOW WAS YOUR TALK?
HE IS... A SIMPLE CREATURE.
OVERWHELMED. EXHAUSTED. DOES NOT UNDERSTAND WHAT'S HAPPENING.
DO YOU UNDERSTAND WHAT'S HAPPENING?
HAHAHA NOW THAT'S A TRIP!
HMM...
NO.

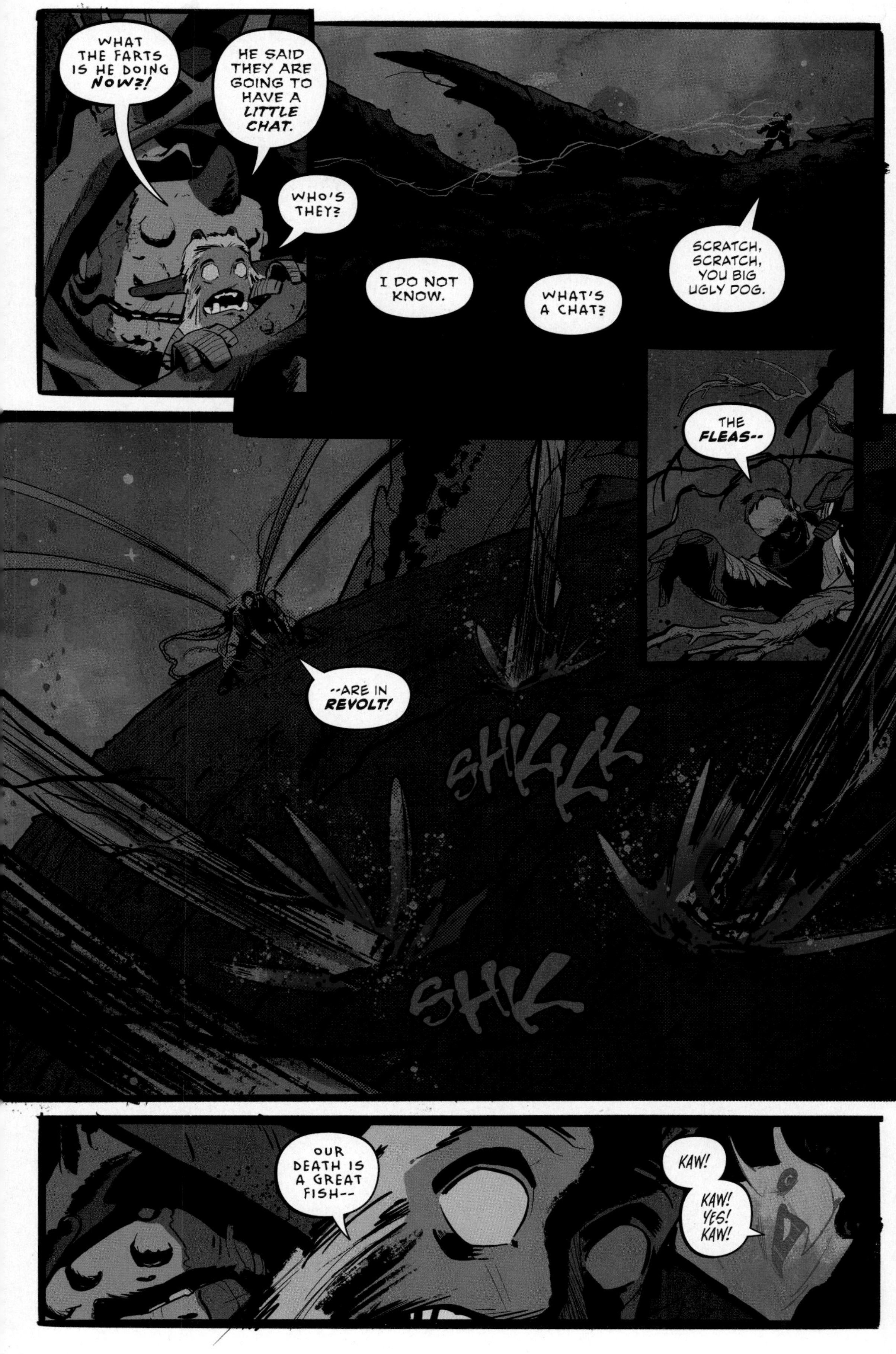
WHAT THE FARTS IS HE DOING NOW?!
HE SAID THEY ARE GOING TO HAVE A LITTLE CHAT.
WHO'S THEY?
I DO NOT KNOW.
WHAT'S A CHAT?
SCRATCH, SCRATCH, YOU BIG UGLY DOG.
THE FLEAS--
--ARE IN REVOLT!
SHKKK
SHK
OUR DEATH IS A GREAT FISH--
KAW!
KAW! YES! KAW!

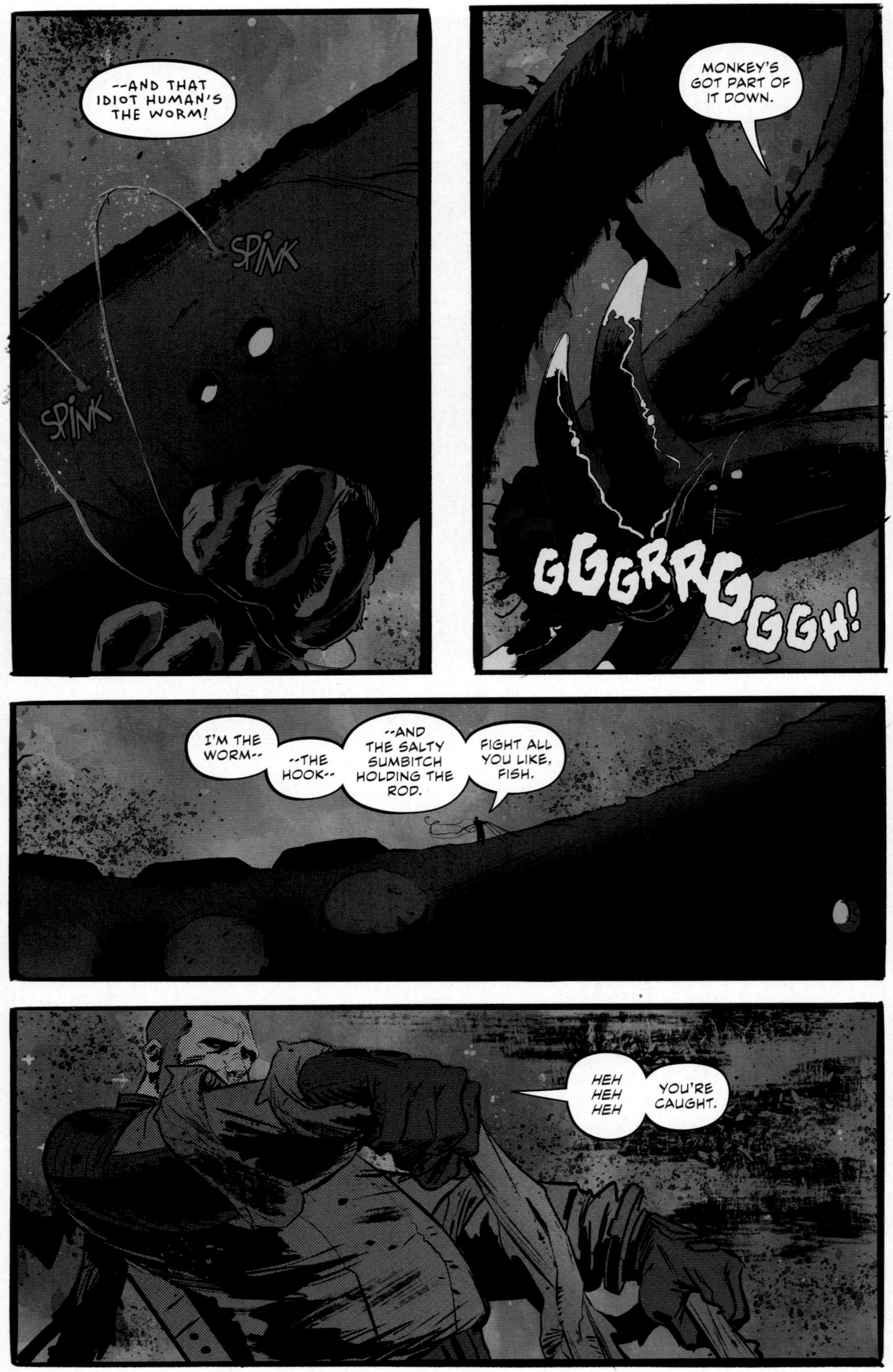
--AND THAT IDIOT HUMAN'S THE WORM!
SPINK
SPINK
MONKEY'S GOT PART OF IT DOWN.
GGGRRRGGGH!
I'M THE WORM--
--THE HOOK--
--AND THE SALTY SUMBITCH HOLDING THE ROD.
FIGHT ALL YOU LIKE, FISH.
HEH HEH HEH
YOU'RE CAUGHT.

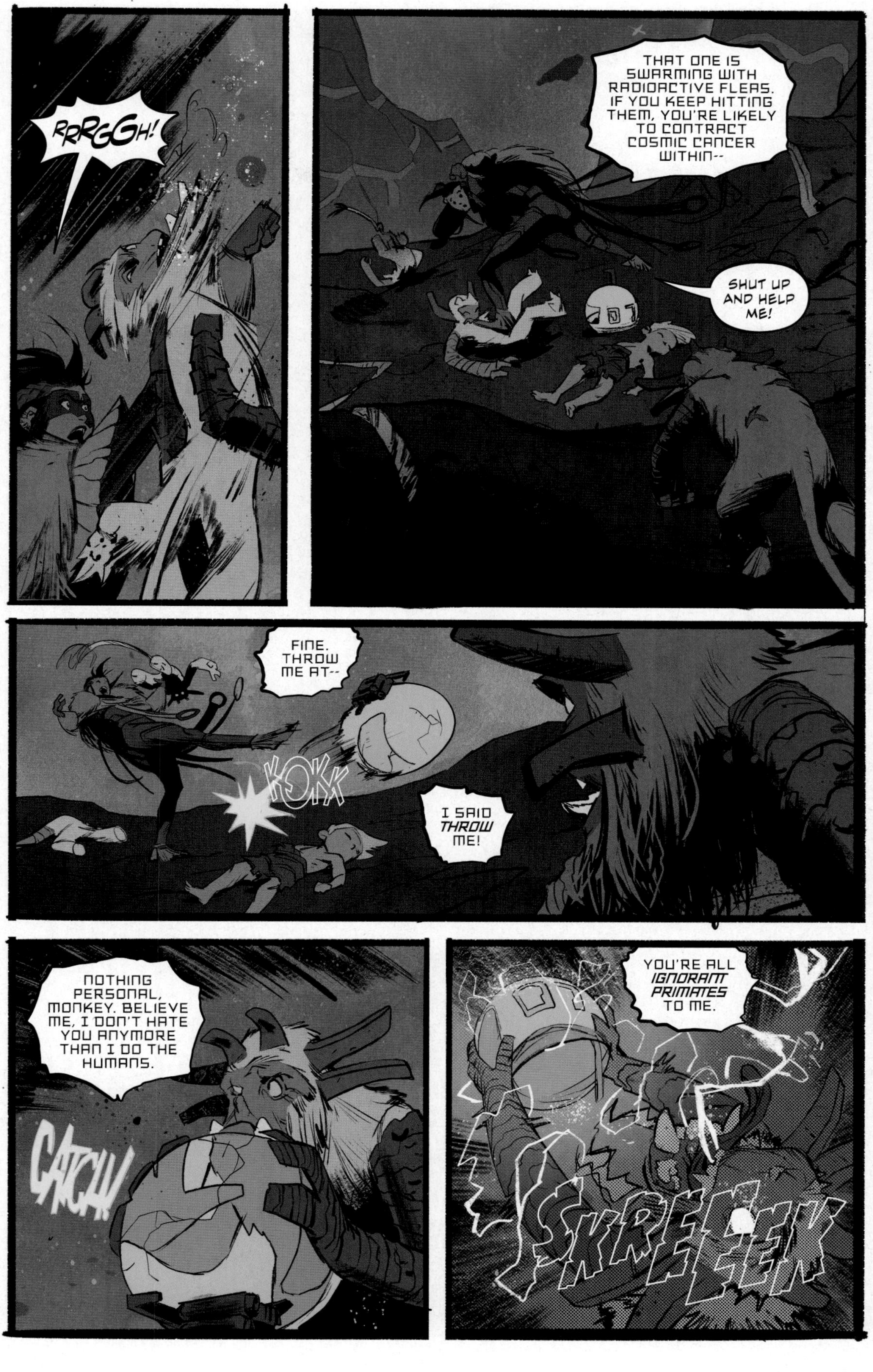
RRRGGH!
THAT ONE IS SWARMING WITH RADIOACTIVE FLEAS. IF YOU KEEP HITTING THEM, YOU'RE LIKELY TO CONTRACT COSMIC CANCER WITHIN--
SHUT UP AND HELP ME!
FINE. THROW ME AT--
KOKK
I SAID *THROW* ME!
NOTHING PERSONAL, MONKEY. BELIEVE ME, I DON'T HATE YOU ANYMORE THAN I DO THE HUMANS.
CATCH
YOU'RE ALL *IGNORANT PRIMATES* TO ME.
SKREEEEK

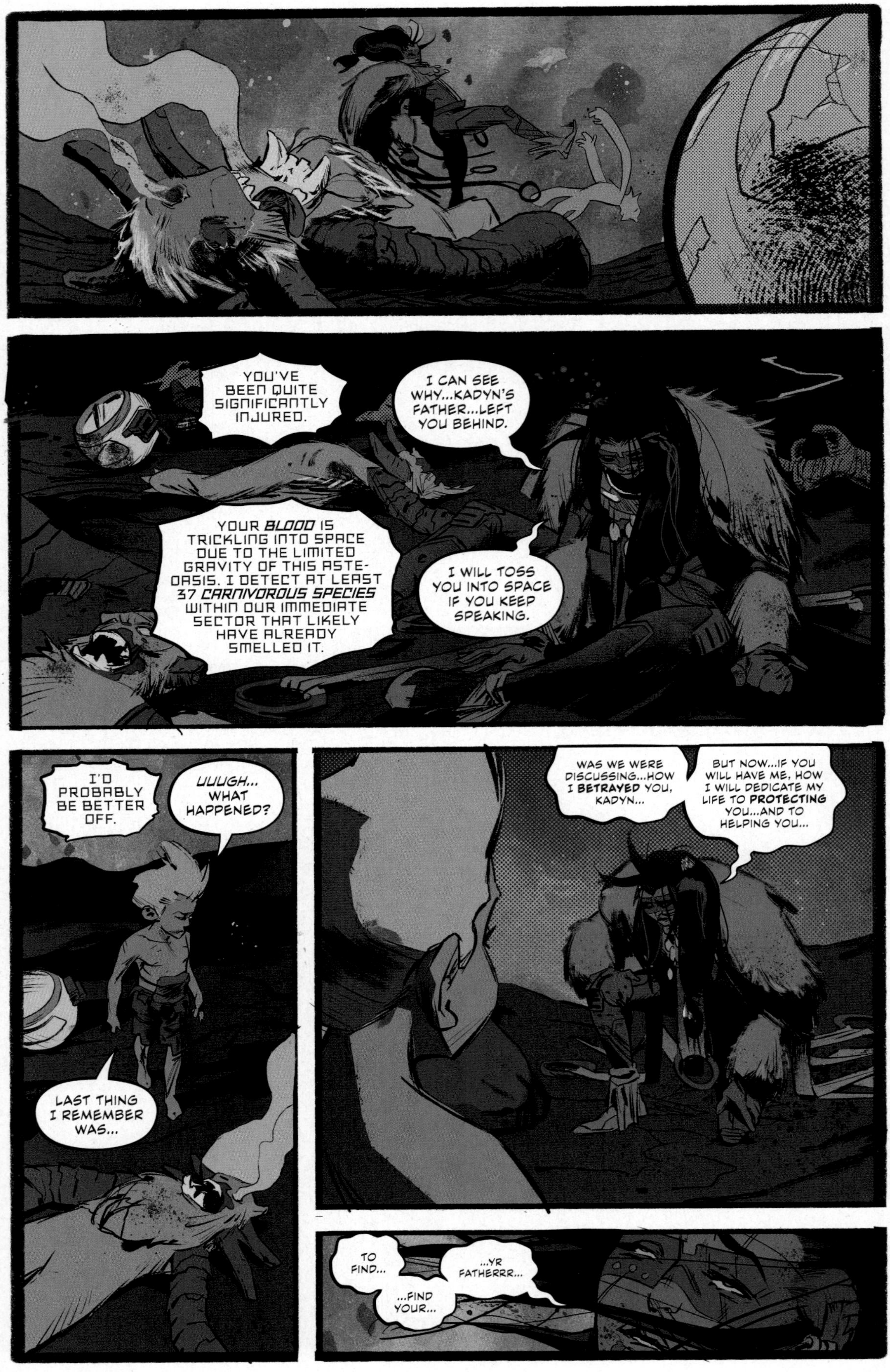
YOU'VE BEEN QUITE SIGNIFICANTLY INJURED.
I CAN SEE WHY...KADYN'S FATHER...LEFT YOU BEHIND.
YOUR BLOOD IS TRICKLING INTO SPACE DUE TO THE LIMITED GRAVITY OF THIS ASTE-OASIS. I DETECT AT LEAST 37 CARNIVOROUS SPECIES WITHIN OUR IMMEDIATE SECTOR THAT LIKELY HAVE ALREADY SMELLED IT.
I WILL TOSS YOU INTO SPACE IF YOU KEEP SPEAKING.
I'D PROBABLY BE BETTER OFF.
UUUGH... WHAT HAPPENED?
LAST THING I REMEMBER WAS...
WAS WE WERE DISCUSSING...HOW I BETRAYED YOU, KADYN...
BUT NOW...IF YOU WILL HAVE ME, HOW I WILL DEDICATE MY LIFE TO PROTECTING YOU...AND TO HELPING YOU...
TO FIND...
...FIND YOUR...
...YR FATHERRR...

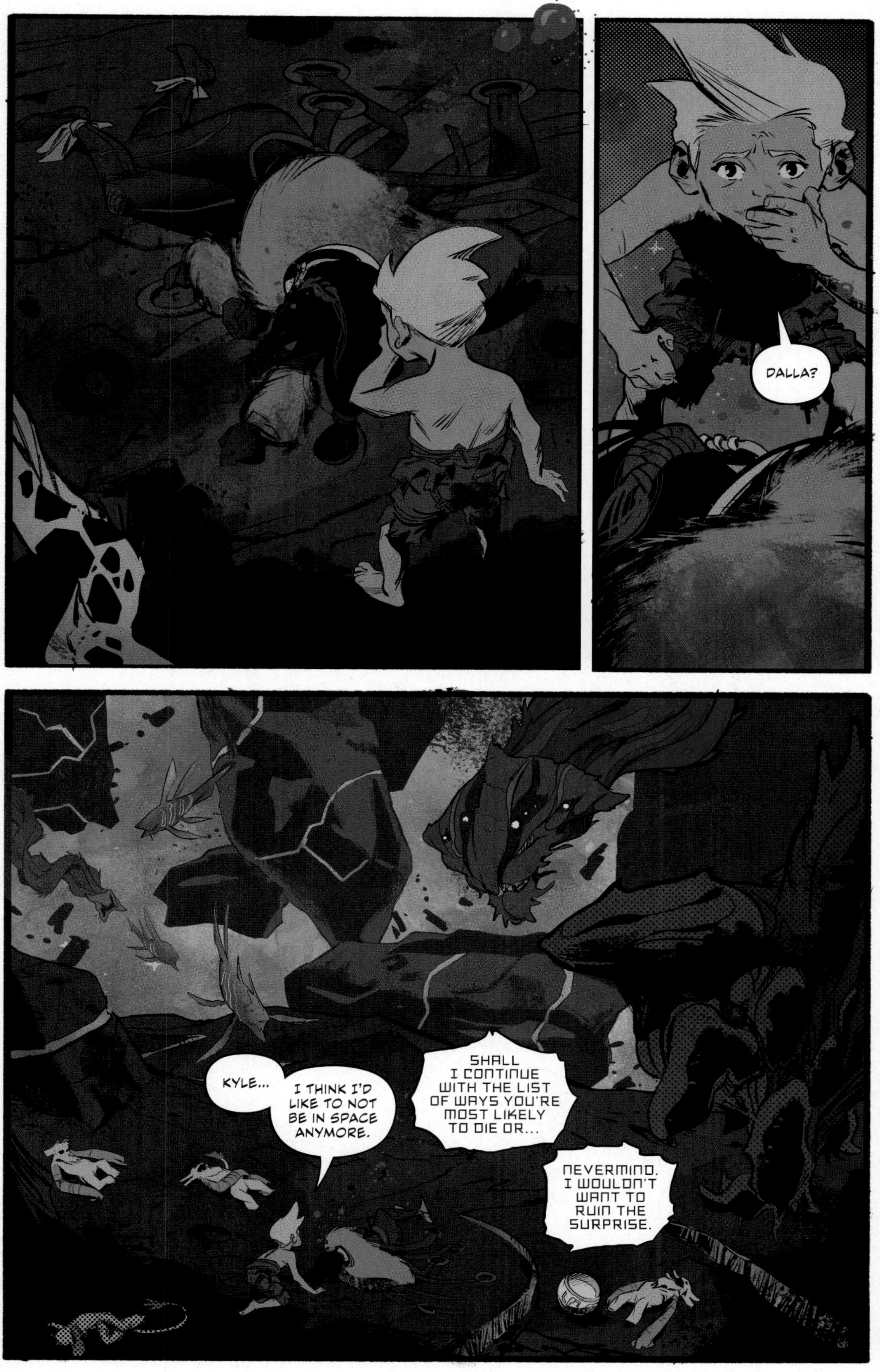
DALLA?
KYLE...
I THINK I'D LIKE TO NOT BE IN SPACE ANYMORE.
SHALL I CONTINUE WITH THE LIST OF WAYS YOU'RE MOST LIKELY TO DIE OR...
NEVERMIND. I WOULDN'T WANT TO RUIN THE SURPRISE.

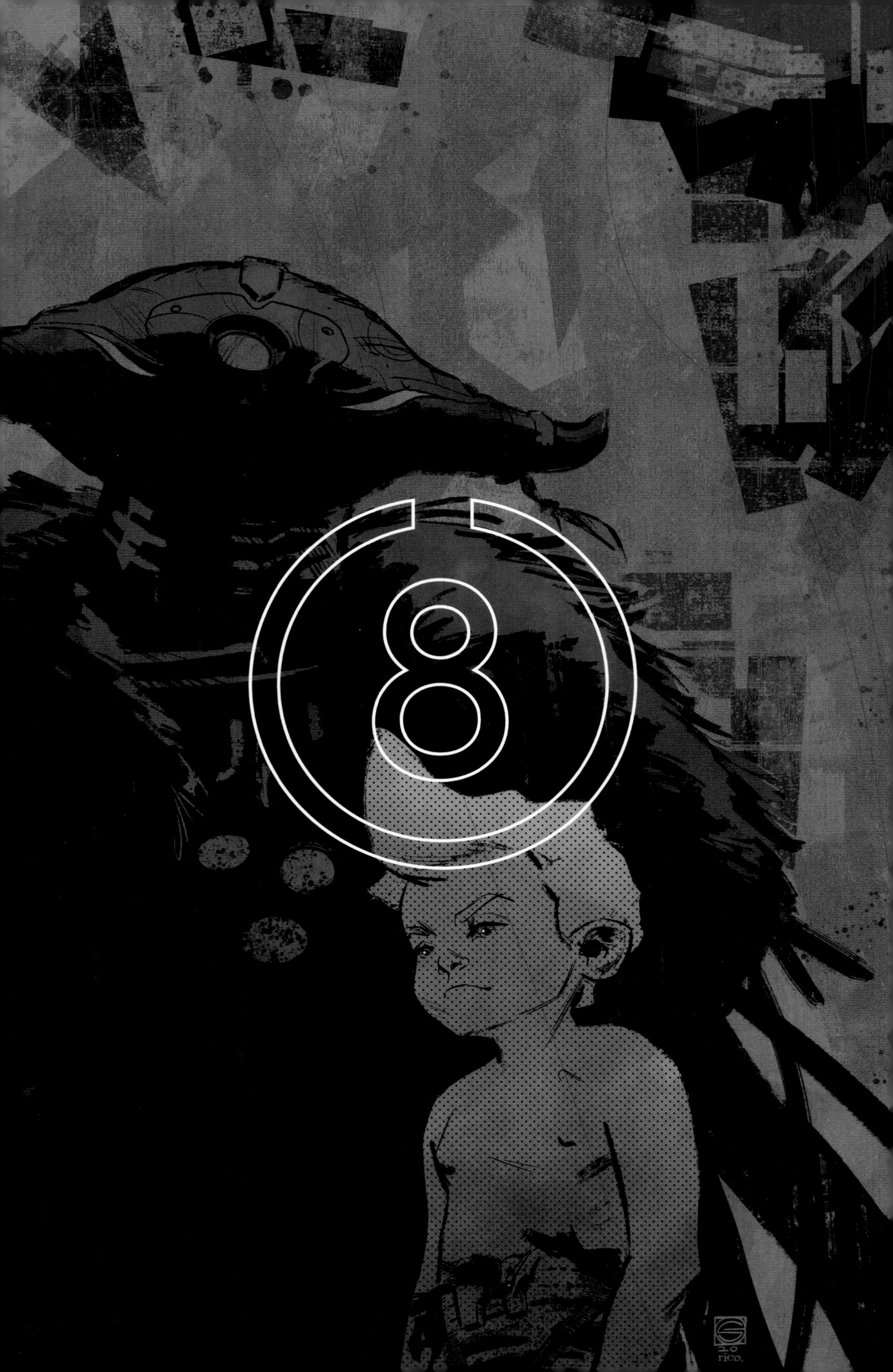
8

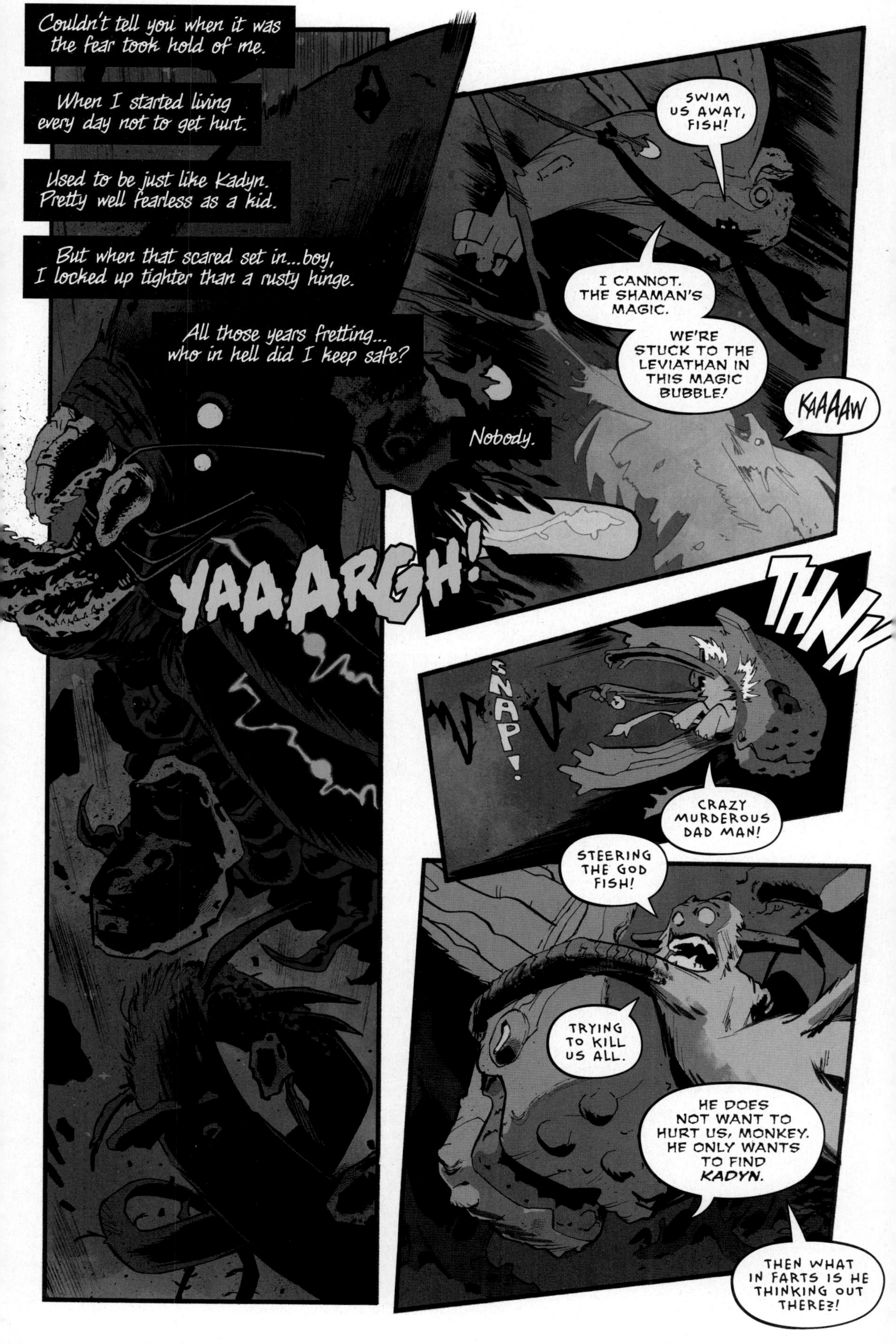
Couldn't tell you when it was the fear took hold of me.
When I started living every day not to get hurt.
Used to be just like Kadyn. Pretty well fearless as a kid.
But when that scared set in...boy, I locked up tighter than a rusty hinge.
All those years fretting... who in hell did I keep safe?
Nobody.
YAAARGH!
SWIM US AWAY, FISH!
I CANNOT. THE SHAMAN'S MAGIC.
WE'RE STUCK TO THE LEVIATHAN IN THIS MAGIC BUBBLE!
KAAAAW
THNK
SNAP!
CRAZY MURDEROUS DAD MAN!
STEERING THE GOD FISH!
TRYING TO KILL US ALL.
HE DOES NOT WANT TO HURT US, MONKEY. HE ONLY WANTS TO FIND KADYN.
THEN WHAT IN FARTS IS HE THINKING OUT THERE?!

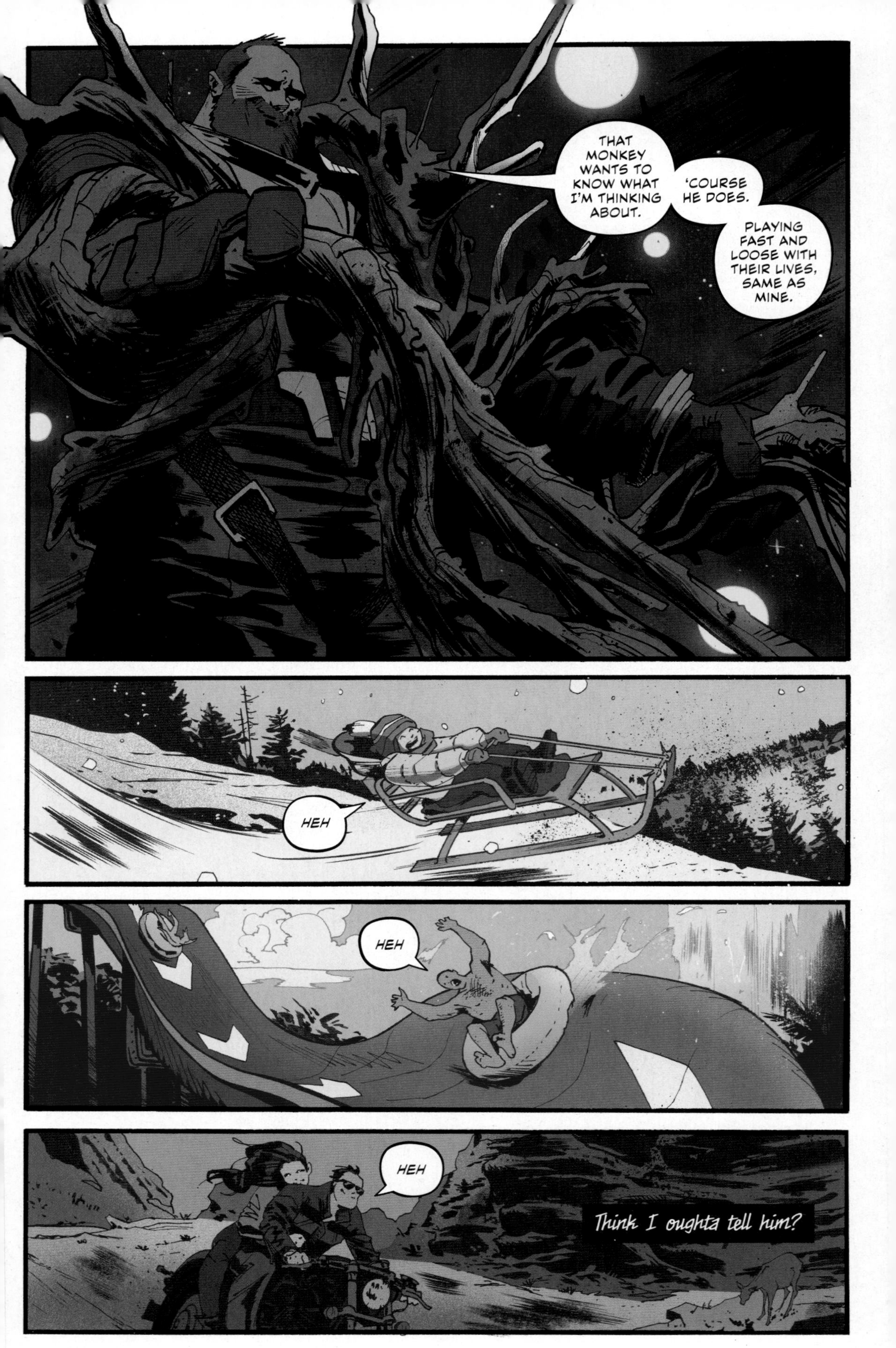
THAT MONKEY WANTS TO KNOW WHAT I'M THINKING ABOUT.
'COURSE HE DOES.
PLAYING FAST AND LOOSE WITH THEIR LIVES, SAME AS MINE.
HEH
HEH
HEH
Think I oughta tell him?

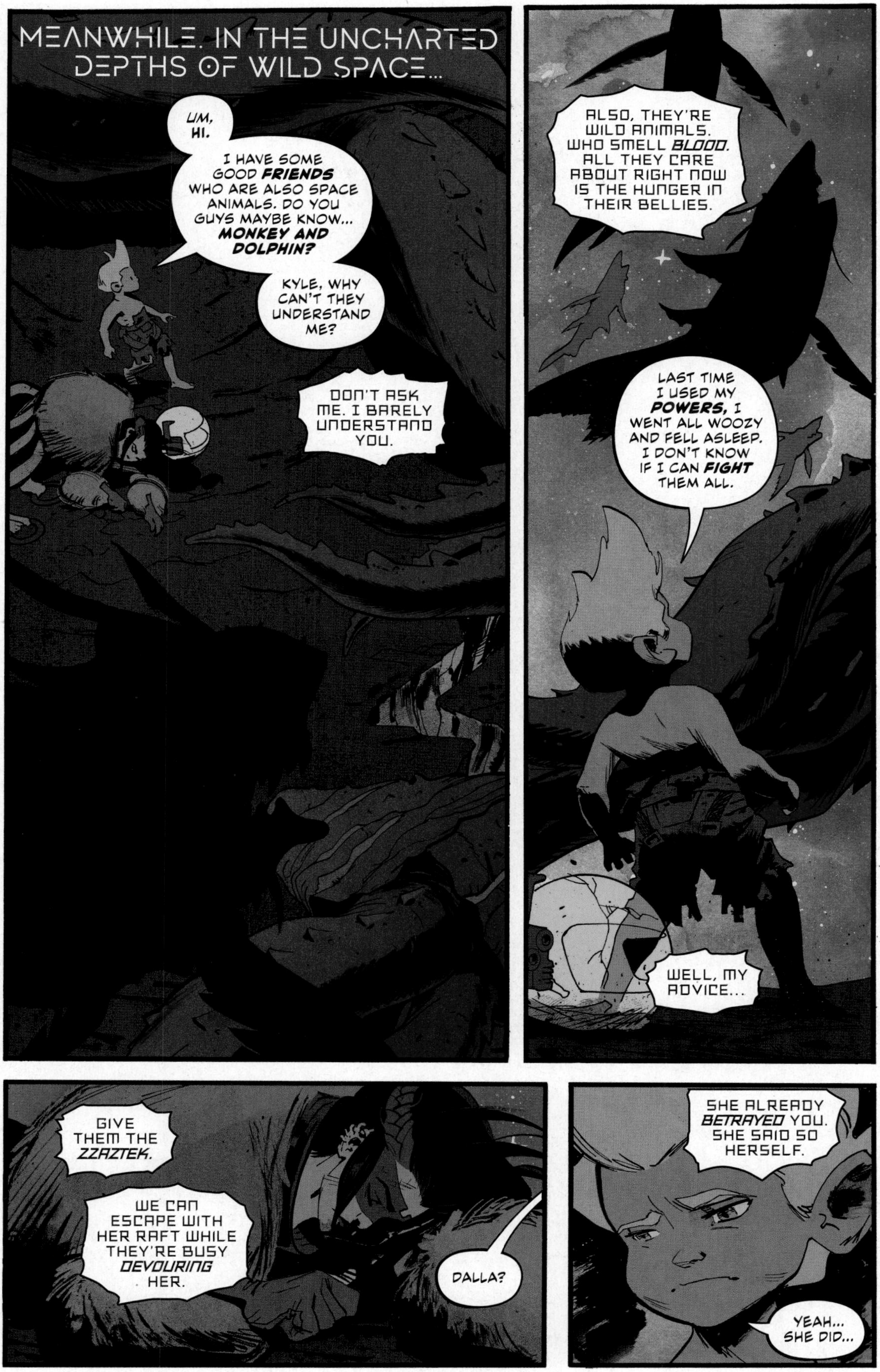
MEANWHILE, IN THE UNCHARTED DEPTHS OF WILD SPACE...
UM, HI.
I HAVE SOME GOOD FRIENDS WHO ARE ALSO SPACE ANIMALS. DO YOU GUYS MAYBE KNOW... MONKEY AND DOLPHIN?
KYLE, WHY CAN'T THEY UNDERSTAND ME?
DON'T ASK ME. I BARELY UNDERSTAND YOU.
ALSO, THEY'RE WILD ANIMALS. WHO SMELL BLOOD. ALL THEY CARE ABOUT RIGHT NOW IS THE HUNGER IN THEIR BELLIES.
LAST TIME I USED MY POWERS, I WENT ALL WOOZY AND FELL ASLEEP. I DON'T KNOW IF I CAN FIGHT THEM ALL.
WELL, MY ADVICE...
GIVE THEM THE ZZAZTEK.
WE CAN ESCAPE WITH HER RAFT WHILE THEY'RE BUSY DEVOURING HER.
DALLA?
SHE ALREADY BETRAYED YOU. SHE SAID SO HERSELF.
YEAH... SHE DID...

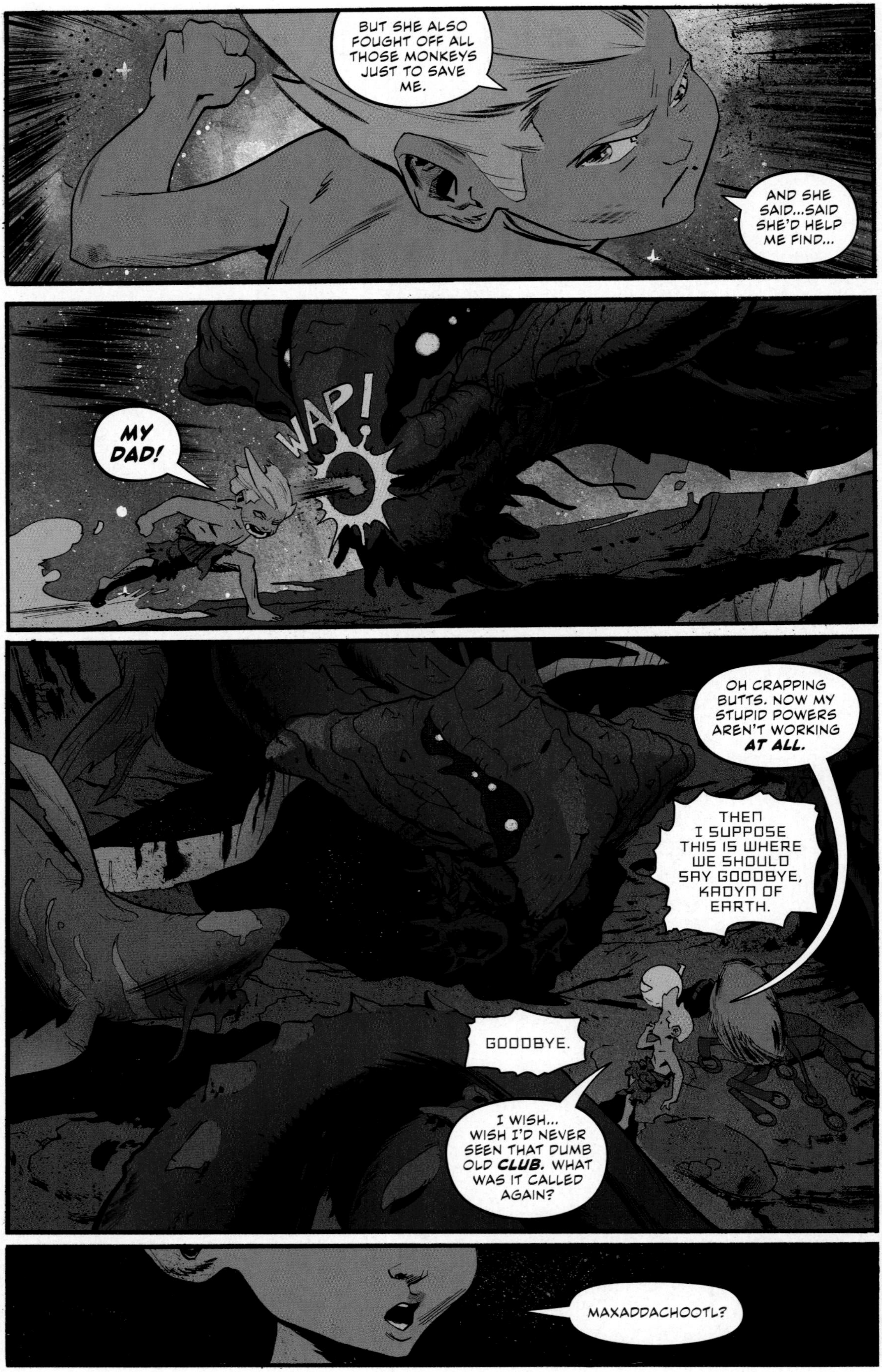

BUT SHE ALSO FOUGHT OFF ALL THOSE MONKEYS JUST TO SAVE ME.
AND SHE SAID...SAID SHE'D HELP ME FIND...
MY DAD!
WAP!
OH CRAPPING BUTTS. NOW MY STUPID POWERS AREN'T WORKING AT ALL.
THEN I SUPPOSE THIS IS WHERE WE SHOULD SAY GOODBYE, KADYN OF EARTH.
GOODBYE.
I WISH... WISH I'D NEVER SEEN THAT DUMB OLD CLUB. WHAT WAS IT CALLED AGAIN?
MAXADDACHOOTL?

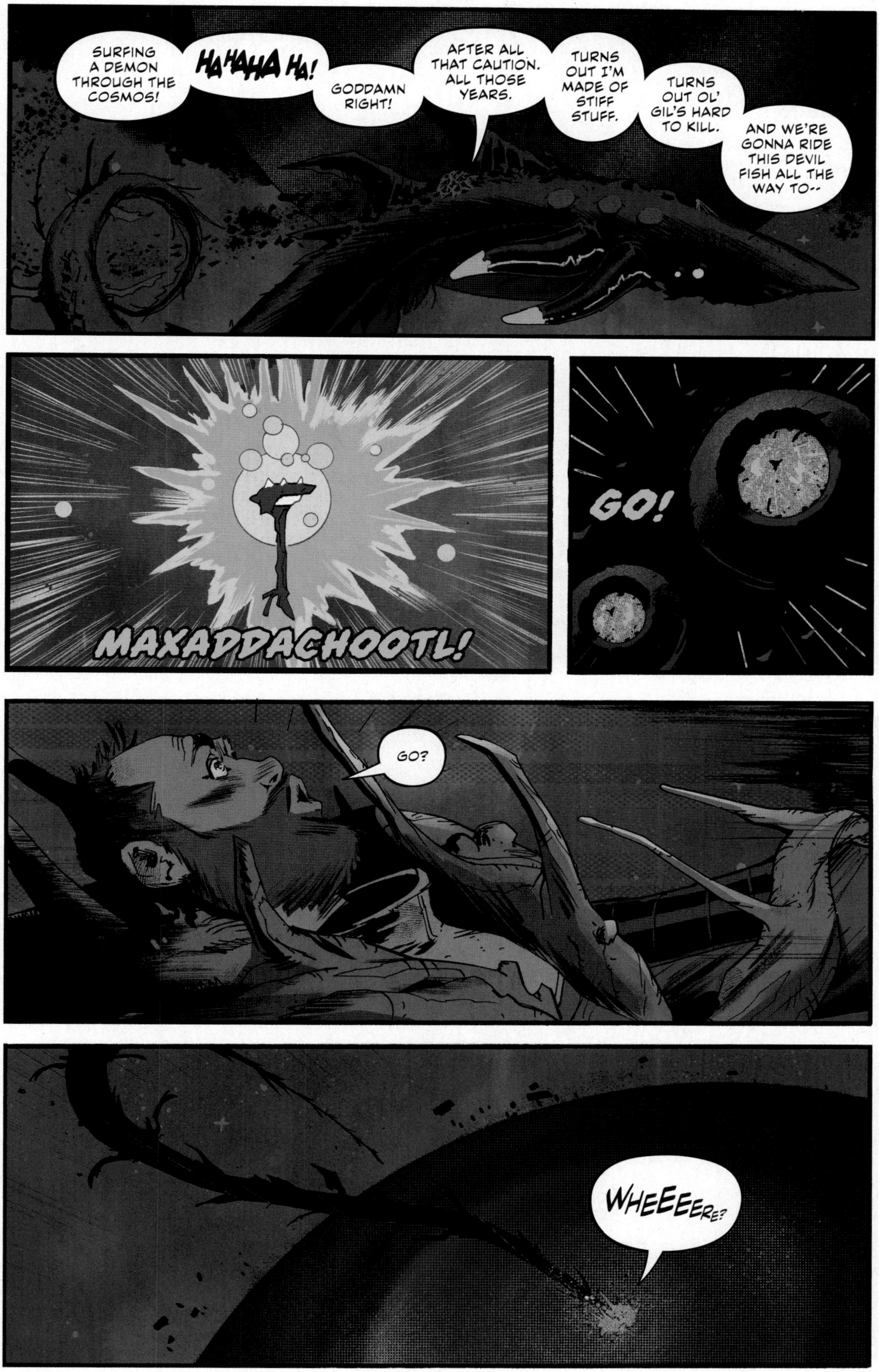

SURFING A DEMON THROUGH THE COSMOS!
HAHAHA HA!
GODDAMN RIGHT!
AFTER ALL THAT CAUTION. ALL THOSE YEARS.
TURNS OUT I'M MADE OF STIFF STUFF.
TURNS OUT OL' GIL'S HARD TO KILL.
AND WE'RE GONNA RIDE THIS DEVIL FISH ALL THE WAY TO--
MAXADDACHOOTL!
GO!
GO?
WHEEEEEre?

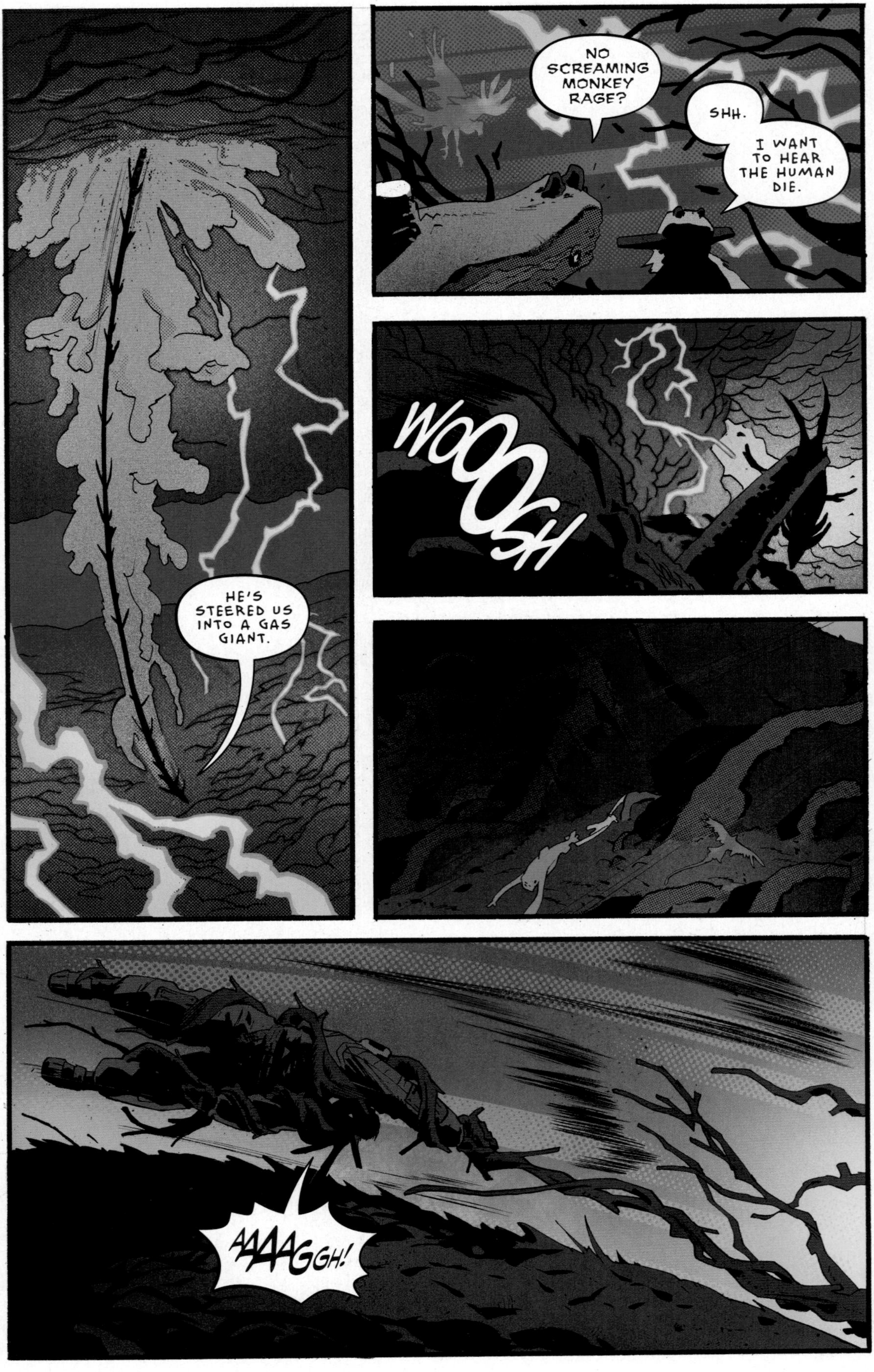
HE'S STEERED US INTO A GAS GIANT.
NO SCREAMING MONKEY RAGE?
SHH.
I WANT TO HEAR THE HUMAN DIE.
WOOOSH
AAAAGGH!

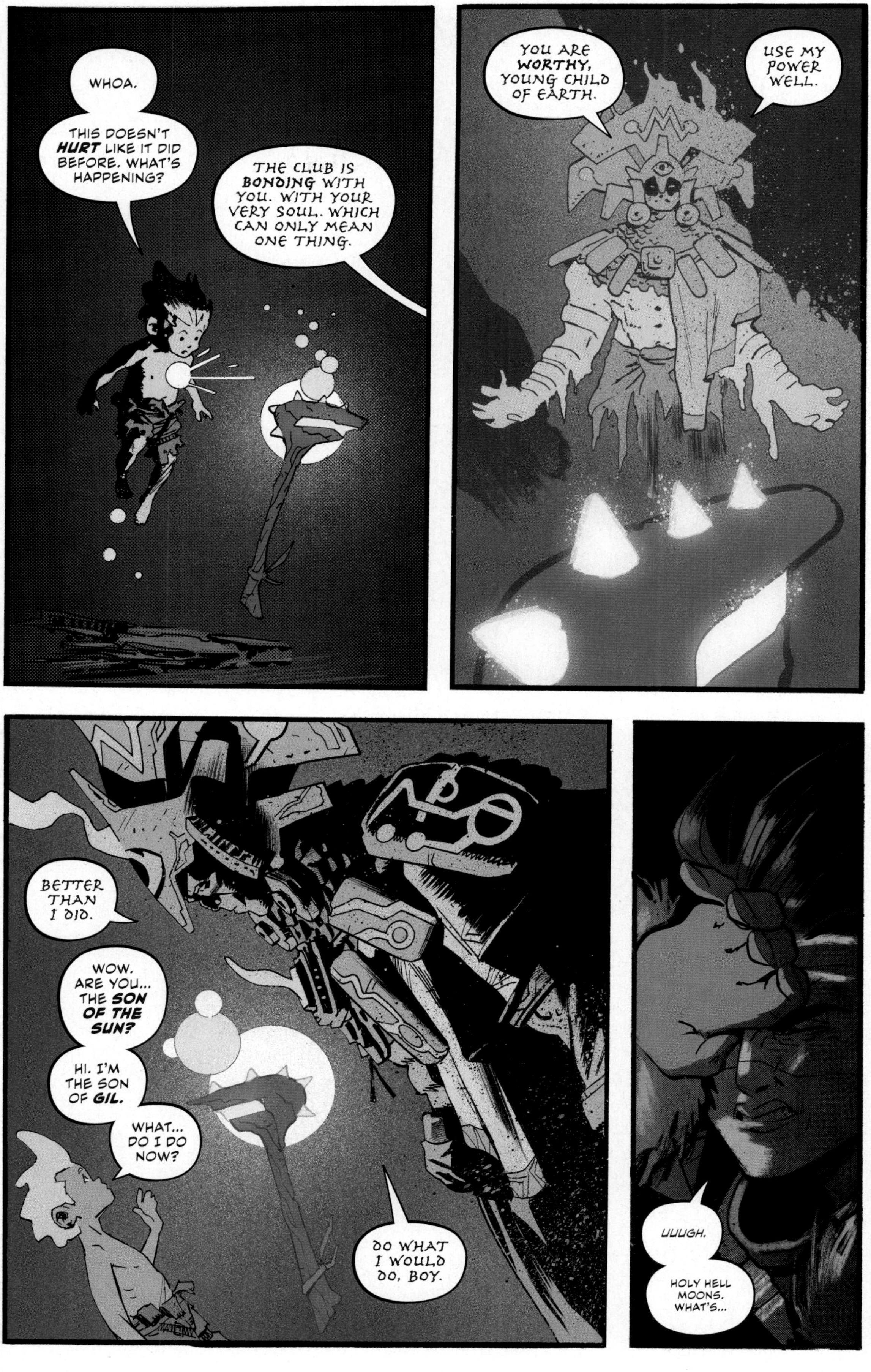
WHOA.
THIS DOESN'T HURT LIKE IT DID BEFORE. WHAT'S HAPPENING?
THE CLUB IS BONDING WITH YOU. WITH YOUR VERY SOUL. WHICH CAN ONLY MEAN ONE THING.
YOU ARE WORTHY, YOUNG CHILD OF EARTH.
USE MY POWER WELL.
BETTER THAN I DID.
WOW. ARE YOU... THE SON OF THE SUN?
HI. I'M THE SON OF GIL.
WHAT... DO I DO NOW?
DO WHAT I WOULD DO, BOY.
UUUGH.
HOLY HELL MOONS. WHAT'S...

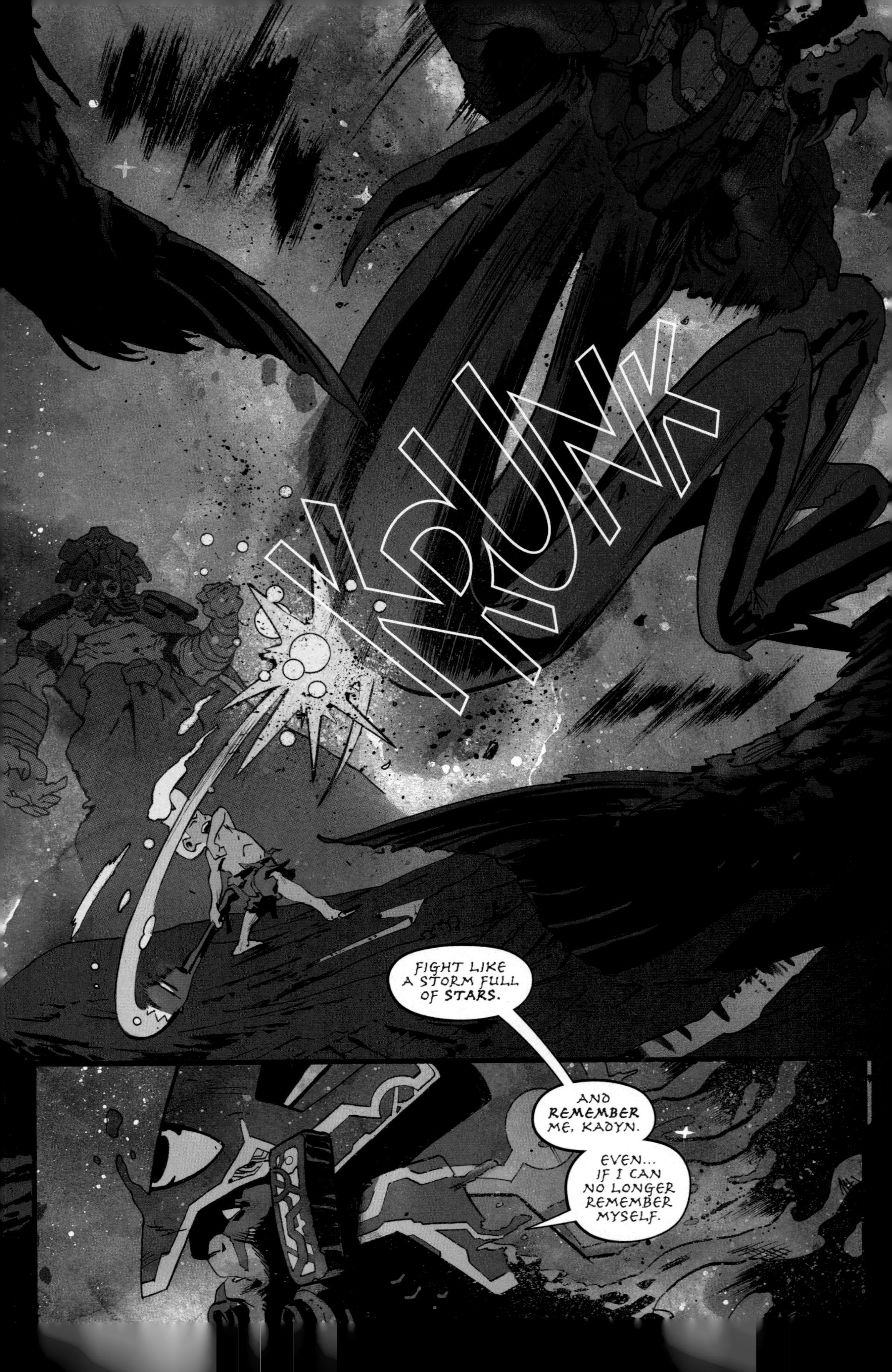

KRUNK
FIGHT LIKE A STORM FULL OF STARS.
AND REMEMBER ME, KADYN.
EVEN... IF I CAN NO LONGER REMEMBER MYSELF.

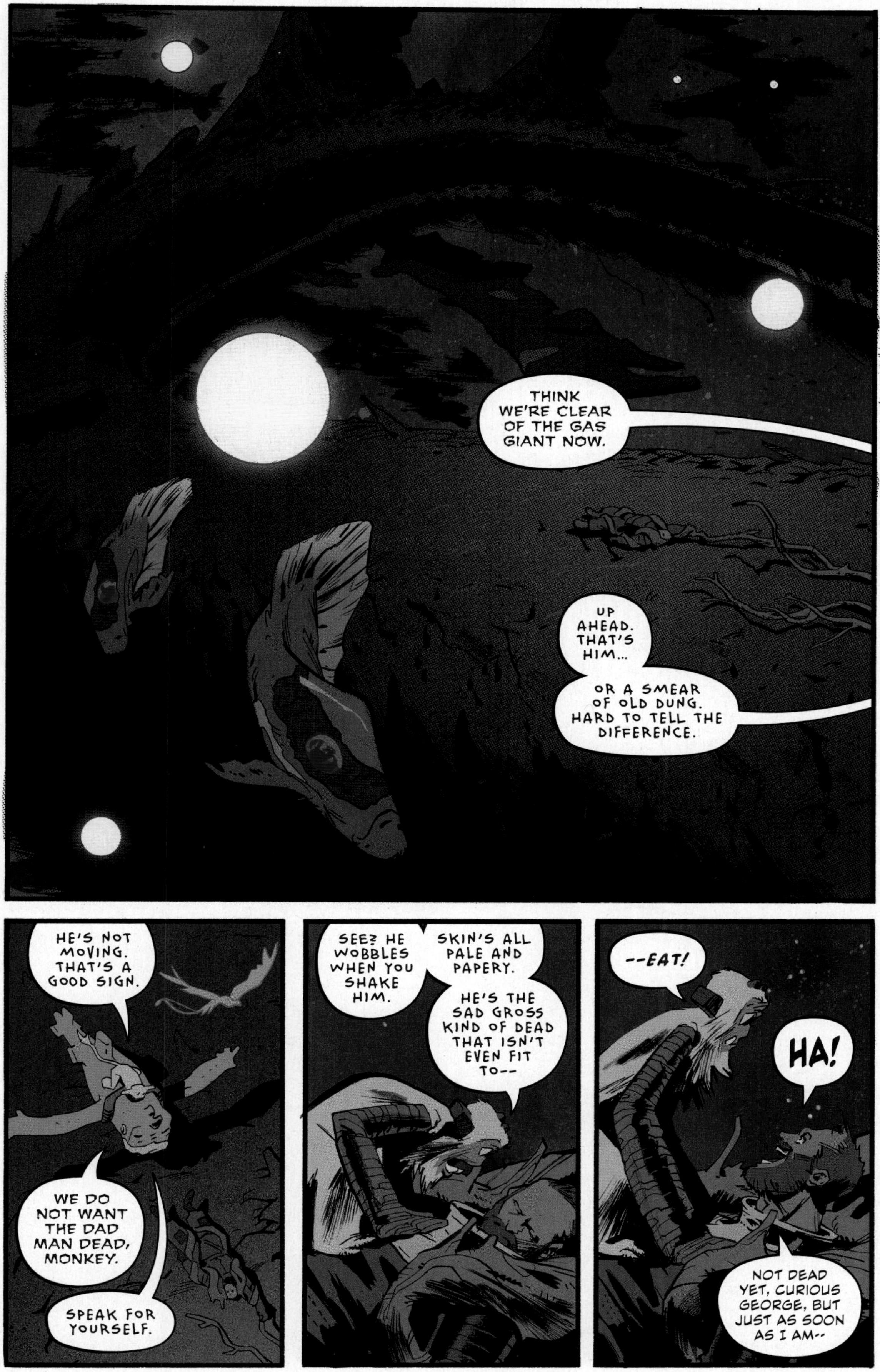
THINK WE'RE CLEAR OF THE GAS GIANT NOW.
UP AHEAD. THAT'S HIM...
OR A SMEAR OF OLD DUNG. HARD TO TELL THE DIFFERENCE.
HE'S NOT MOVING. THAT'S A GOOD SIGN.
WE DO NOT WANT THE DAD MAN DEAD, MONKEY.
SPEAK FOR YOURSELF.
SEE? HE WOBBLES WHEN YOU SHAKE HIM.
SKIN'S ALL PALE AND PAPERY.
HE'S THE SAD GROSS KIND OF DEAD THAT ISN'T EVEN FIT TO--
--EAT!
HA!
NOT DEAD YET, CURIOUS GEORGE, BUT JUST AS SOON AS I AM--

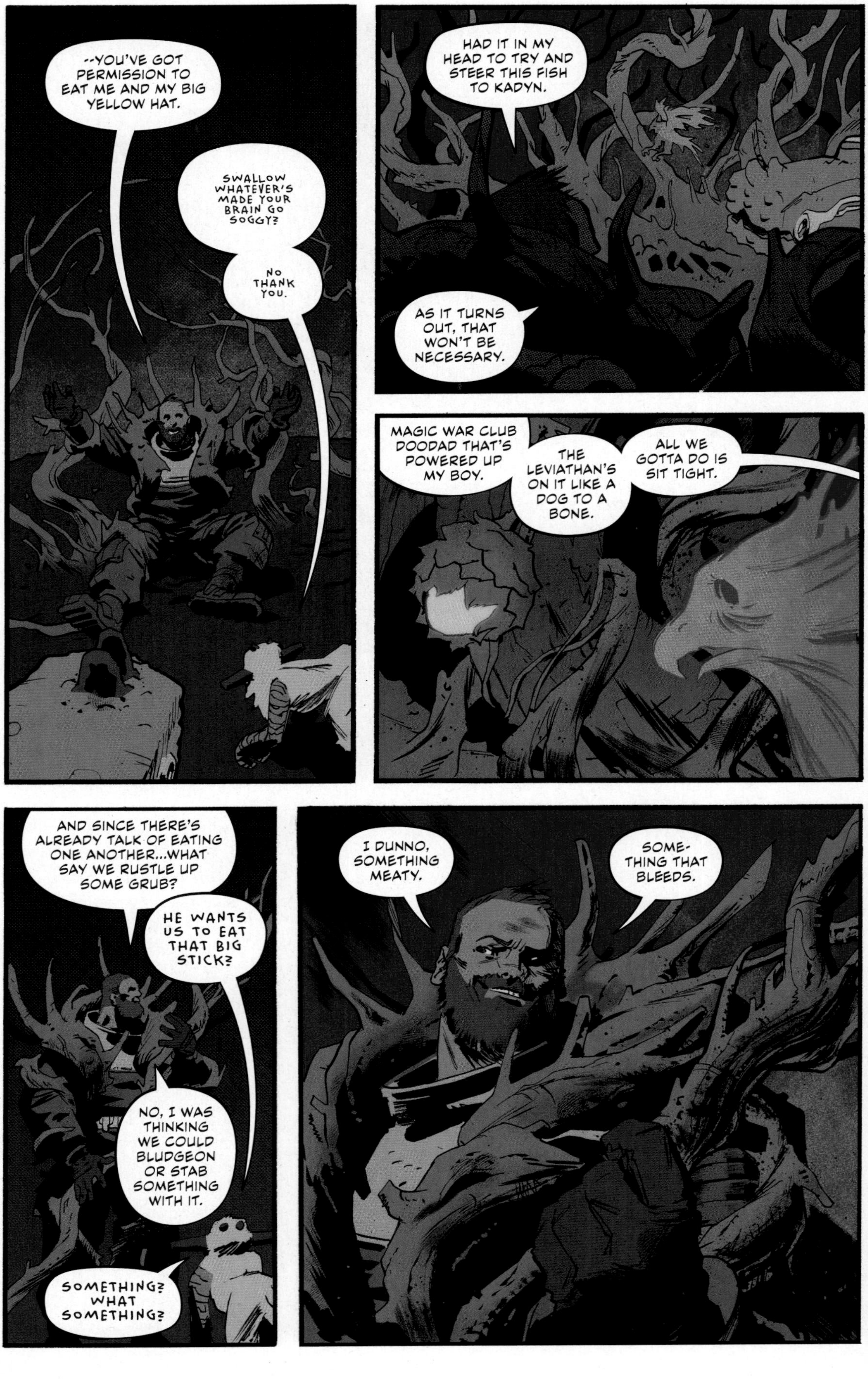
--YOU'VE GOT PERMISSION TO EAT ME AND MY BIG YELLOW HAT.
SWALLOW WHATEVER'S MADE YOUR BRAIN GO SOGGY?
NO THANK YOU.
HAD IT IN MY HEAD TO TRY AND STEER THIS FISH TO KADYN.
AS IT TURNS OUT, THAT WON'T BE NECESSARY.
MAGIC WAR CLUB DOODAD THAT'S POWERED UP MY BOY.
THE LEVIATHAN'S ON IT LIKE A DOG TO A BONE.
ALL WE GOTTA DO IS SIT TIGHT.
AND SINCE THERE'S ALREADY TALK OF EATING ONE ANOTHER...WHAT SAY WE RUSTLE UP SOME GRUB?
HE WANTS US TO EAT THAT BIG STICK?
NO, I WAS THINKING WE COULD BLUDGEON OR STAB SOMETHING WITH IT.
SOMETHING? WHAT SOMETHING?
I DUNNO, SOMETHING MEATY.
SOME-THING THAT BLEEDS.

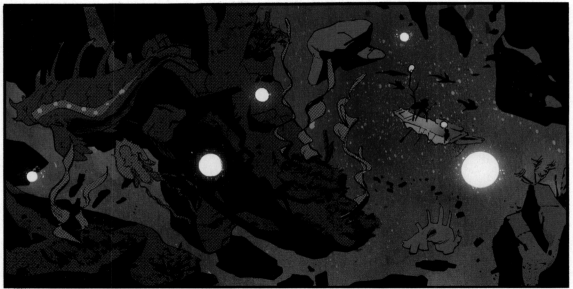

THIS COULD BE A VERY **LONG** JOURNEY, KADYN.

IT'LL BE EVEN LONGER IF YOU WON'T **SPEAK** TO ME THE ENTIRE WAY.

I DON'T EXPECT YOU TO FORGIVE MY BETRAYAL. I **OWE** YOU. EVEN BEFORE YOU SAVED MY LIFE WITH YOUR CLUB.

I KNOW YOU'VE **RE-ABSORBED** IT AGAIN, BUT WHEN YOU WERE FIGHTING, I SWEAR...

...I SAW A GLIMPSE OF **QUASARRO** HIMSELF.

IF ANYONE CAN HELP US UNDERSTAND WHAT'S HAPPENED TO YOU, KADYN... **TRULY** UNDERSTAND, IT'LL BE THE PEOPLE WE'RE SAILING TO...

YOU HAVE TO **PROMISE,** DALLA.

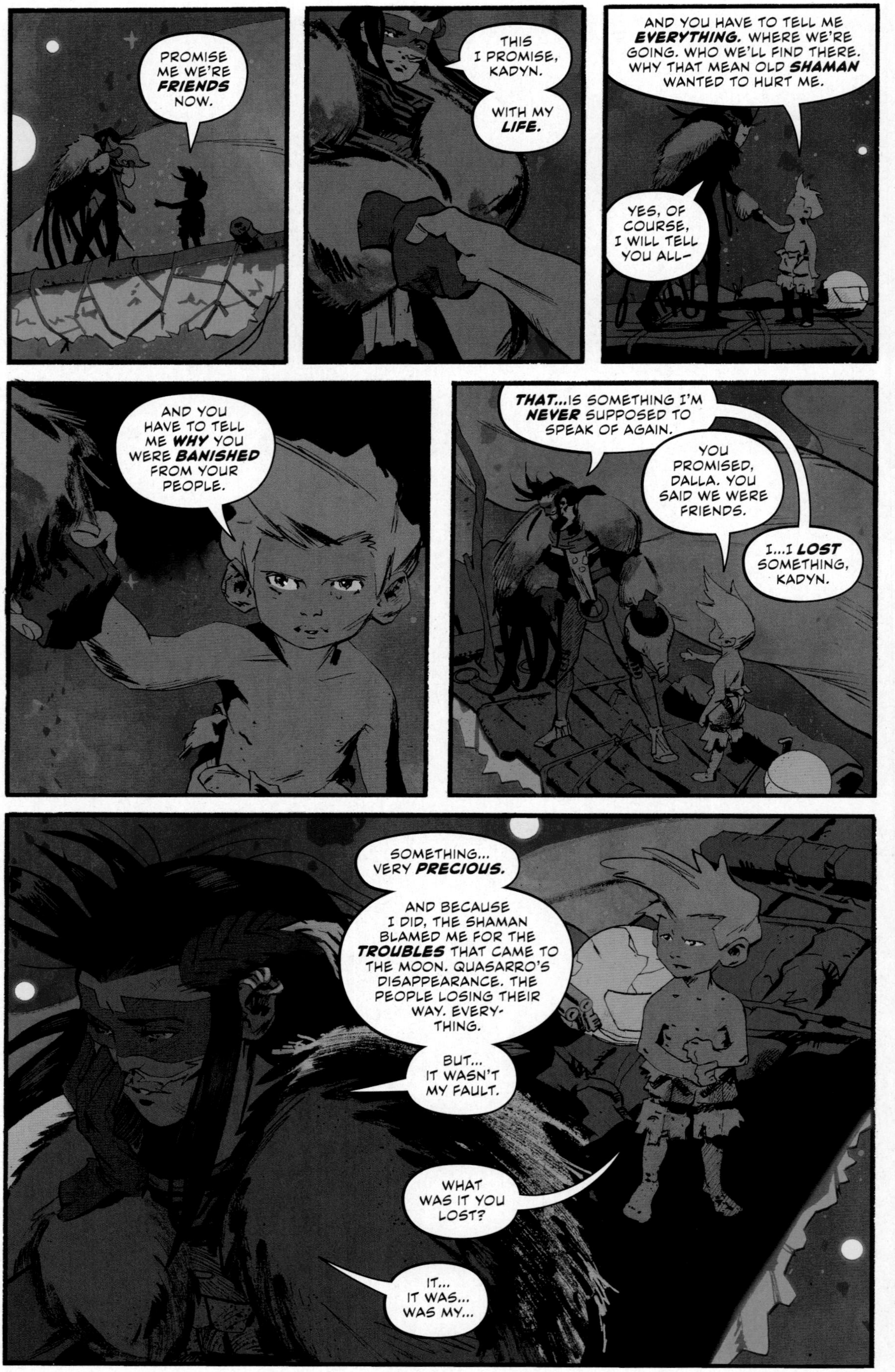

PROMISE ME WE'RE FRIENDS NOW.
THIS I PROMISE, KADYN.
WITH MY LIFE.
AND YOU HAVE TO TELL ME EVERYTHING. WHERE WE'RE GOING. WHO WE'LL FIND THERE. WHY THAT MEAN OLD SHAMAN WANTED TO HURT ME.
YES, OF COURSE, I WILL TELL YOU ALL—
AND YOU HAVE TO TELL ME WHY YOU WERE BANISHED FROM YOUR PEOPLE.
THAT...IS SOMETHING I'M NEVER SUPPOSED TO SPEAK OF AGAIN.
YOU PROMISED, DALLA. YOU SAID WE WERE FRIENDS.
I...I LOST SOMETHING, KADYN.
SOMETHING... VERY PRECIOUS.
AND BECAUSE I DID, THE SHAMAN BLAMED ME FOR THE TROUBLES THAT CAME TO THE MOON. QUASARRO'S DISAPPEARANCE. THE PEOPLE LOSING THEIR WAY. EVERY-THING.
BUT... IT WASN'T MY FAULT.
WHAT WAS IT YOU LOST?
IT... IT WAS... WAS MY...

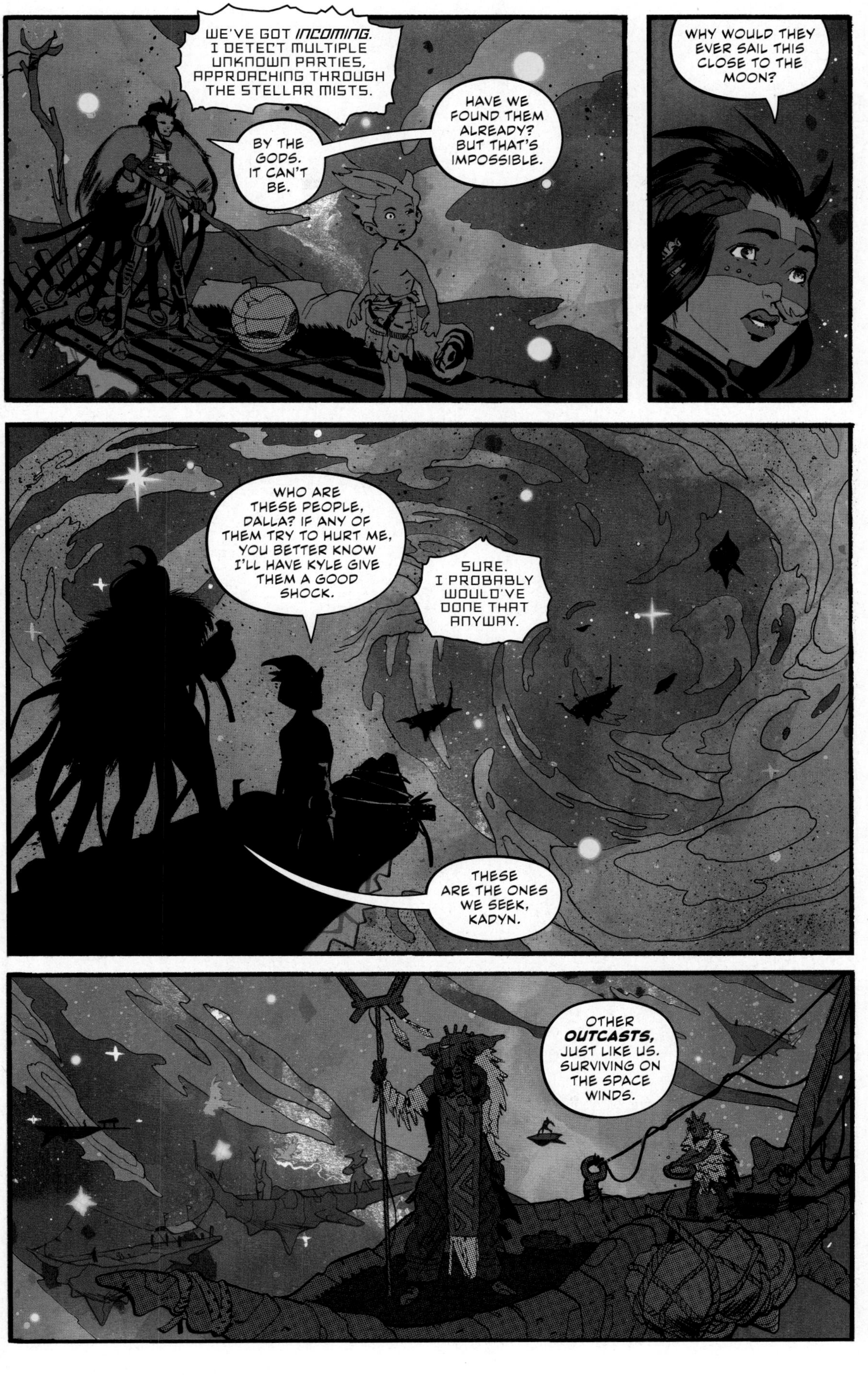
WE'VE GOT INCOMING. I DETECT MULTIPLE UNKNOWN PARTIES, APPROACHING THROUGH THE STELLAR MISTS.
BY THE GODS. IT CAN'T BE.
HAVE WE FOUND THEM ALREADY? BUT THAT'S IMPOSSIBLE.
WHY WOULD THEY EVER SAIL THIS CLOSE TO THE MOON?
WHO ARE THESE PEOPLE, DALLA? IF ANY OF THEM TRY TO HURT ME, YOU BETTER KNOW I'LL HAVE KYLE GIVE THEM A GOOD SHOCK.
SURE. I PROBABLY WOULD'VE DONE THAT ANYWAY.
THESE ARE THE ONES WE SEEK, KADYN.
OTHER OUTCASTS, JUST LIKE US. SURVIVING ON THE SPACE WINDS.

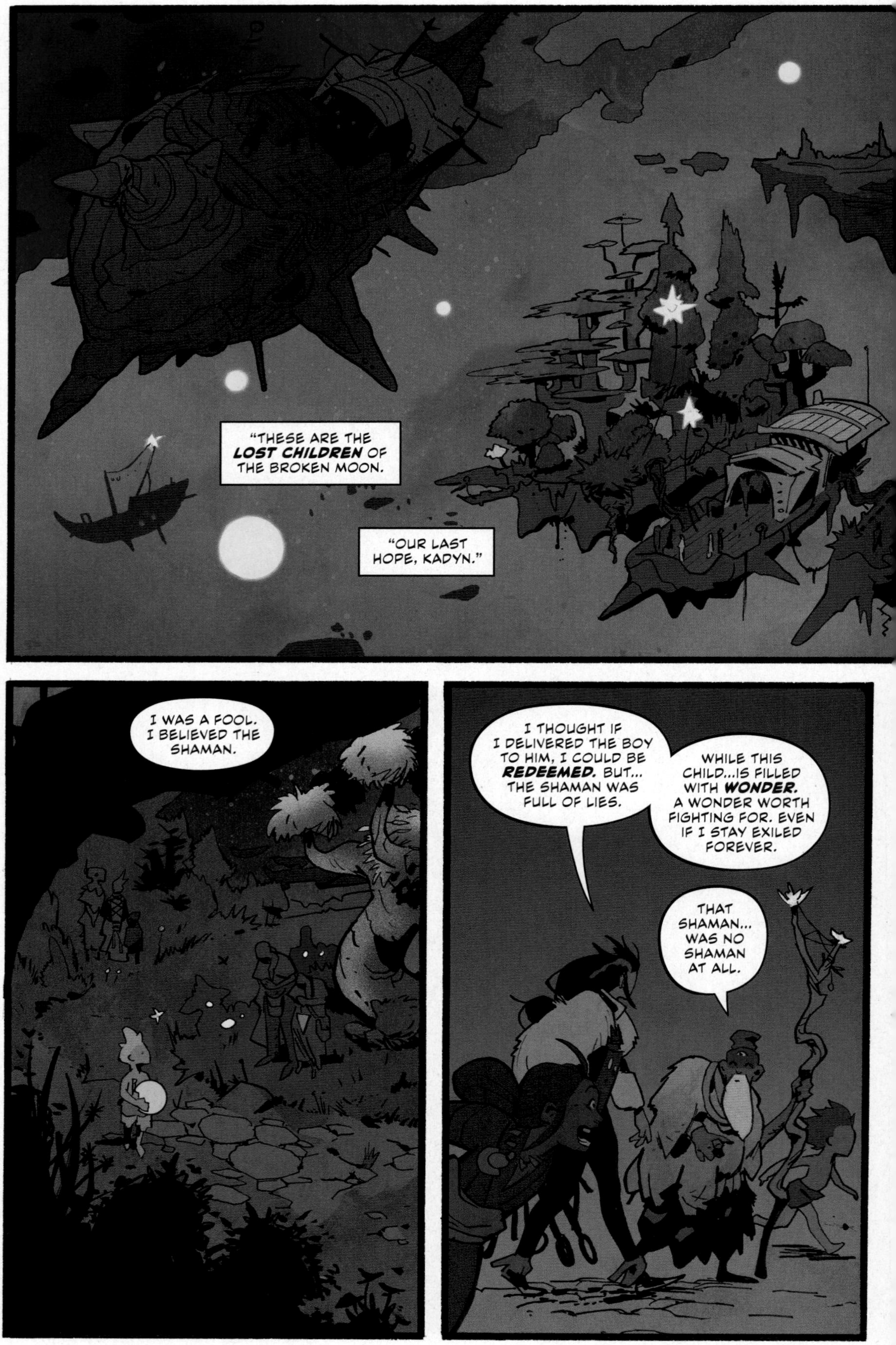
"THESE ARE THE **LOST CHILDREN** OF THE BROKEN MOON.
"OUR LAST HOPE, KADYN."
I WAS A FOOL. I BELIEVED THE SHAMAN.
I THOUGHT IF I DELIVERED THE BOY TO HIM, I COULD BE **REDEEMED.** BUT... THE SHAMAN WAS FULL OF LIES.
WHILE THIS CHILD...IS FILLED WITH **WONDER.** A WONDER WORTH FIGHTING FOR. EVEN IF I STAY EXILED FOREVER.
THAT SHAMAN... WAS NO SHAMAN AT ALL.

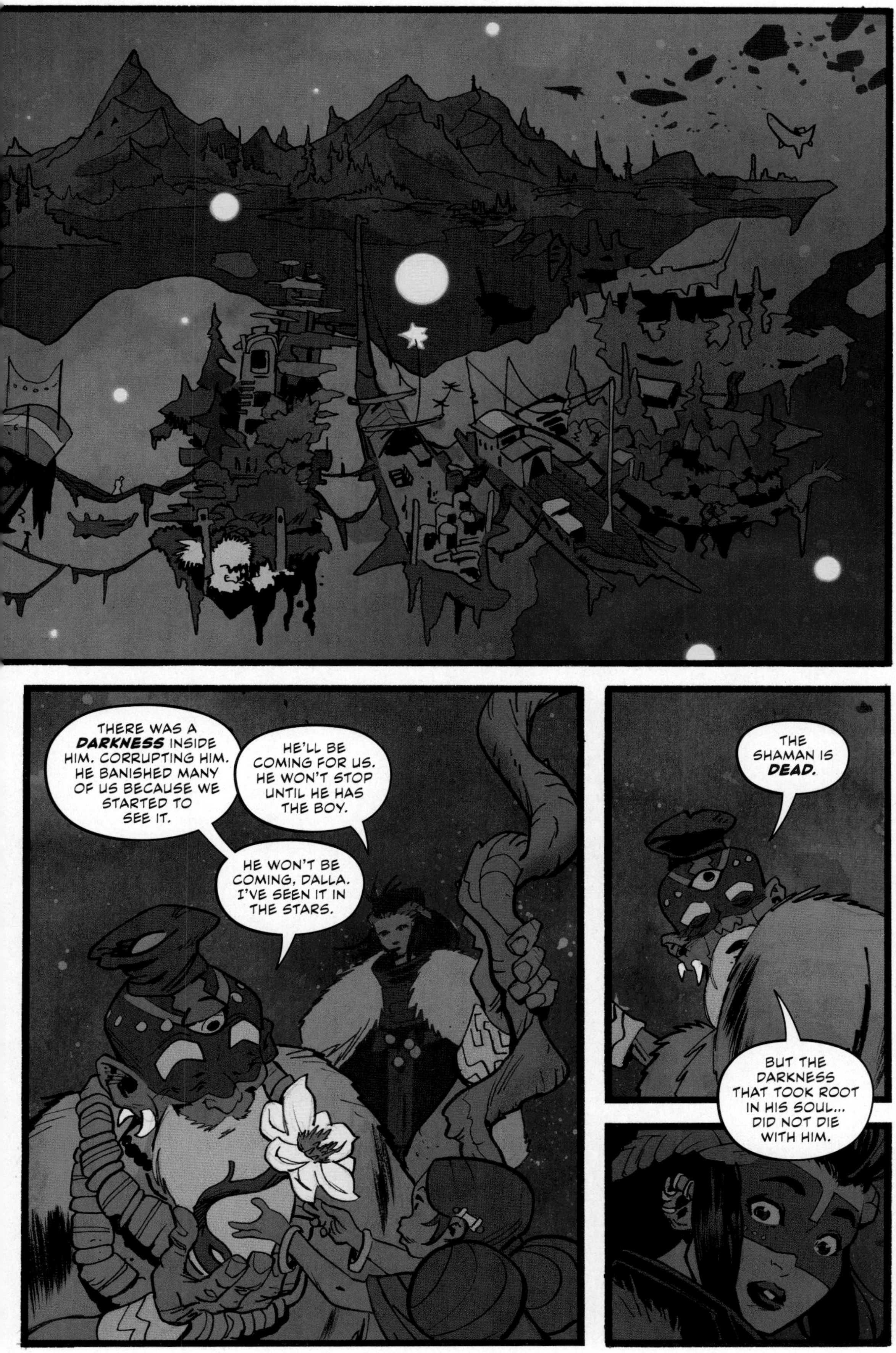
THERE WAS A DARKNESS INSIDE HIM. CORRUPTING HIM. HE BANISHED MANY OF US BECAUSE WE STARTED TO SEE IT.
HE'LL BE COMING FOR US. HE WON'T STOP UNTIL HE HAS THE BOY.
HE WON'T BE COMING, DALLA. I'VE SEEN IT IN THE STARS.
THE SHAMAN IS DEAD.
BUT THE DARKNESS THAT TOOK ROOT IN HIS SOUL... DID NOT DIE WITH HIM.

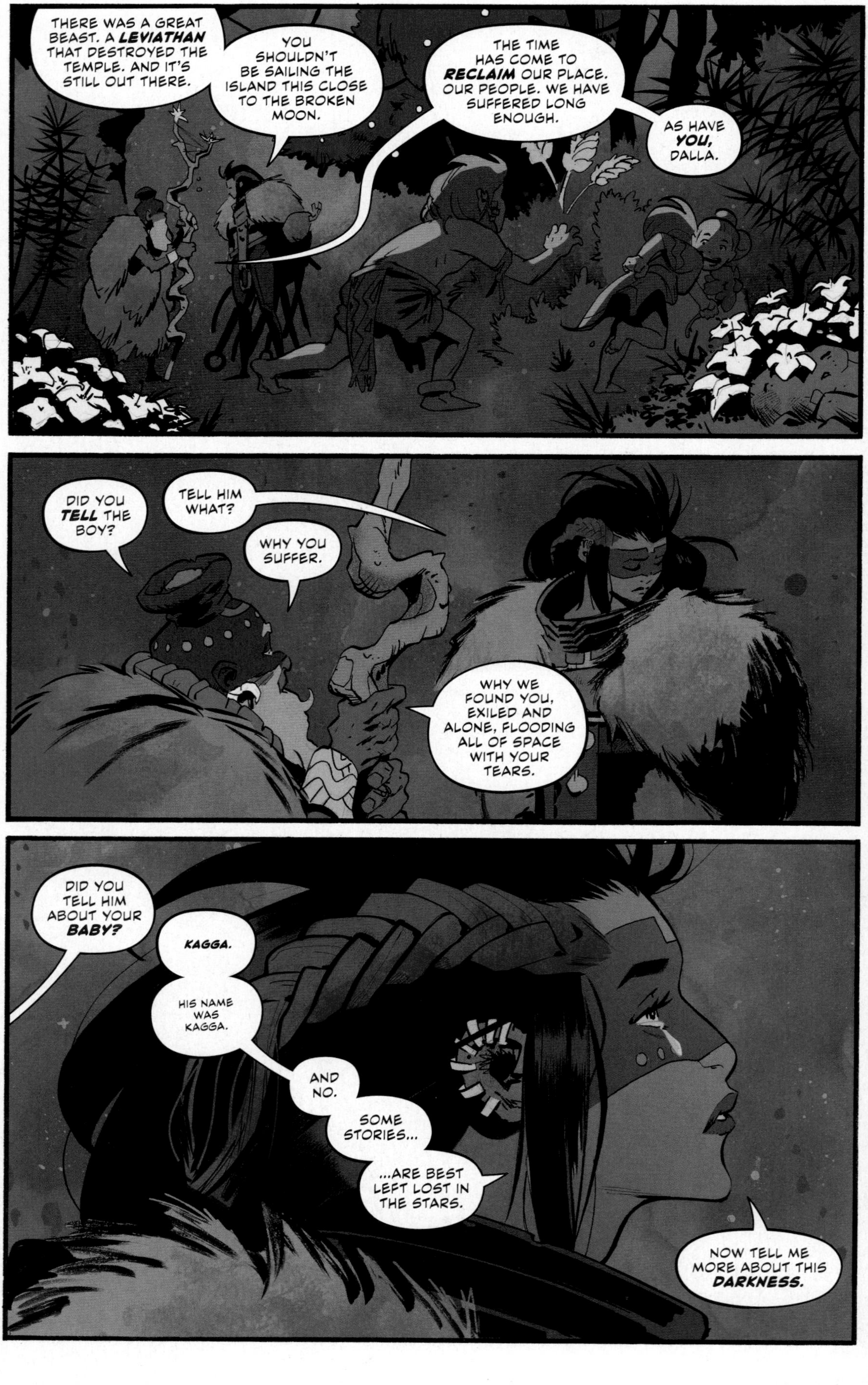
THERE WAS A GREAT BEAST. A LEVIATHAN THAT DESTROYED THE TEMPLE. AND IT'S STILL OUT THERE.
YOU SHOULDN'T BE SAILING THE ISLAND THIS CLOSE TO THE BROKEN MOON.
THE TIME HAS COME TO RECLAIM OUR PLACE. OUR PEOPLE. WE HAVE SUFFERED LONG ENOUGH.
AS HAVE YOU, DALLA.
DID YOU TELL THE BOY?
TELL HIM WHAT?
WHY YOU SUFFER.
WHY WE FOUND YOU, EXILED AND ALONE, FLOODING ALL OF SPACE WITH YOUR TEARS.
DID YOU TELL HIM ABOUT YOUR BABY?
KAGGA.
HIS NAME WAS KAGGA.
AND NO.
SOME STORIES...
...ARE BEST LEFT LOST IN THE STARS.
NOW TELL ME MORE ABOUT THIS DARKNESS.

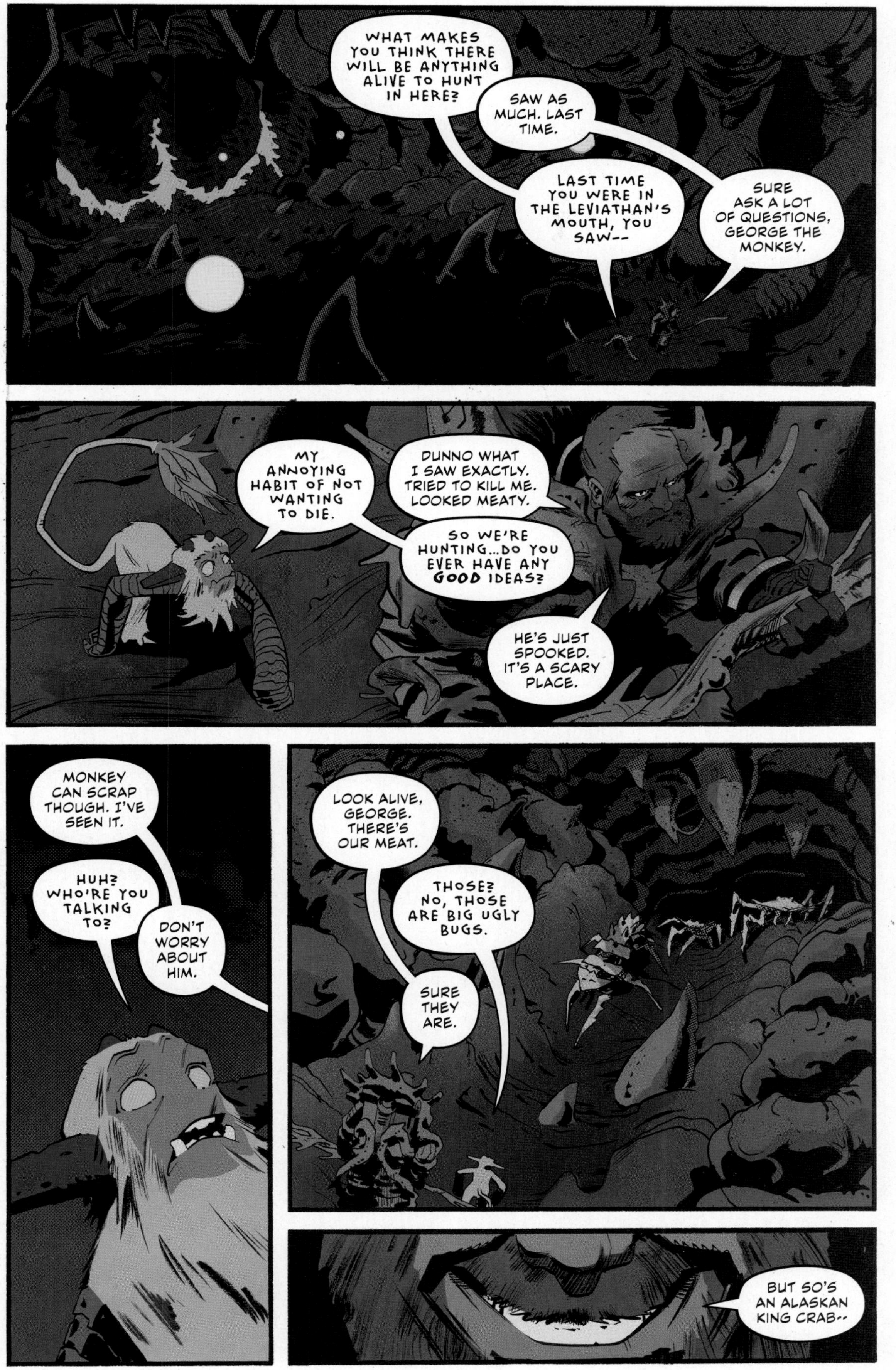
WHAT MAKES YOU THINK THERE WILL BE ANYTHING ALIVE TO HUNT IN HERE?
SAW AS MUCH. LAST TIME.
LAST TIME YOU WERE IN THE LEVIATHAN'S MOUTH, YOU SAW--
SURE ASK A LOT OF QUESTIONS, GEORGE THE MONKEY.
DUNNO WHAT I SAW EXACTLY. TRIED TO KILL ME. LOOKED MEATY.
MY ANNOYING HABIT OF NOT WANTING TO DIE.
SO WE'RE HUNTING...DO YOU EVER HAVE ANY GOOD IDEAS?
HE'S JUST SPOOKED. IT'S A SCARY PLACE.
MONKEY CAN SCRAP THOUGH. I'VE SEEN IT.
HUH? WHO'RE YOU TALKING TO?
DON'T WORRY ABOUT HIM.
LOOK ALIVE, GEORGE. THERE'S OUR MEAT.
THOSE? NO, THOSE ARE BIG UGLY BUGS.
SURE THEY ARE.
BUT SO'S AN ALASKAN KING CRAB--

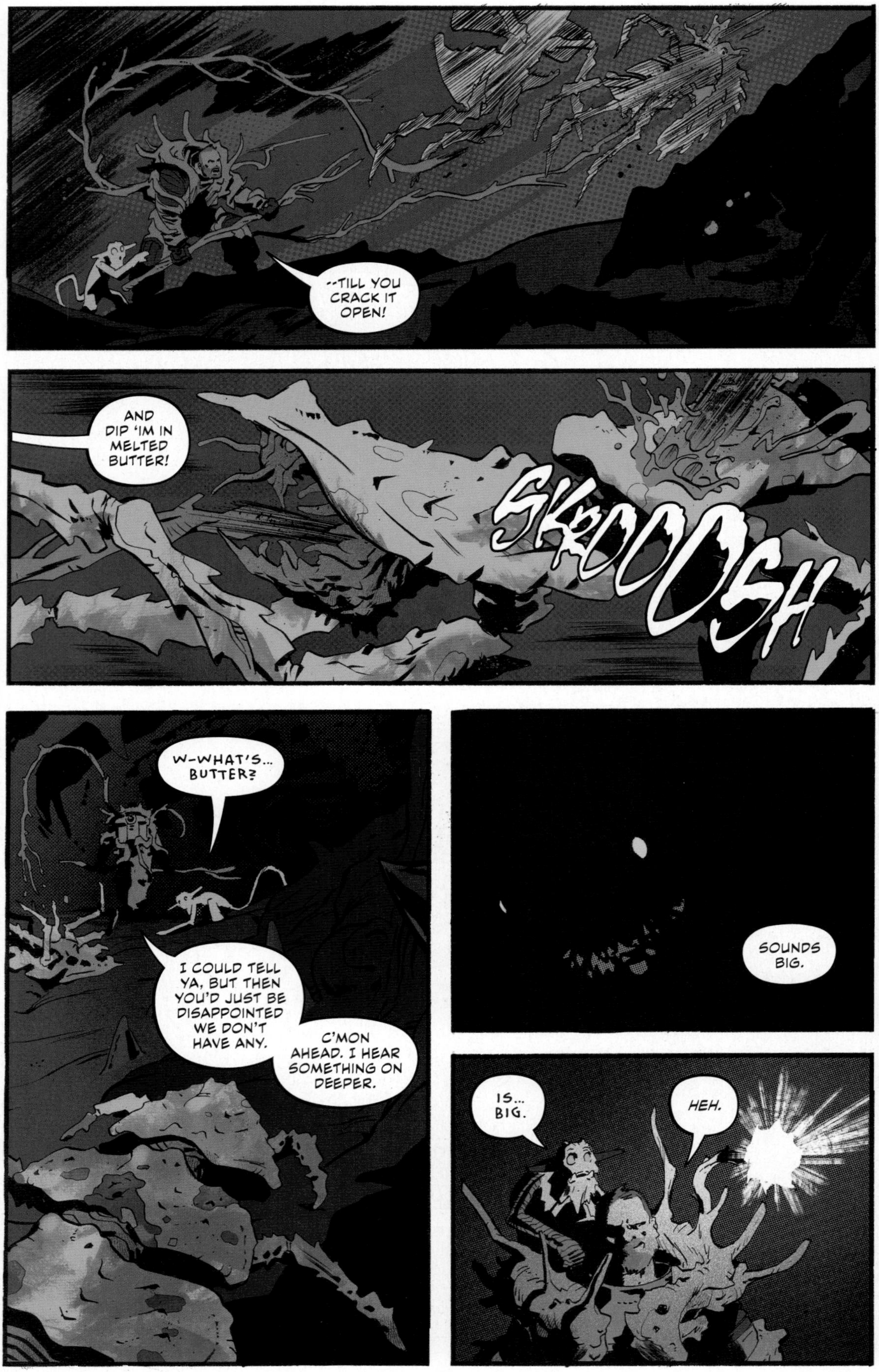
--TILL YOU CRACK IT OPEN!
AND DIP 'IM IN MELTED BUTTER!
SKROOOSH
W-WHAT'S... BUTTER?
I COULD TELL YA, BUT THEN YOU'D JUST BE DISAPPOINTED WE DON'T HAVE ANY.
C'MON AHEAD. I HEAR SOMETHING ON DEEPER.
SOUNDS BIG.
IS... BIG.
HEH.

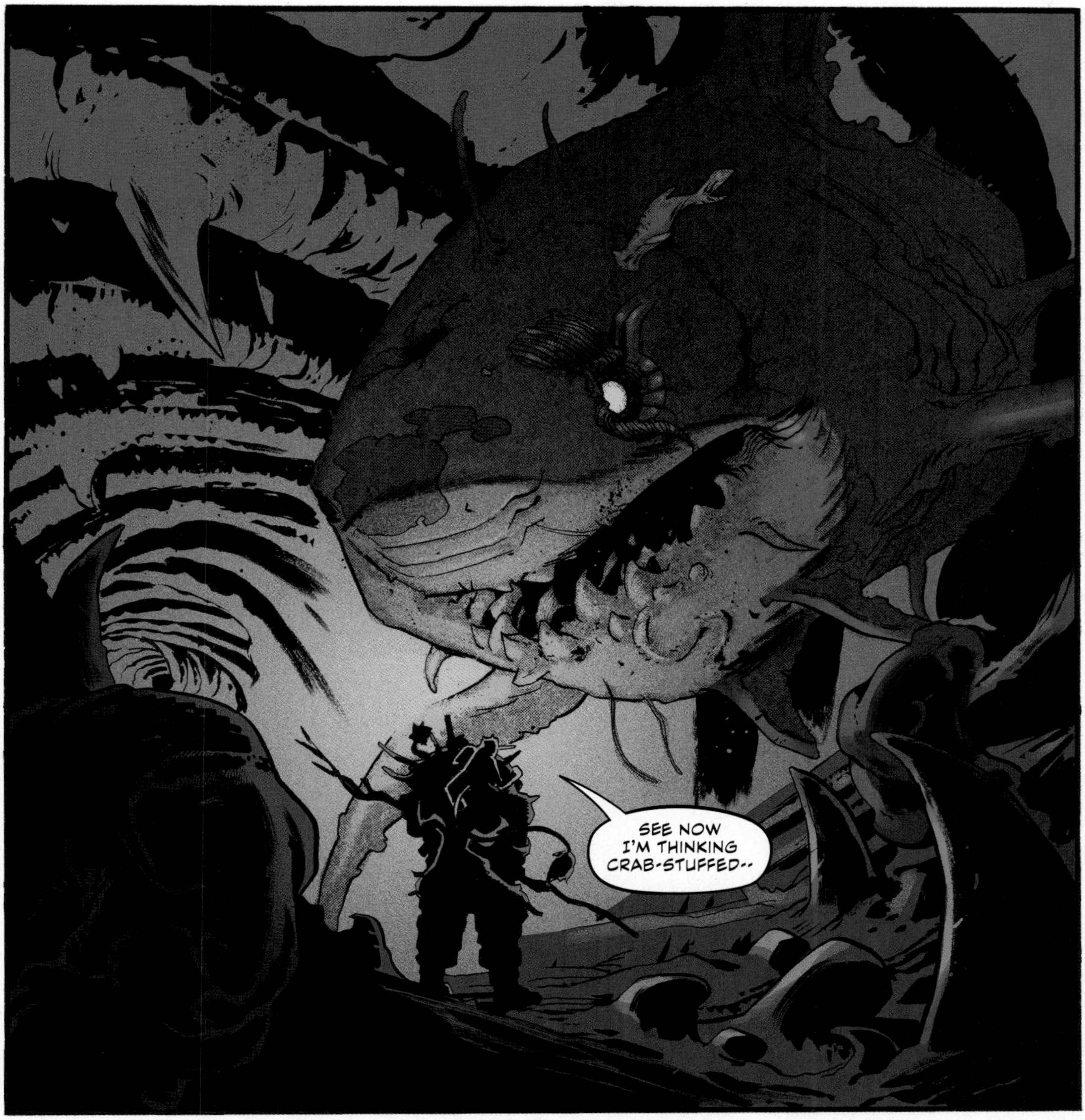
SEE NOW I'M THINKING CRAB-STUFFED--

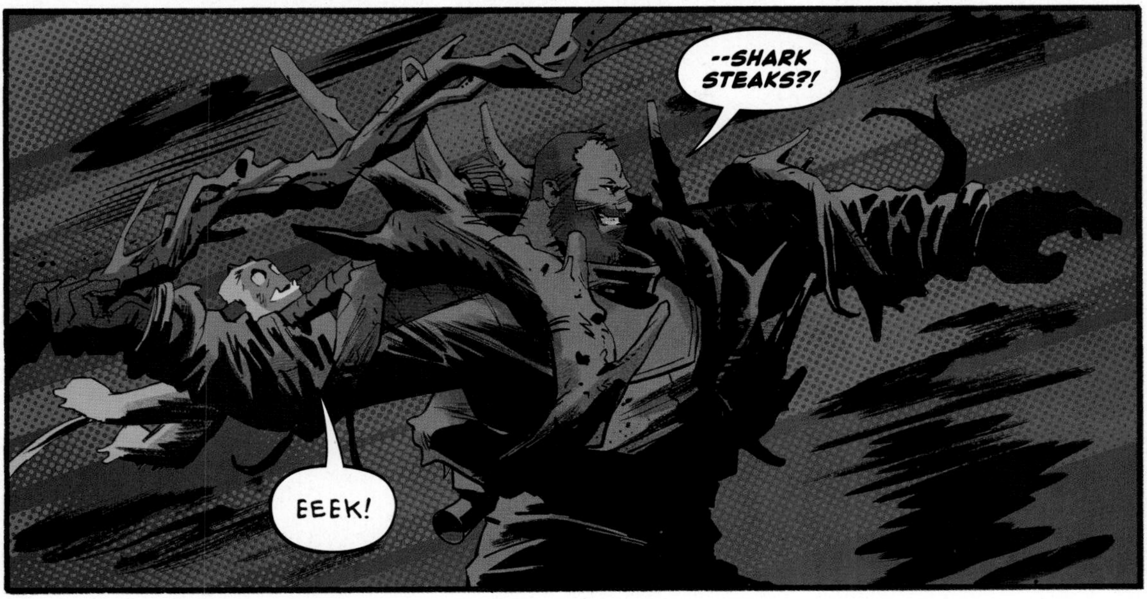
--SHARK STEAKS?!
EEEK!

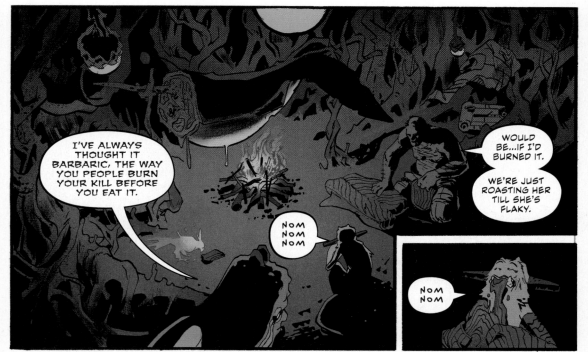

I'VE ALWAYS THOUGHT IT BARBARIC, THE WAY YOU PEOPLE BURN YOUR KILL BEFORE YOU EAT IT.

WOULD BE...IF I'D BURNED IT.

WE'RE JUST ROASTING HER TILL SHE'S FLAKY.

NOM NOM NOM

NOM NOM

HERE. HAVE A LITTLE TASTE. TELL ME I'M WRONG.

HE'S NOT WRONG. THE SHARK ≡BURRRP≡ IS STUPID DELICIOUS.

AND WITH OUR BELLIES FULL OF THIS MAGICAL FOOD--

--WE ARE NOW POWERLESS TO STOP--

FoOOm

--THE MELTED BUTTER MANIAC WHO PUT IT THERE.

HEH HEH HEH.

RELAX. GEORGE IS ONLY JOKING.

LOOK AT HIM.

HE'S GOT THE MONKEY MEAT SWEATS.

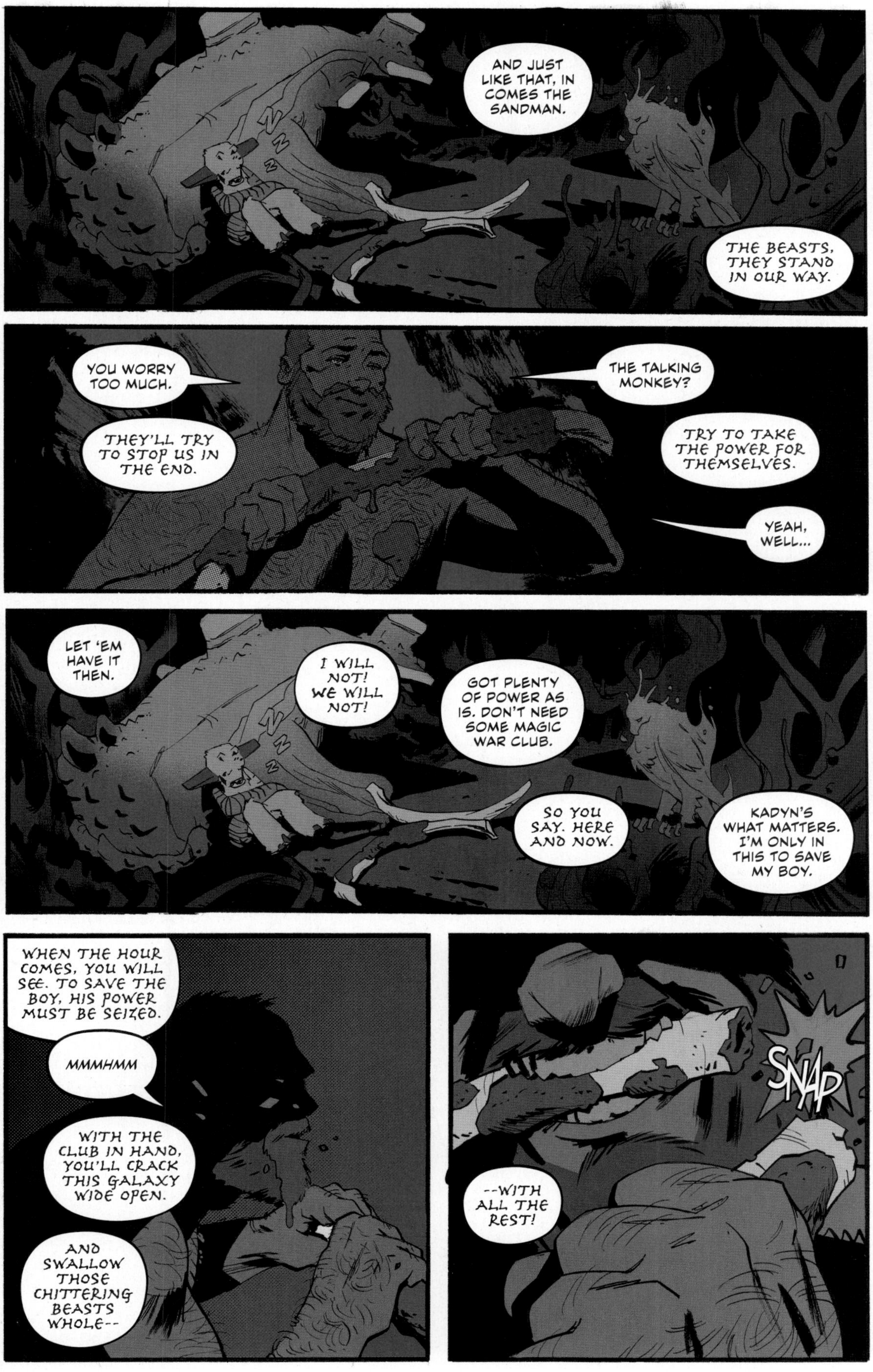
AND JUST LIKE THAT, IN COMES THE SANDMAN.
THE BEASTS, THEY STAND IN OUR WAY.
YOU WORRY TOO MUCH.
THE TALKING MONKEY?
THEY'LL TRY TO STOP US IN THE END.
TRY TO TAKE THE POWER FOR THEMSELVES.
YEAH, WELL...
LET 'EM HAVE IT THEN.
I WILL NOT! WE WILL NOT!
GOT PLENTY OF POWER AS IS. DON'T NEED SOME MAGIC WAR CLUB.
SO YOU SAY. HERE AND NOW.
KADYN'S WHAT MATTERS. I'M ONLY IN THIS TO SAVE MY BOY.
WHEN THE HOUR COMES, YOU WILL SEE. TO SAVE THE BOY, HIS POWER MUST BE SEIZED.
MMMHMM
WITH THE CLUB IN HAND, YOU'LL CRACK THIS GALAXY WIDE OPEN.
AND SWALLOW THOSE CHITTERING BEASTS WHOLE--
SNAP
--WITH ALL THE REST!

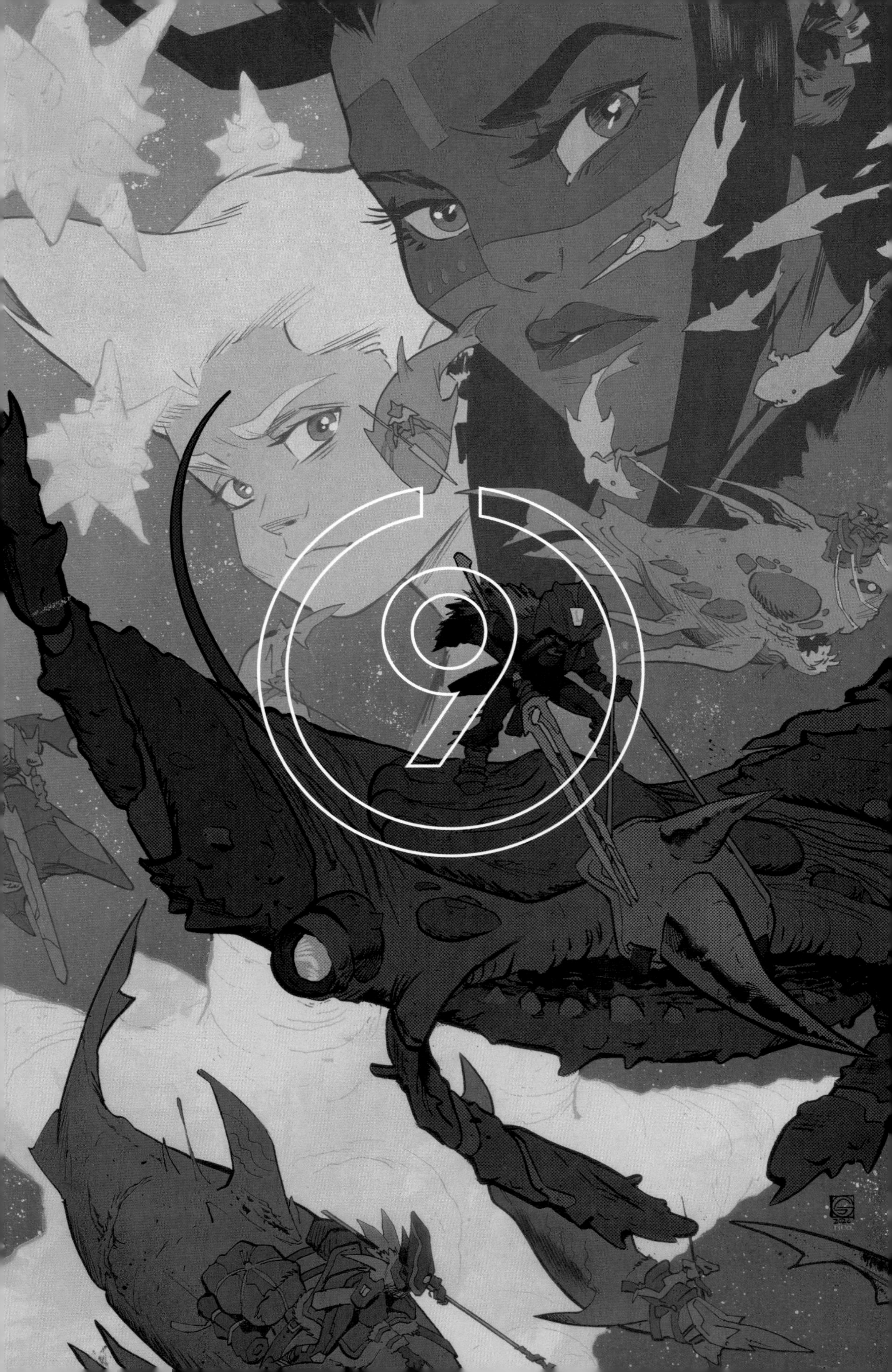

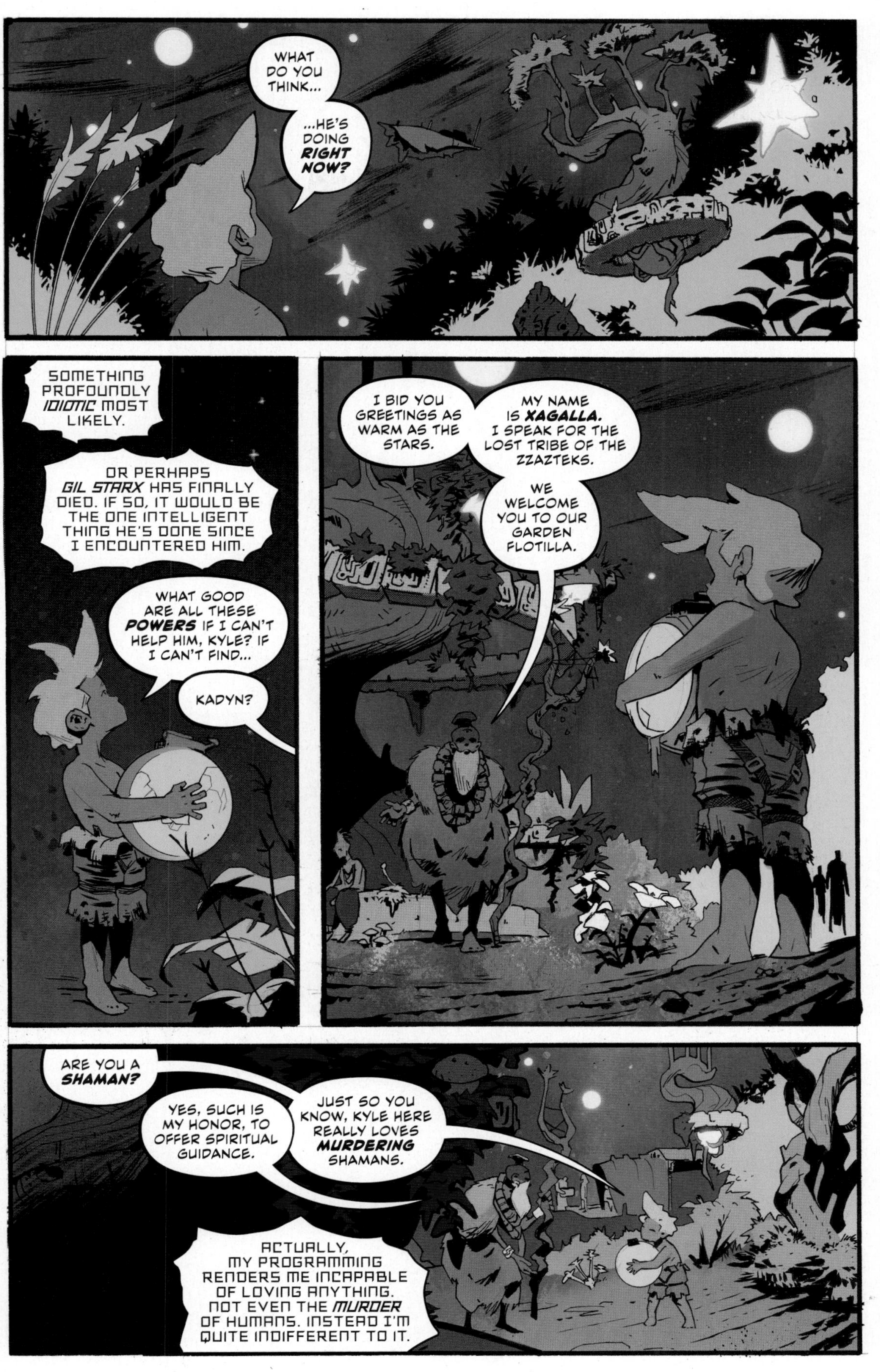
WHAT DO YOU THINK...
...HE'S DOING **RIGHT NOW?**
SOMETHING PROFOUNDLY *IDIOTIC* MOST LIKELY.
OR PERHAPS *GIL STARX* HAS FINALLY DIED. IF SO, IT WOULD BE THE ONE INTELLIGENT THING HE'S DONE SINCE I ENCOUNTERED HIM.
WHAT GOOD ARE ALL THESE **POWERS** IF I CAN'T HELP HIM, KYLE? IF I CAN'T FIND...
KADYN?
I BID YOU GREETINGS AS WARM AS THE STARS.
MY NAME IS **XAGALLA.** I SPEAK FOR THE LOST TRIBE OF THE ZZAZTEKS.
WE WELCOME YOU TO OUR GARDEN FLOTILLA.
ARE YOU A **SHAMAN?**
YES, SUCH IS MY HONOR, TO OFFER SPIRITUAL GUIDANCE.
JUST SO YOU KNOW, KYLE HERE REALLY LOVES **MURDERING** SHAMANS.
ACTUALLY, MY PROGRAMMING RENDERS ME INCAPABLE OF LOVING ANYTHING. NOT EVEN THE *MURDER* OF HUMANS. INSTEAD I'M QUITE INDIFFERENT TO IT.

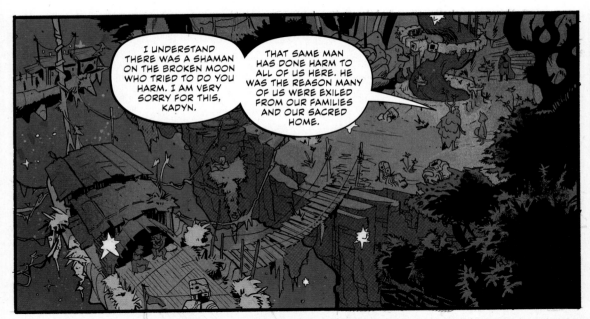

I UNDERSTAND THERE WAS A SHAMAN ON THE BROKEN MOON WHO TRIED TO DO YOU HARM. I AM VERY SORRY FOR THIS, KADYN.

THAT SAME MAN HAS DONE HARM TO ALL OF US HERE. HE WAS THE REASON MANY OF US WERE EXILED FROM OUR FAMILIES AND OUR SACRED HOME.

THAT SHAMAN HAD BEEN CORRUPTED BY A GREAT EVIL. AN EVIL WE HERE WILL FIGHT, IF GIVEN THE CHANCE.

JUST AS *YOU* HAVE FOUGHT TO PROTECT YOURSELF THROUGH COUNTLESS PERILS. AND TO SAVE YOUR *FRIENDS.*

MY POWERS...

YOU WANT TO TAKE MY POWERS!

YOU CAN'T! I *NEED* THEM!

NO.

I WOULD NEVER WANT TO TAKE WHAT THE STARS HAVE GIFTED YOU.

BUT IF YOU LIKE, KADYN, PERHAPS I CAN HELP YOU *LEARN* TO UNDERSTAND THEM.

AND BE THE HERO MIGHTY *QUASARRO* WOULD WANT YOU TO BE.

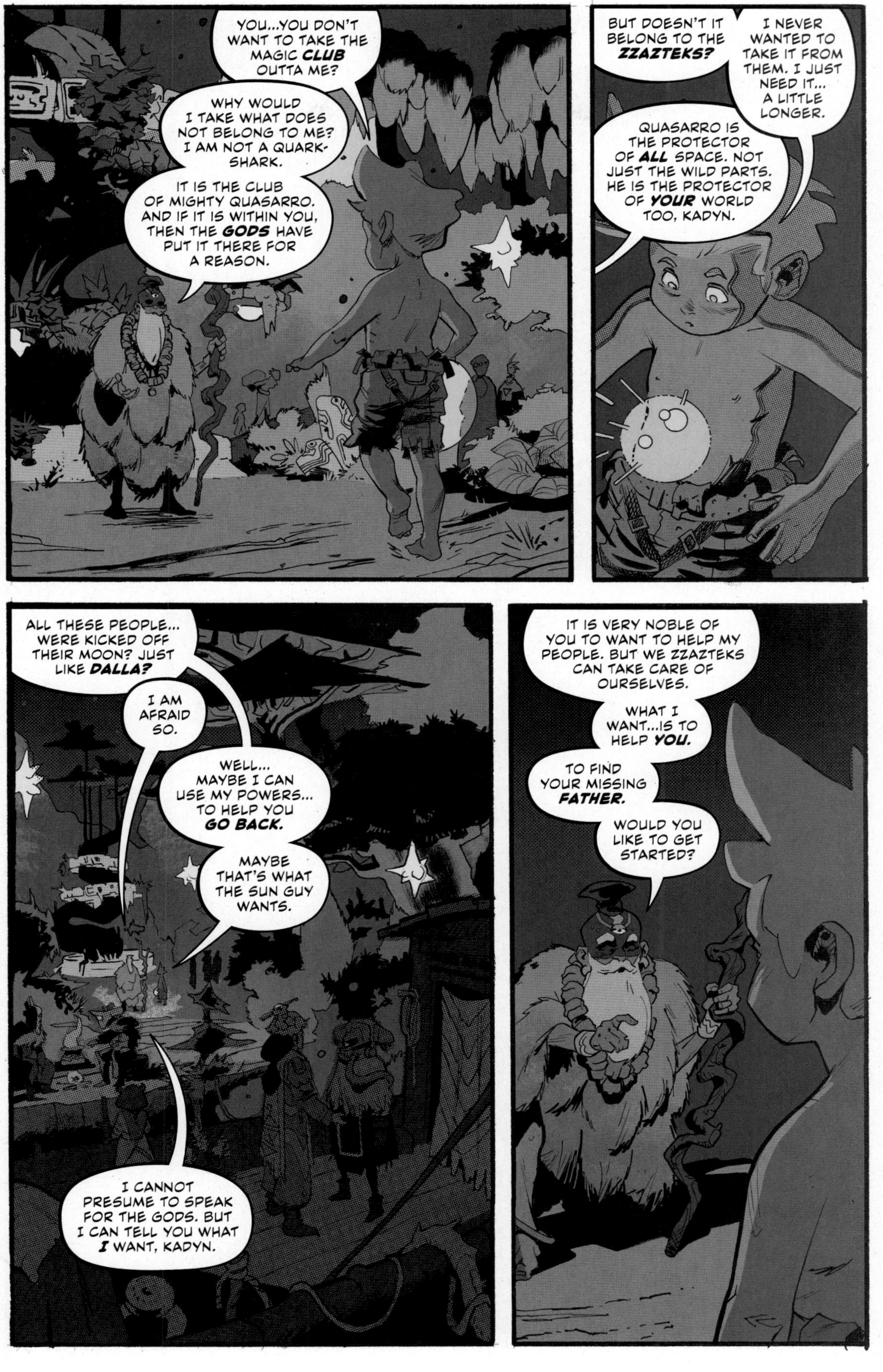

YOU...YOU DON'T WANT TO TAKE THE MAGIC CLUB OUTTA ME?
WHY WOULD I TAKE WHAT DOES NOT BELONG TO ME? I AM NOT A QUARK-SHARK.
IT IS THE CLUB OF MIGHTY QUASARRO. AND IF IT IS WITHIN YOU, THEN THE GODS HAVE PUT IT THERE FOR A REASON.
BUT DOESN'T IT BELONG TO THE ZZAZTEKS?
I NEVER WANTED TO TAKE IT FROM THEM. I JUST NEED IT... A LITTLE LONGER.
QUASARRO IS THE PROTECTOR OF ALL SPACE. NOT JUST THE WILD PARTS. HE IS THE PROTECTOR OF YOUR WORLD TOO, KADYN.
ALL THESE PEOPLE... WERE KICKED OFF THEIR MOON? JUST LIKE DALLA?
I AM AFRAID SO.
WELL... MAYBE I CAN USE MY POWERS... TO HELP YOU GO BACK.
MAYBE THAT'S WHAT THE SUN GUY WANTS.
I CANNOT PRESUME TO SPEAK FOR THE GODS. BUT I CAN TELL YOU WHAT I WANT, KADYN.
IT IS VERY NOBLE OF YOU TO WANT TO HELP MY PEOPLE. BUT WE ZZAZTEKS CAN TAKE CARE OF OURSELVES.
WHAT I WANT...IS TO HELP YOU.
TO FIND YOUR MISSING FATHER.
WOULD YOU LIKE TO GET STARTED?

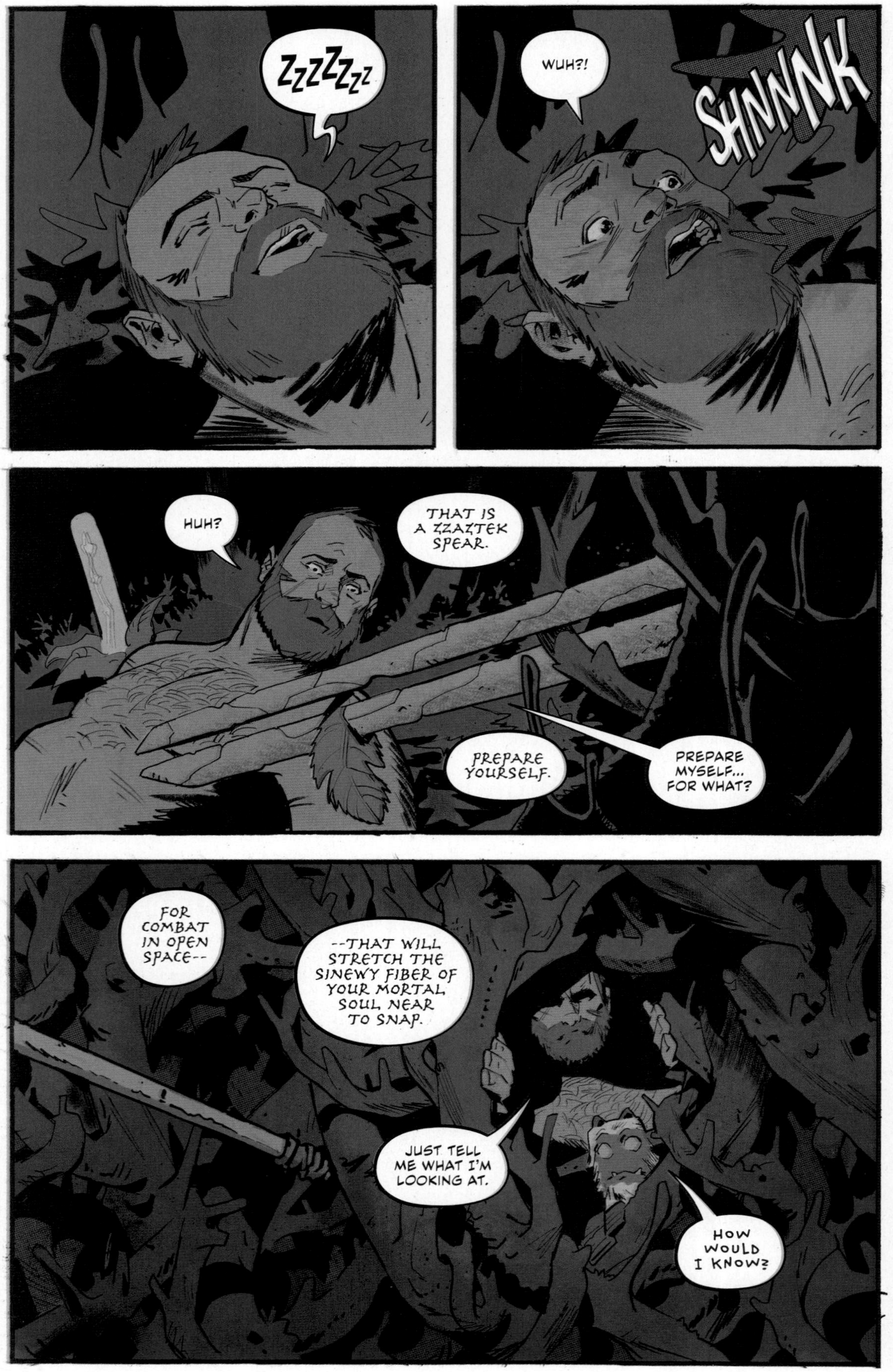
ZZZZZZZ
WUH?!
SHNNNK
HUH?
THAT IS A ZZAZTEK SPEAR.
PREPARE YOURSELF.
PREPARE MYSELF... FOR WHAT?
FOR COMBAT IN OPEN SPACE--
--THAT WILL STRETCH THE SINEWY FIBER OF YOUR MORTAL SOUL NEAR TO SNAP.
JUST TELL ME WHAT I'M LOOKING AT.
HOW WOULD I KNOW?

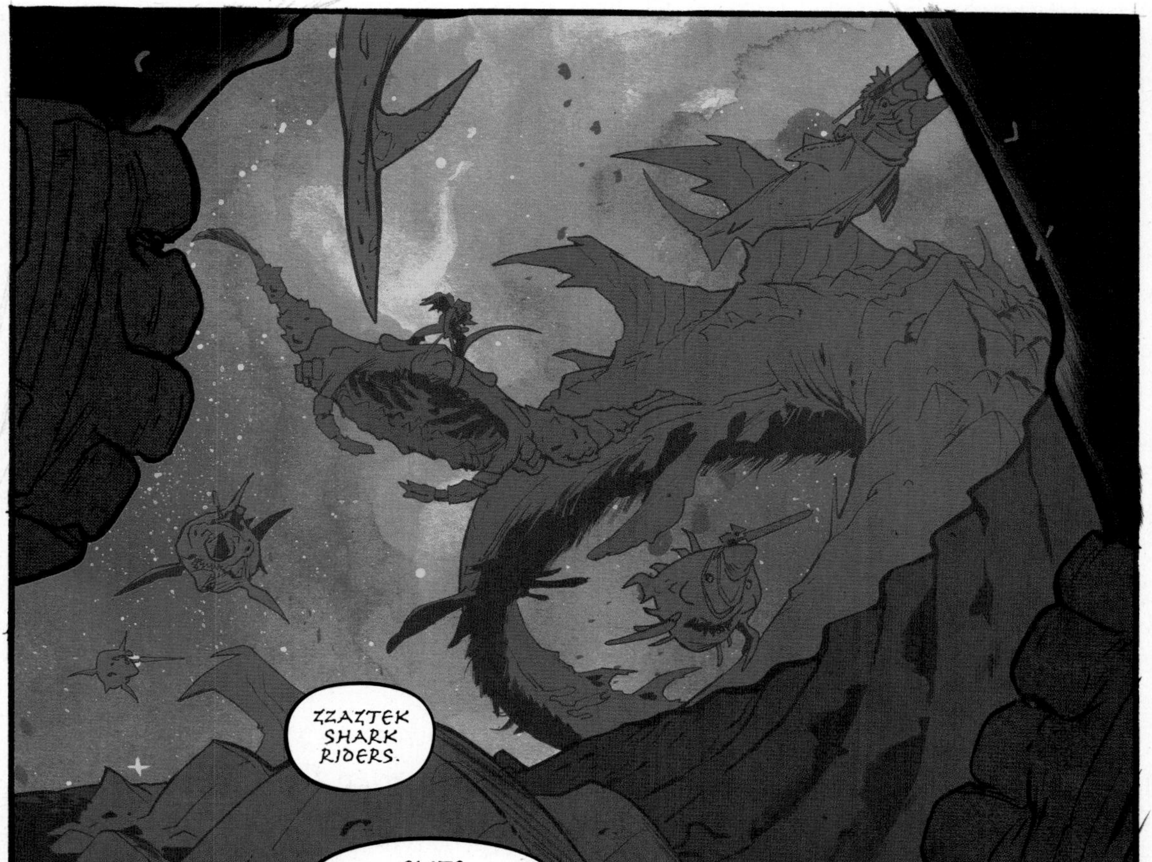
ZZAZTEK SHARK RIDERS.
ELITE PRACTITIONERS OF VENGEANCE.
THEY'VE COME FOR THE LEVIATHAN.
GREAT.

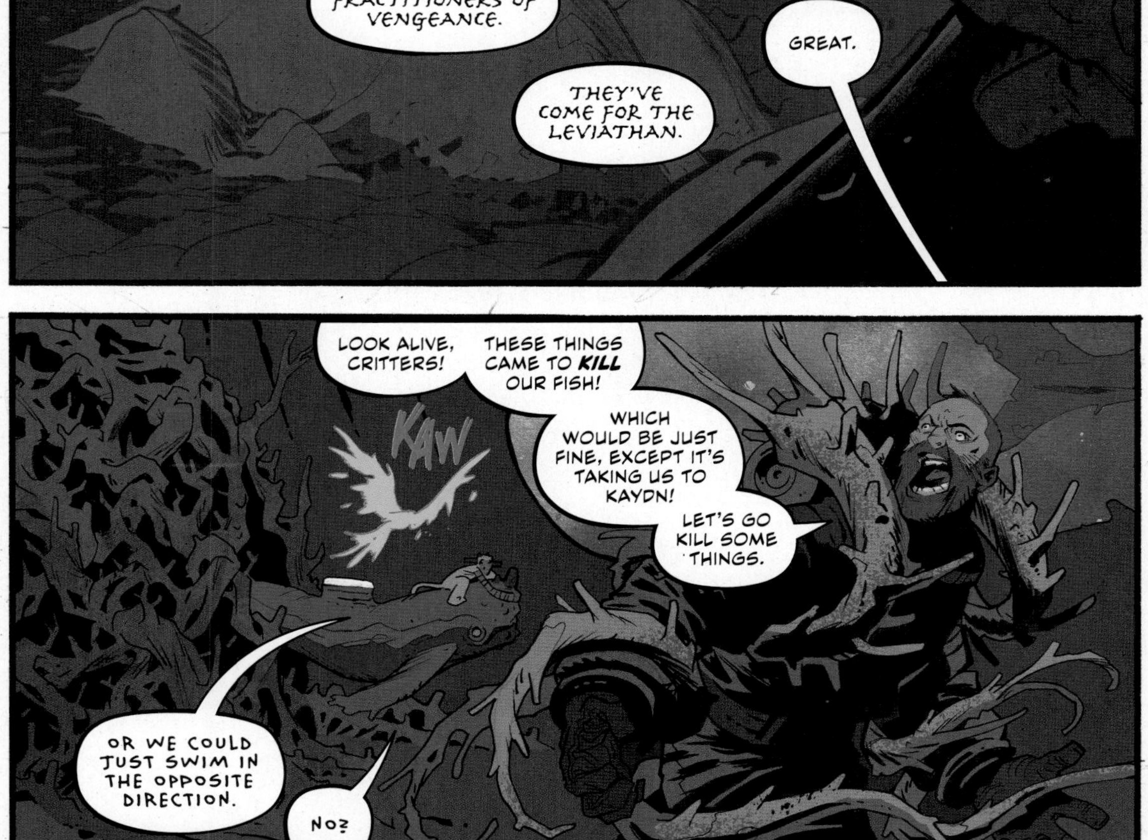
LOOK ALIVE, CRITTERS!
THESE THINGS CAME TO **KILL** OUR FISH!
WHICH WOULD BE JUST FINE, EXCEPT IT'S TAKING US TO KAYDN!
LET'S GO KILL SOME THINGS.
KAW
OR WE COULD JUST SWIM IN THE OPPOSITE DIRECTION.
NO?

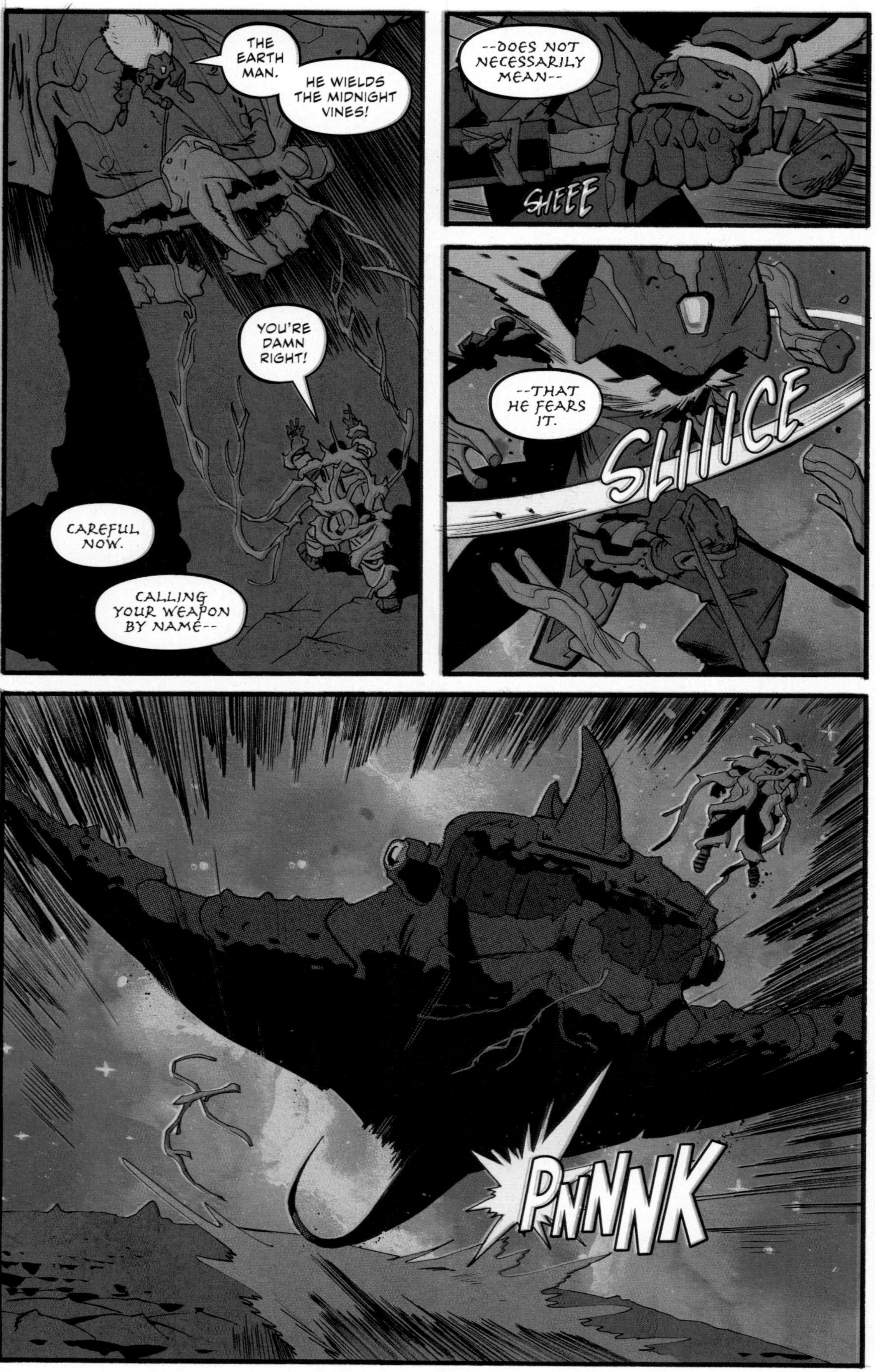
THE EARTH MAN.
HE WIELDS THE MIDNIGHT VINES!
YOU'RE DAMN RIGHT!
CAREFUL NOW.
CALLING YOUR WEAPON BY NAME--
--DOES NOT NECESSARILY MEAN--
SHEEE
--THAT HE FEARS IT.
SLIIICE
PNNNK

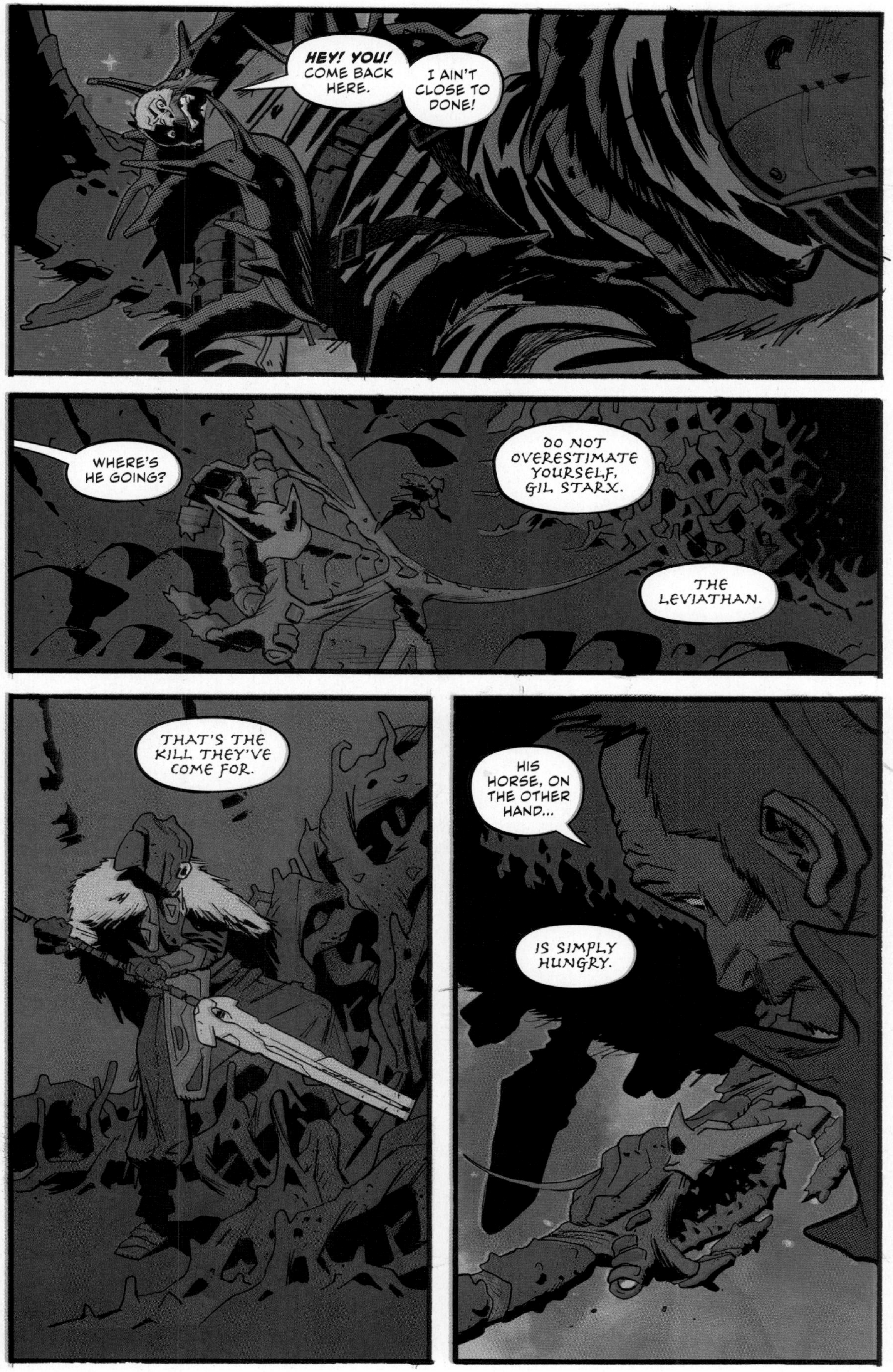
HEY! YOU! COME BACK HERE.
I AIN'T CLOSE TO DONE!
WHERE'S HE GOING?
DO NOT OVERESTIMATE YOURSELF, GIL STARX.
THE LEVIATHAN.
THAT'S THE KILL THEY'VE COME FOR.
HIS HORSE, ON THE OTHER HAND...
IS SIMPLY HUNGRY.

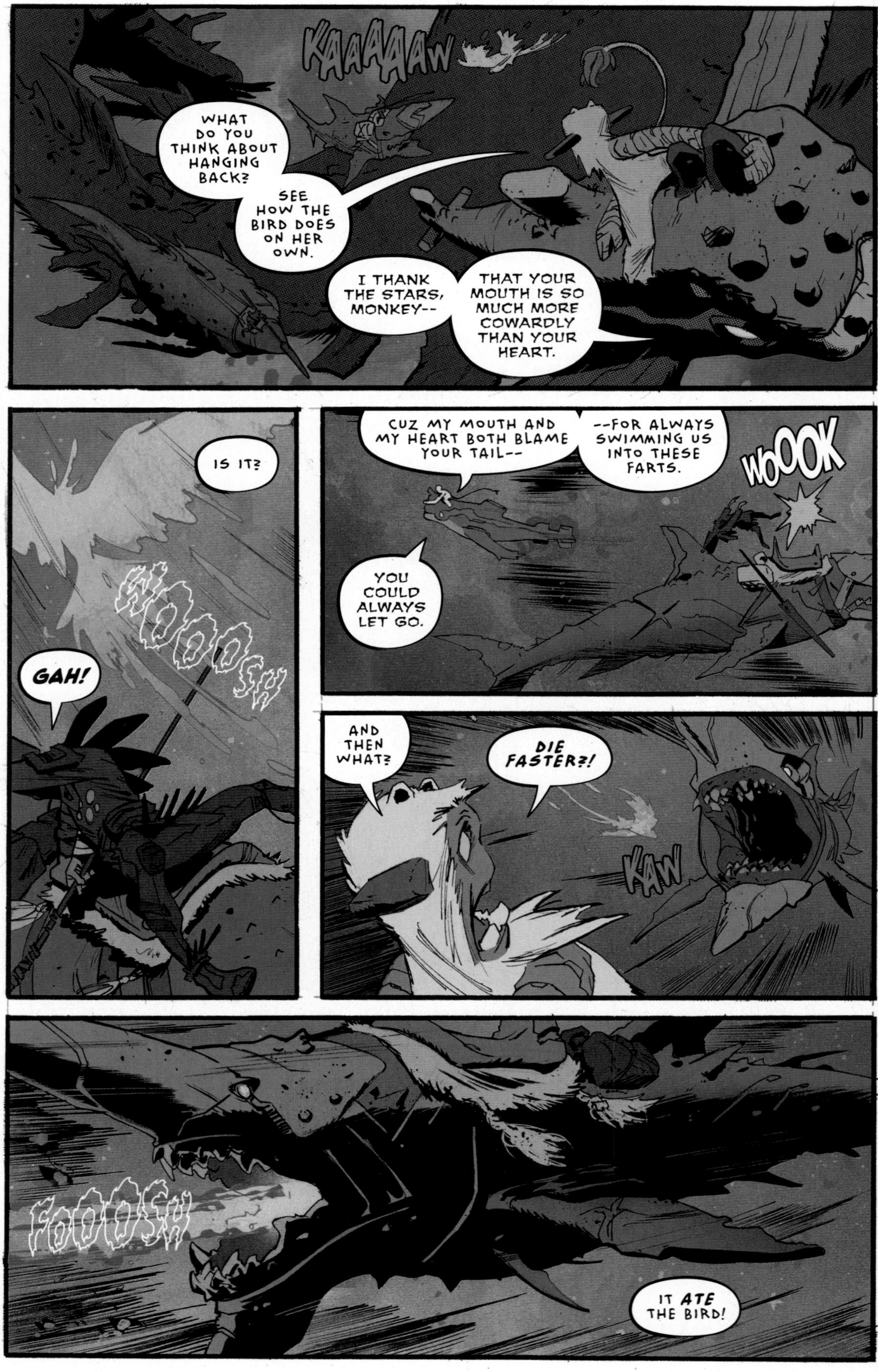
KAAAAAAW
WHAT DO YOU THINK ABOUT HANGING BACK?
SEE HOW THE BIRD DOES ON HER OWN.
I THANK THE STARS, MONKEY--
THAT YOUR MOUTH IS SO MUCH MORE COWARDLY THAN YOUR HEART.
IS IT?
WOOOSH
GAH!
CUZ MY MOUTH AND MY HEART BOTH BLAME YOUR TAIL--
--FOR ALWAYS SWIMMING US INTO THESE FARTS.
WOOOK
YOU COULD ALWAYS LET GO.
AND THEN WHAT?
DIE FASTER?!
KAW
FOOOSH
IT ATE THE BIRD!

IT ATE THE FIREBIRD *LIKE* YOU DID!

KAAAW

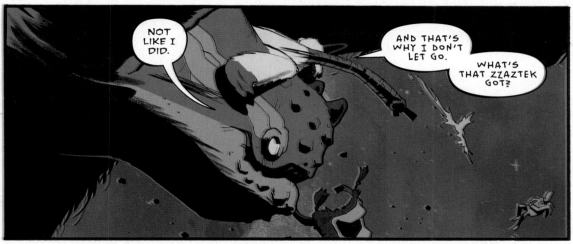

NOT LIKE I DID.

AND THAT'S WHY I DON'T LET GO.

WHAT'S THAT ZZAZTEK GOT?

CLICK

WORM-HOLE.

WHOA

KAAAAAAW

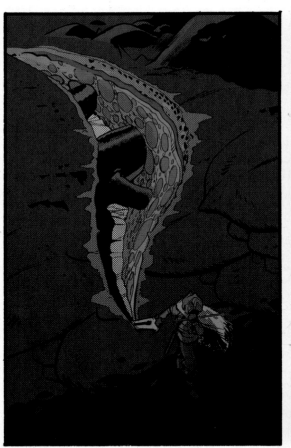

SQUIT

FLOOOSH

LOOK AT YOU,
ALL SURGICAL
WITH YOUR
KILLIN'.

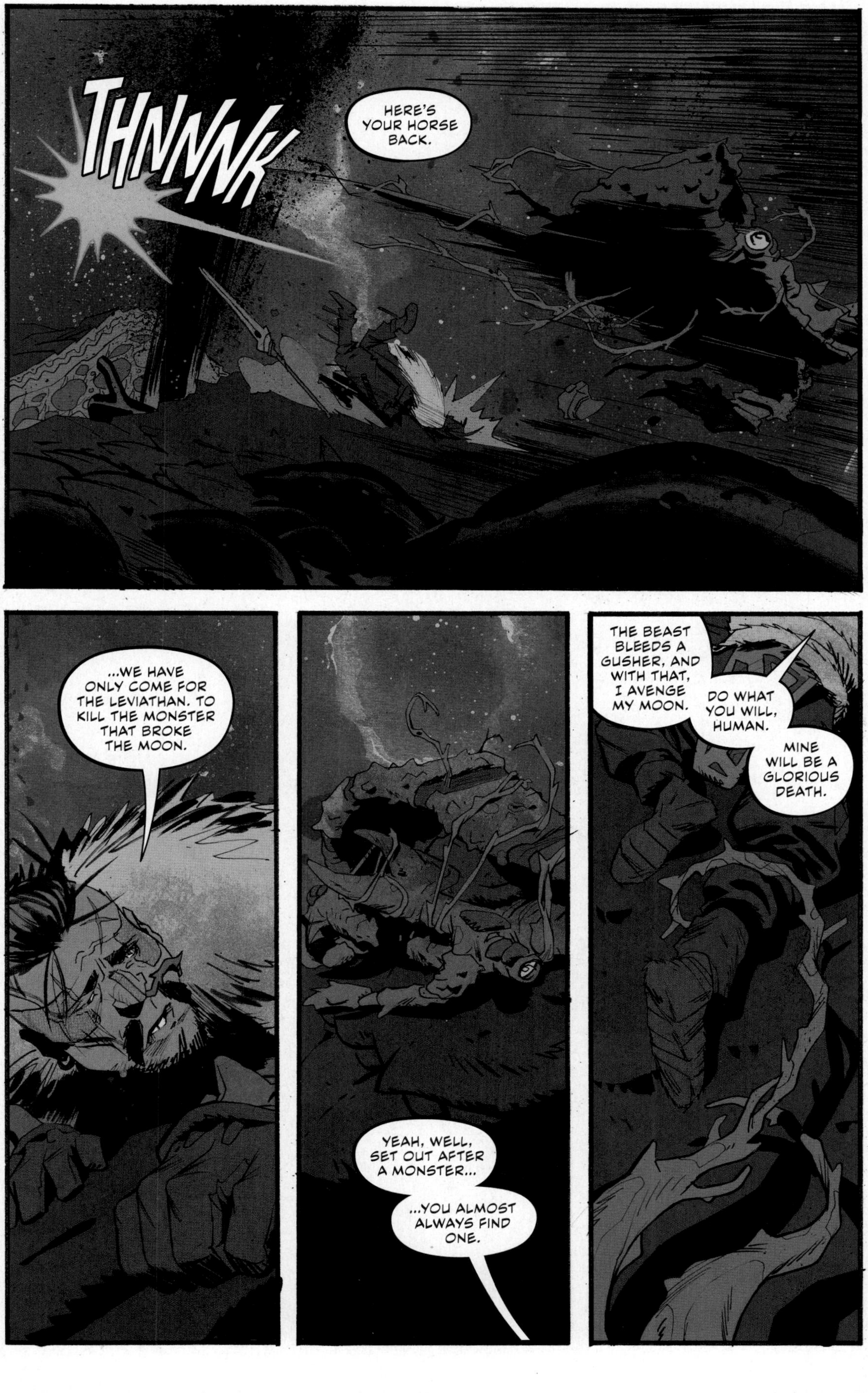
THHNNK
HERE'S YOUR HORSE BACK.
...WE HAVE ONLY COME FOR THE LEVIATHAN. TO KILL THE MONSTER THAT BROKE THE MOON.
YEAH, WELL, SET OUT AFTER A MONSTER...
...YOU ALMOST ALWAYS FIND ONE.
THE BEAST BLEEDS A GUSHER, AND WITH THAT, I AVENGE MY MOON.
DO WHAT YOU WILL, HUMAN.
MINE WILL BE A GLORIOUS DEATH.

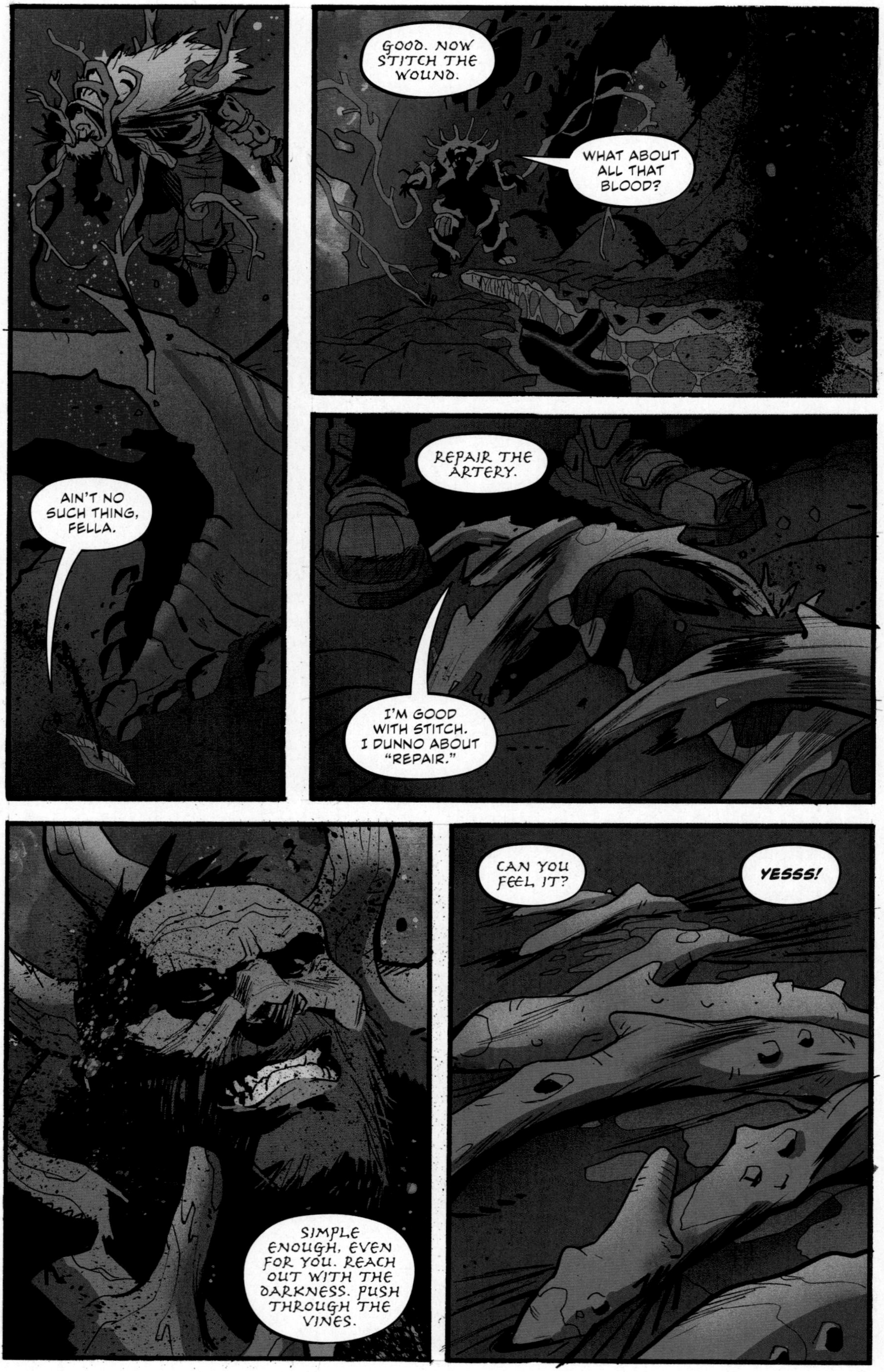
GOOD. NOW STITCH THE WOUND.
WHAT ABOUT ALL THAT BLOOD?
AIN'T NO SUCH THING, FELLA.
REPAIR THE ARTERY.
I'M GOOD WITH STITCH. I DUNNO ABOUT "REPAIR."
SIMPLE ENOUGH, EVEN FOR YOU. REACH OUT WITH THE DARKNESS. PUSH THROUGH THE VINES.
CAN YOU FEEL, IT?
YESSS!

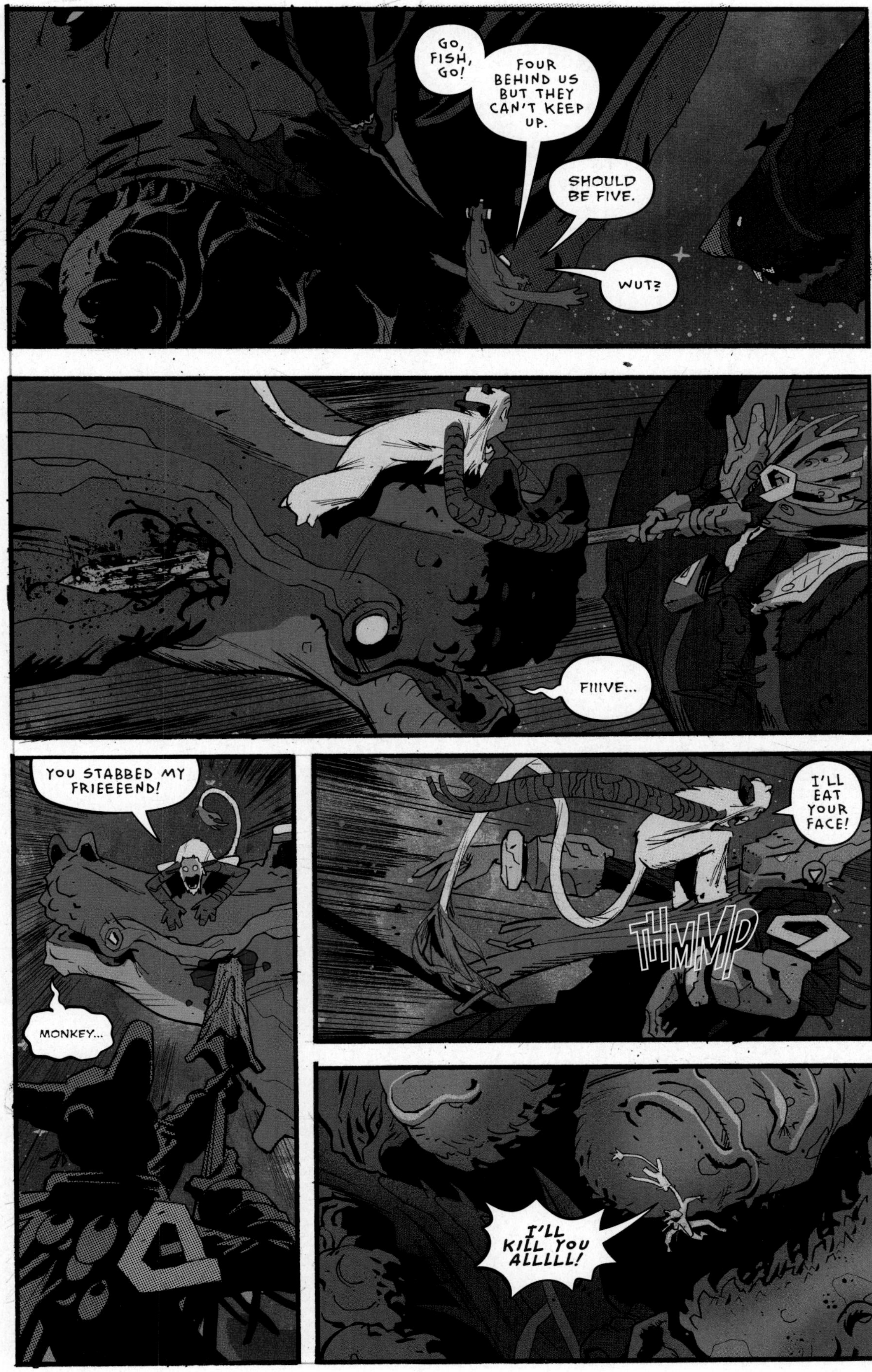
GO, FISH, GO!
FOUR BEHIND US BUT THEY CAN'T KEEP UP.
SHOULD BE FIVE.
WUT?
FIIIVE...
YOU STABBED MY FRIEEEEND!
MONKEY...
I'LL EAT YOUR FACE!
THMMP
I'LL KILL YOU ALLLLL!

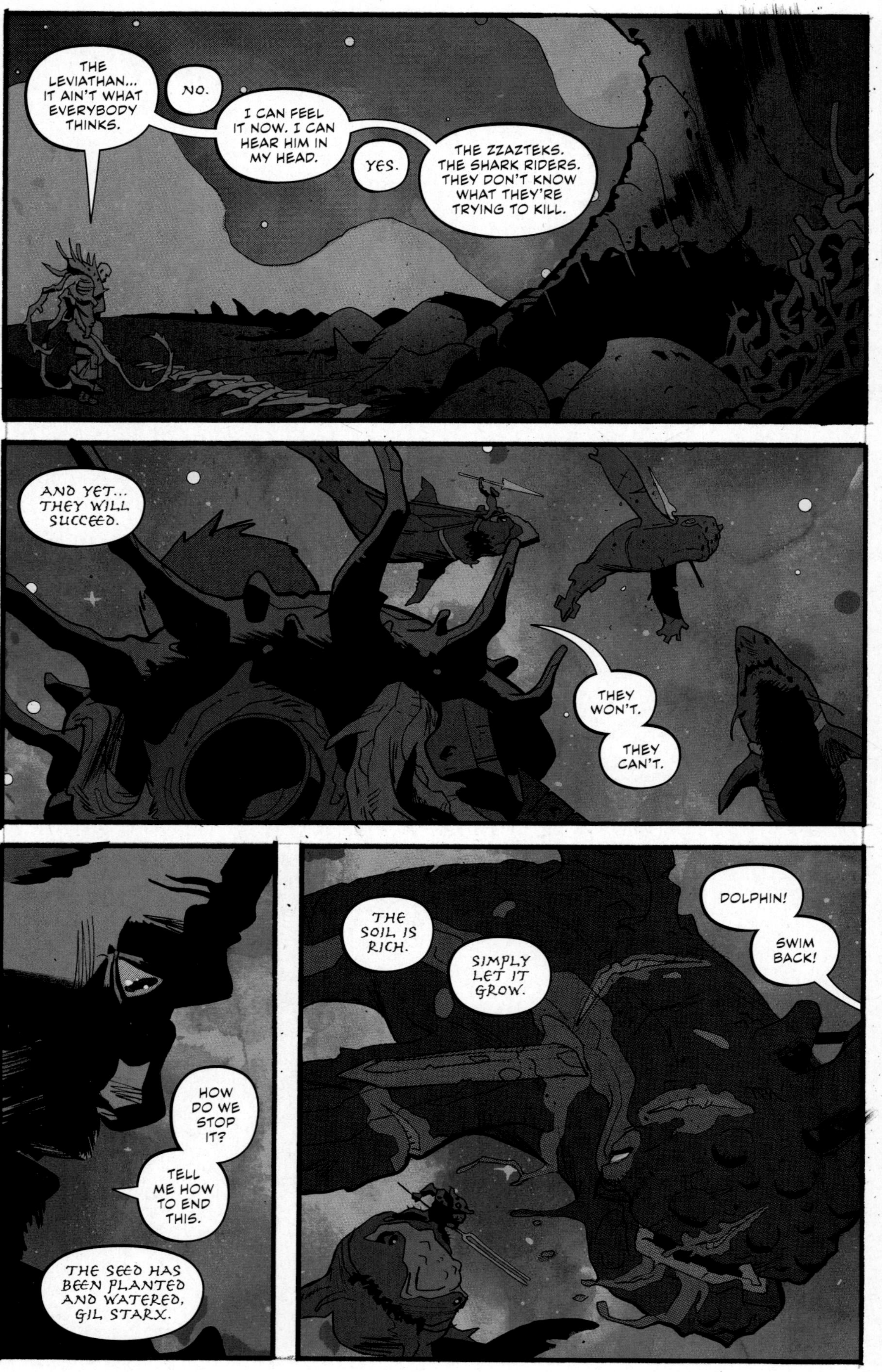
THE LEVIATHAN... IT AIN'T WHAT EVERYBODY THINKS.
NO.
I CAN FEEL IT NOW. I CAN HEAR HIM IN MY HEAD.
YES.
THE ZZAZTEKS. THE SHARK RIDERS. THEY DON'T KNOW WHAT THEY'RE TRYING TO KILL.
AND YET... THEY WILL SUCCEED.
THEY WON'T.
THEY CAN'T.
HOW DO WE STOP IT?
TELL ME HOW TO END THIS.
THE SEED HAS BEEN PLANTED AND WATERED, GIL STARX.
THE SOIL IS RICH.
SIMPLY LET IT GROW.
DOLPHIN!
SWIM BACK!

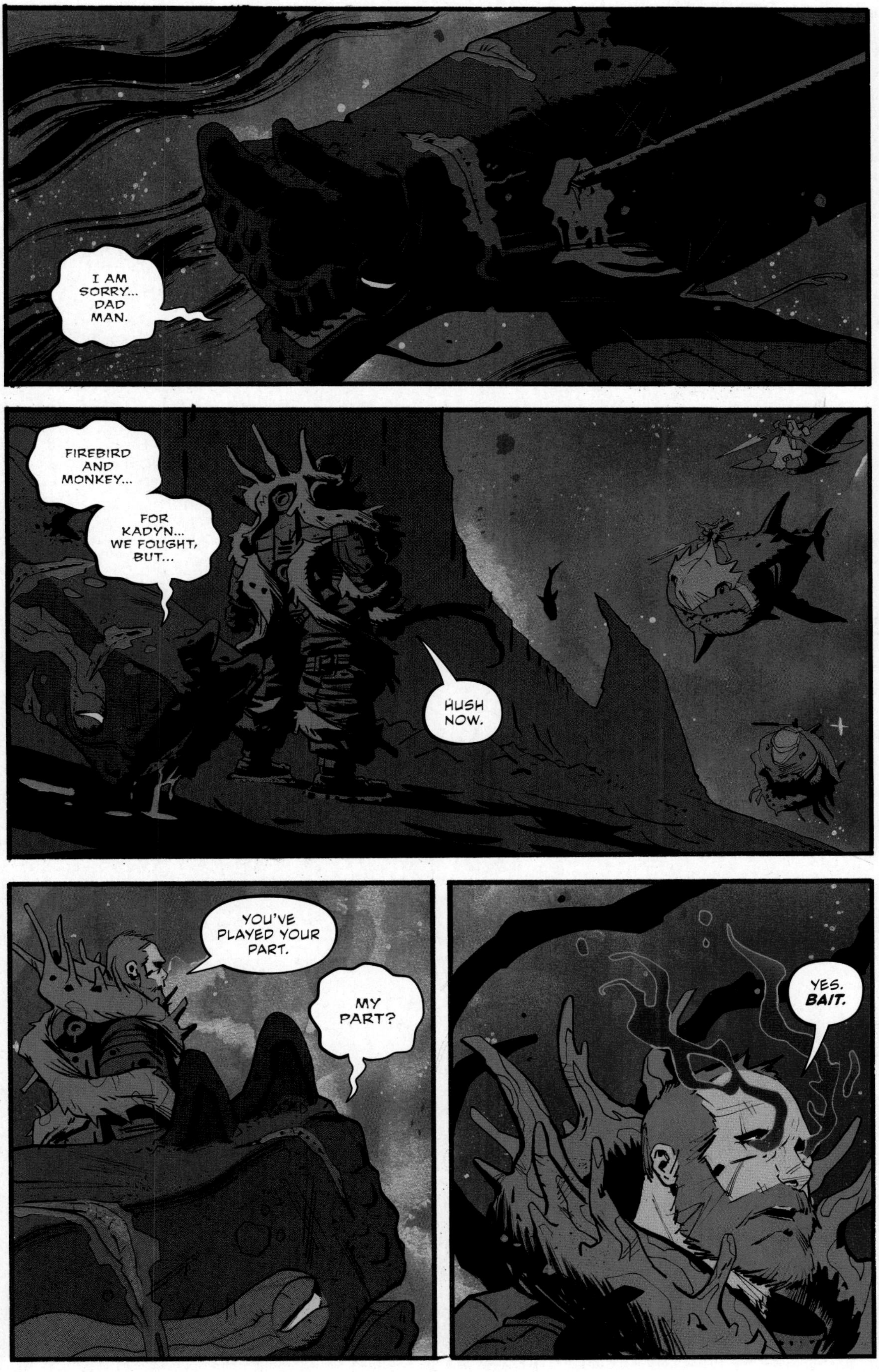
I AM SORRY... DAD MAN.
FIREBIRD AND MONKEY...
FOR KADYN... WE FOUGHT, BUT...
HUSH NOW.
YOU'VE PLAYED YOUR PART.
MY PART?
YES. *BAIT.*

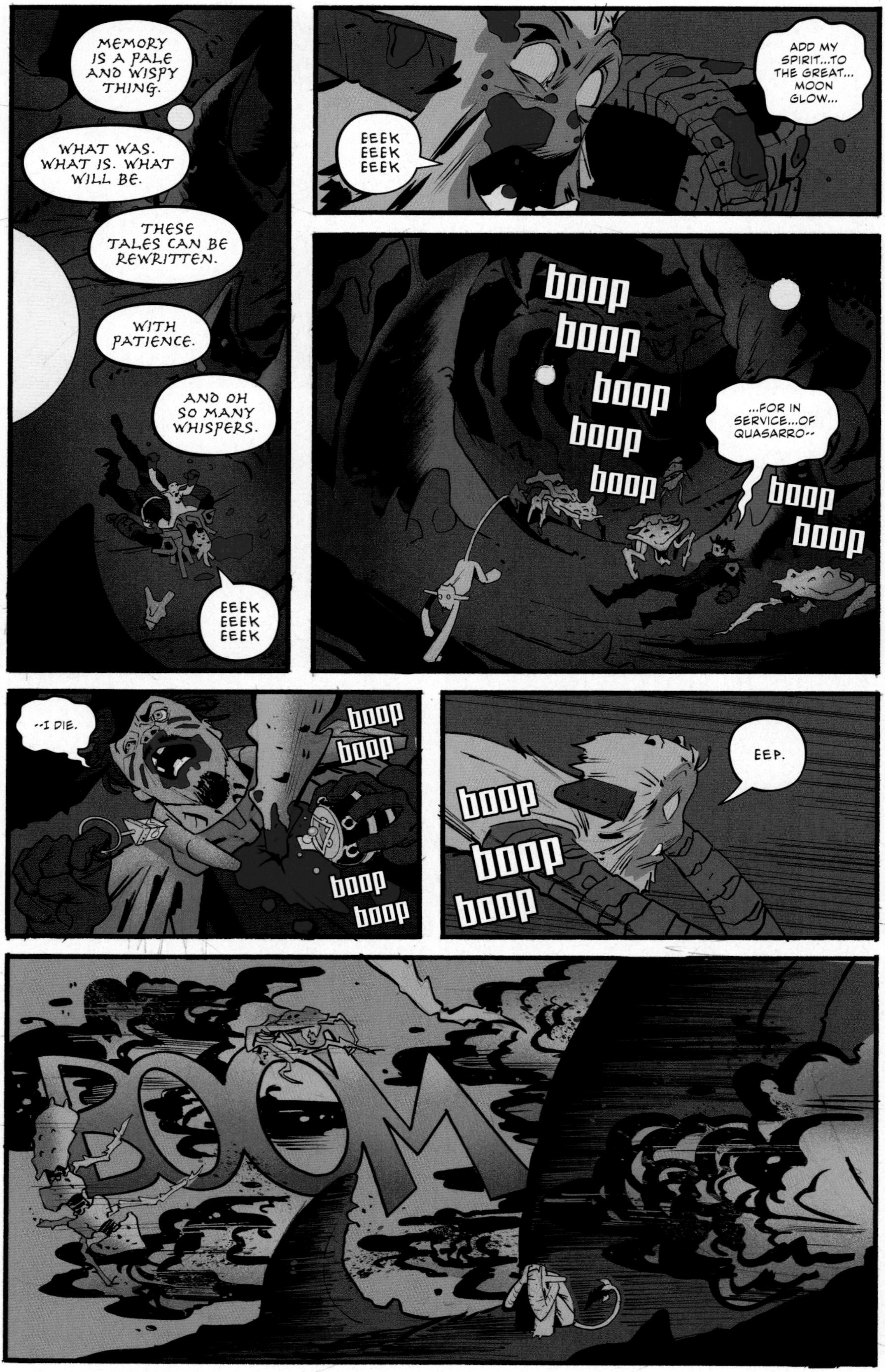

MEMORY IS A PALE AND WISPY THING.
WHAT WAS. WHAT IS. WHAT WILL BE.
THESE TALES CAN BE REWRITTEN.
WITH PATIENCE.
AND OH SO MANY WHISPERS.
EEEK EEEK EEEK
EEEK EEEK EEEK
ADD MY SPIRIT...TO THE GREAT... MOON GLOW...
boop boop boop boop boop
...FOR IN SERVICE...OF QUASARRO--
boop boop
--I DIE.
boop boop
boop boop
EEP.
boop boop boop
BOOM

WHAT WAS IT THAT BROKE THE MOON?

TELL ME AGAIN.

WHO CAME AND ATE THE STARS?

NO. NO. NO.

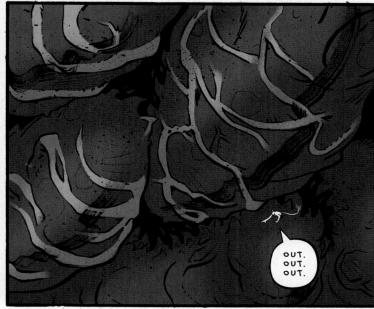

OUT. OUT. OUT.

FISH!

I'M OUT! I'M HERE!

COME AND FIND--

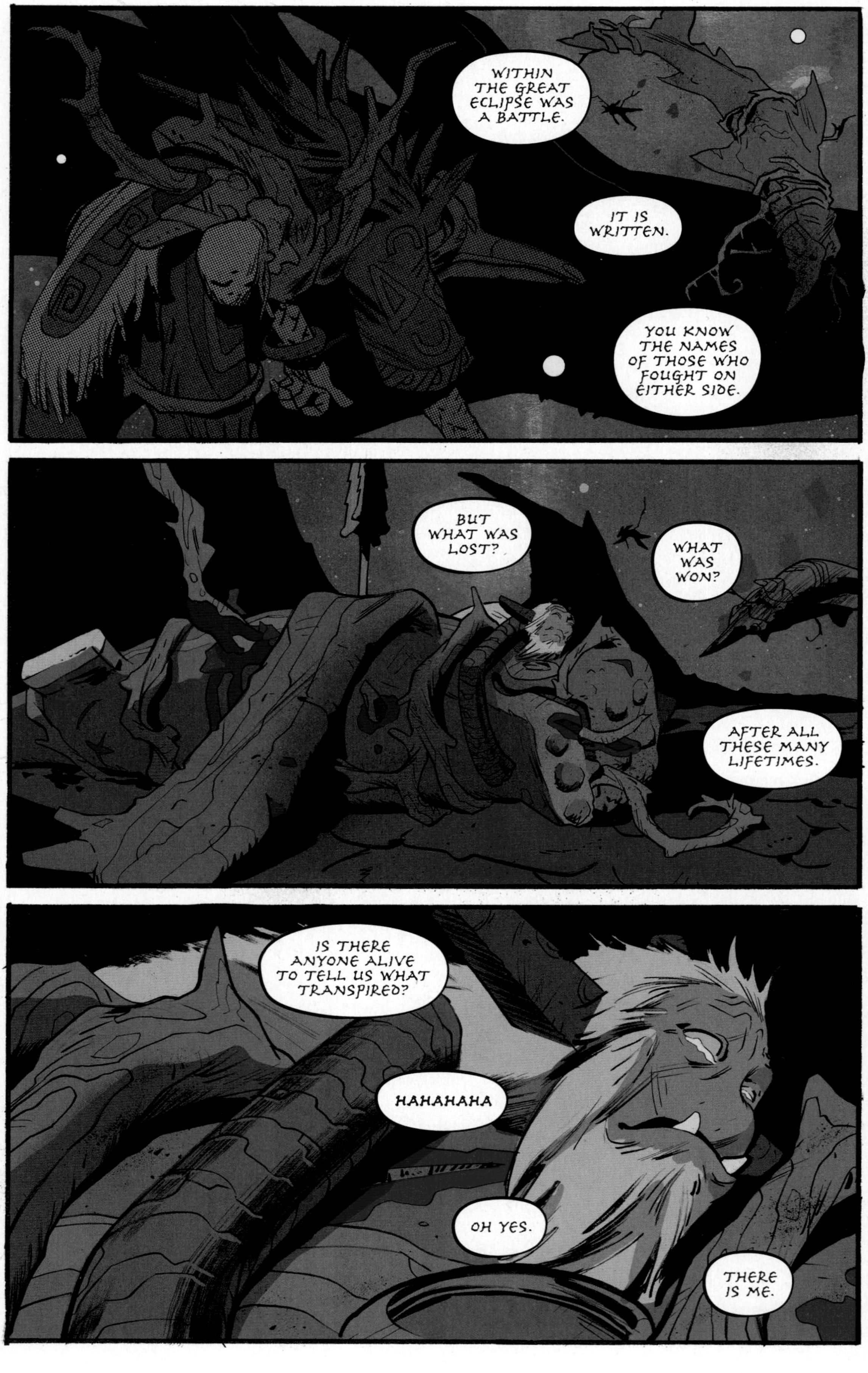
WITHIN THE GREAT ECLIPSE WAS A BATTLE.
IT IS WRITTEN.
YOU KNOW THE NAMES OF THOSE WHO FOUGHT ON EITHER SIDE.
BUT WHAT WAS LOST?
WHAT WAS WON?
AFTER ALL THESE MANY LIFETIMES.
IS THERE ANYONE ALIVE TO TELL US WHAT TRANSPIRED?
HAHAHAHA
OH YES.
THERE IS ME.

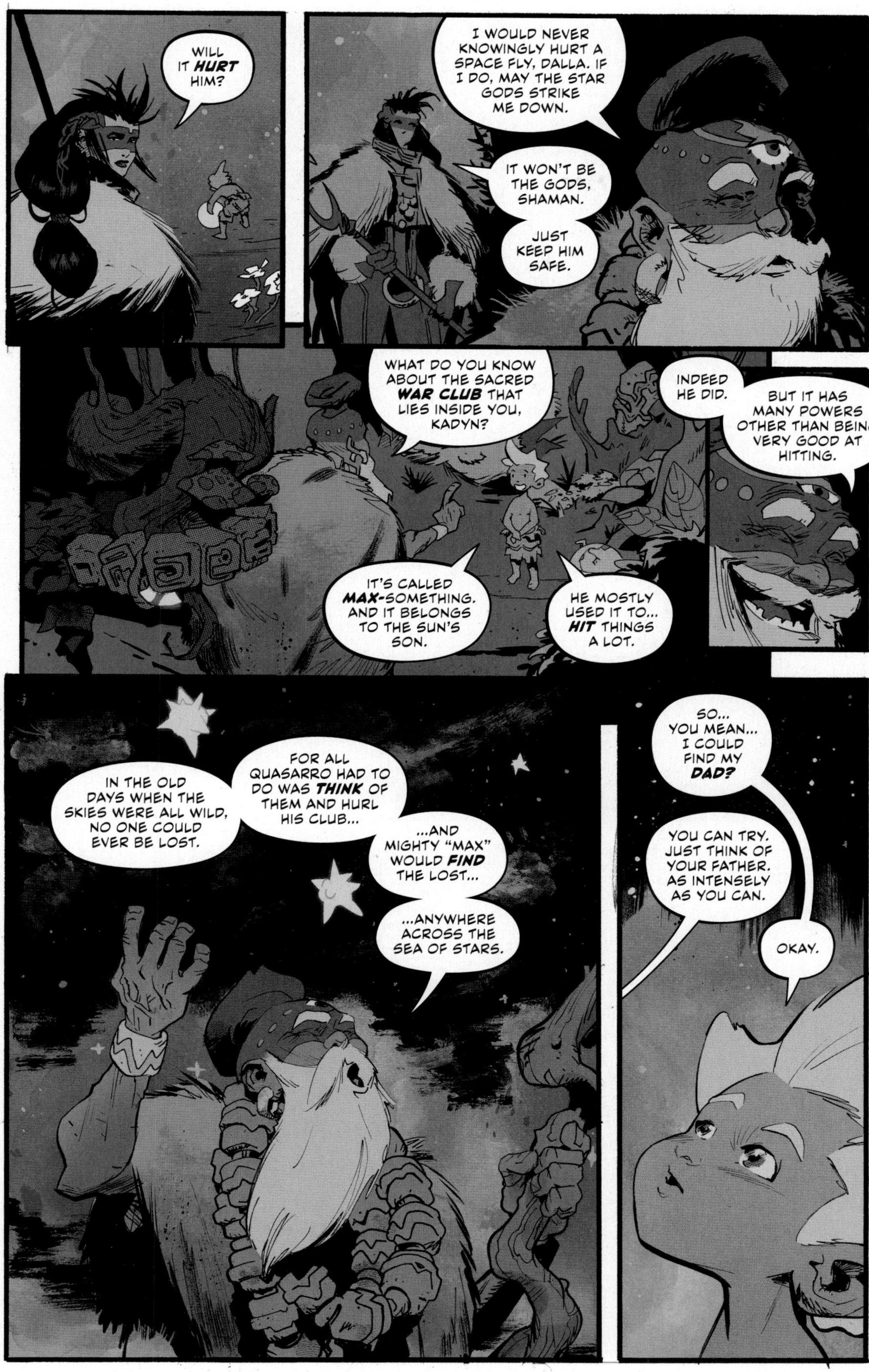
WILL IT HURT HIM?
I WOULD NEVER KNOWINGLY HURT A SPACE FLY, DALLA. IF I DO, MAY THE STAR GODS STRIKE ME DOWN.
IT WON'T BE THE GODS, SHAMAN.
JUST KEEP HIM SAFE.
WHAT DO YOU KNOW ABOUT THE SACRED WAR CLUB THAT LIES INSIDE YOU, KADYN?
IT'S CALLED MAX-SOMETHING. AND IT BELONGS TO THE SUN'S SON.
HE MOSTLY USED IT TO... HIT THINGS A LOT.
INDEED HE DID.
BUT IT HAS MANY POWERS OTHER THAN BEING VERY GOOD AT HITTING.
IN THE OLD DAYS WHEN THE SKIES WERE ALL WILD, NO ONE COULD EVER BE LOST.
FOR ALL QUASARRO HAD TO DO WAS THINK OF THEM AND HURL HIS CLUB...
...AND MIGHTY "MAX" WOULD FIND THE LOST...
...ANYWHERE ACROSS THE SEA OF STARS.
SO... YOU MEAN... I COULD FIND MY DAD?
YOU CAN TRY. JUST THINK OF YOUR FATHER. AS INTENSELY AS YOU CAN.
OKAY.

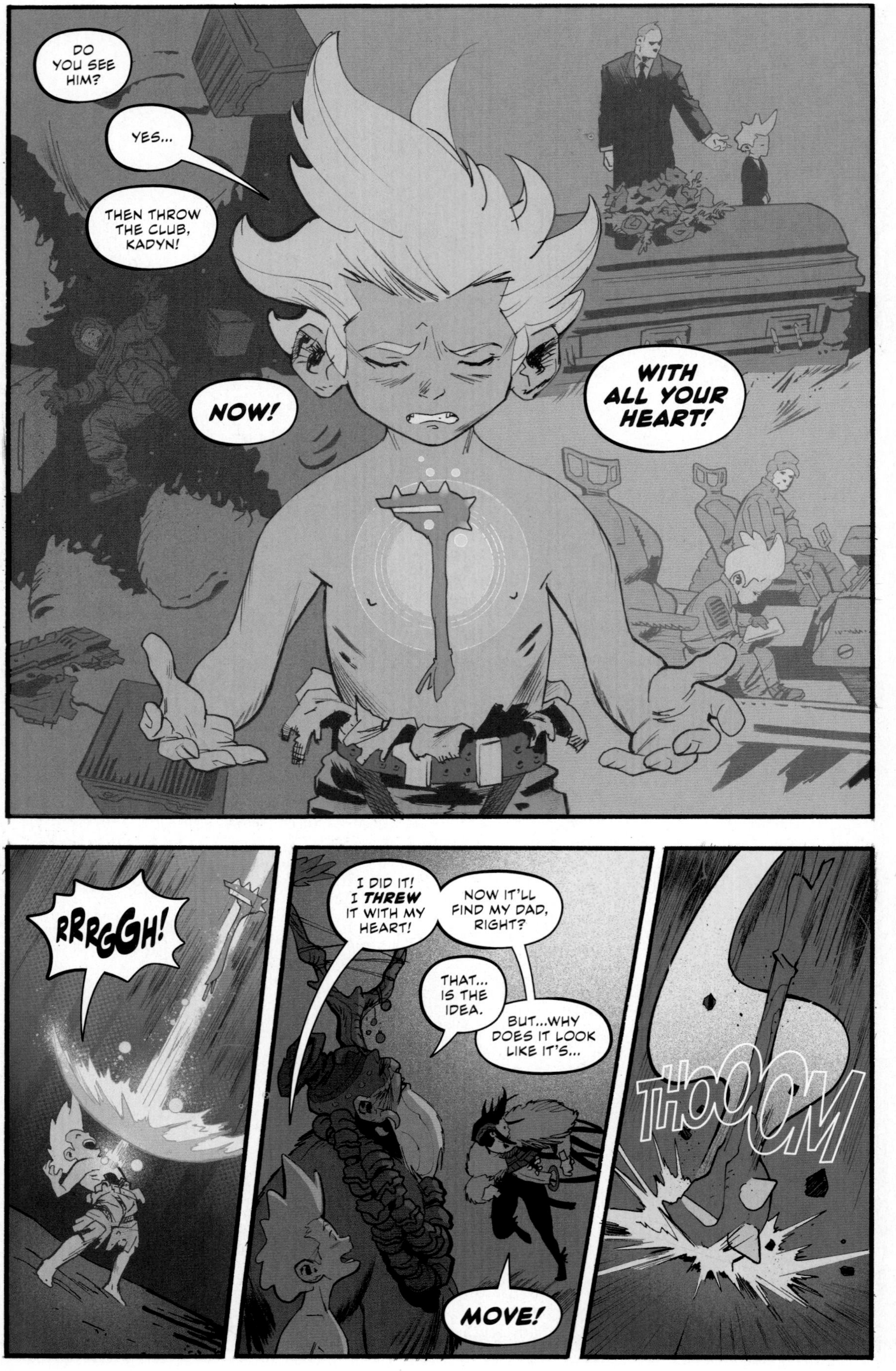
DO YOU SEE HIM?
YES...
THEN THROW THE CLUB, KADYN!
NOW!
WITH ALL YOUR HEART!
RRRGGH!
I DID IT! I THREW IT WITH MY HEART!
NOW IT'LL FIND MY DAD, RIGHT?
THAT... IS THE IDEA.
BUT...WHY DOES IT LOOK LIKE IT'S...
MOVE!
THOOOOM

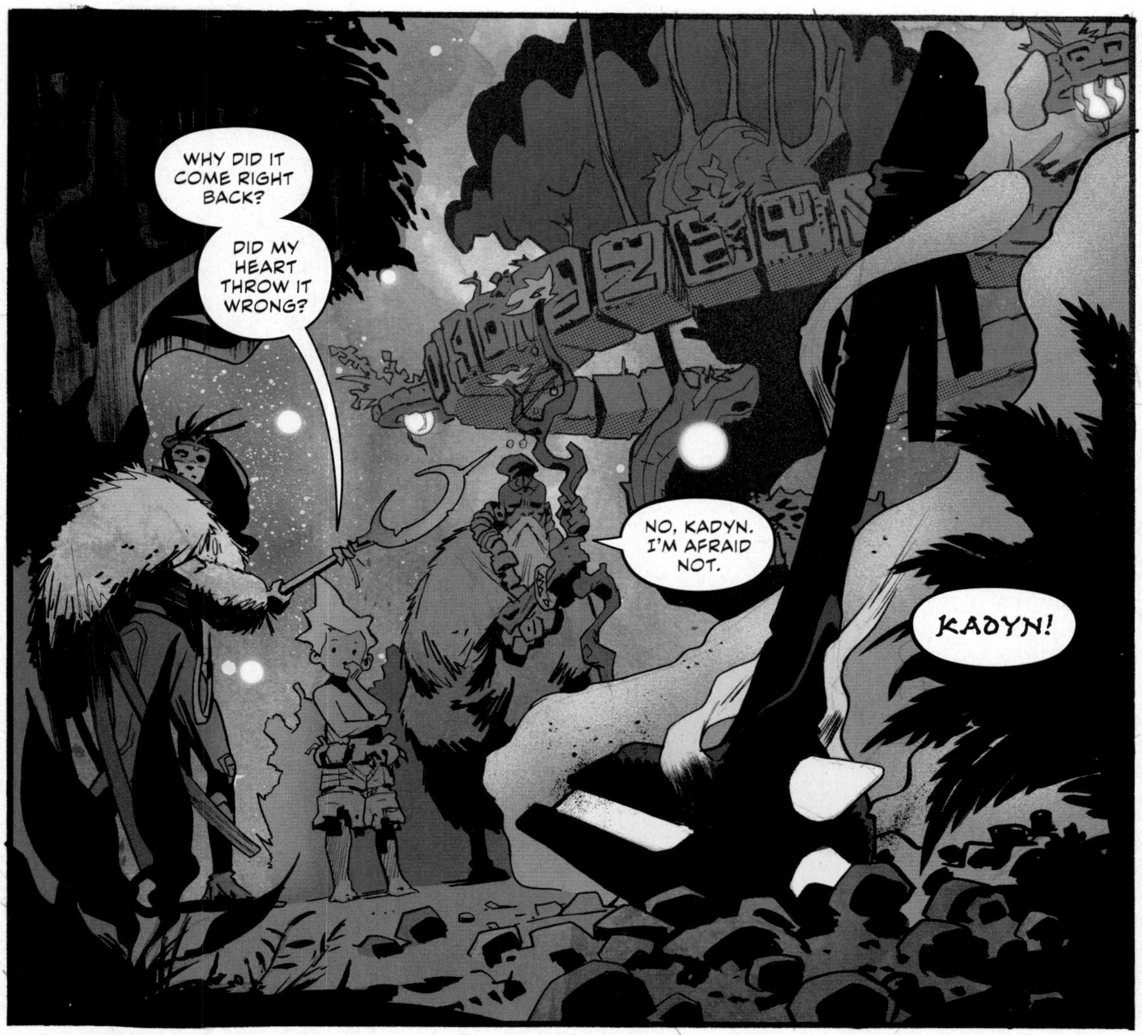
WHY DID IT COME RIGHT BACK?
DID MY HEART THROW IT WRONG?
NO, KADYN. I'M AFRAID NOT.
KADYN!

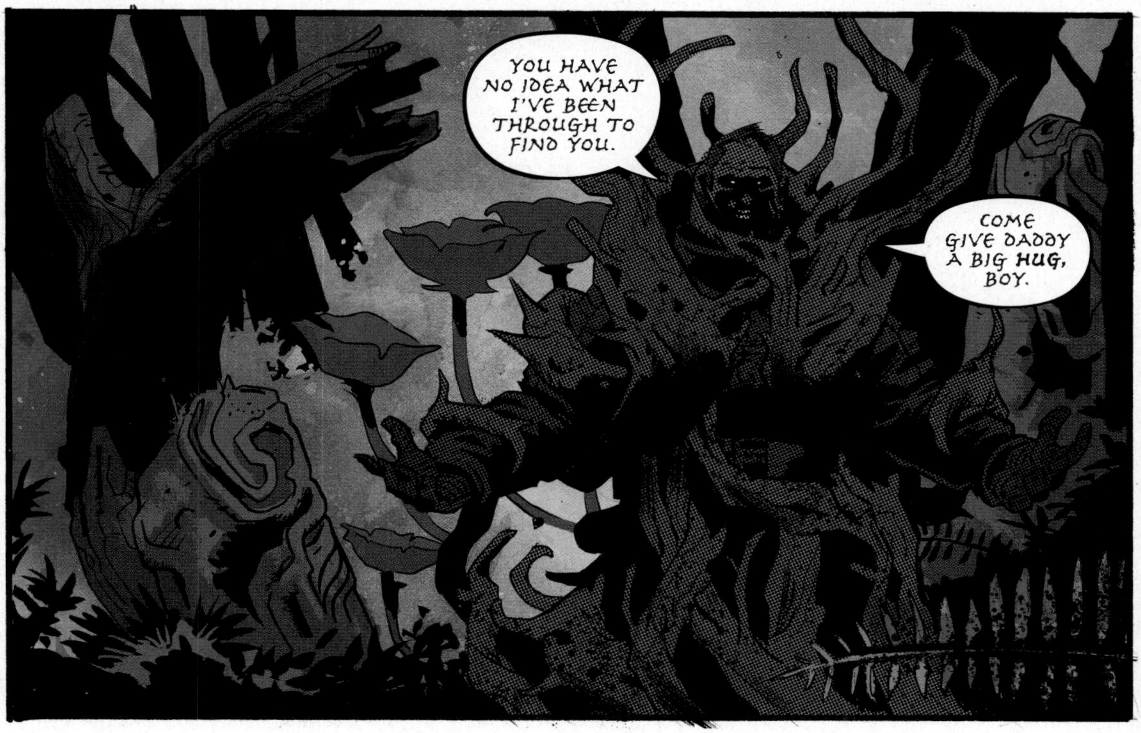
YOU HAVE NO IDEA WHAT I'VE BEEN THROUGH TO FIND YOU.
COME GIVE DADDY A BIG HUG, BOY.

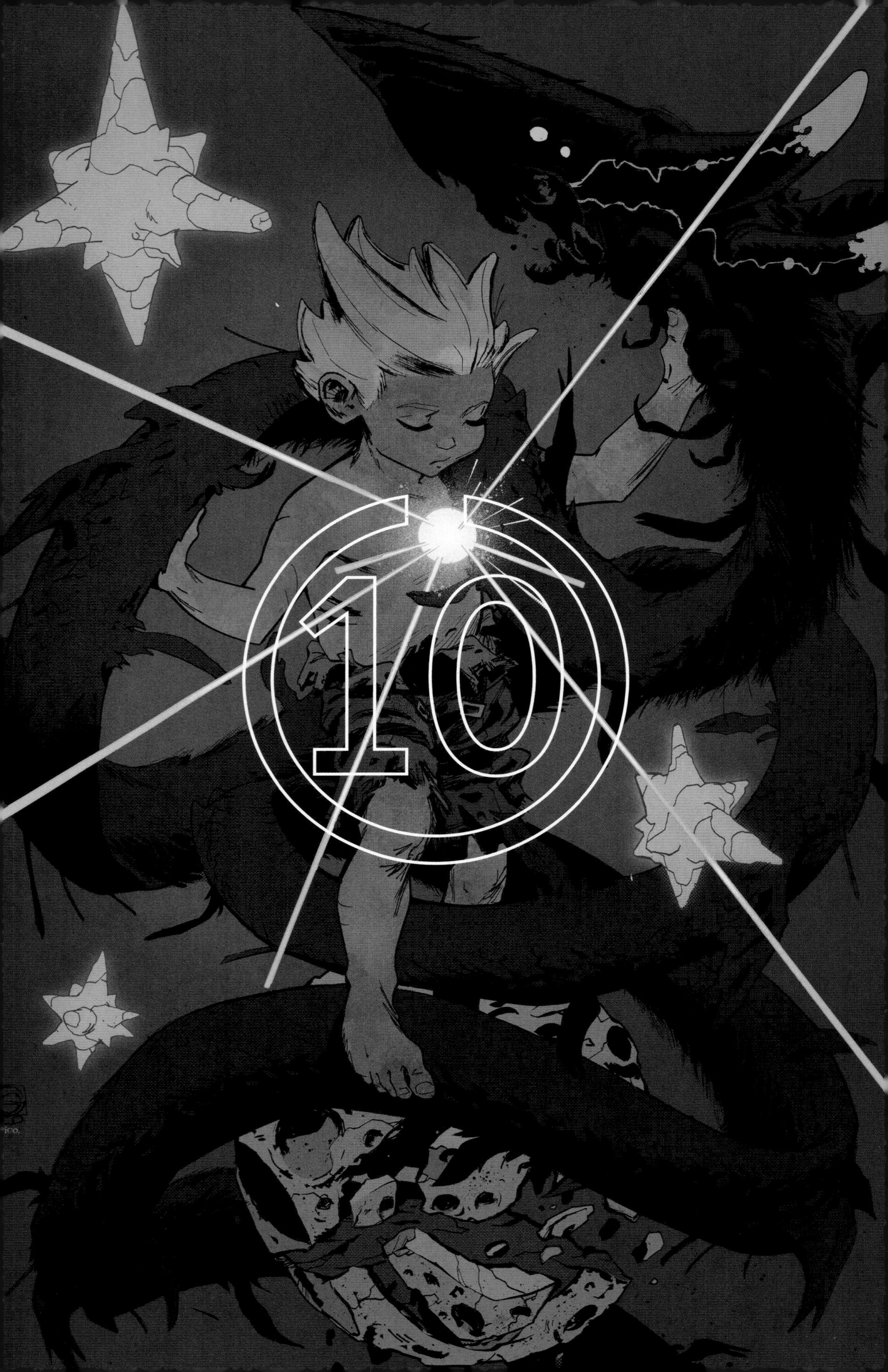
10

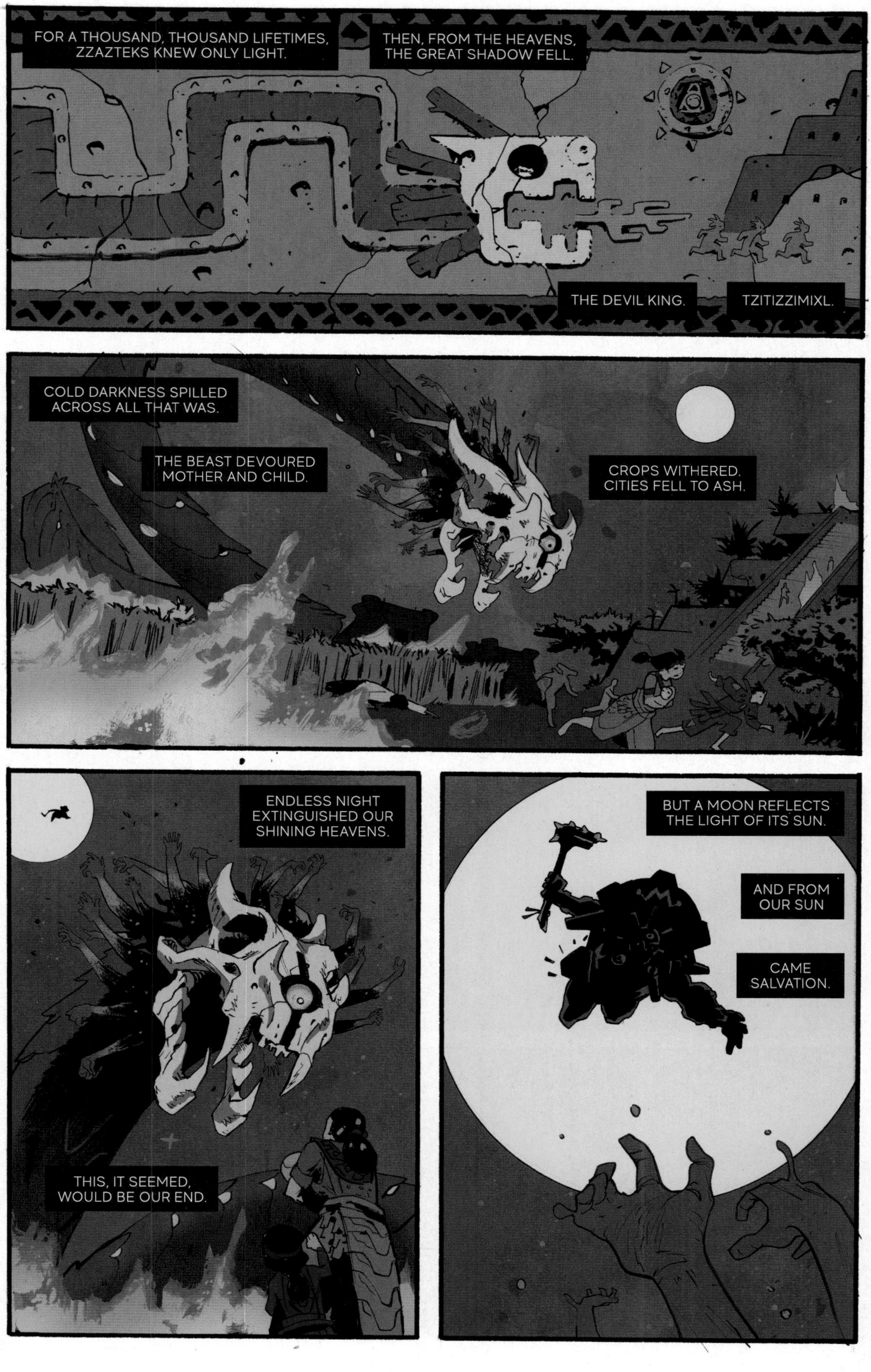
FOR A THOUSAND, THOUSAND LIFETIMES, ZZAZTEKS KNEW ONLY LIGHT.
THEN, FROM THE HEAVENS, THE GREAT SHADOW FELL.
THE DEVIL KING.
TZITIZZIMIXL.
COLD DARKNESS SPILLED ACROSS ALL THAT WAS.
THE BEAST DEVOURED MOTHER AND CHILD.
CROPS WITHERED. CITIES FELL TO ASH.
ENDLESS NIGHT EXTINGUISHED OUR SHINING HEAVENS.
THIS, IT SEEMED, WOULD BE OUR END.
BUT A MOON REFLECTS THE LIGHT OF ITS SUN.
AND FROM OUR SUN
CAME SALVATION.

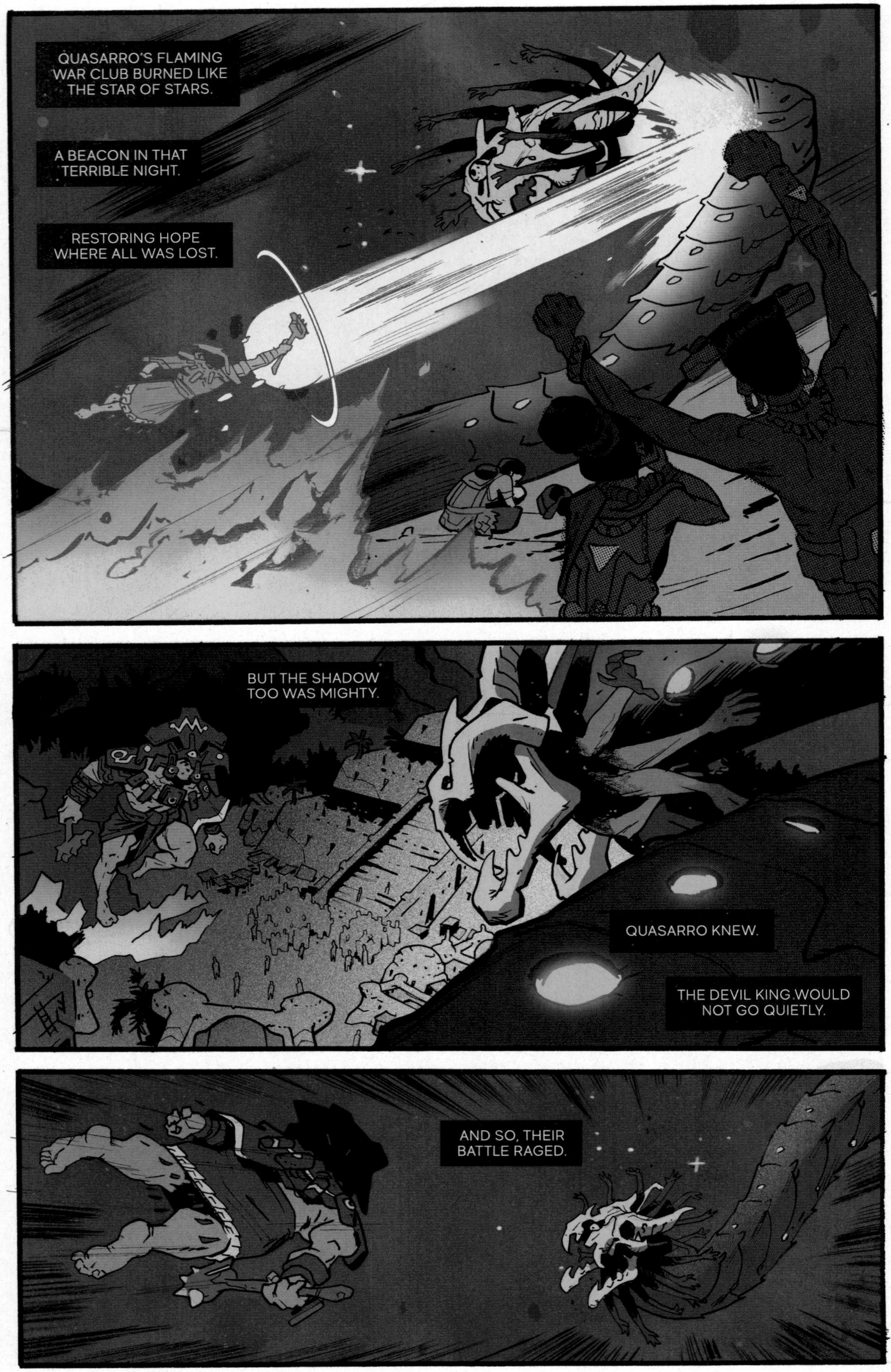
QUASARRO'S FLAMING WAR CLUB BURNED LIKE THE STAR OF STARS.
A BEACON IN THAT TERRIBLE NIGHT.
RESTORING HOPE WHERE ALL WAS LOST.
BUT THE SHADOW TOO WAS MIGHTY.
QUASARRO KNEW.
THE DEVIL KING.WOULD NOT GO QUIETLY.
AND SO, THEIR BATTLE RAGED.

THE GREAT ECLIPSE.

DARKNESS AND LIGHT.

AT WAR FOR THE HEAVENS.

THE SKY ITSELF DID QUAKE.

AS QUASARRO STRUCK HIS KILLING BLOW.

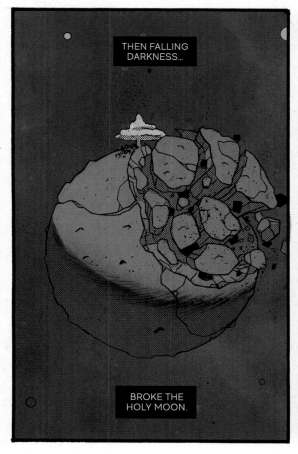

THEN FALLING DARKNESS...

BROKE THE HOLY MOON.

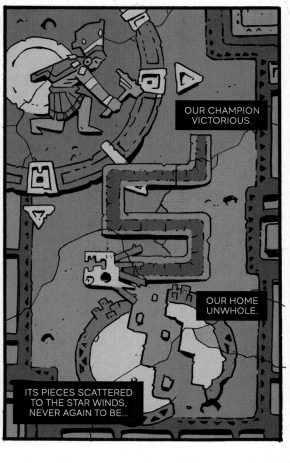

OUR CHAMPION VICTORIOUS.

OUR HOME UNWHOLE.

ITS PIECES SCATTERED TO THE STAR WINDS, NEVER AGAIN TO BE...

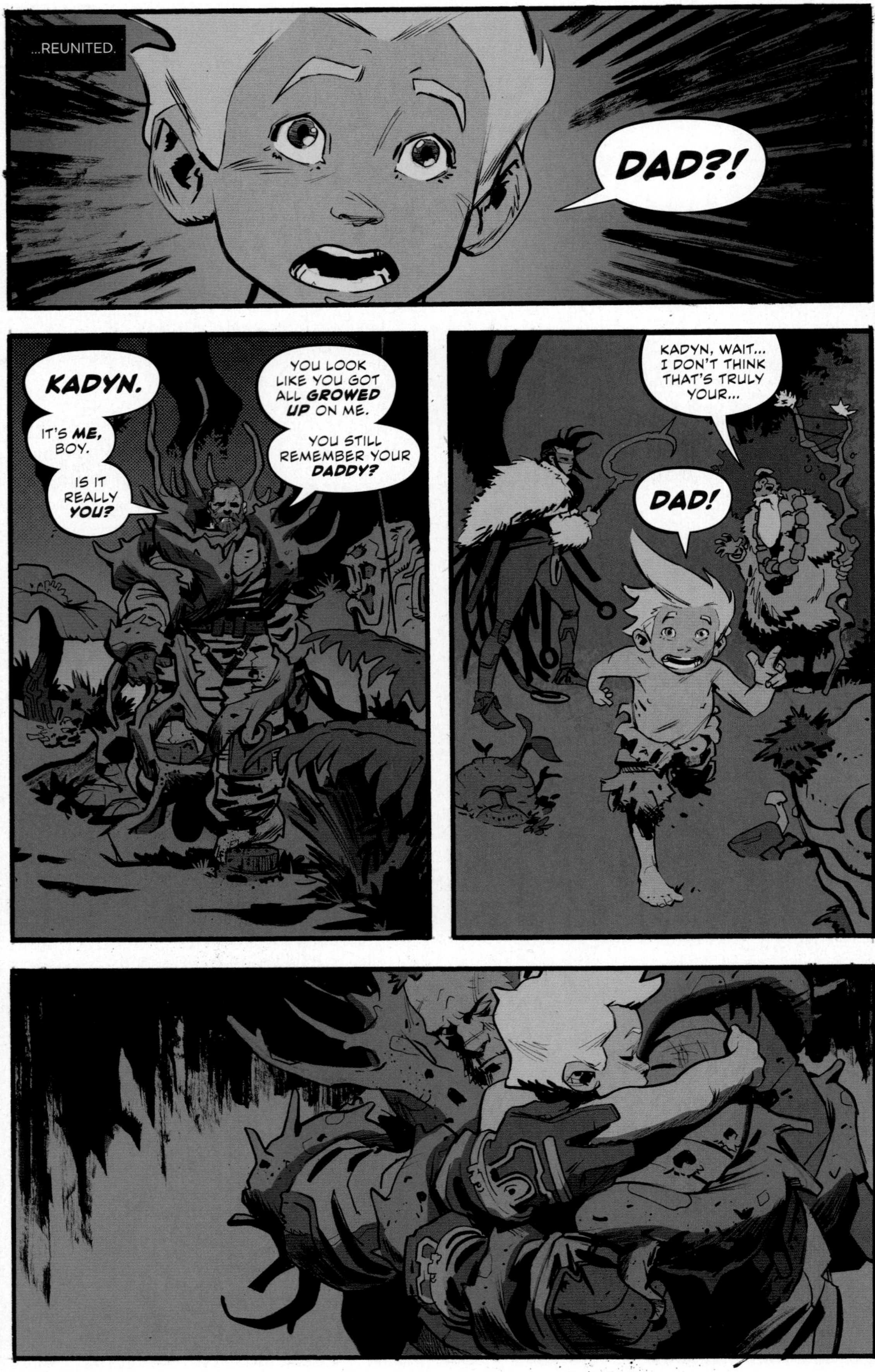
...REUNITED.
DAD?!
KADYN.
IT'S **ME,** BOY.
IS IT REALLY **YOU?**
YOU LOOK LIKE YOU GOT ALL **GROWED UP** ON ME.
YOU STILL REMEMBER YOUR **DADDY?**
KADYN, WAIT... I DON'T THINK THAT'S TRULY YOUR...
DAD!

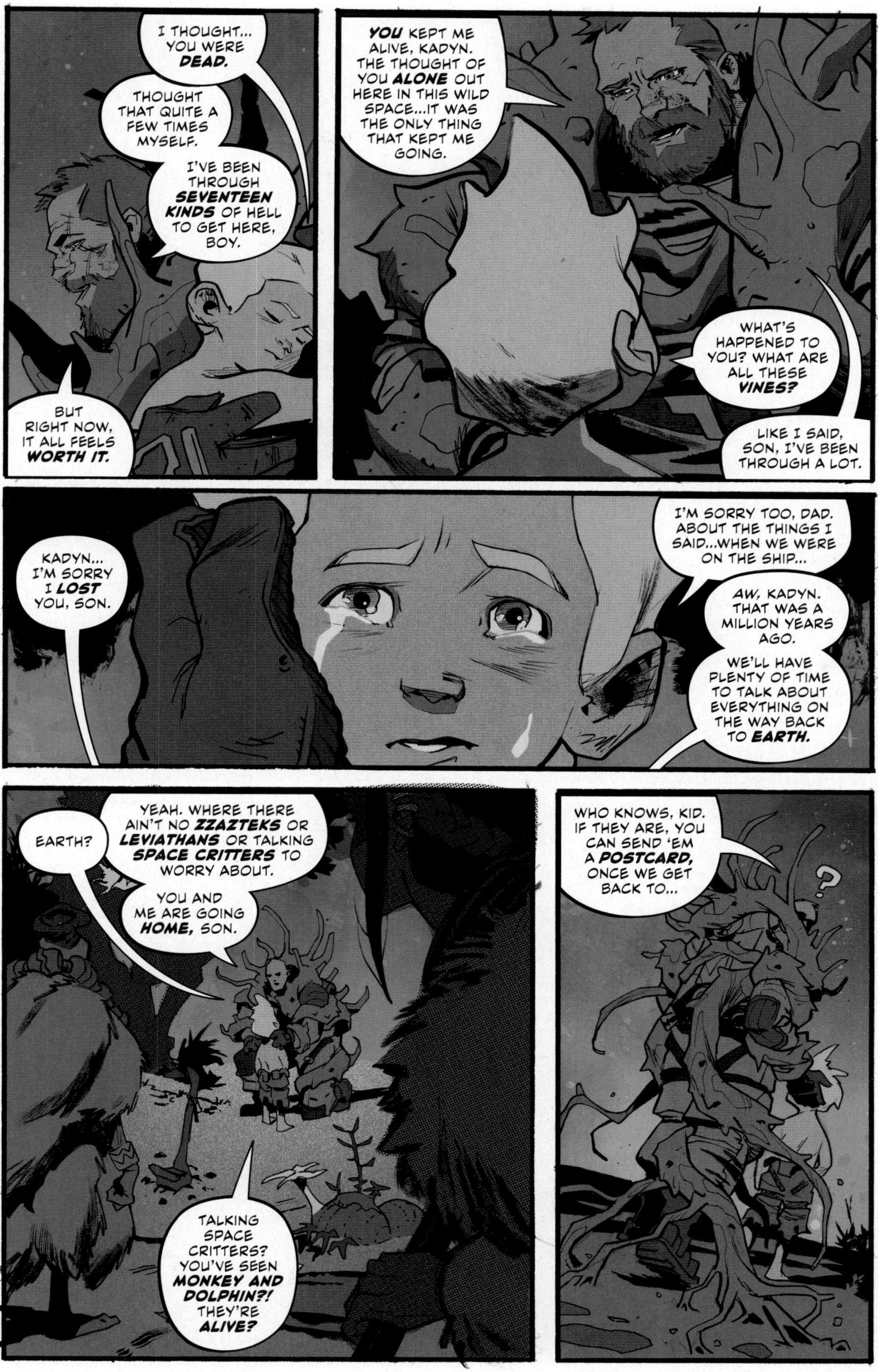
I THOUGHT... YOU WERE DEAD.
THOUGHT THAT QUITE A FEW TIMES MYSELF.
I'VE BEEN THROUGH SEVENTEEN KINDS OF HELL TO GET HERE, BOY.
BUT RIGHT NOW, IT ALL FEELS WORTH IT.
YOU KEPT ME ALIVE, KADYN. THE THOUGHT OF YOU ALONE OUT HERE IN THIS WILD SPACE...IT WAS THE ONLY THING THAT KEPT ME GOING.
WHAT'S HAPPENED TO YOU? WHAT ARE ALL THESE VINES?
LIKE I SAID, SON, I'VE BEEN THROUGH A LOT.
KADYN... I'M SORRY I LOST YOU, SON.
I'M SORRY TOO, DAD. ABOUT THE THINGS I SAID...WHEN WE WERE ON THE SHIP...
AW, KADYN. THAT WAS A MILLION YEARS AGO.
WE'LL HAVE PLENTY OF TIME TO TALK ABOUT EVERYTHING ON THE WAY BACK TO EARTH.
EARTH?
YEAH. WHERE THERE AIN'T NO ZZAZTEKS OR LEVIATHANS OR TALKING SPACE CRITTERS TO WORRY ABOUT.
YOU AND ME ARE GOING HOME, SON.
TALKING SPACE CRITTERS? YOU'VE SEEN MONKEY AND DOLPHIN?! THEY'RE ALIVE?
WHO KNOWS, KID. IF THEY ARE, YOU CAN SEND 'EM A POSTCARD, ONCE WE GET BACK TO...
?

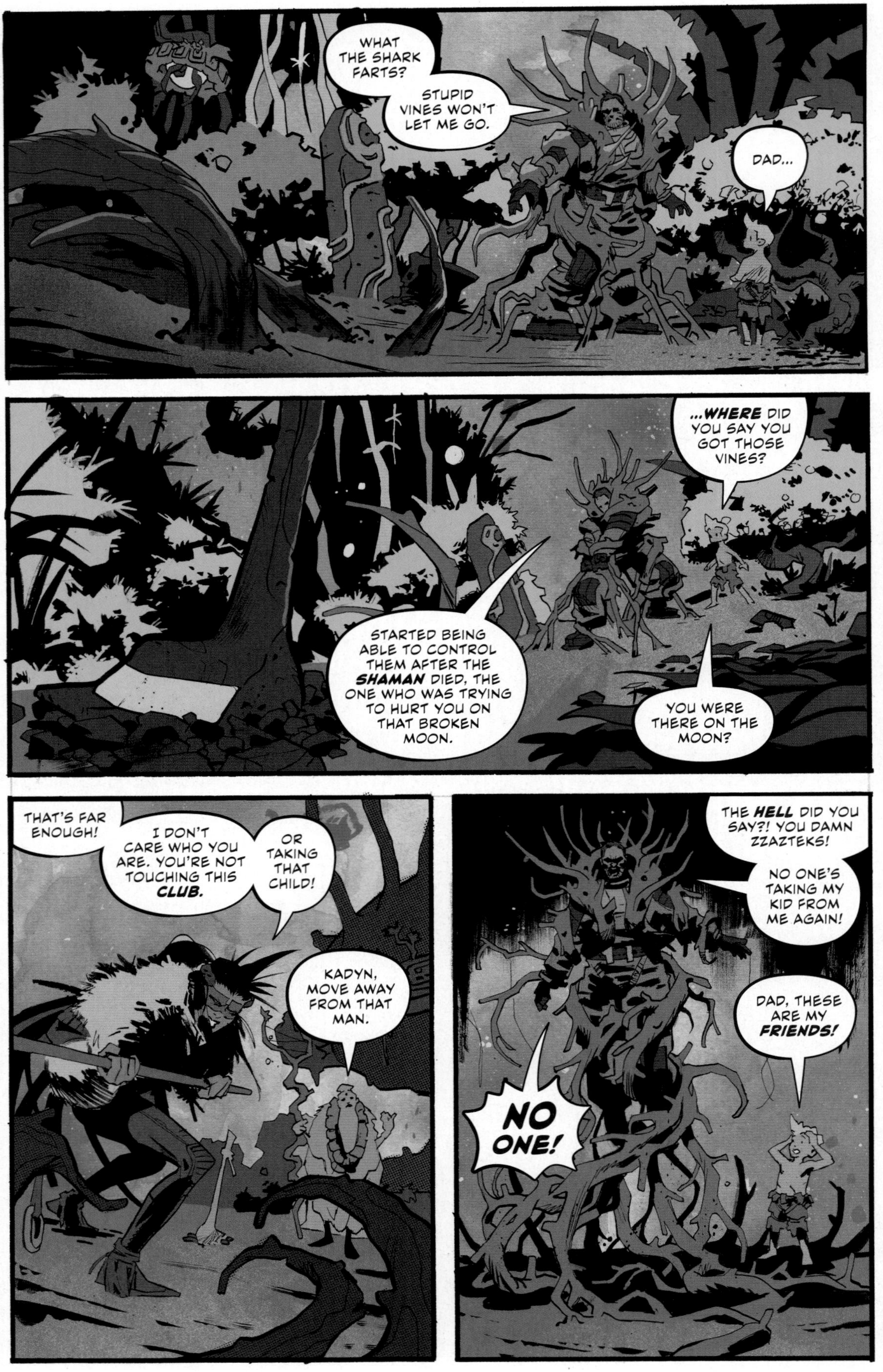
WHAT THE SHARK FARTS?
STUPID VINES WON'T LET ME GO.
DAD...
...WHERE DID YOU SAY YOU GOT THOSE VINES?
STARTED BEING ABLE TO CONTROL THEM AFTER THE SHAMAN DIED, THE ONE WHO WAS TRYING TO HURT YOU ON THAT BROKEN MOON.
YOU WERE THERE ON THE MOON?
THAT'S FAR ENOUGH!
I DON'T CARE WHO YOU ARE. YOU'RE NOT TOUCHING THIS CLUB.
OR TAKING THAT CHILD!
KADYN, MOVE AWAY FROM THAT MAN.
THE HELL DID YOU SAY?! YOU DAMN ZZAZTEKS!
NO ONE'S TAKING MY KID FROM ME AGAIN!
DAD, THESE ARE MY FRIENDS!
NO ONE!

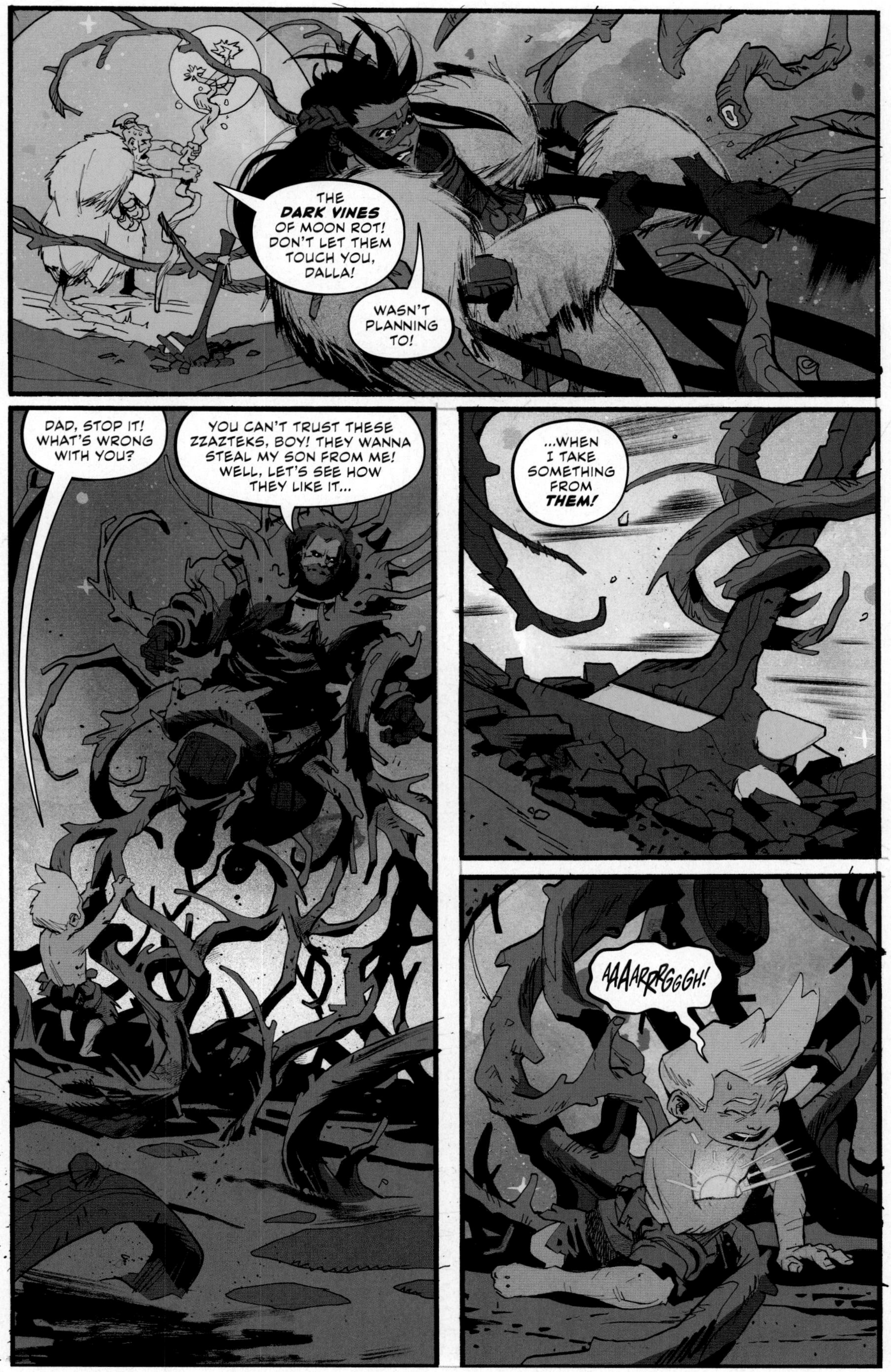
THE DARK VINES OF MOON ROT! DON'T LET THEM TOUCH YOU, DALLA!
WASN'T PLANNING TO!
DAD, STOP IT! WHAT'S WRONG WITH YOU?
YOU CAN'T TRUST THESE ZZAZTEKS, BOY! THEY WANNA STEAL MY SON FROM ME! WELL, LET'S SEE HOW THEY LIKE IT...
...WHEN I TAKE SOMETHING FROM THEM!
AAAARRRGGGH!

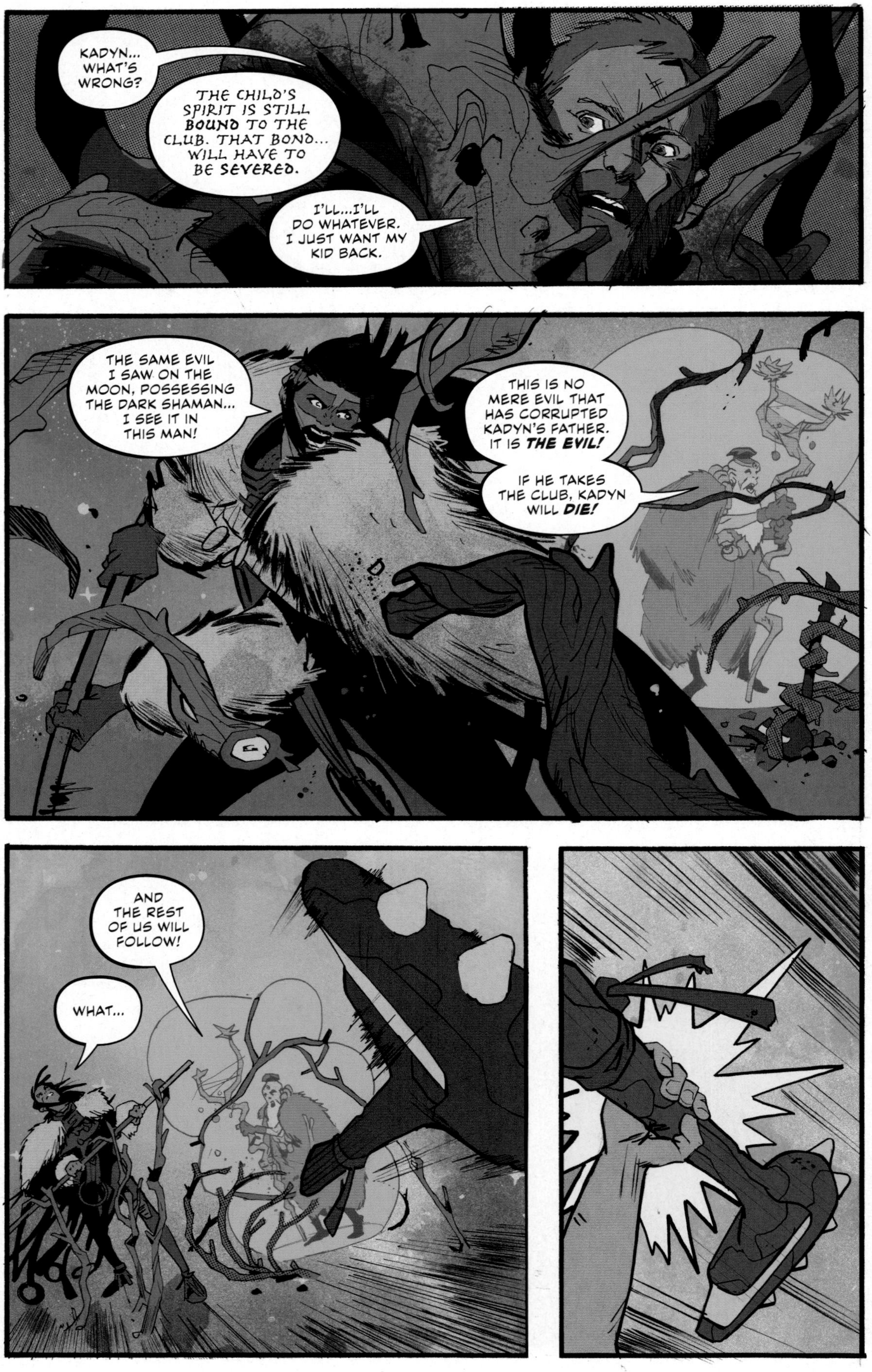
KADYN... WHAT'S WRONG?
THE CHILD'S SPIRIT IS STILL BOUND TO THE CLUB. THAT BOND... WILL HAVE TO BE SEVERED.
I'LL...I'LL DO WHATEVER. I JUST WANT MY KID BACK.
THE SAME EVIL I SAW ON THE MOON, POSSESSING THE DARK SHAMAN... I SEE IT IN THIS MAN!
THIS IS NO MERE EVIL THAT HAS CORRUPTED KADYN'S FATHER. IT IS THE EVIL!
IF HE TAKES THE CLUB, KADYN WILL DIE!
AND THE REST OF US WILL FOLLOW!
WHAT...

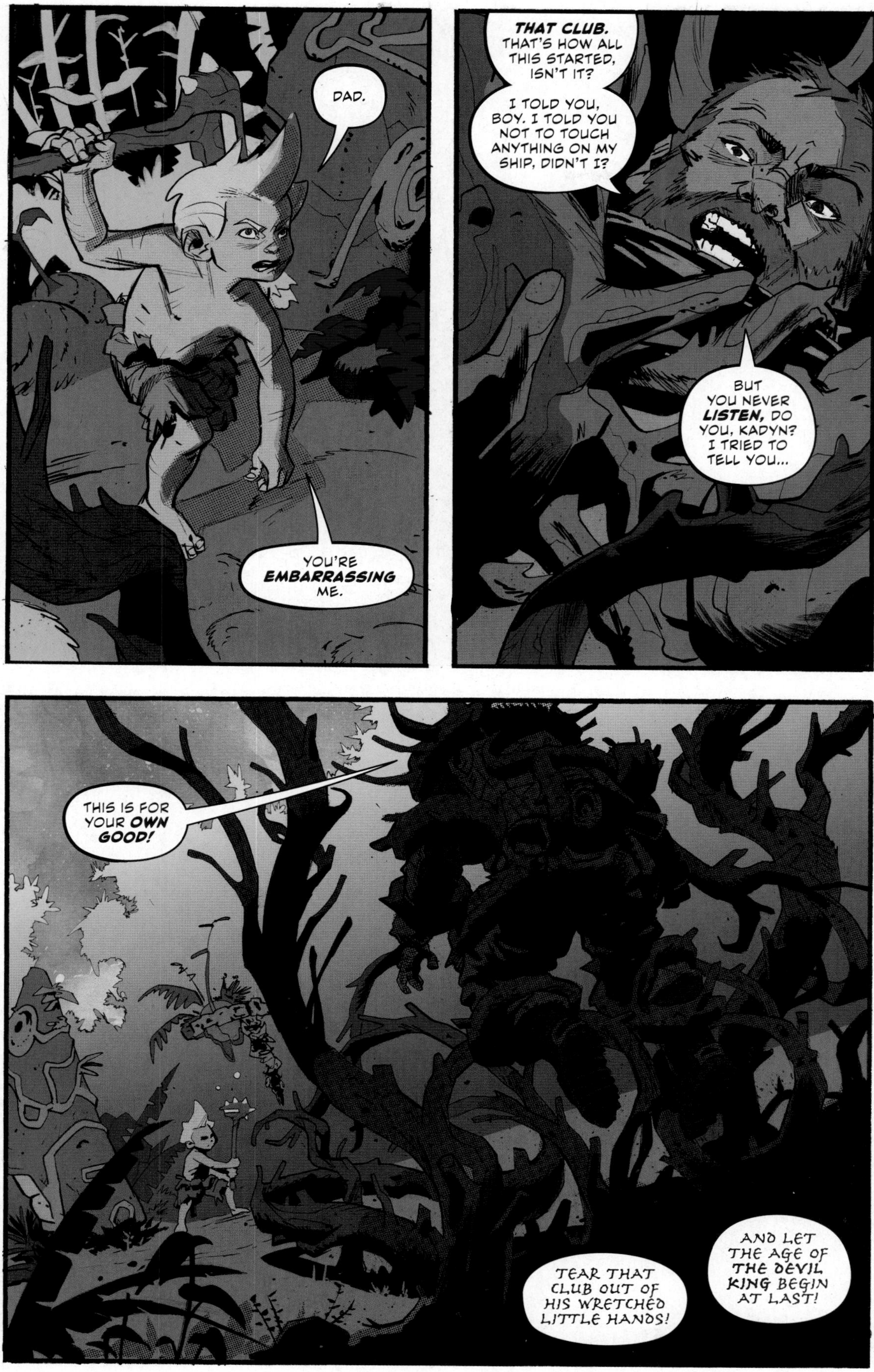
DAD.
YOU'RE EMBARRASSING ME.
THAT CLUB. THAT'S HOW ALL THIS STARTED, ISN'T IT?
I TOLD YOU, BOY. I TOLD YOU NOT TO TOUCH ANYTHING ON MY SHIP, DIDN'T I?
BUT YOU NEVER LISTEN, DO YOU, KADYN? I TRIED TO TELL YOU...
THIS IS FOR YOUR OWN GOOD!
TEAR THAT CLUB OUT OF HIS WRETCHED LITTLE HANDS!
AND LET THE AGE OF THE DEVIL KING BEGIN AT LAST!

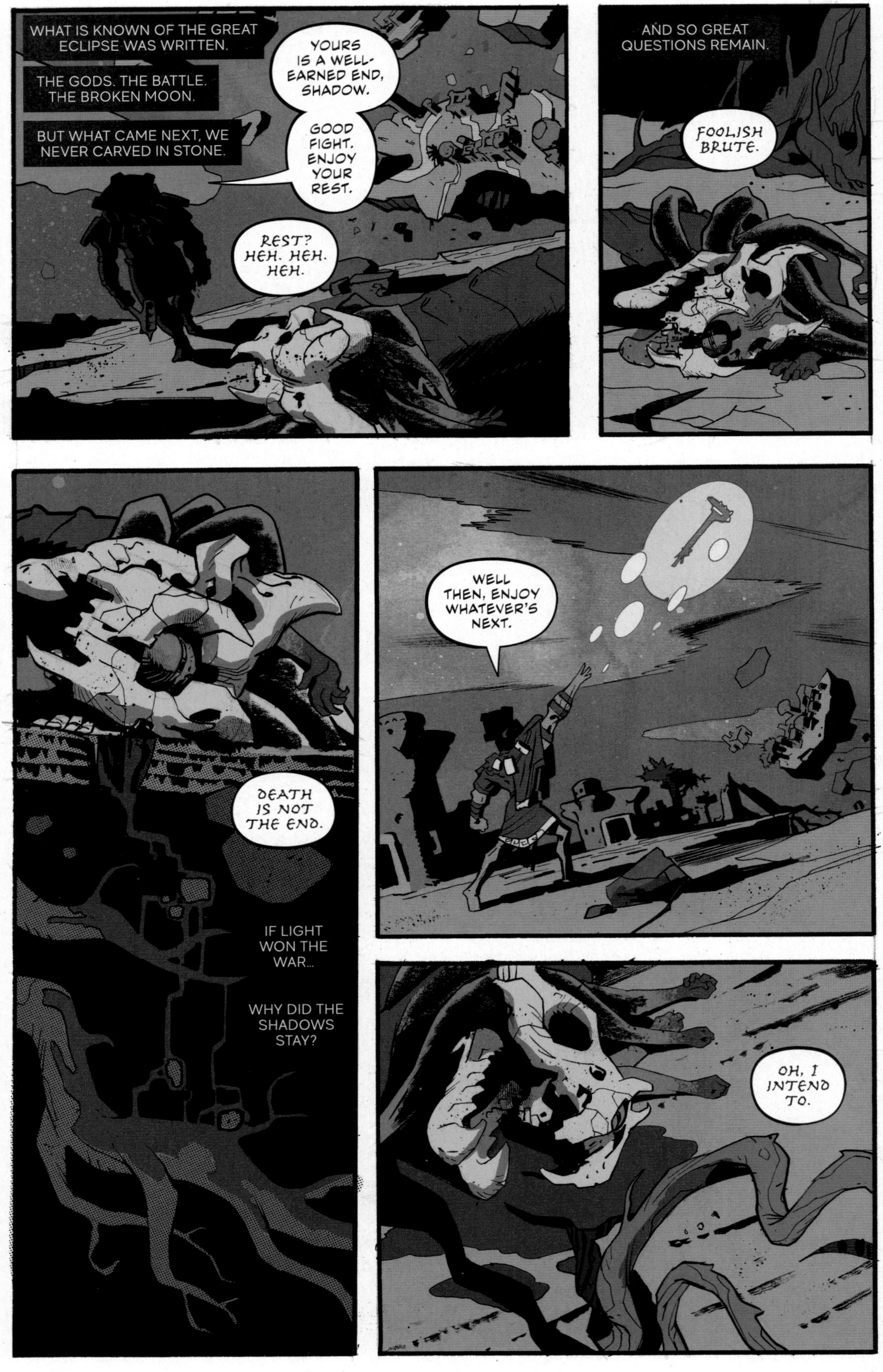
WHAT IS KNOWN OF THE GREAT ECLIPSE WAS WRITTEN.
THE GODS. THE BATTLE. THE BROKEN MOON.
BUT WHAT CAME NEXT, WE NEVER CARVED IN STONE.
YOURS IS A WELL-EARNED END, SHADOW.
GOOD FIGHT. ENJOY YOUR REST.
REST? HEH. HEH. HEH.
AND SO GREAT QUESTIONS REMAIN.
FOOLISH BRUTE.
DEATH IS NOT THE END.
IF LIGHT WON THE WAR...
WHY DID THE SHADOWS STAY?
WELL THEN, ENJOY WHATEVER'S NEXT.
OH, I INTEND TO.

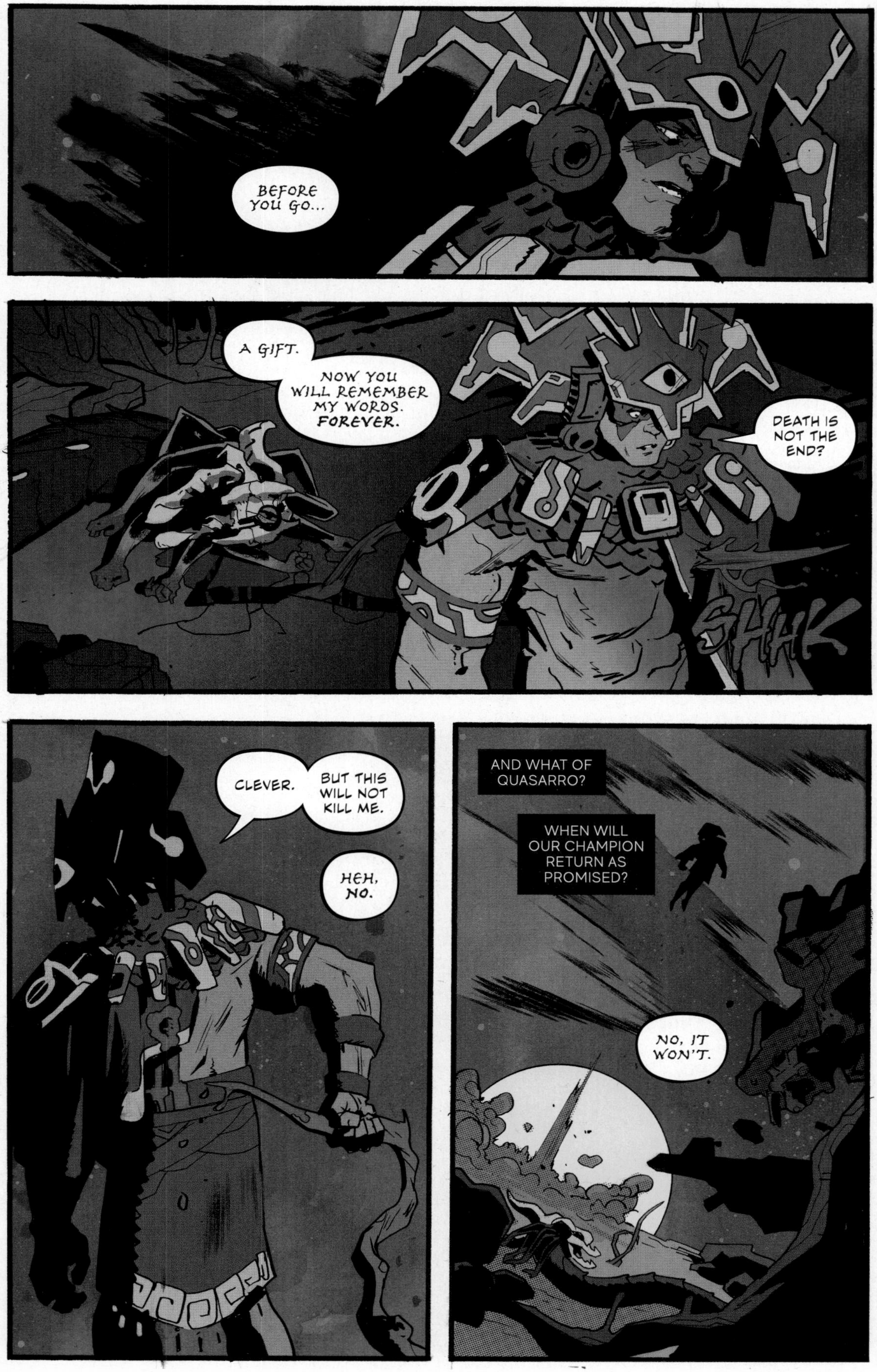
BEFORE YOU GO...
A GIFT.
NOW YOU WILL REMEMBER MY WORDS. FOREVER.
DEATH IS NOT THE END?
SHHK
CLEVER.
BUT THIS WILL NOT KILL ME.
HEH, NO.
AND WHAT OF QUASARRO?
WHEN WILL OUR CHAMPION RETURN AS PROMISED?
NO, IT WON'T.

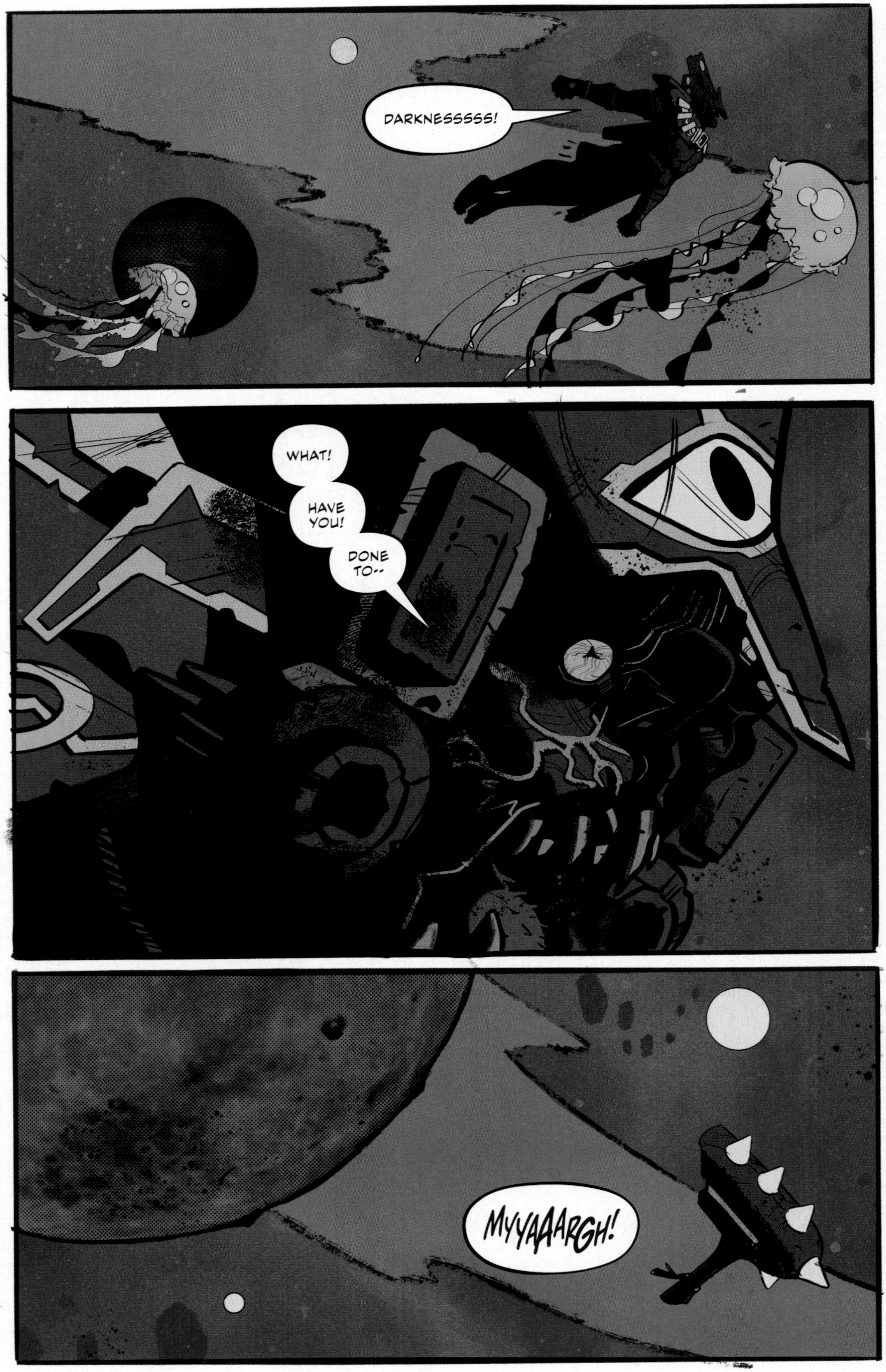
DARKNESSSSS!
WHAT!
HAVE YOU!
DONE TO--
MYYAAARGH!

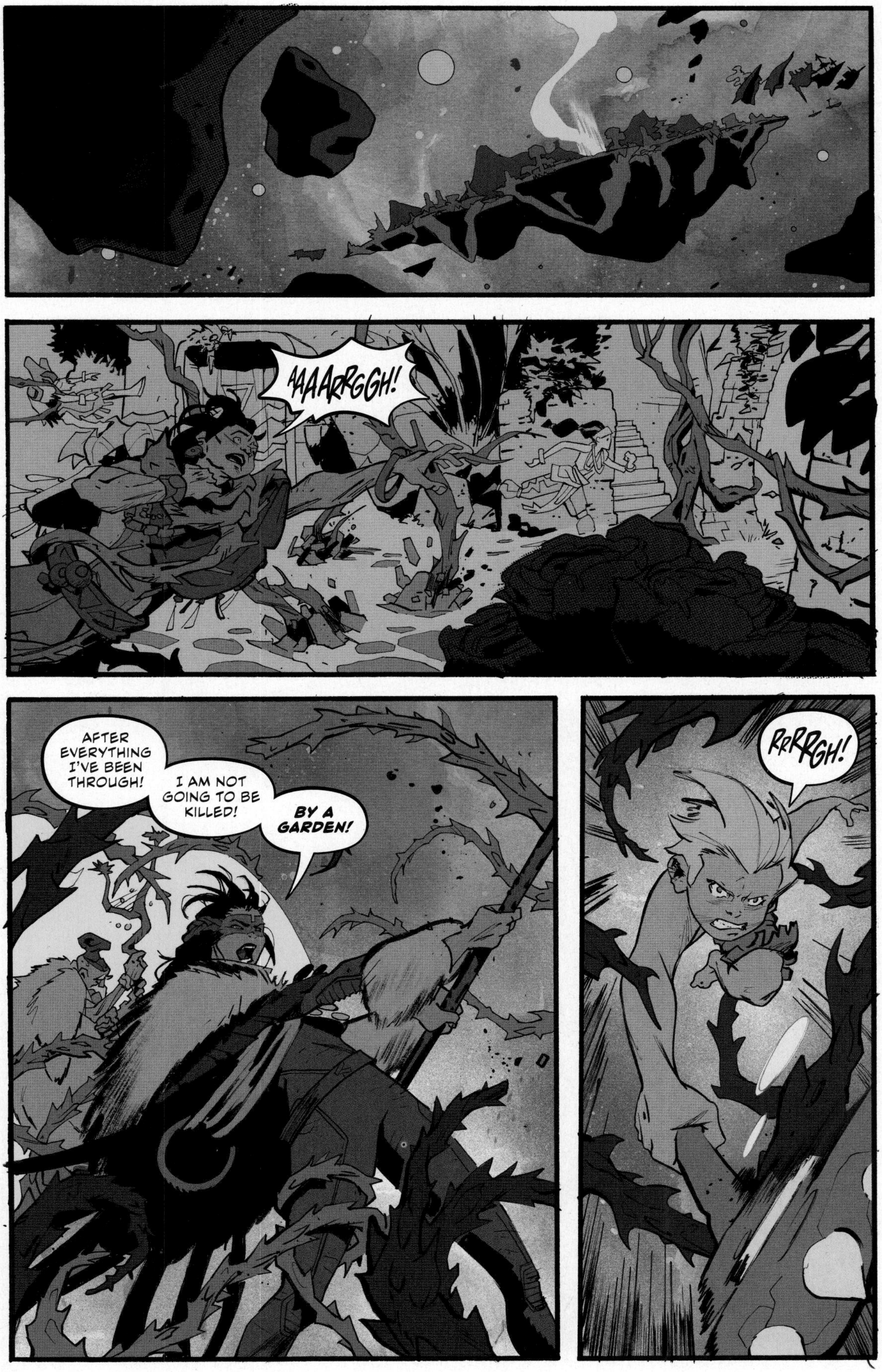
AAAARRGGH!
AFTER EVERYTHING I'VE BEEN THROUGH!
I AM NOT GOING TO BE KILLED!
BY A GARDEN!
RRRRGH!

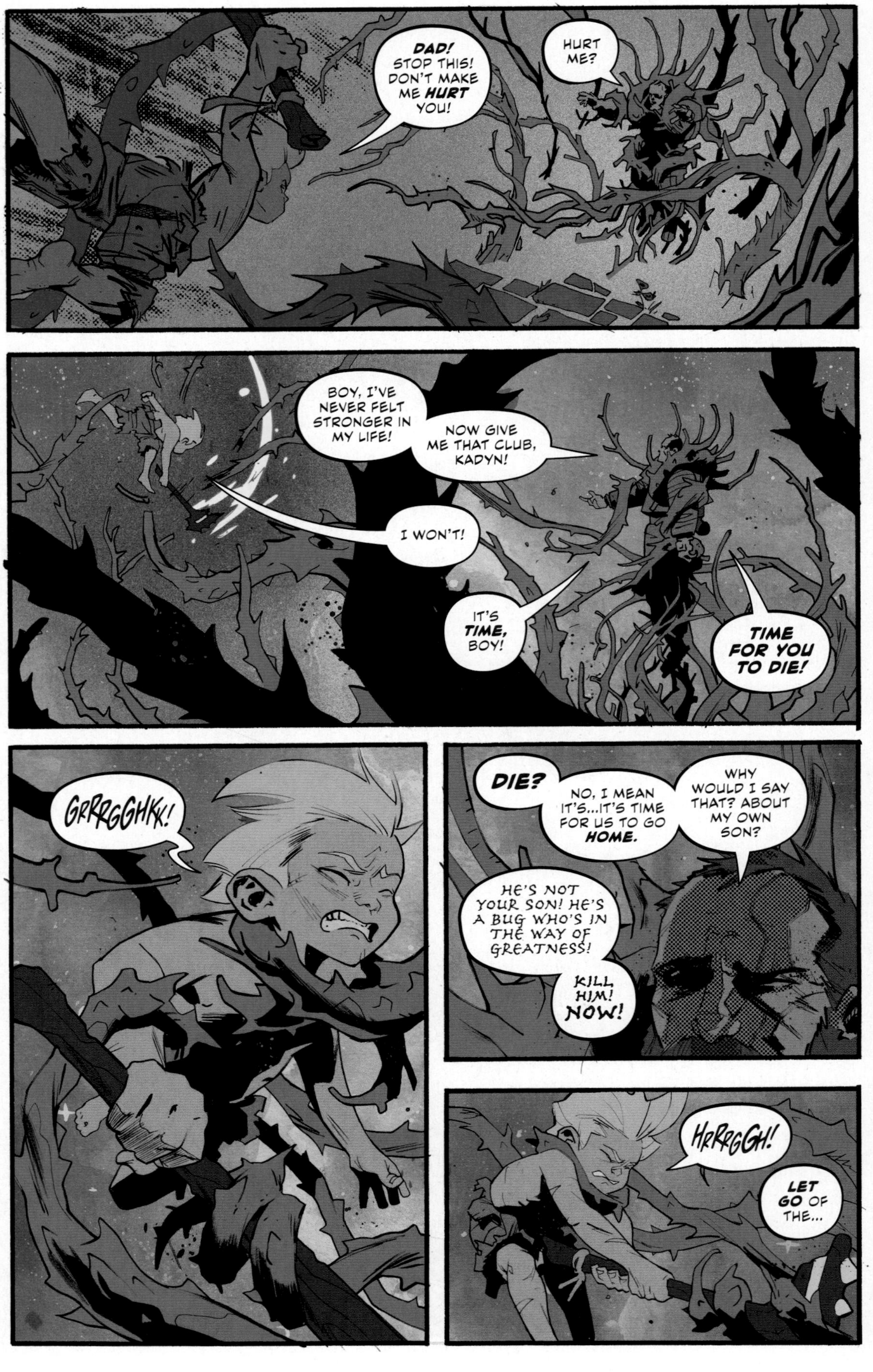

DAD! STOP THIS! DON'T MAKE ME HURT YOU!
HURT ME?
BOY, I'VE NEVER FELT STRONGER IN MY LIFE!
NOW GIVE ME THAT CLUB, KADYN!
I WON'T!
IT'S TIME, BOY!
TIME FOR YOU TO DIE!
GRRRGGHKK!
DIE?
NO, I MEAN IT'S...IT'S TIME FOR US TO GO HOME.
WHY WOULD I SAY THAT? ABOUT MY OWN SON?
HE'S NOT YOUR SON! HE'S A BUG WHO'S IN THE WAY OF GREATNESS!
KILL HIM! NOW!
HRRRGGH!
LET GO OF THE...

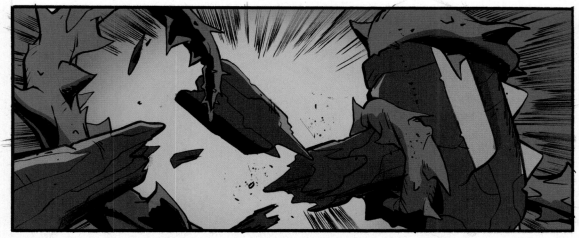

OH NO.

MAX?

KADYN...

I **LOVE** YOU, SON.

I'D ALWAYS DO ANYTHING TO KEEP YOU **SAFE**.

STOP FIGHTING ME, YOU FOOL!

ANYTHING.

NOOOO!

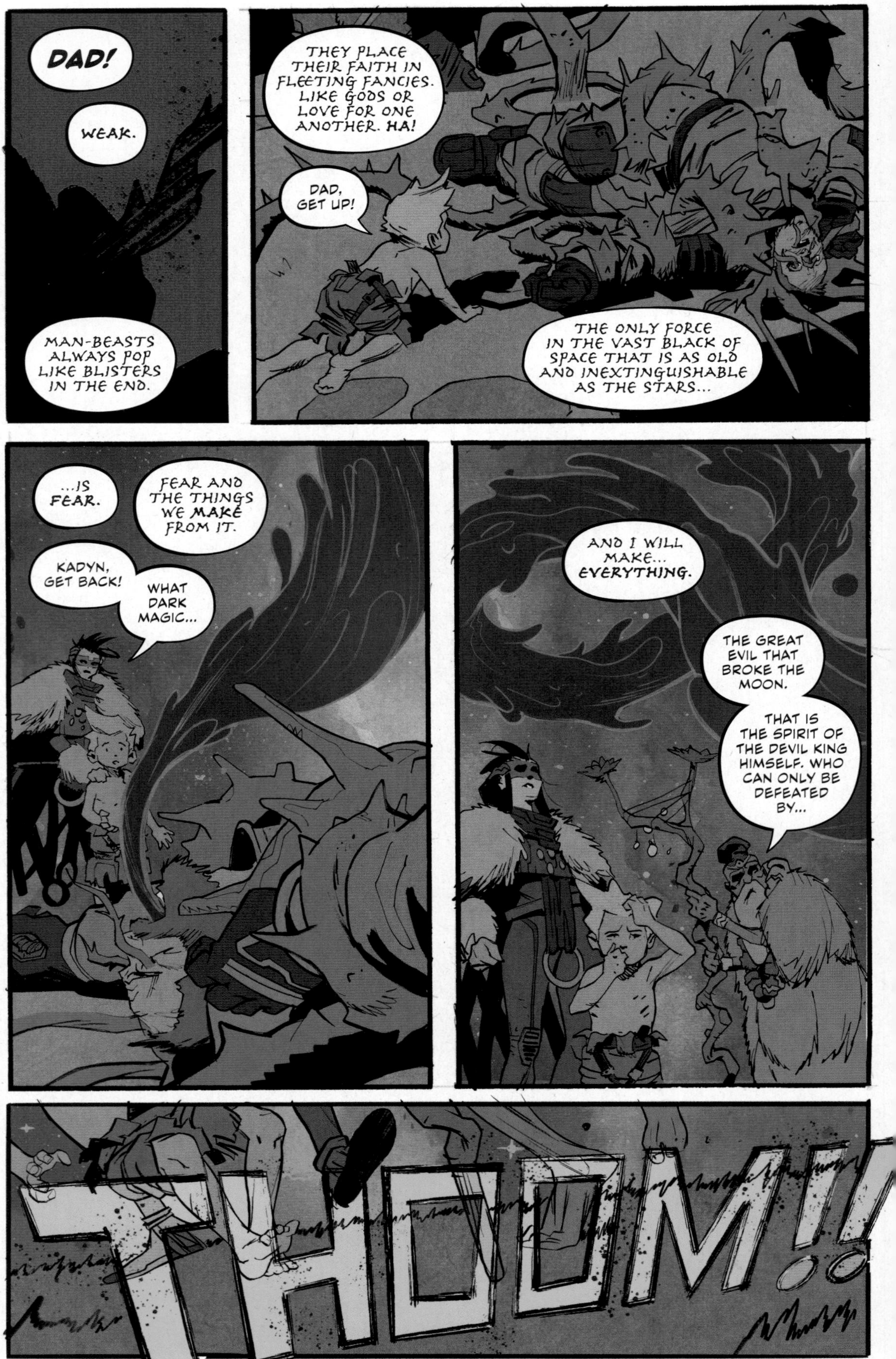
DAD!
WEAK.
MAN-BEASTS ALWAYS POP LIKE BLISTERS IN THE END.
THEY PLACE THEIR FAITH IN FLEETING FANCIES. LIKE GODS OR LOVE FOR ONE ANOTHER. HA!
DAD, GET UP!
THE ONLY FORCE IN THE VAST BLACK OF SPACE THAT IS AS OLD AND INEXTINGUISHABLE AS THE STARS...
...IS FEAR.
FEAR AND THE THINGS WE MAKE FROM IT.
KADYN, GET BACK!
WHAT DARK MAGIC...
AND I WILL MAKE... EVERYTHING.
THE GREAT EVIL THAT BROKE THE MOON.
THAT IS THE SPIRIT OF THE DEVIL KING HIMSELF. WHO CAN ONLY BE DEFEATED BY...
THOOM!!

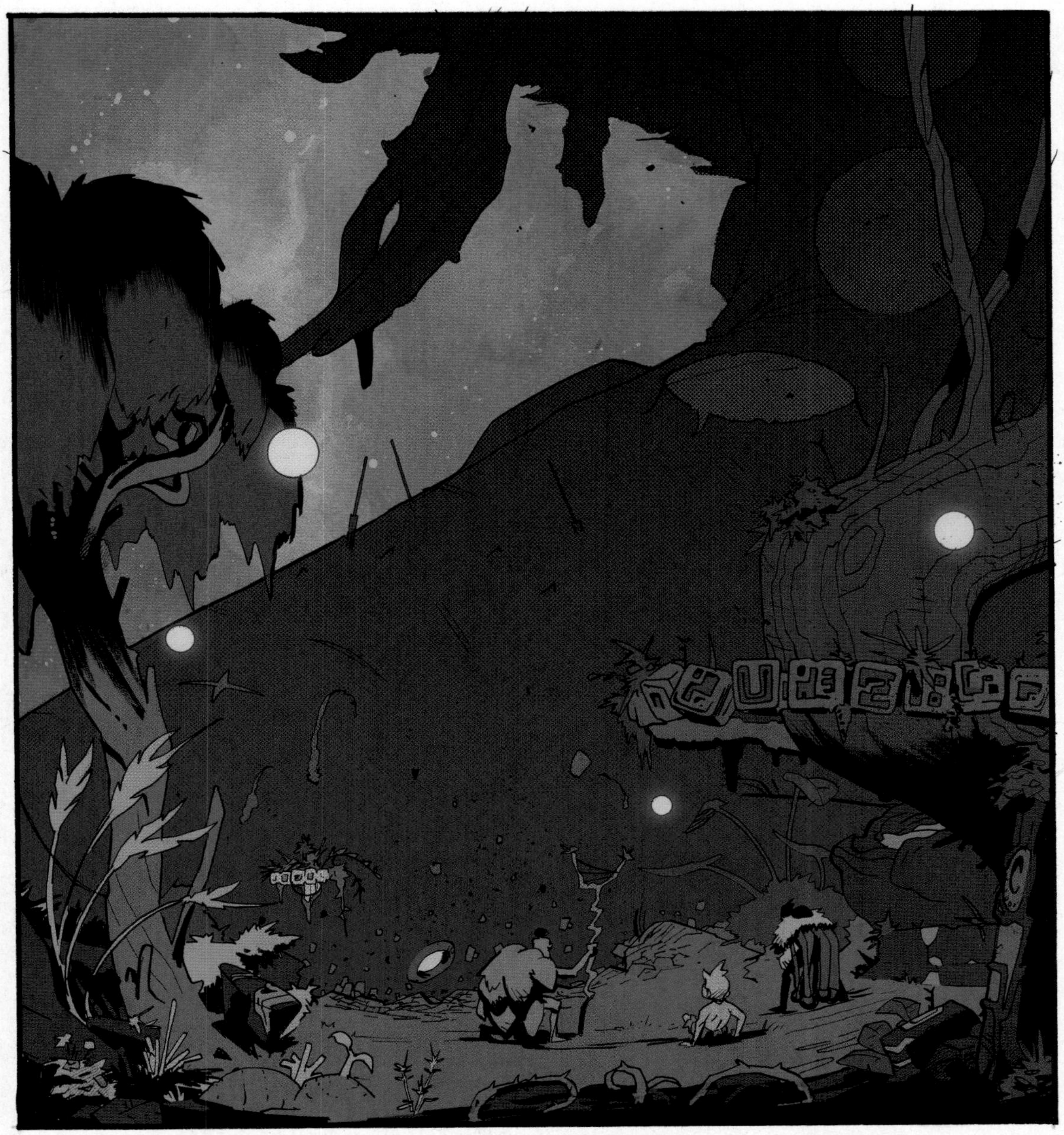

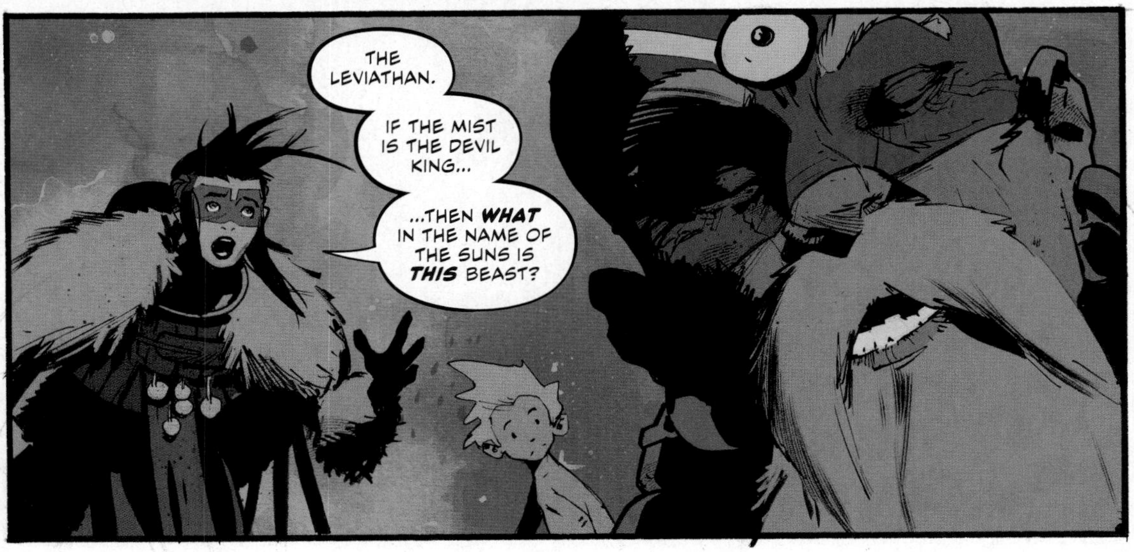
THE LEVIATHAN.
IF THE MIST IS THE DEVIL KING...
...THEN **WHAT** IN THE NAME OF THE SUNS IS **THIS** BEAST?

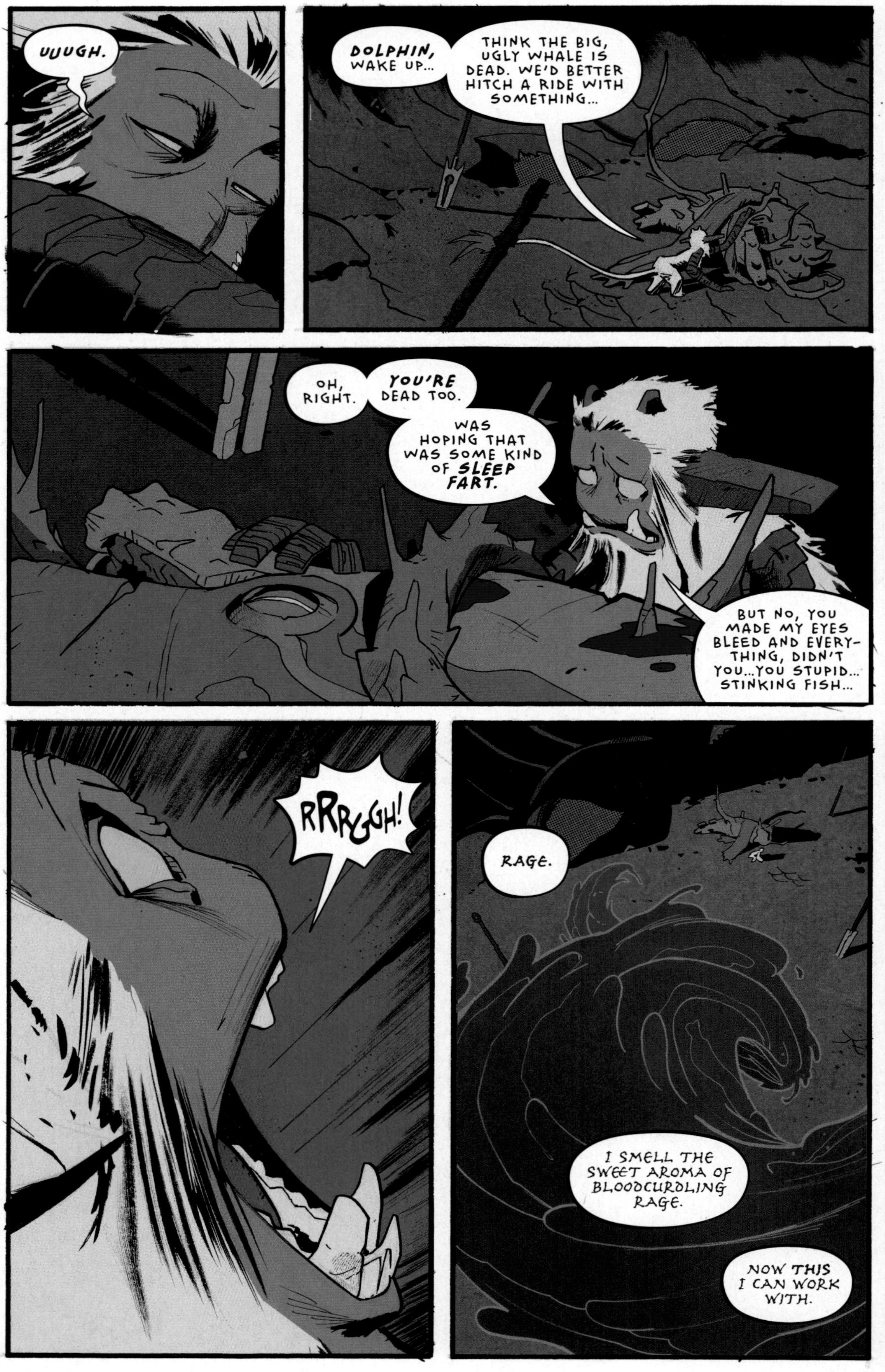
UUUGH.
DOLPHIN, WAKE UP...
THINK THE BIG, UGLY WHALE IS DEAD. WE'D BETTER HITCH A RIDE WITH SOMETHING...
OH, RIGHT.
YOU'RE DEAD TOO.
WAS HOPING THAT WAS SOME KIND OF SLEEP FART.
BUT NO, YOU MADE MY EYES BLEED AND EVERYTHING, DIDN'T YOU...YOU STUPID... STINKING FISH...
RRRGGH!
RAGE.
I SMELL THE SWEET AROMA OF BLOODCURDLING RAGE.
NOW THIS I CAN WORK WITH.

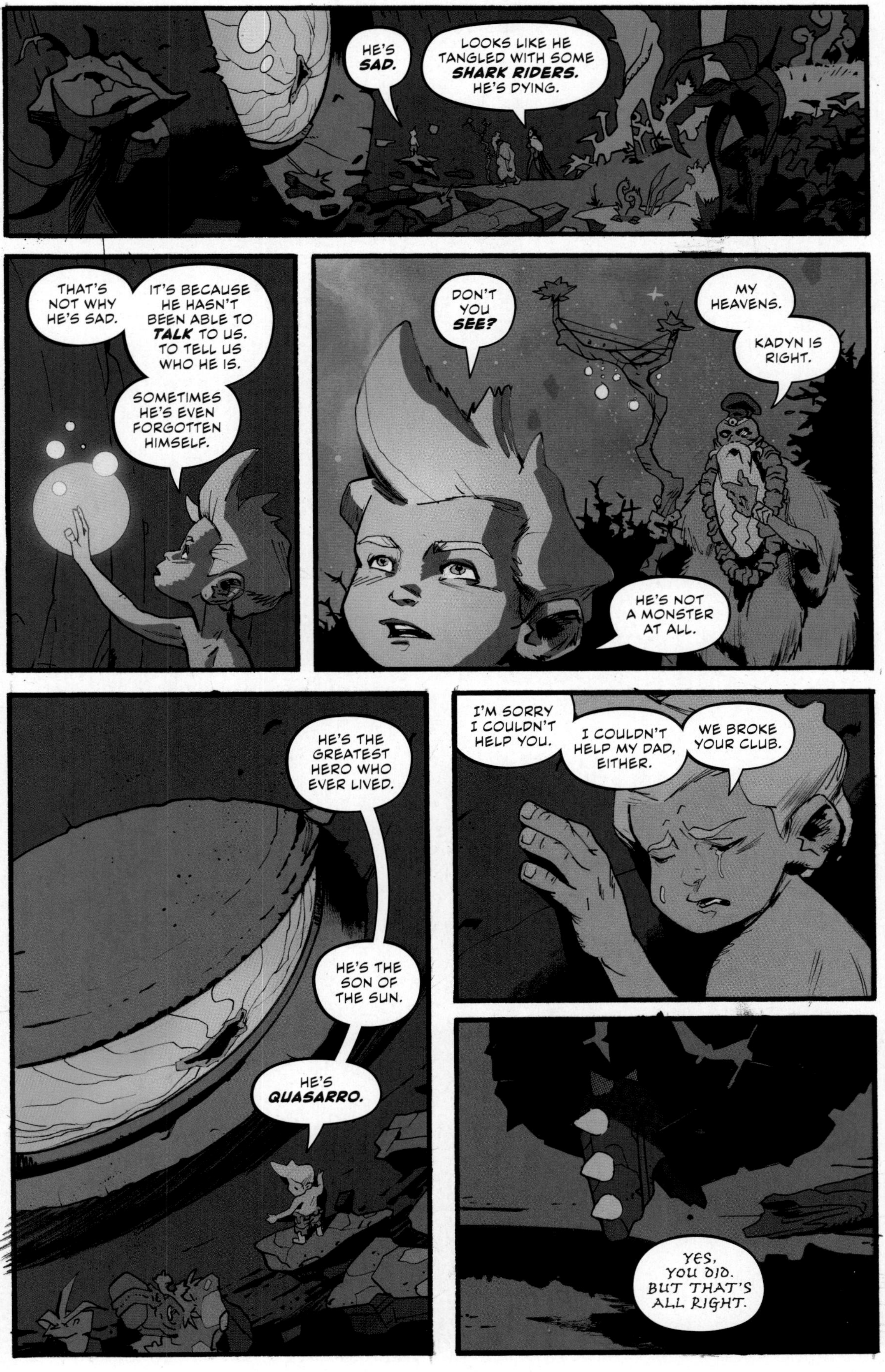
HE'S **SAD.**
LOOKS LIKE HE TANGLED WITH SOME **SHARK RIDERS.** HE'S DYING.
THAT'S NOT WHY HE'S SAD.
IT'S BECAUSE HE HASN'T BEEN ABLE TO **TALK** TO US. TO TELL US WHO HE IS.
SOMETIMES HE'S EVEN FORGOTTEN HIMSELF.
DON'T YOU **SEE?**
MY HEAVENS.
KADYN IS RIGHT.
HE'S NOT A MONSTER AT ALL.
HE'S THE GREATEST HERO WHO EVER LIVED.
HE'S THE SON OF THE SUN.
HE'S **QUASARRO.**
I'M SORRY I COULDN'T HELP YOU.
I COULDN'T HELP MY DAD, EITHER.
WE BROKE YOUR CLUB.
YES, YOU DID. BUT THAT'S ALL RIGHT.

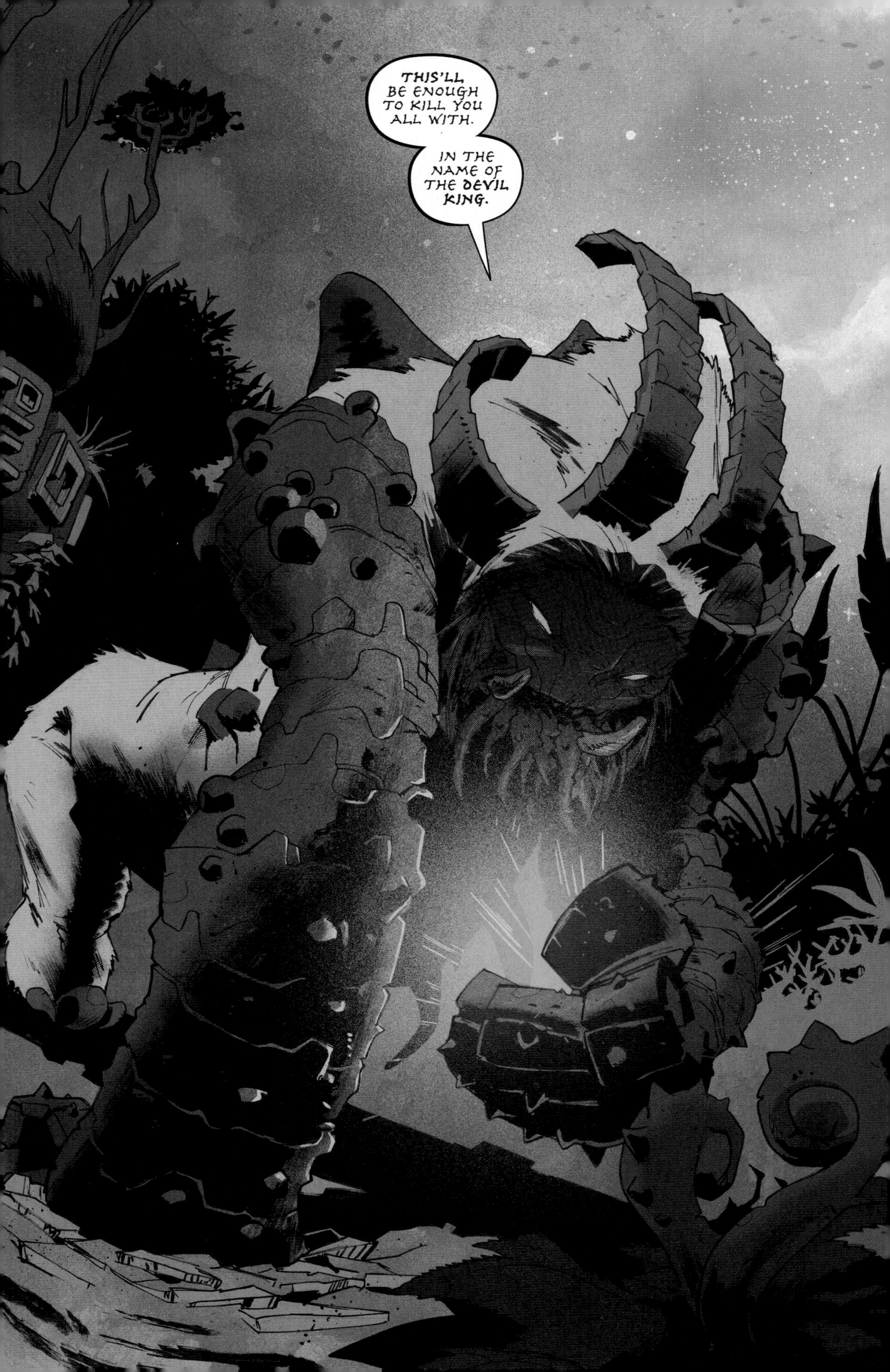
THIS'LL BE ENOUGH TO KILL YOU ALL WITH.
IN THE NAME OF THE DEVIL KING.

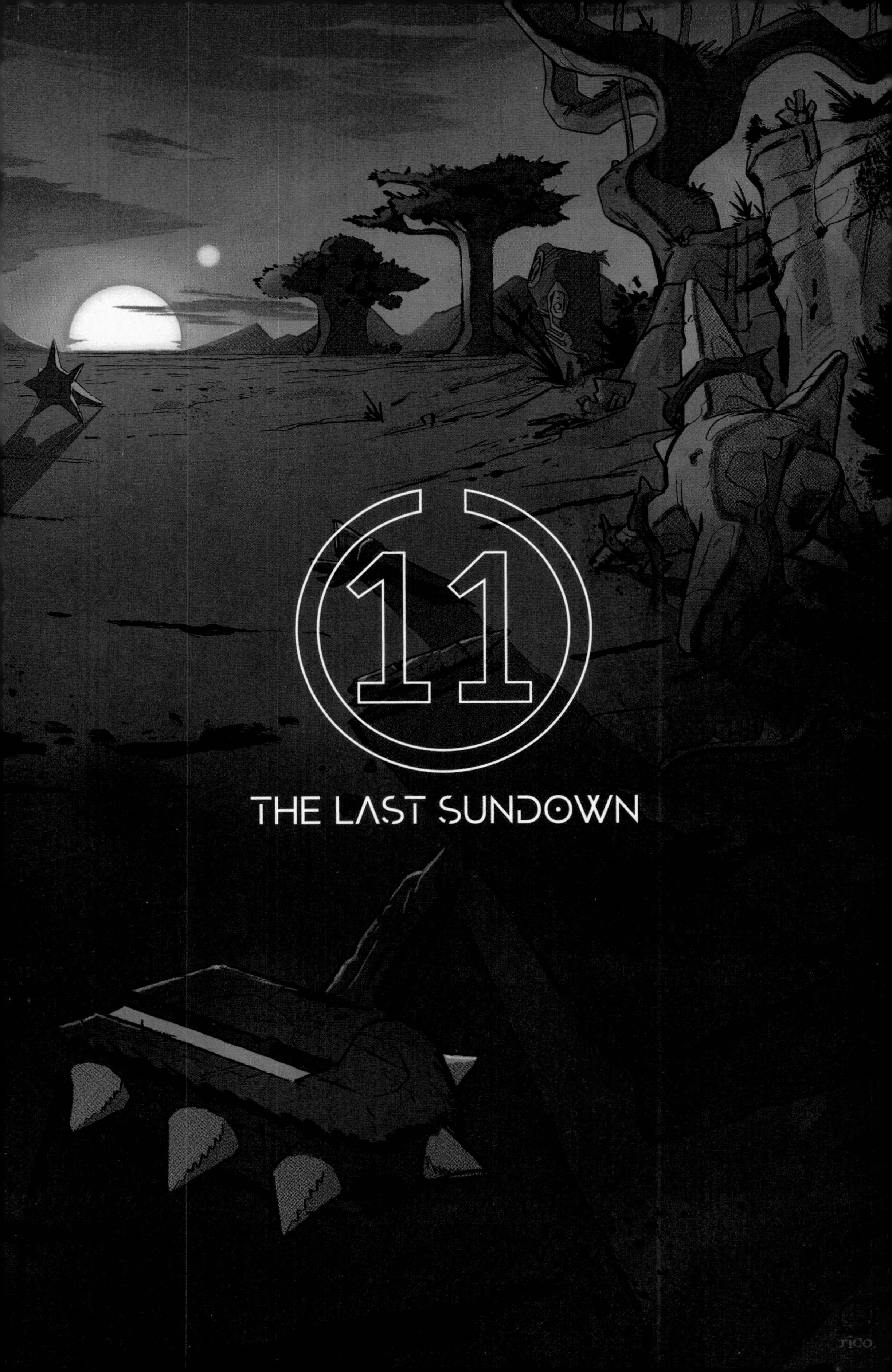
11
THE LAST SUNDOWN

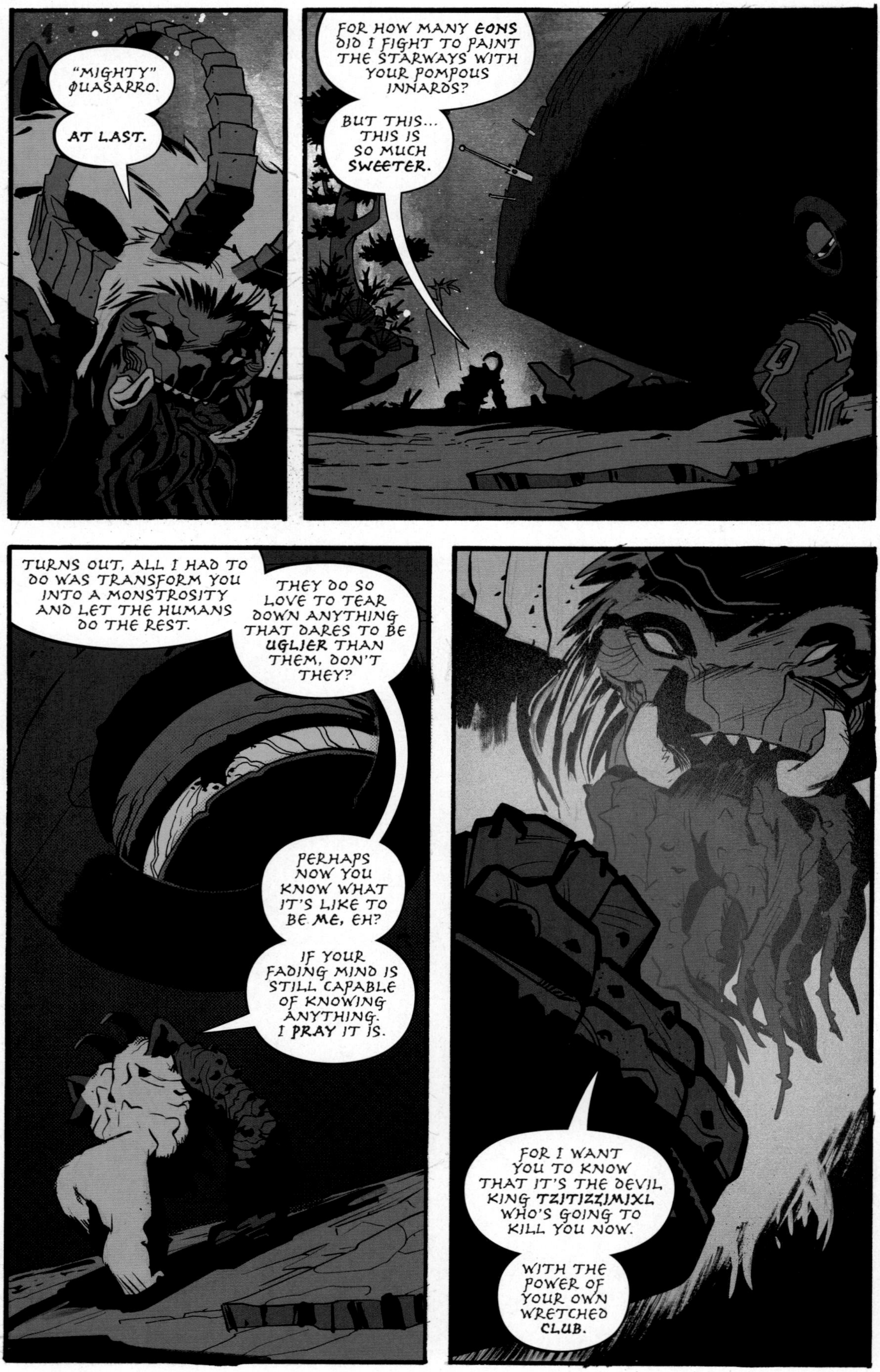
"MIGHTY" QUASARRO.
AT LAST.
FOR HOW MANY EONS DID I FIGHT TO PAINT THE STARWAYS WITH YOUR POMPOUS INNARDS?
BUT THIS... THIS IS SO MUCH SWEETER.
TURNS OUT, ALL I HAD TO DO WAS TRANSFORM YOU INTO A MONSTROSITY AND LET THE HUMANS DO THE REST.
THEY DO SO LOVE TO TEAR DOWN ANYTHING THAT DARES TO BE UGLIER THAN THEM, DON'T THEY?
PERHAPS NOW YOU KNOW WHAT IT'S LIKE TO BE ME, EH?
IF YOUR FADING MIND IS STILL CAPABLE OF KNOWING ANYTHING. I PRAY IT IS.
FOR I WANT YOU TO KNOW THAT IT'S THE DEVIL KING TZITIZZIMIXL WHO'S GOING TO KILL YOU NOW.
WITH THE POWER OF YOUR OWN WRETCHED CLUB.

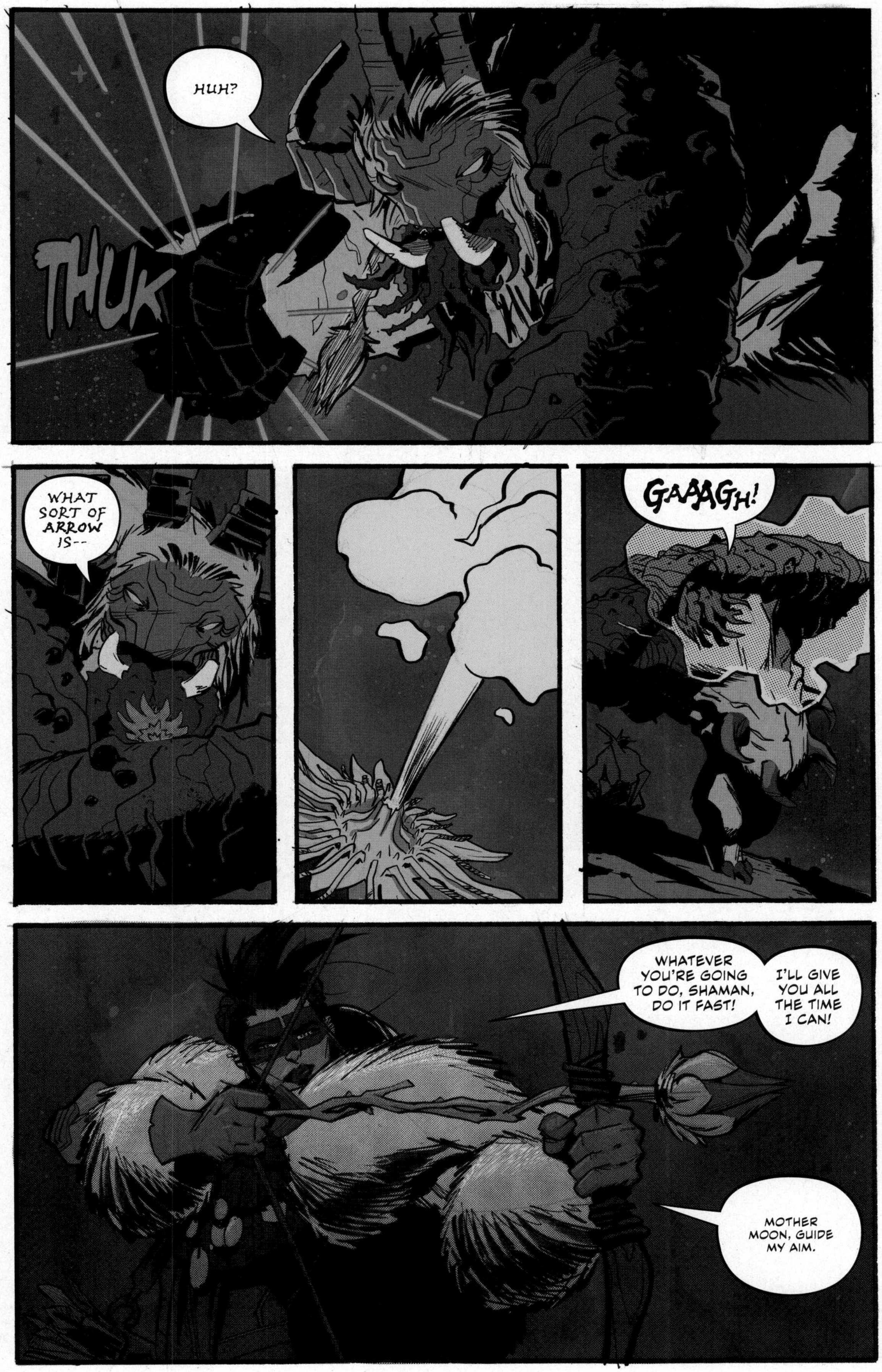
HUH?
THUK
WHAT SORT OF ARROW IS--
GAAAGH!
WHATEVER YOU'RE GOING TO DO, SHAMAN, DO IT FAST!
I'LL GIVE YOU ALL THE TIME I CAN!
MOTHER MOON, GUIDE MY AIM.

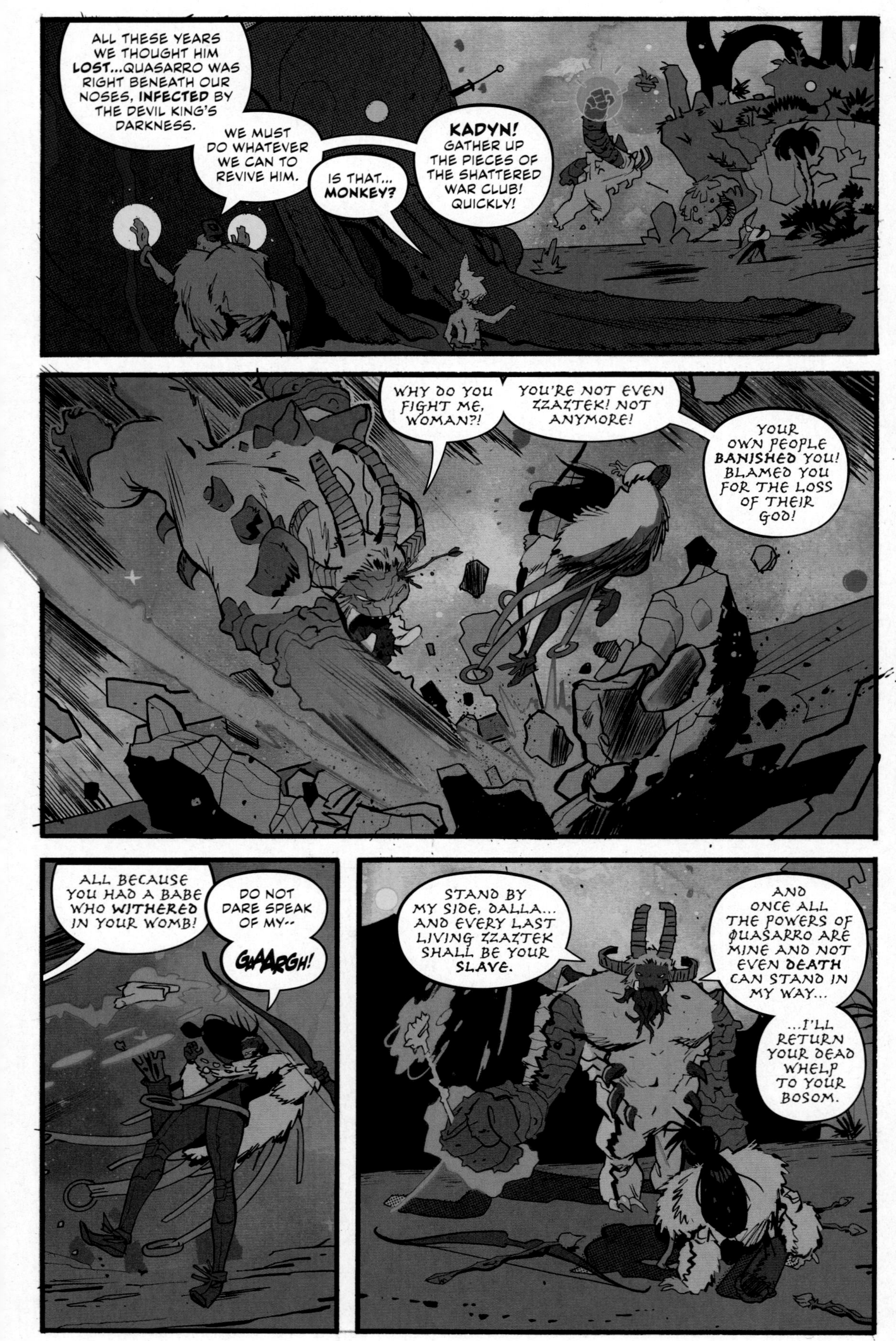
ALL THESE YEARS WE THOUGHT HIM LOST...QUASARRO WAS RIGHT BENEATH OUR NOSES, INFECTED BY THE DEVIL KING'S DARKNESS.
WE MUST DO WHATEVER WE CAN TO REVIVE HIM.
IS THAT... MONKEY?
KADYN! GATHER UP THE PIECES OF THE SHATTERED WAR CLUB! QUICKLY!
WHY DO YOU FIGHT ME, WOMAN?!
YOU'RE NOT EVEN ZZAZTEK! NOT ANYMORE!
YOUR OWN PEOPLE BANISHED YOU! BLAMED YOU FOR THE LOSS OF THEIR GOD!
ALL BECAUSE YOU HAD A BABE WHO WITHERED IN YOUR WOMB!
DO NOT DARE SPEAK OF MY--
GAAARGH!
STAND BY MY SIDE, DALLA... AND EVERY LAST LIVING ZZAZTEK SHALL BE YOUR SLAVE.
AND ONCE ALL THE POWERS OF QUASARRO ARE MINE AND NOT EVEN DEATH CAN STAND IN MY WAY...
...I'LL RETURN YOUR DEAD WHELP TO YOUR BOSOM.

YOU WANT TO REUNITE ME WITH MY KAGGA?!

THEN KILL ME IF YOU CAN, DEVIL MONKEY!

SO BE IT.

UUNGH!

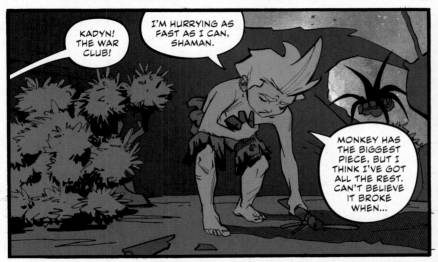

KADYN! THE WAR CLUB!

I'M HURRYING AS FAST AS I CAN, SHAMAN.

MONKEY HAS THE BIGGEST PIECE, BUT I THINK I'VE GOT ALL THE REST. CAN'T BELIEVE IT BROKE WHEN...

QUASARRO WILL FIX IT.

HE'LL FIX EVERYTHING.

EVERYTHING I MESSED UP.

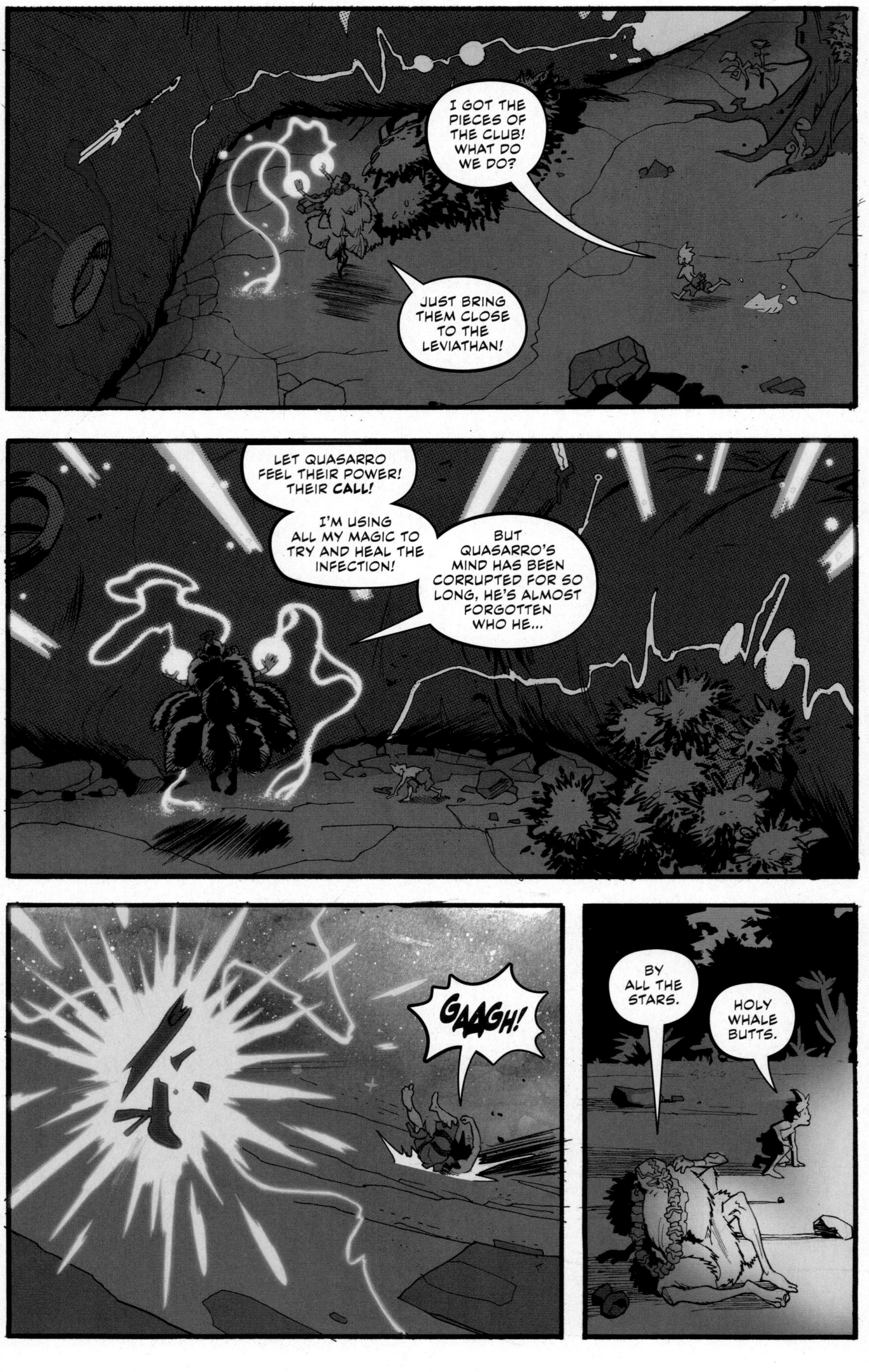
I GOT THE PIECES OF THE CLUB! WHAT DO WE DO?
JUST BRING THEM CLOSE TO THE LEVIATHAN!
LET QUASARRO FEEL THEIR POWER! THEIR **CALL!**
I'M USING ALL MY MAGIC TO TRY AND HEAL THE INFECTION!
BUT QUASARRO'S MIND HAS BEEN CORRUPTED FOR SO LONG, HE'S ALMOST FORGOTTEN WHO HE...
GAAGH!
BY ALL THE STARS.
HOLY WHALE BUTTS.

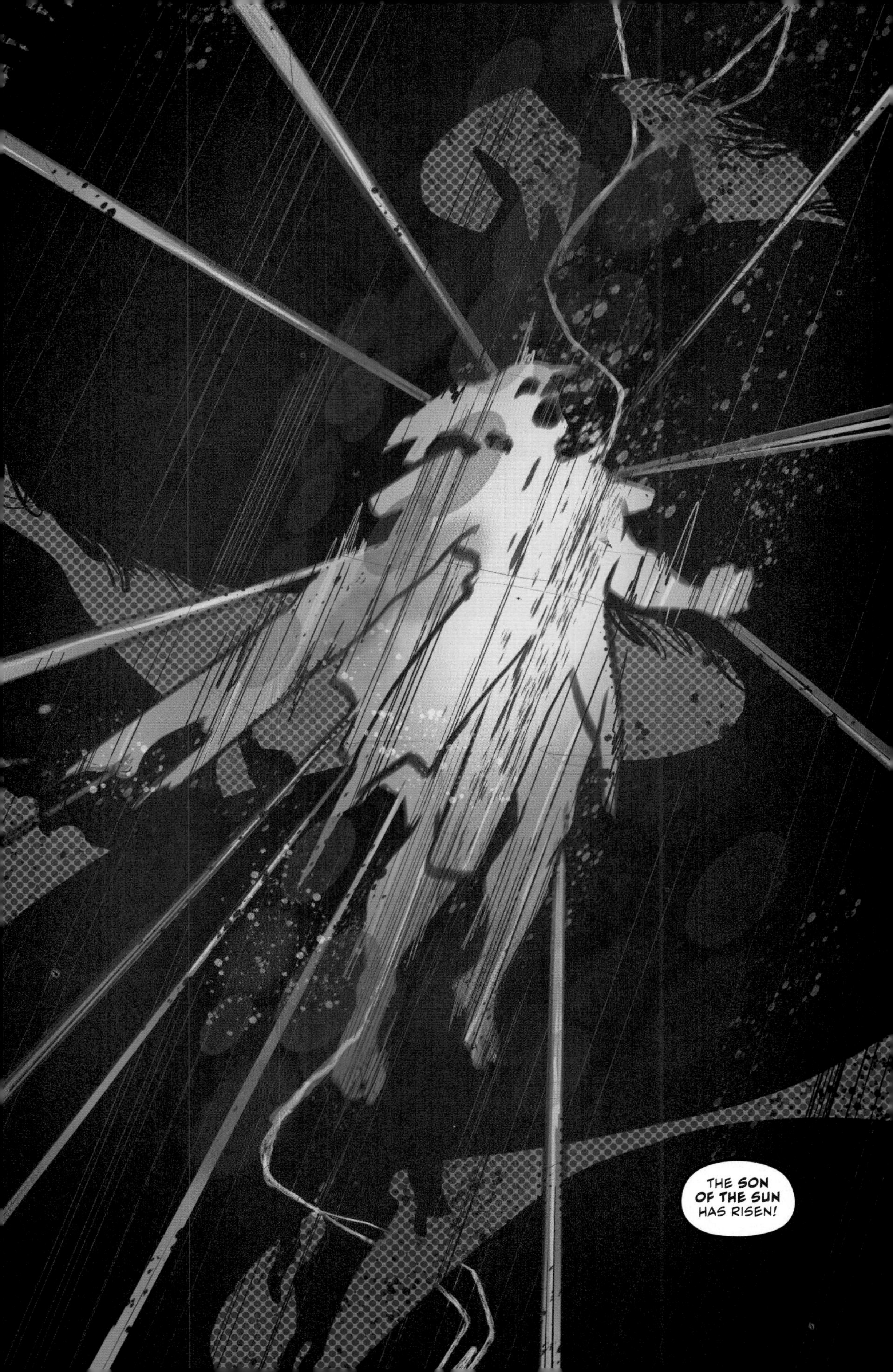
THE SON OF THE SUN HAS RISEN!

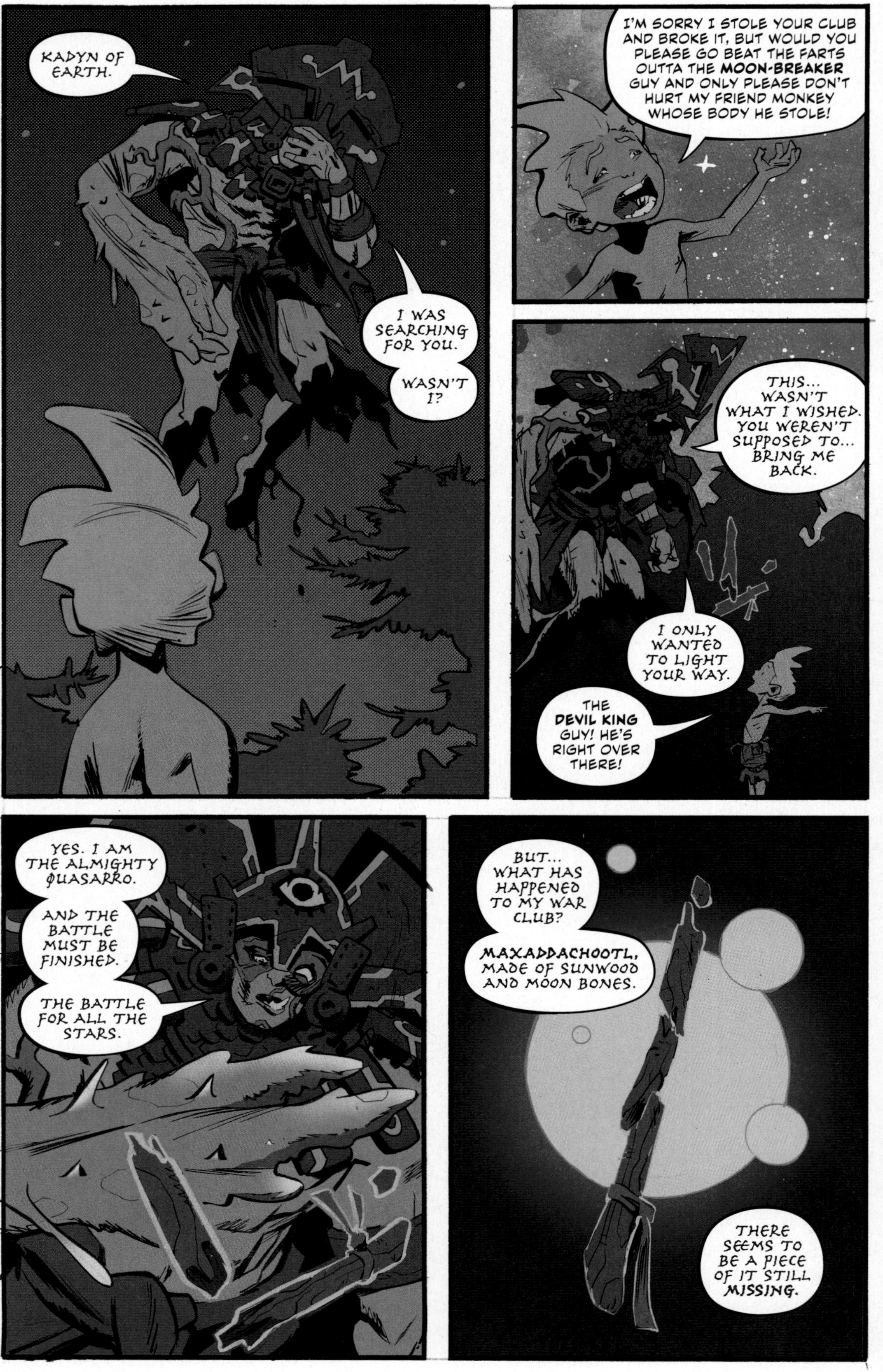
KADYN OF EARTH.
I WAS SEARCHING FOR YOU.
WASN'T I?
I'M SORRY I STOLE YOUR CLUB AND BROKE IT, BUT WOULD YOU PLEASE GO BEAT THE FARTS OUTTA THE MOON-BREAKER GUY AND ONLY PLEASE DON'T HURT MY FRIEND MONKEY WHOSE BODY HE STOLE!
THIS... WASN'T WHAT I WISHED. YOU WEREN'T SUPPOSED TO... BRING ME BACK.
I ONLY WANTED TO LIGHT YOUR WAY.
THE DEVIL KING GUY! HE'S RIGHT OVER THERE!
YES. I AM THE ALMIGHTY QUASARRO.
AND THE BATTLE MUST BE FINISHED.
THE BATTLE FOR ALL THE STARS.
BUT... WHAT HAS HAPPENED TO MY WAR CLUB?
MAXADDACHOOTL, MADE OF SUNWOOD AND MOON BONES.
THERE SEEMS TO BE A PIECE OF IT STILL MISSING.

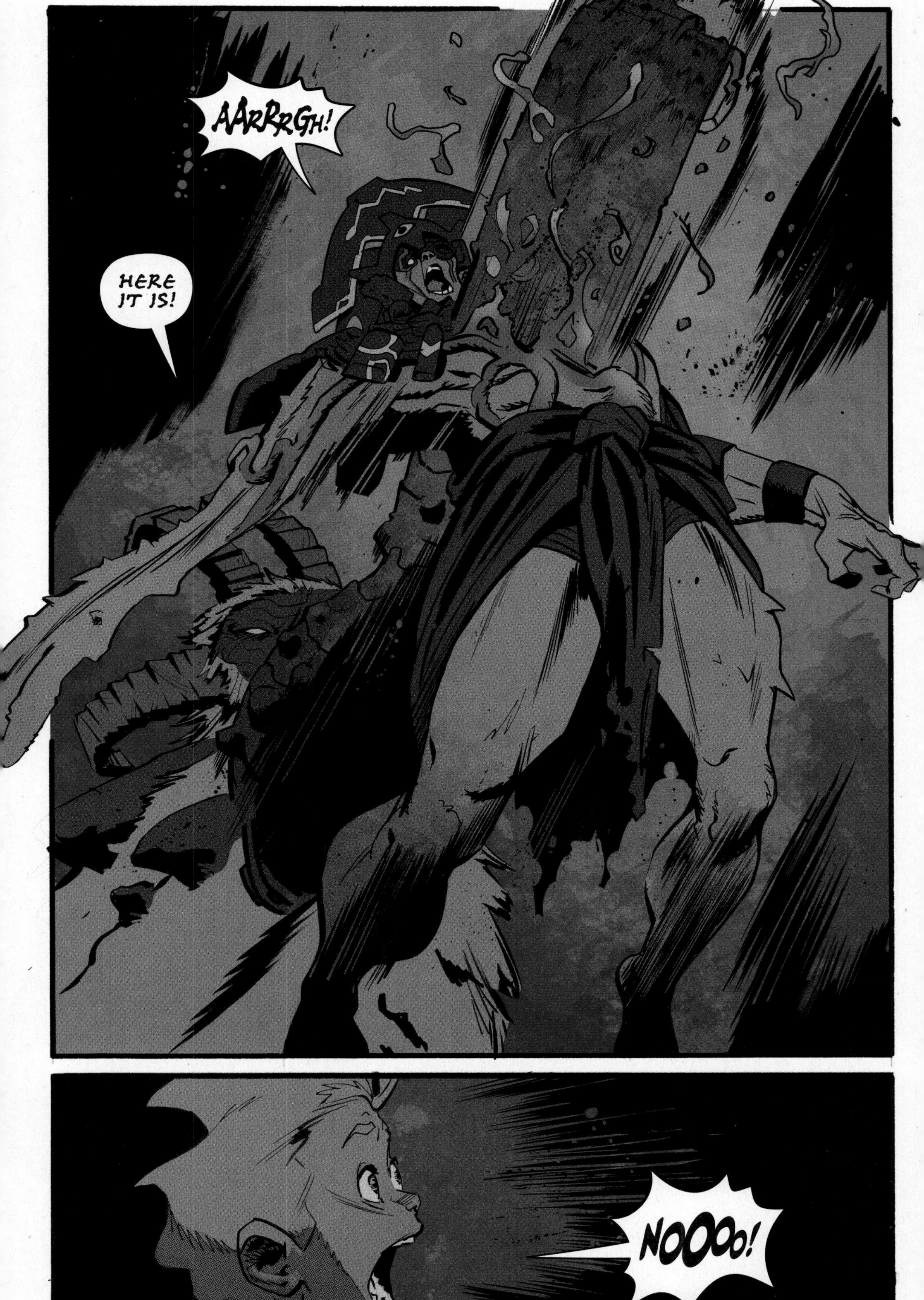
AARRRGH!
HERE IT IS!
NOOOo!

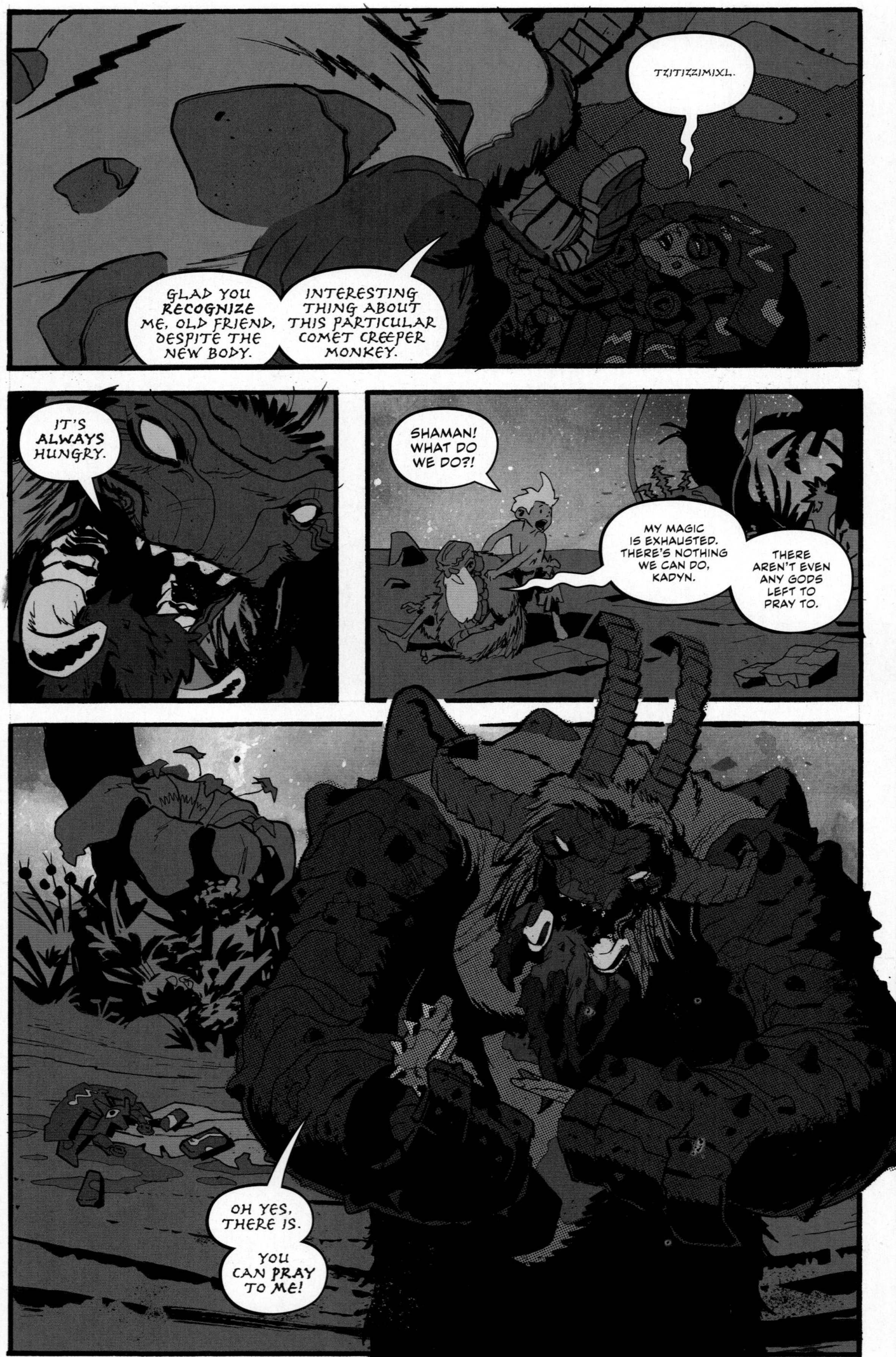
TZITIZZIMIXL.
GLAD YOU RECOGNIZE ME, OLD FRIEND, DESPITE THE NEW BODY.
INTERESTING THING ABOUT THIS PARTICULAR COMET CREEPER MONKEY.
IT'S ALWAYS HUNGRY.
SHAMAN! WHAT DO WE DO?!
MY MAGIC IS EXHAUSTED. THERE'S NOTHING WE CAN DO, KADYN.
THERE AREN'T EVEN ANY GODS LEFT TO PRAY TO.
OH YES, THERE IS.
YOU CAN PRAY TO ME!

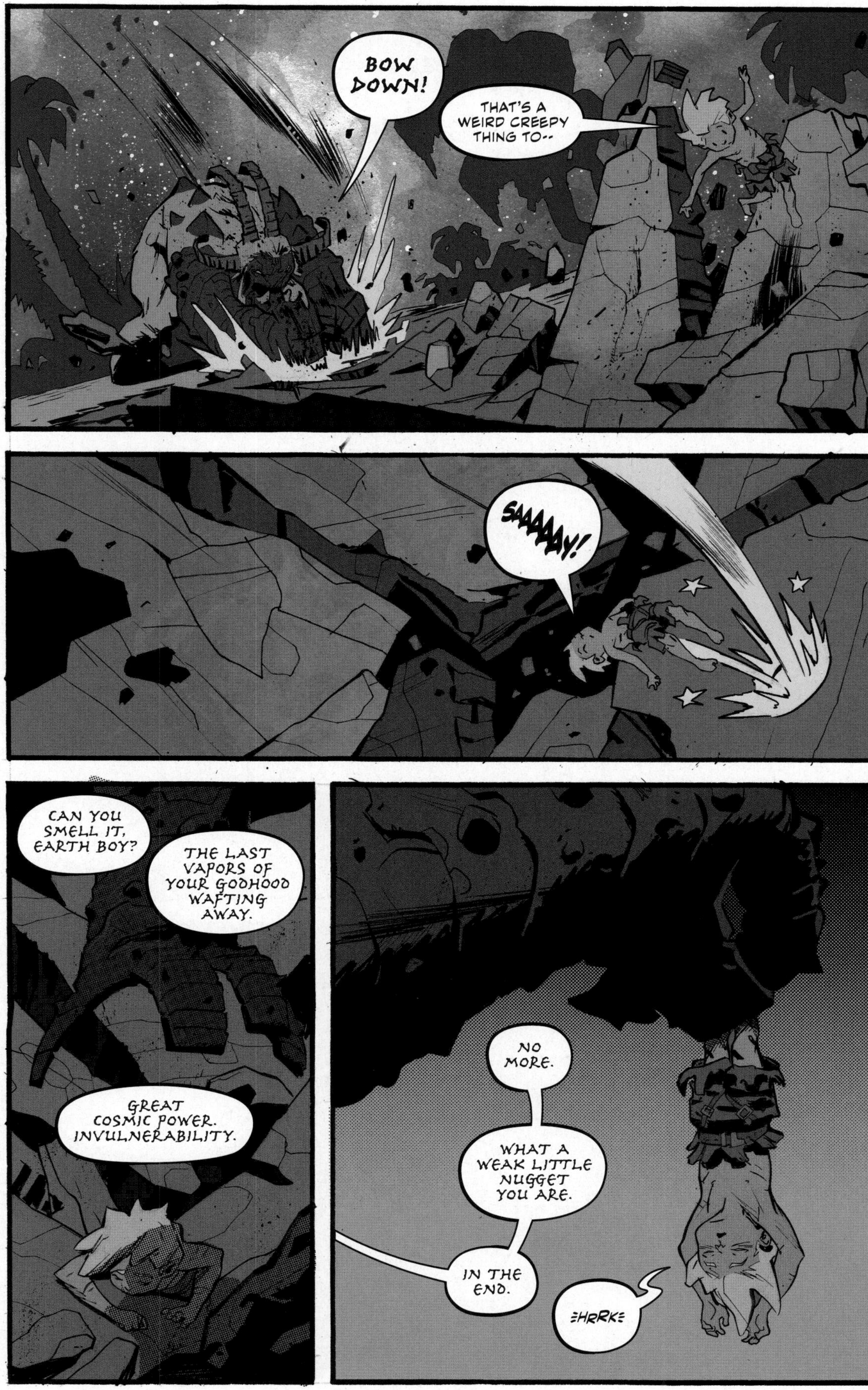
BOW DOWN!
THAT'S A WEIRD CREEPY THING TO--
SAAAAAY!
CAN YOU SMELL IT, EARTH BOY?
THE LAST VAPORS OF YOUR GODHOOD WAFTING AWAY.
GREAT COSMIC POWER. INVULNERABILITY.
NO MORE.
WHAT A WEAK LITTLE NUGGET YOU ARE.
IN THE END.
HRRK

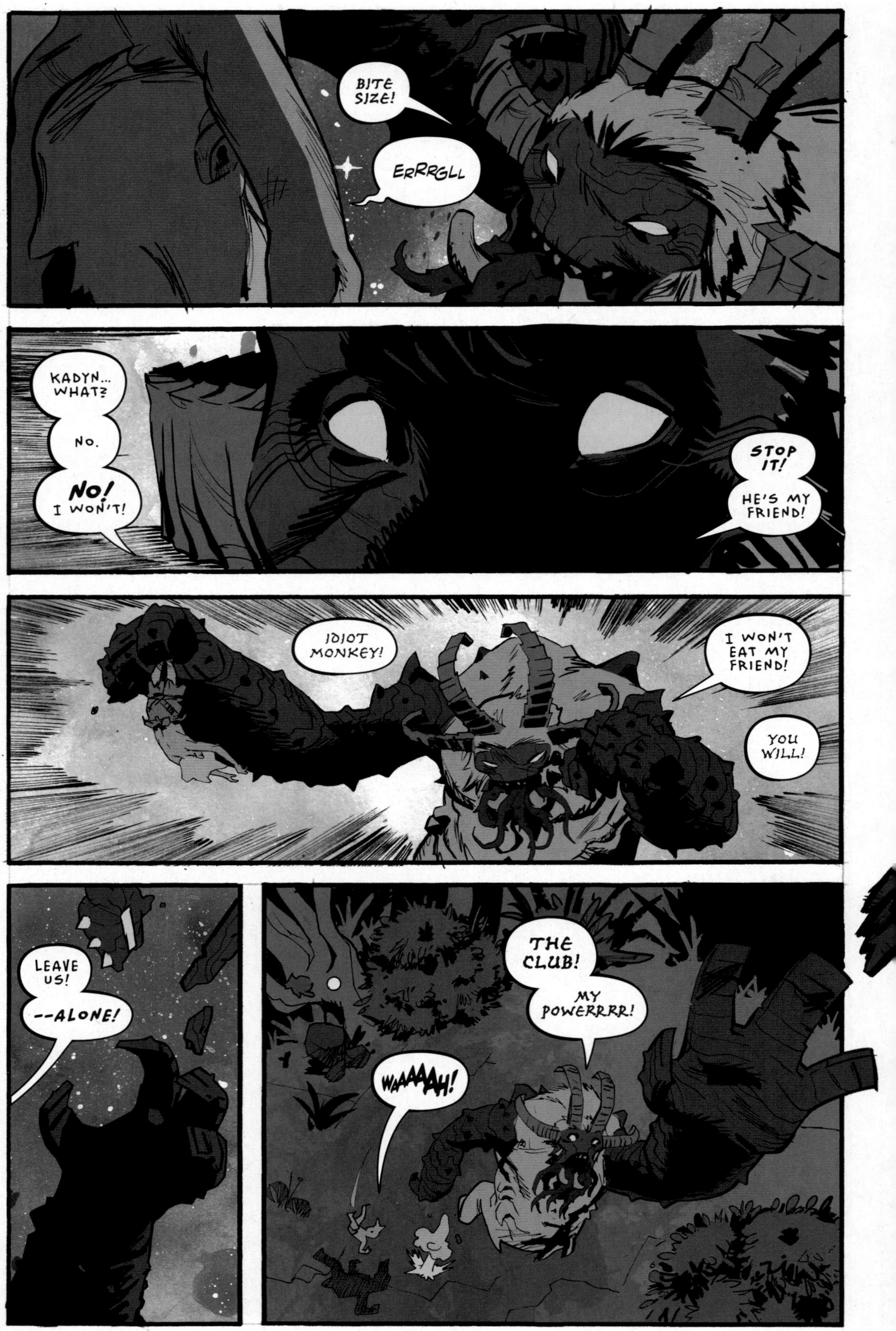
BITE SIZE!
ERRRGLL
KADYN... WHAT?
NO.
NO! I WON'T!
STOP IT!
HE'S MY FRIEND!
IDIOT MONKEY!
I WON'T EAT MY FRIEND!
YOU WILL!
LEAVE US!
--ALONE!
THE CLUB!
MY POWERRRR!
WAAAAAH!

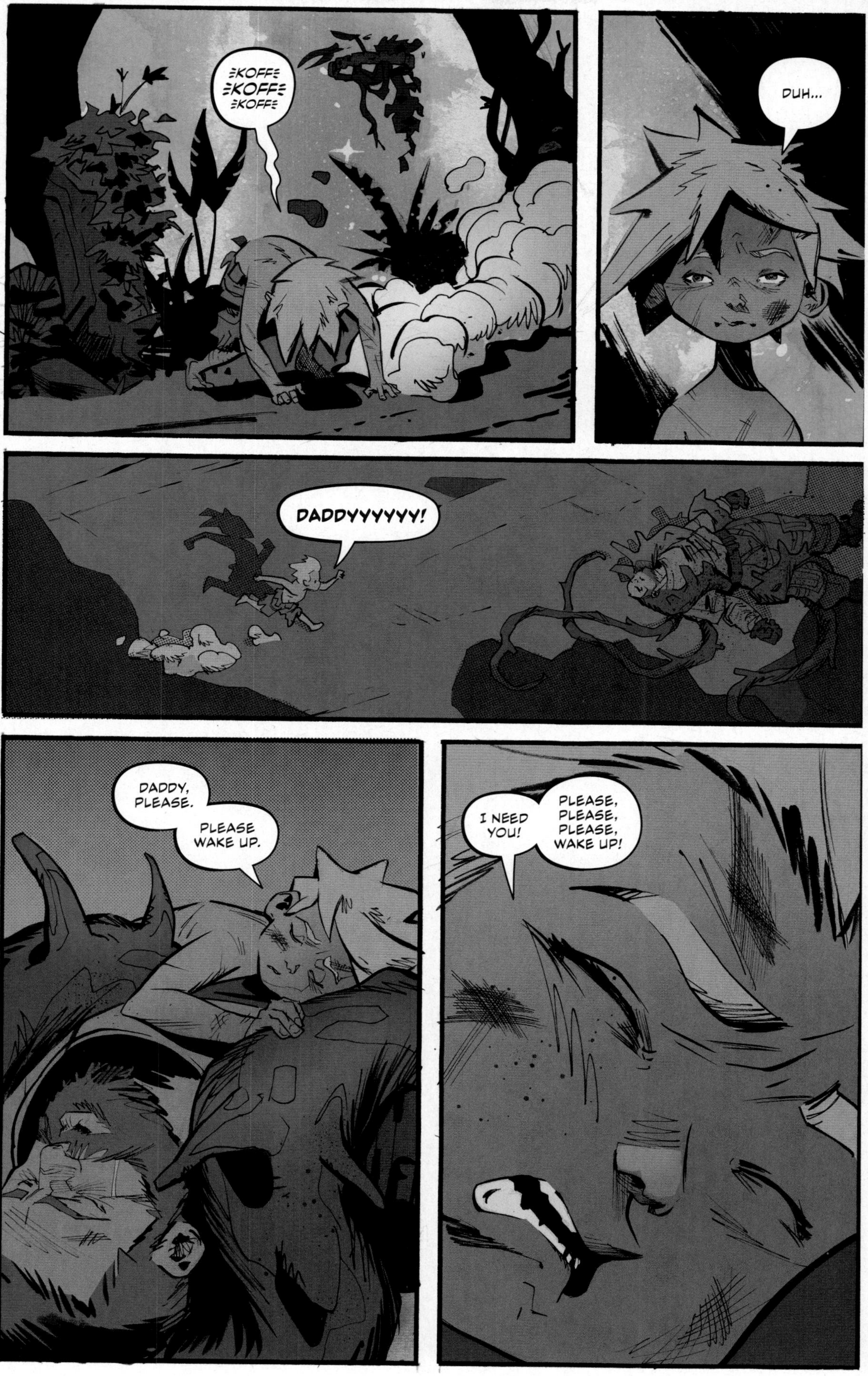

KOFF KOFF KOFF
DUH...
DADDYYYYYY!
DADDY, PLEASE.
PLEASE WAKE UP.
PLEASE, PLEASE, PLEASE, WAKE UP!
I NEED YOU!

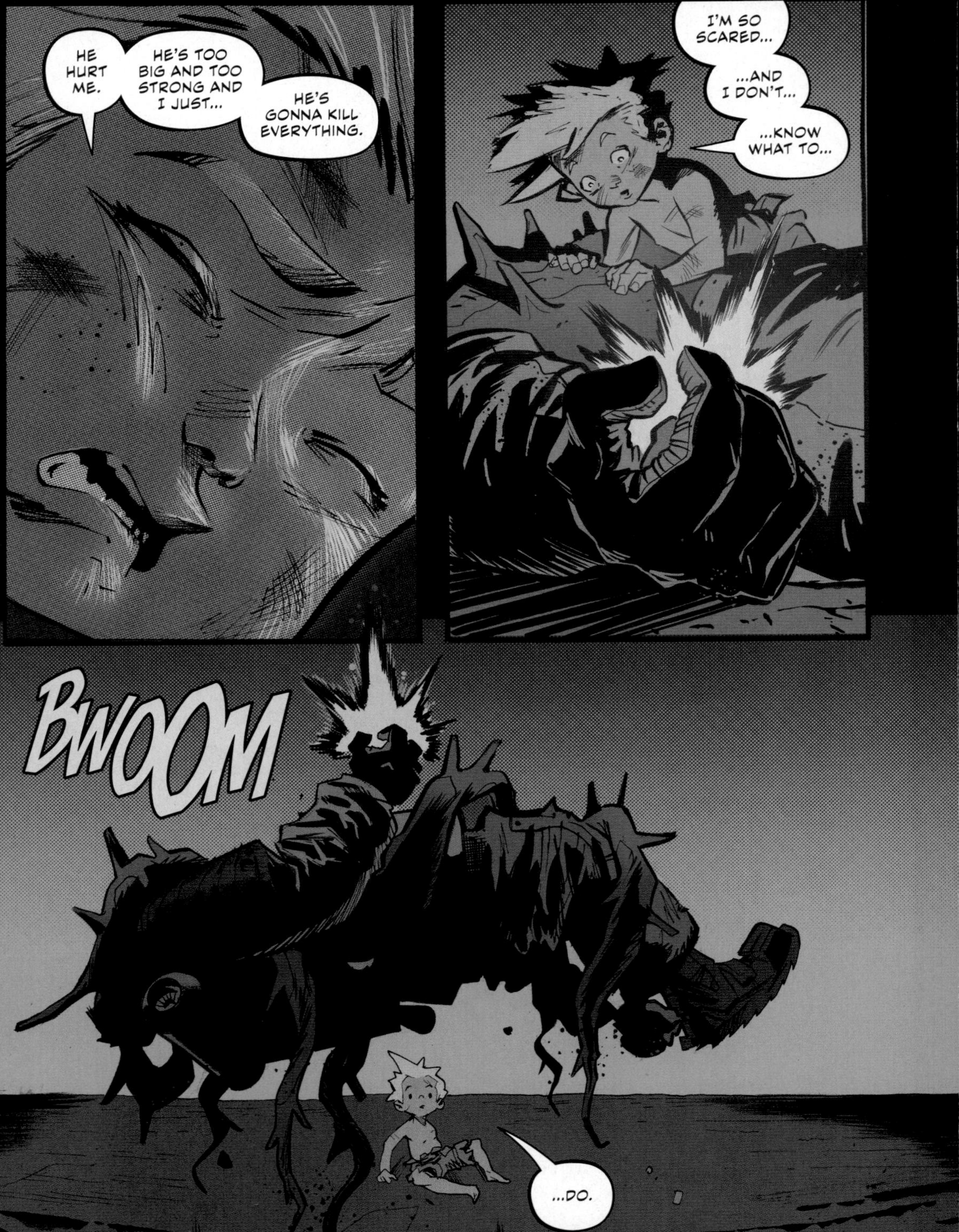
HE HURT ME.
HE'S TOO BIG AND TOO STRONG AND I JUST...
HE'S GONNA KILL EVERYTHING.
I'M SO SCARED...
...AND I DON'T...
...KNOW WHAT TO...
BWOOM
...DO.

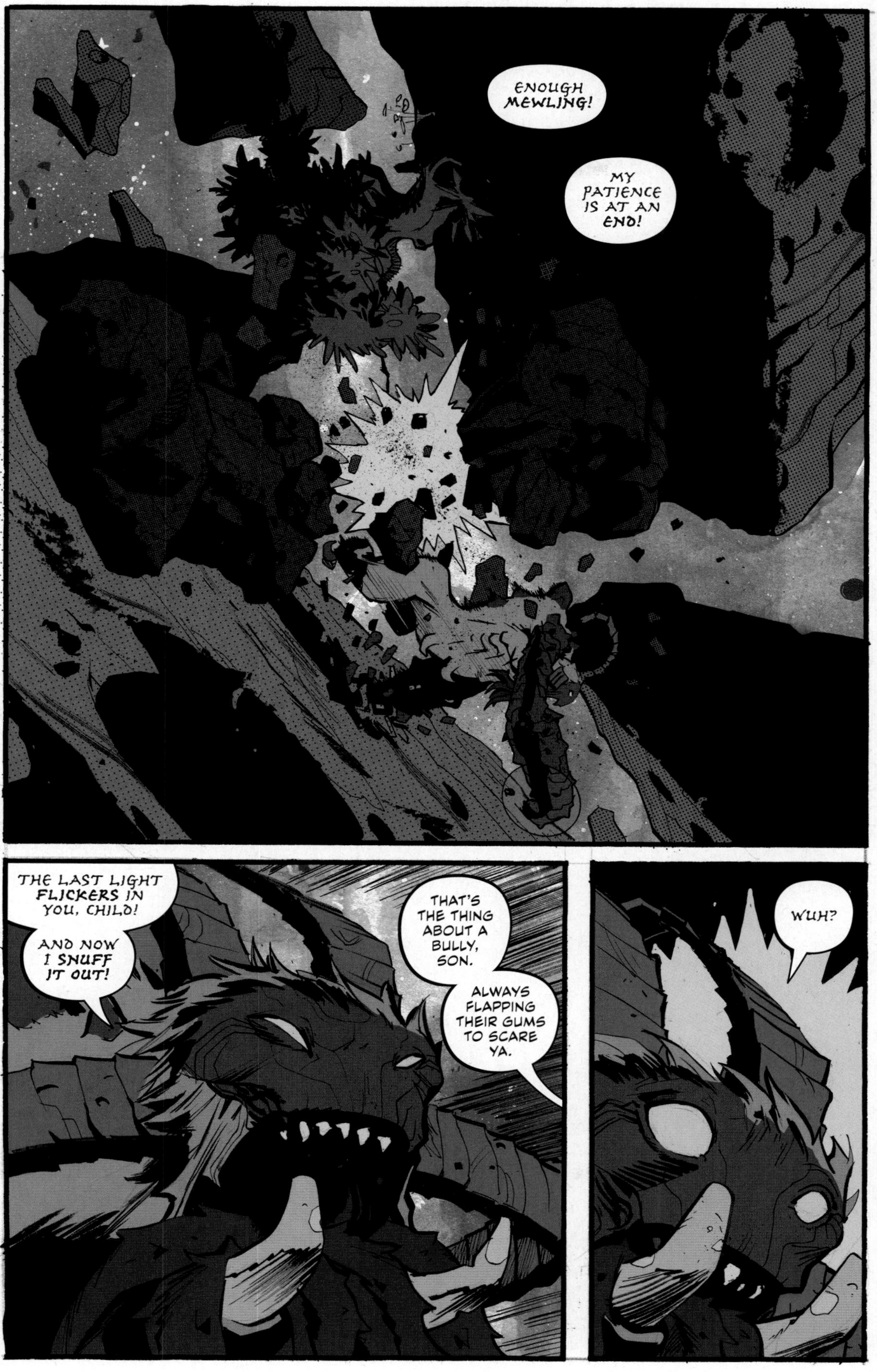
ENOUGH MEWLING!
MY PATIENCE IS AT AN END!
THE LAST LIGHT FLICKERS IN YOU, CHILD!
AND NOW I SNUFF IT OUT!
THAT'S THE THING ABOUT A BULLY, SON.
ALWAYS FLAPPING THEIR GUMS TO SCARE YA.
WUH?

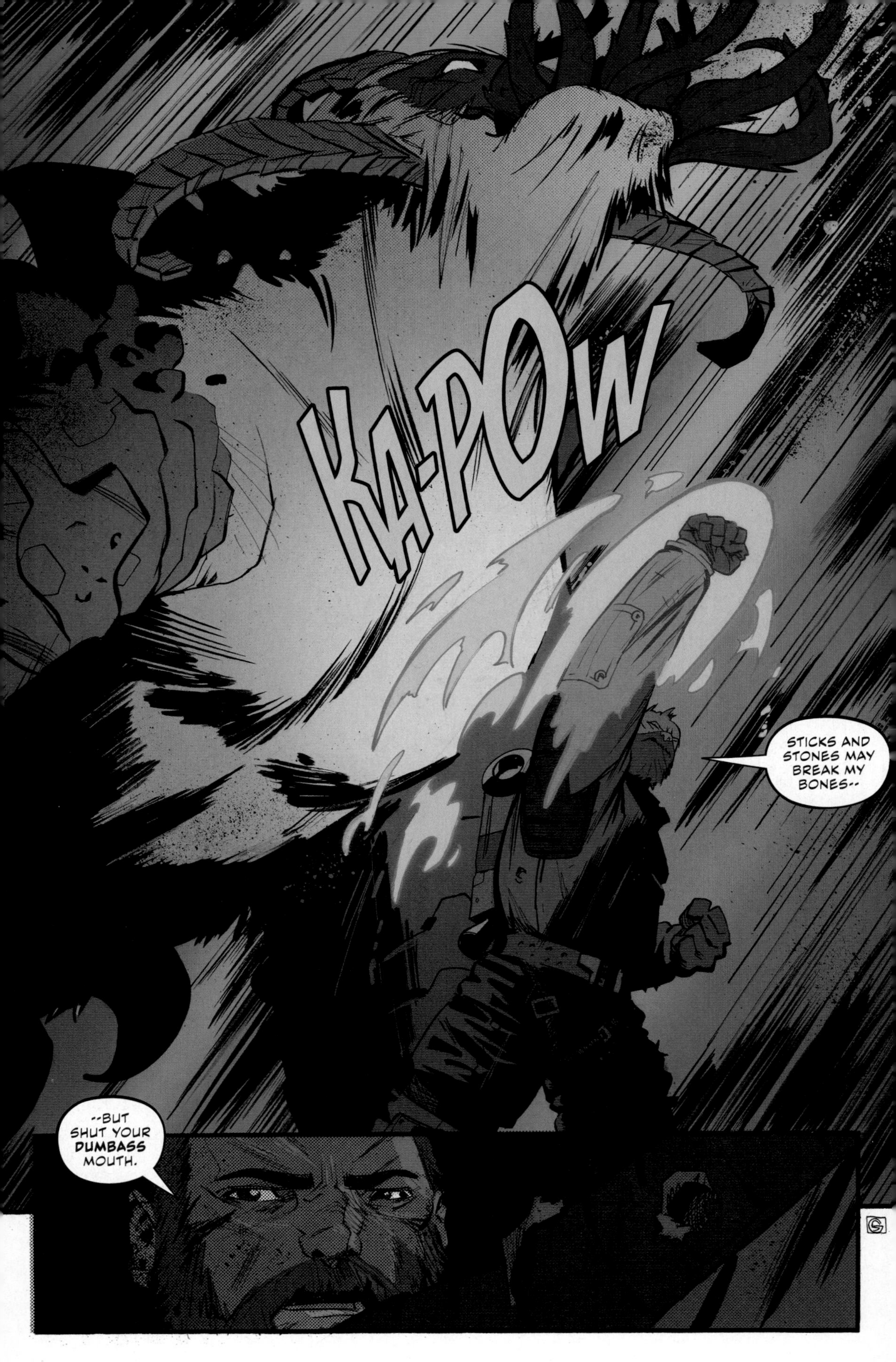
KA-POW
STICKS AND STONES MAY BREAK MY BONES--
--BUT SHUT YOUR DUMBASS MOUTH.

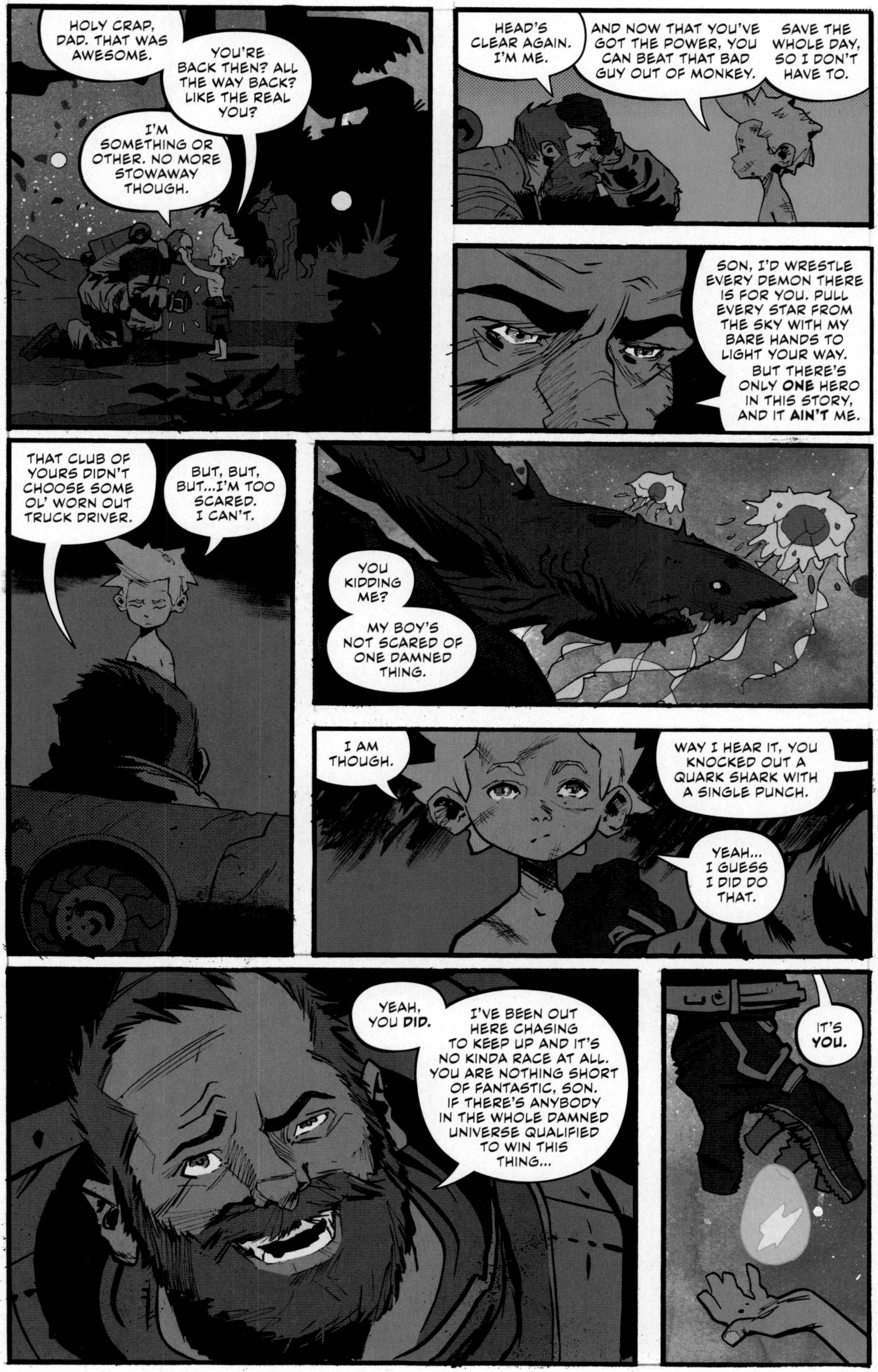
HOLY CRAP, DAD. THAT WAS AWESOME.
YOU'RE BACK THEN? ALL THE WAY BACK? LIKE THE REAL YOU?
I'M SOMETHING OR OTHER. NO MORE STOWAWAY THOUGH.
HEAD'S CLEAR AGAIN. I'M ME.
AND NOW THAT YOU'VE GOT THE POWER, YOU CAN BEAT THAT BAD GUY OUT OF MONKEY.
SAVE THE WHOLE DAY, SO I DON'T HAVE TO.
SON, I'D WRESTLE EVERY DEMON THERE IS FOR YOU. PULL EVERY STAR FROM THE SKY WITH MY BARE HANDS TO LIGHT YOUR WAY.
BUT THERE'S ONLY **ONE** HERO IN THIS STORY, AND IT **AIN'T** ME.
THAT CLUB OF YOURS DIDN'T CHOOSE SOME OL' WORN OUT TRUCK DRIVER.
BUT, BUT, BUT...I'M TOO SCARED. I CAN'T.
YOU KIDDING ME?
MY BOY'S NOT SCARED OF ONE DAMNED THING.
I AM THOUGH.
WAY I HEAR IT, YOU KNOCKED OUT A QUARK SHARK WITH A SINGLE PUNCH.
YEAH... I GUESS I DID DO THAT.
YEAH, YOU **DID.**
I'VE BEEN OUT HERE CHASING TO KEEP UP AND IT'S NO KINDA RACE AT ALL. YOU ARE NOTHING SHORT OF FANTASTIC, SON. IF THERE'S ANYBODY IN THE WHOLE DAMNED UNIVERSE QUALIFIED TO WIN THIS THING...
IT'S **YOU.**

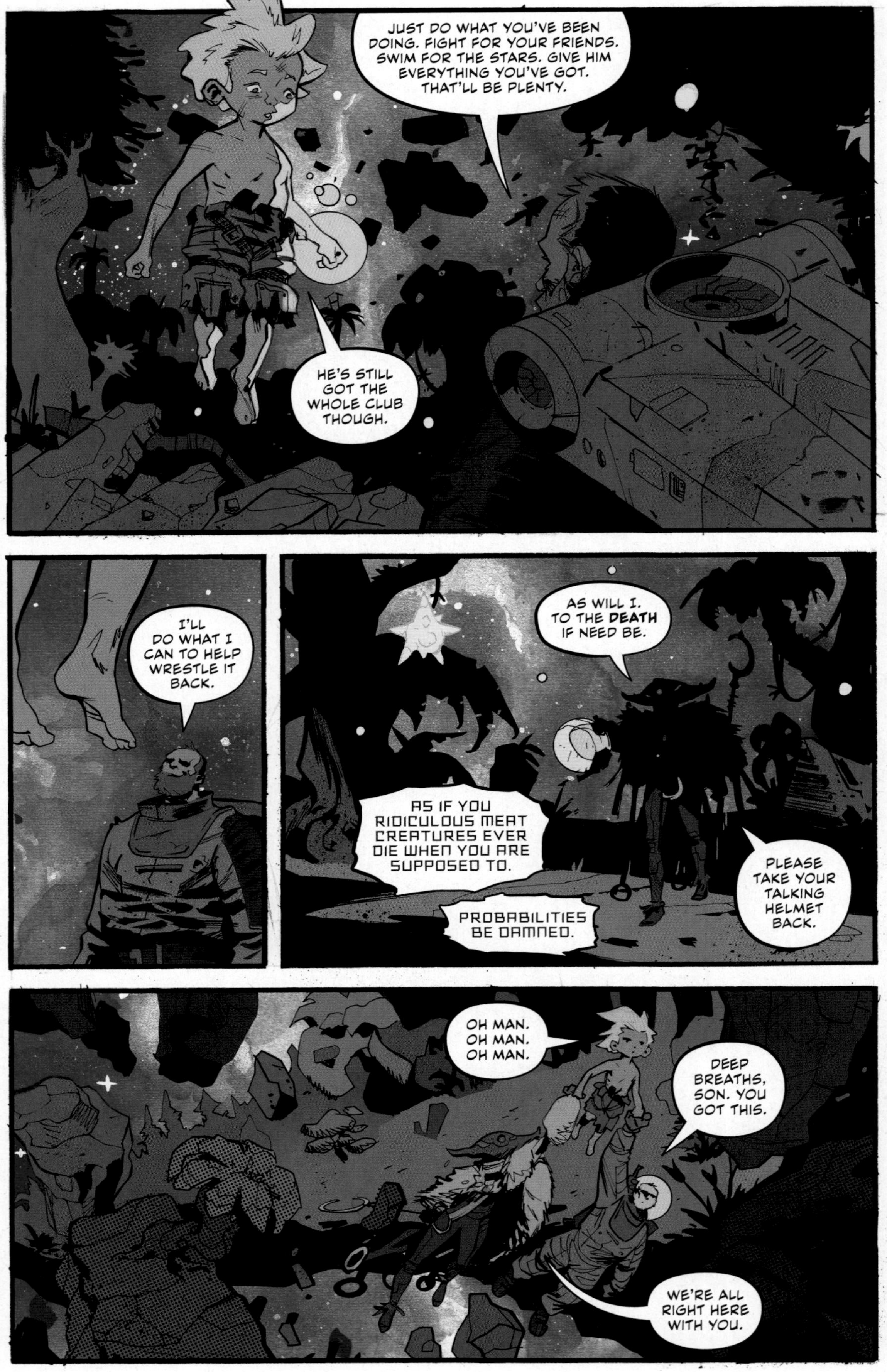

JUST DO WHAT YOU'VE BEEN DOING. FIGHT FOR YOUR FRIENDS. SWIM FOR THE STARS. GIVE HIM EVERYTHING YOU'VE GOT. THAT'LL BE PLENTY.
HE'S STILL GOT THE WHOLE CLUB THOUGH.
I'LL DO WHAT I CAN TO HELP WRESTLE IT BACK.
AS WILL I. TO THE **DEATH** IF NEED BE.
AS IF YOU RIDICULOUS MEAT CREATURES EVER DIE WHEN YOU ARE SUPPOSED TO.
PROBABILITIES BE DAMNED.
PLEASE TAKE YOUR TALKING HELMET BACK.
OH MAN. OH MAN. OH MAN.
DEEP BREATHS, SON. YOU GOT THIS.
WE'RE ALL RIGHT HERE WITH YOU.

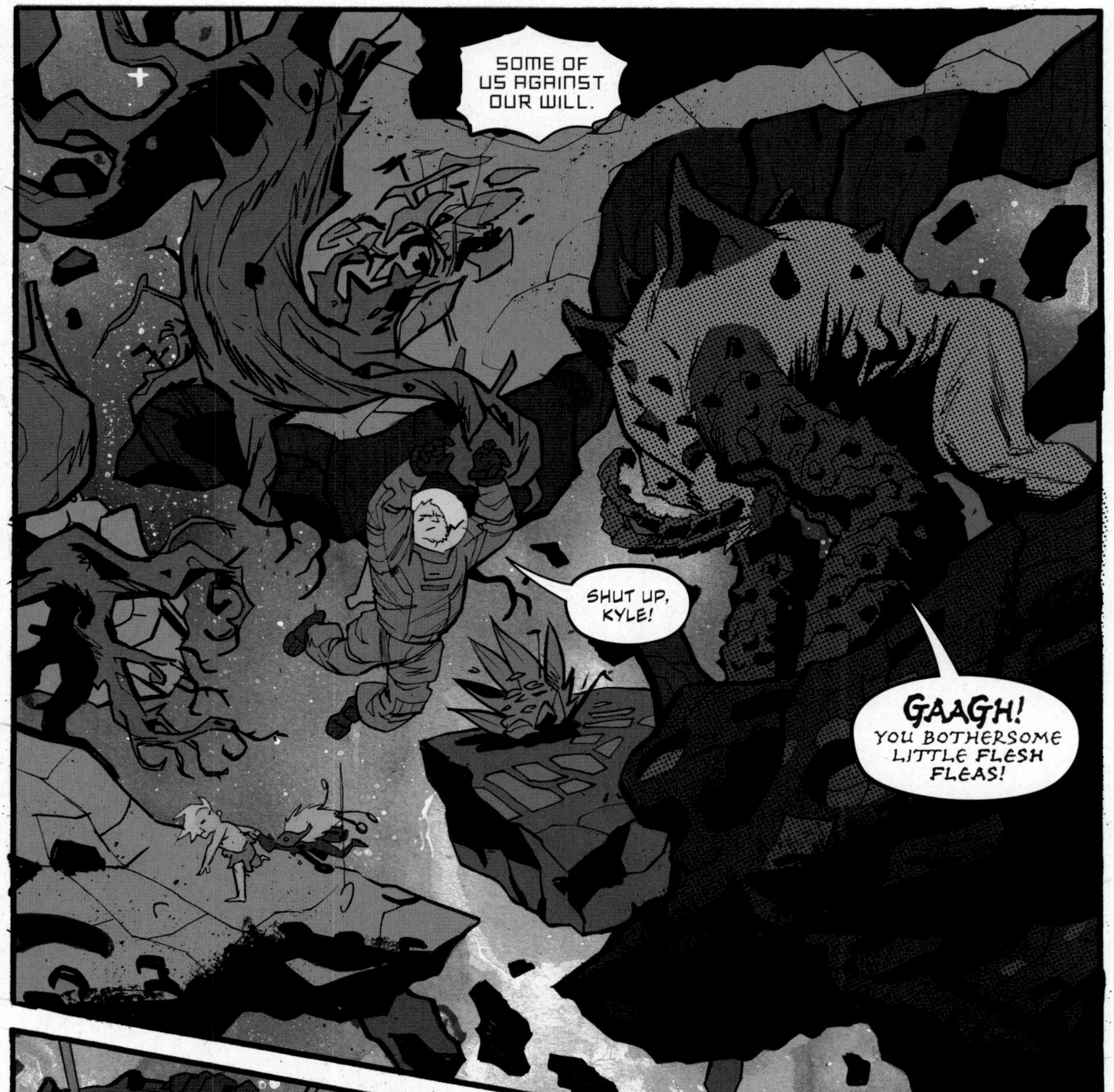
SOME OF US AGAINST OUR WILL.
SHUT UP, KYLE!
GAAGH! YOU BOTHERSOME LITTLE FLESH FLEAS!
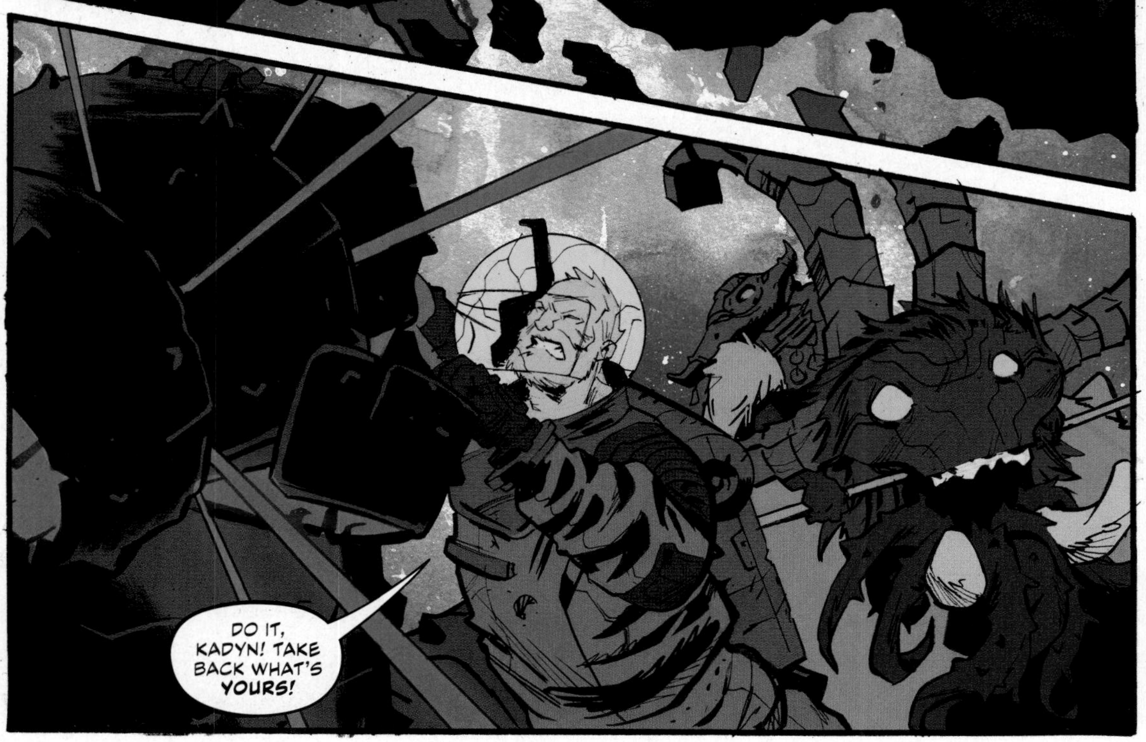
DO IT, KADYN! TAKE BACK WHAT'S YOURS!

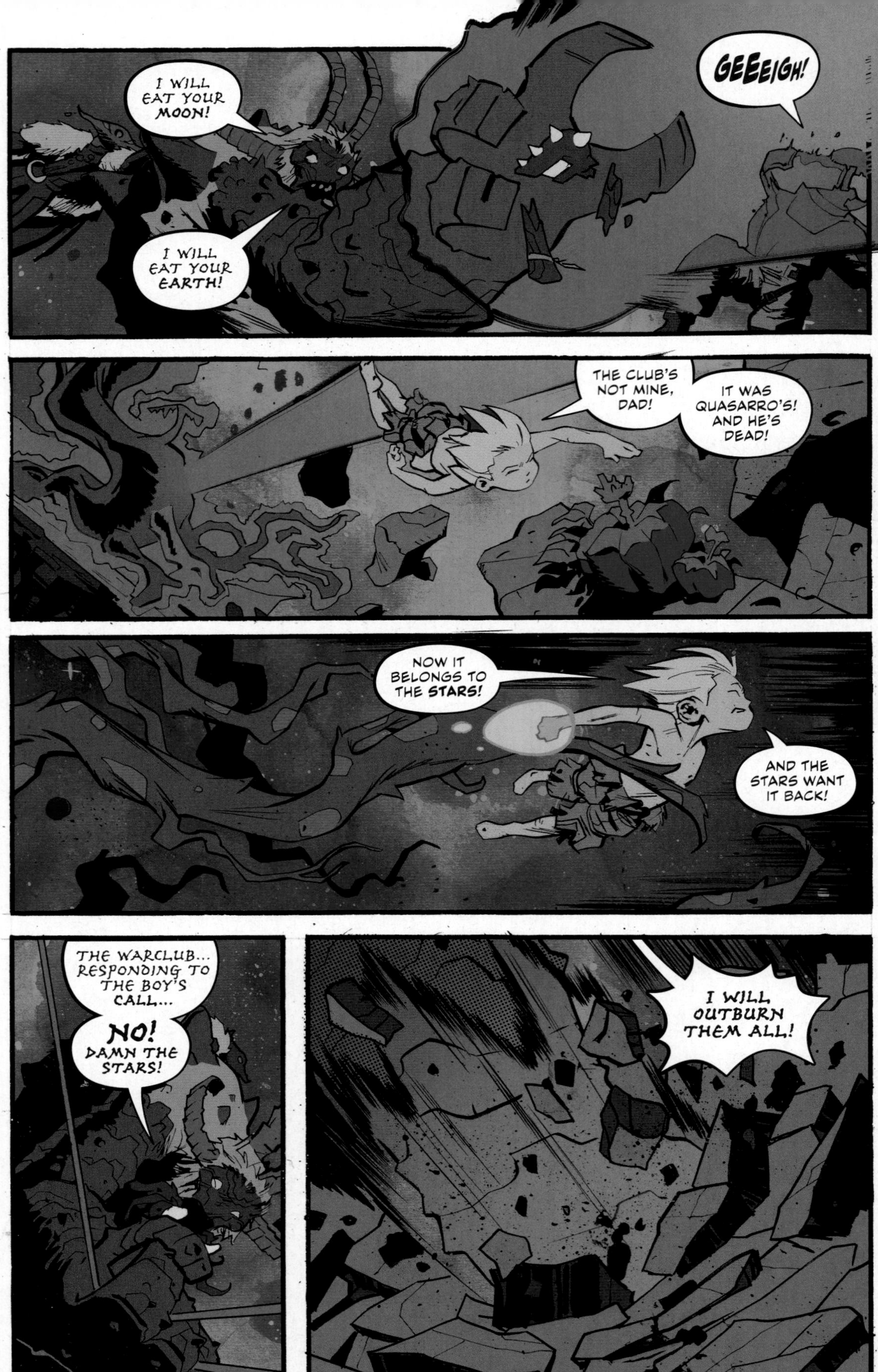
I WILL EAT YOUR MOON!
I WILL EAT YOUR EARTH!
GEEEIGH!
THE CLUB'S NOT MINE, DAD!
IT WAS QUASARRO'S! AND HE'S DEAD!
NOW IT BELONGS TO THE STARS!
AND THE STARS WANT IT BACK!
THE WARCLUB... RESPONDING TO THE BOY'S CALL...
NO! DAMN THE STARS!
I WILL OUTBURN THEM ALL!

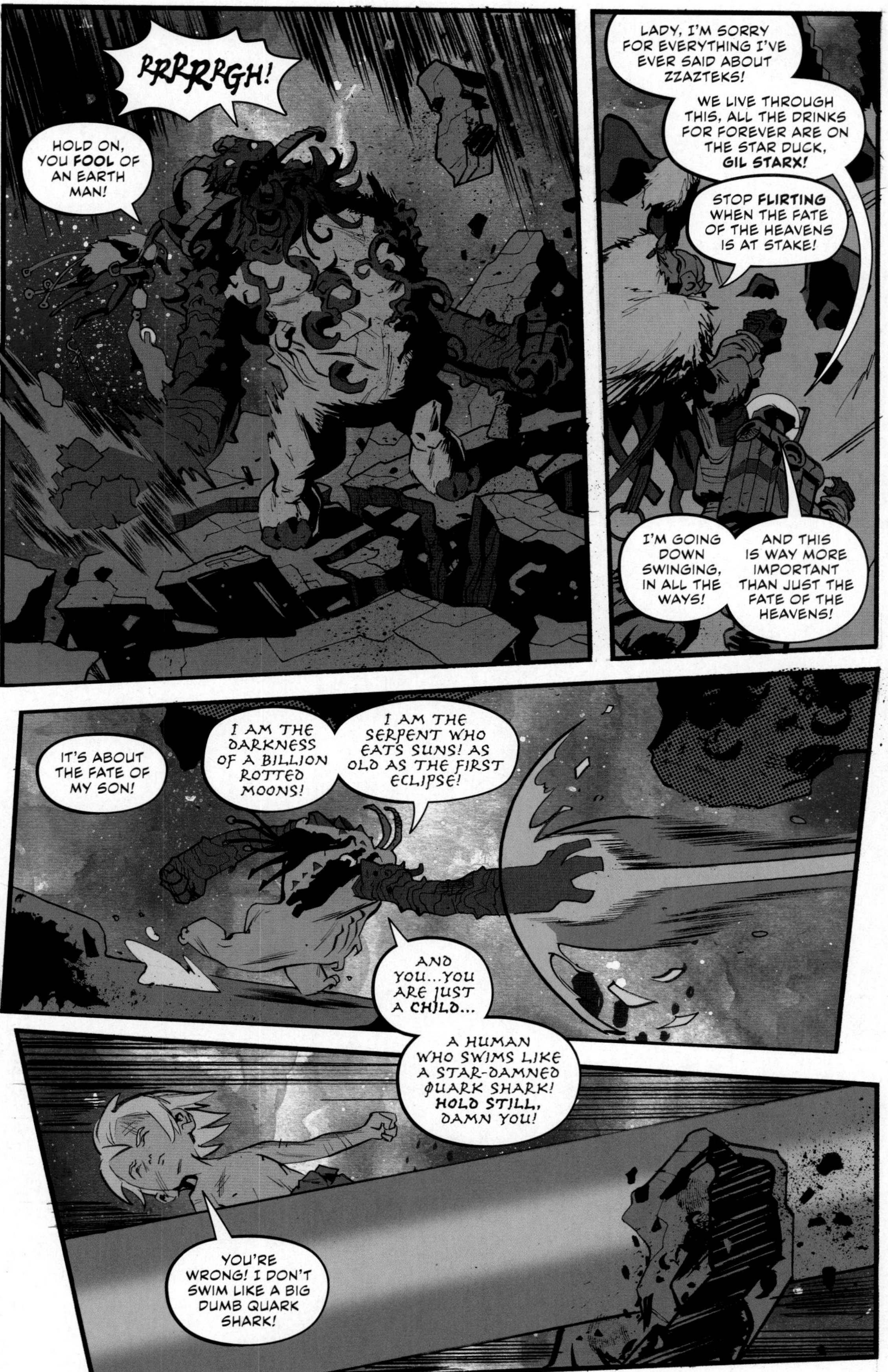
RRRRRGH!
HOLD ON, YOU FOOL OF AN EARTH MAN!
LADY, I'M SORRY FOR EVERYTHING I'VE EVER SAID ABOUT ZZAZTEKS!
WE LIVE THROUGH THIS, ALL THE DRINKS FOR FOREVER ARE ON THE STAR DUCK, GIL STARX!
STOP FLIRTING WHEN THE FATE OF THE HEAVENS IS AT STAKE!
I'M GOING DOWN SWINGING, IN ALL THE WAYS!
AND THIS IS WAY MORE IMPORTANT THAN JUST THE FATE OF THE HEAVENS!
IT'S ABOUT THE FATE OF MY SON!
I AM THE DARKNESS OF A BILLION ROTTED MOONS!
I AM THE SERPENT WHO EATS SUNS! AS OLD AS THE FIRST ECLIPSE!
AND YOU...YOU ARE JUST A CHILD...
A HUMAN WHO SWIMS LIKE A STAR-DAMNED QUARK SHARK! HOLD STILL, DAMN YOU!
YOU'RE WRONG! I DON'T SWIM LIKE A BIG DUMB QUARK SHARK!

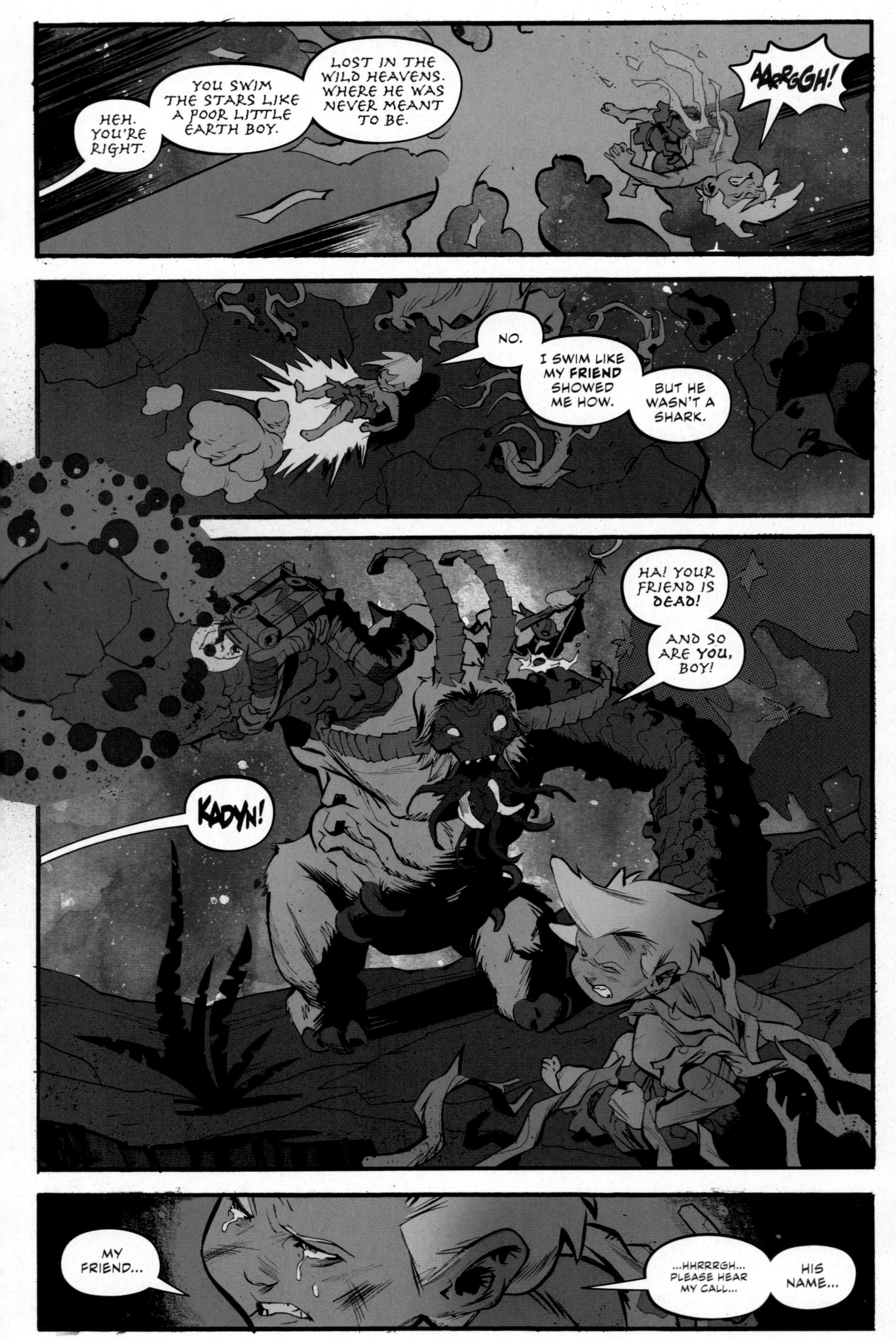
HEH. YOU'RE RIGHT.
YOU SWIM THE STARS LIKE A POOR LITTLE EARTH BOY.
LOST IN THE WILD HEAVENS. WHERE HE WAS NEVER MEANT TO BE.
AARRGGH!
NO.
I SWIM LIKE MY FRIEND SHOWED ME HOW.
BUT HE WASN'T A SHARK.
HA! YOUR FRIEND IS DEAD!
AND SO ARE YOU, BOY!
KADYN!
MY FRIEND...
...HHRRRGH... PLEASE HEAR MY CALL...
HIS NAME...

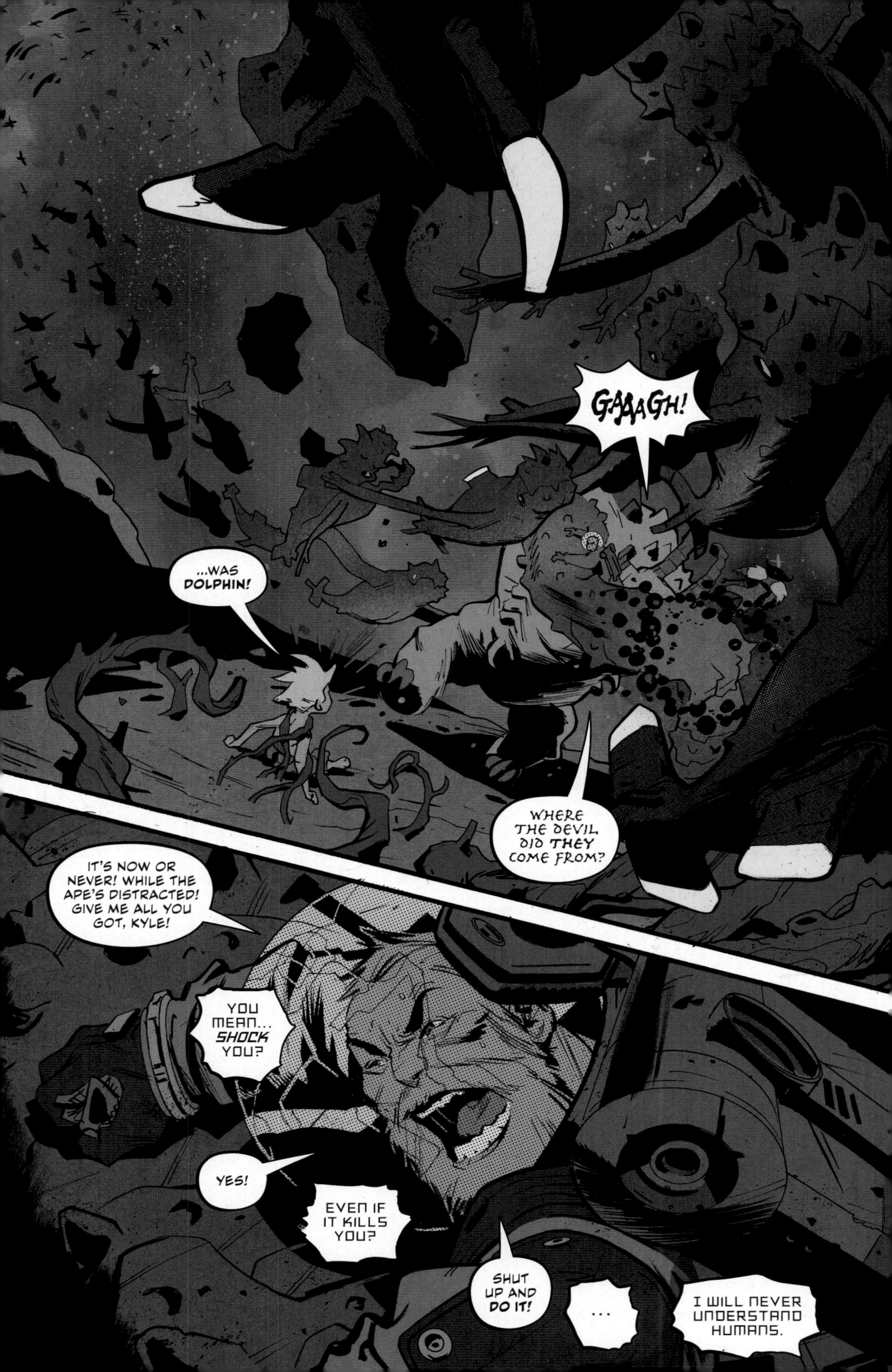
GAAAGH!
...WAS DOLPHIN!
WHERE THE DEVIL DID THEY COME FROM?
IT'S NOW OR NEVER! WHILE THE APE'S DISTRACTED! GIVE ME ALL YOU GOT, KYLE!
YOU MEAN... SHOCK YOU?
YES!
EVEN IF IT KILLS YOU?
SHUT UP AND DO IT!
...
I WILL NEVER UNDERSTAND HUMANS.

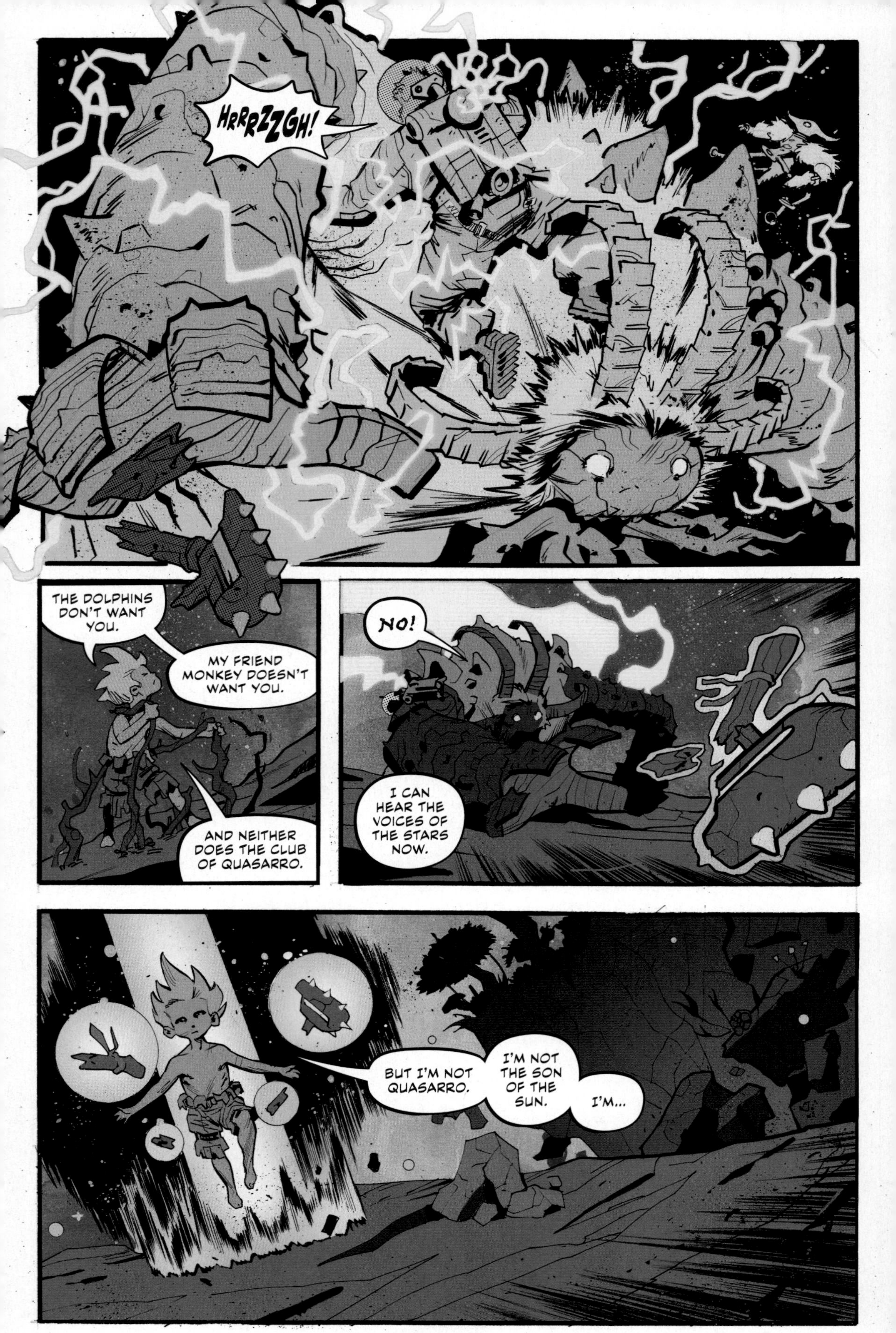
HRRRZZGH!
THE DOLPHINS DON'T WANT YOU.
MY FRIEND MONKEY DOESN'T WANT YOU.
AND NEITHER DOES THE CLUB OF QUASARRO.
NO!
I CAN HEAR THE VOICES OF THE STARS NOW.
BUT I'M NOT QUASARRO.
I'M NOT THE SON OF THE SUN.
I'M...

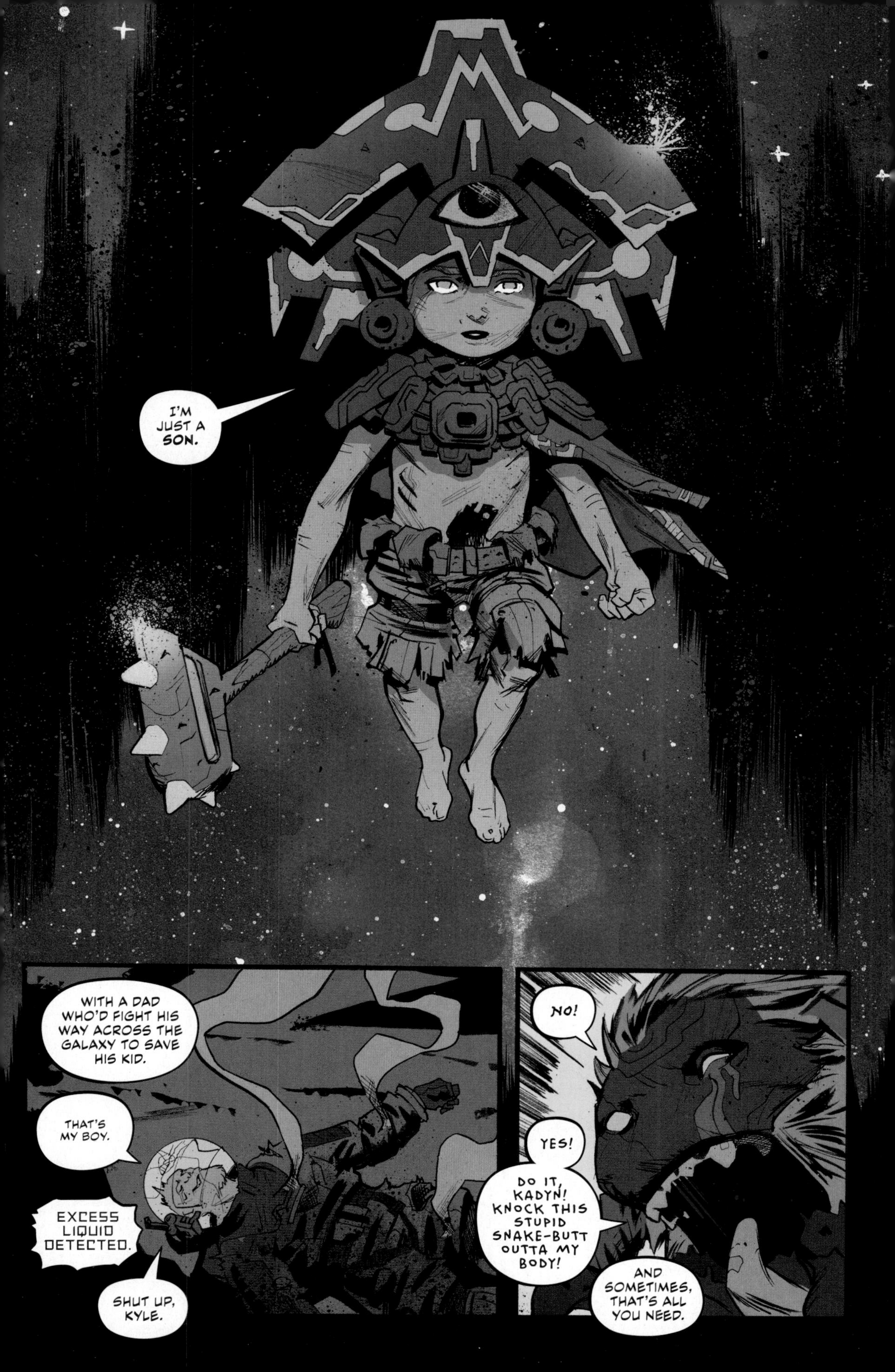
I'M JUST A SON.
WITH A DAD WHO'D FIGHT HIS WAY ACROSS THE GALAXY TO SAVE HIS KID.
THAT'S MY BOY.
EXCESS LIQUID DETECTED.
SHUT UP, KYLE.
NO!
YES!
DO IT, KADYN! KNOCK THIS STUPID SNAKE-BUTT OUTTA MY BODY!
AND SOMETIMES, THAT'S ALL YOU NEED.

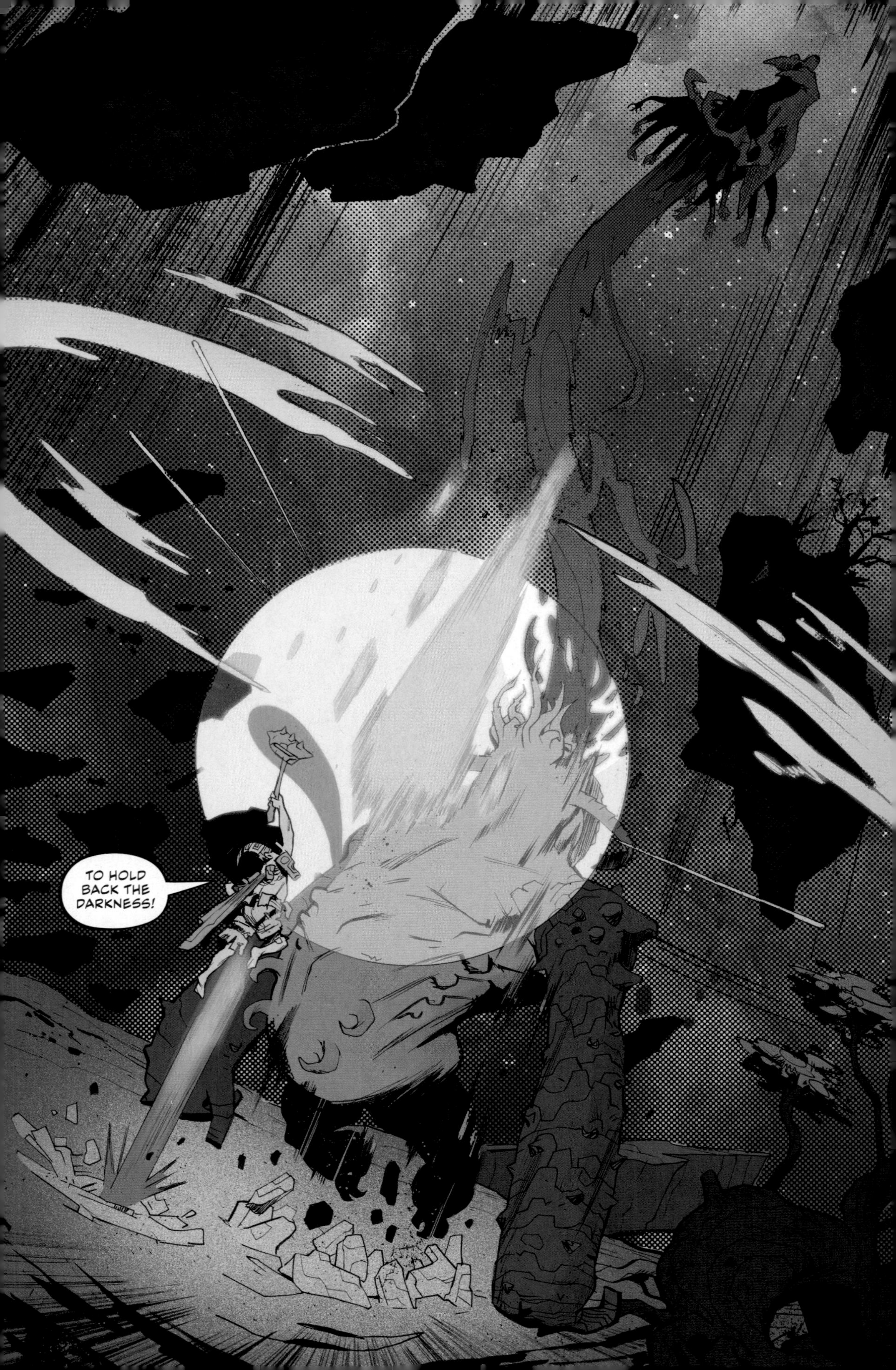
TO HOLD BACK THE DARKNESS!

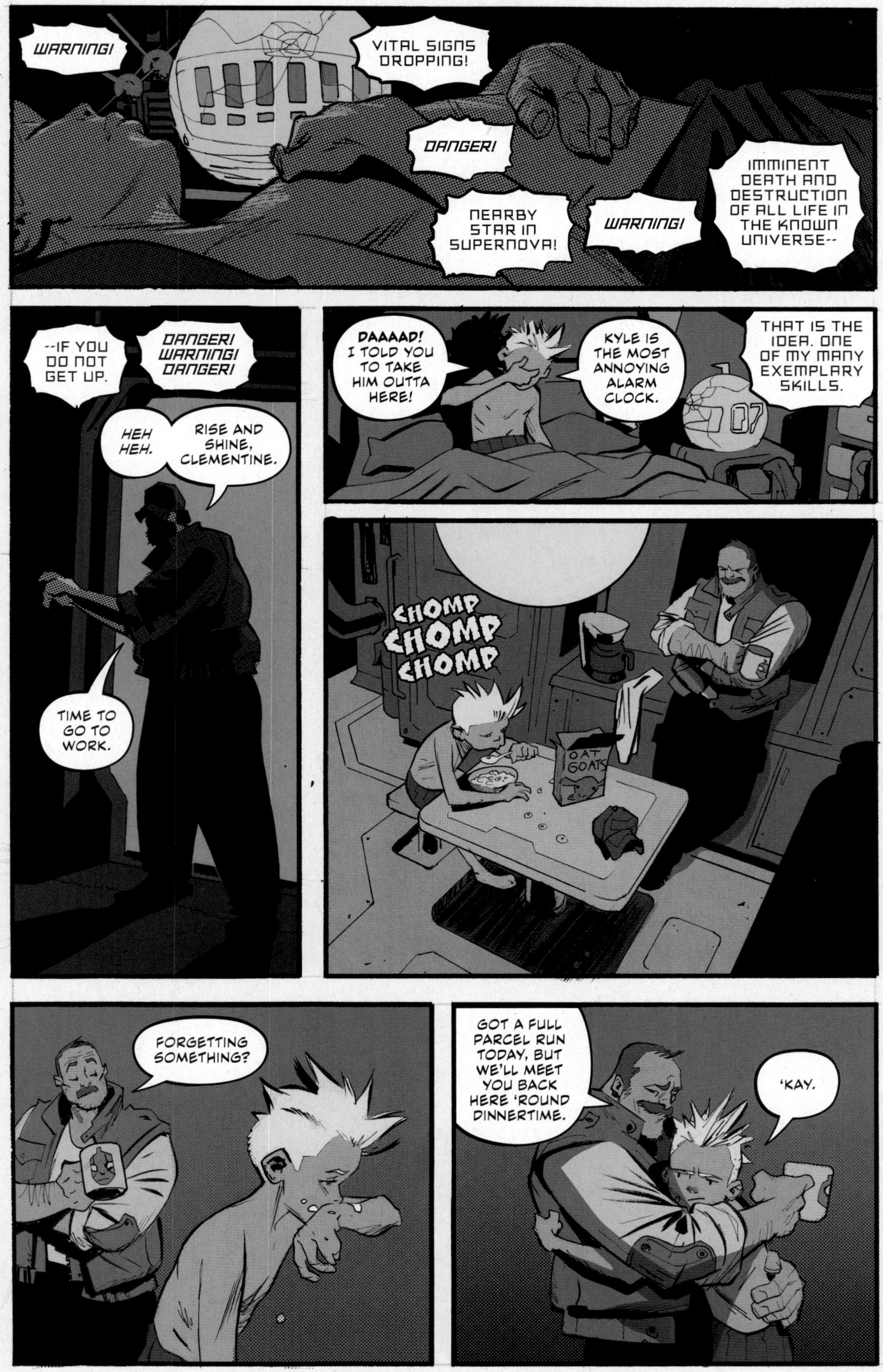
WARNING!
VITAL SIGNS DROPPING!
DANGER!
NEARBY STAR IN SUPERNOVA!
WARNING!
IMMINENT DEATH AND DESTRUCTION OF ALL LIFE IN THE KNOWN UNIVERSE--
--IF YOU DO NOT GET UP.
DANGER! WARNING! DANGER!
HEH HEH.
RISE AND SHINE, CLEMENTINE.
TIME TO GO TO WORK.
DAAAAD! I TOLD YOU TO TAKE HIM OUTTA HERE!
KYLE IS THE MOST ANNOYING ALARM CLOCK.
THAT IS THE IDEA. ONE OF MY MANY EXEMPLARY SKILLS.
07
CHOMP CHOMP CHOMP
OAT GOATS
FORGETTING SOMETHING?
GOT A FULL PARCEL RUN TODAY, BUT WE'LL MEET YOU BACK HERE 'ROUND DINNERTIME.
'KAY.

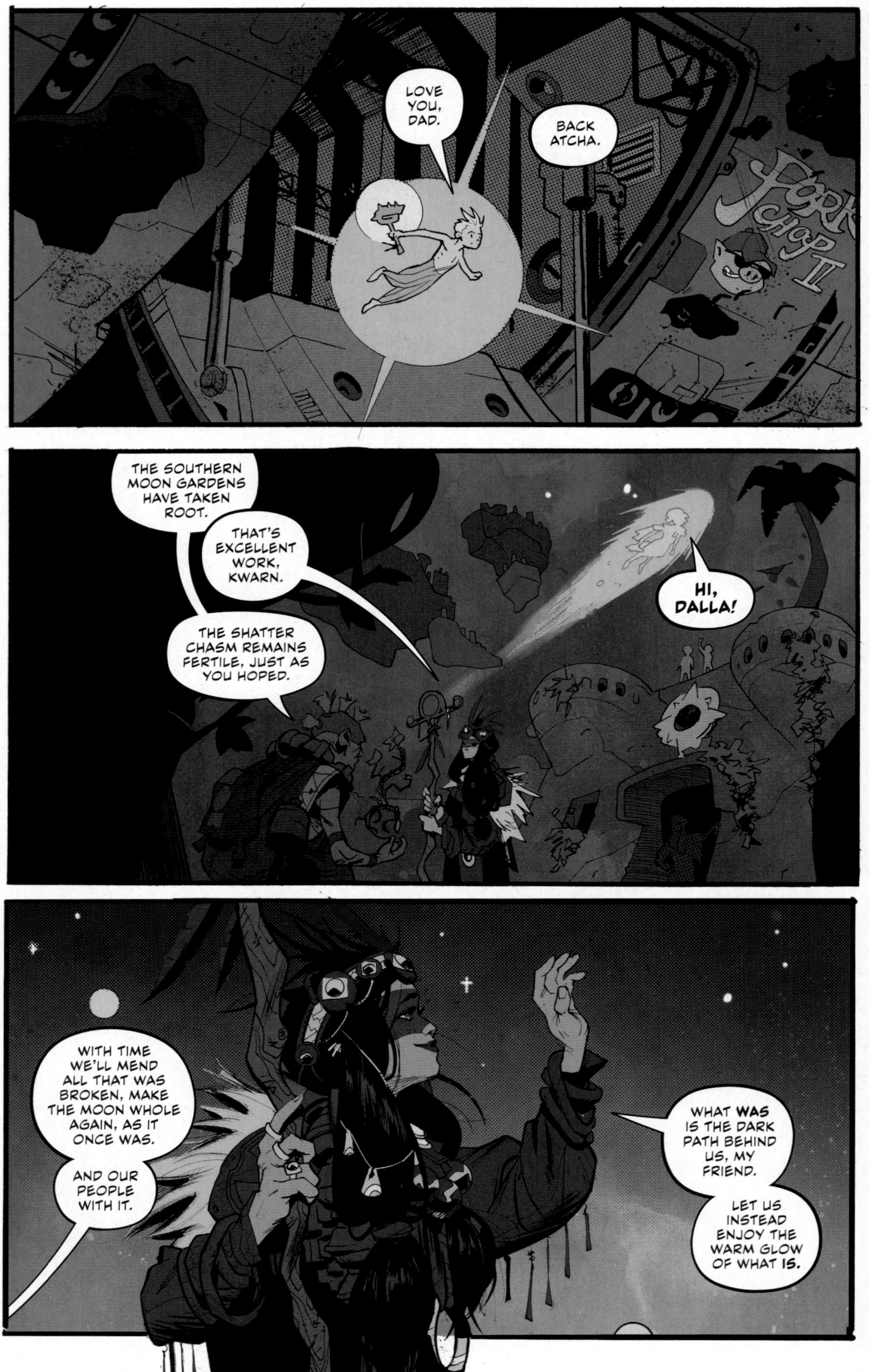
LOVE YOU, DAD.
BACK ATCHA.
PORK CHOP II
THE SOUTHERN MOON GARDENS HAVE TAKEN ROOT.
THAT'S EXCELLENT WORK, KWARN.
THE SHATTER CHASM REMAINS FERTILE, JUST AS YOU HOPED.
HI, DALLA!
WITH TIME WE'LL MEND ALL THAT WAS BROKEN, MAKE THE MOON WHOLE AGAIN, AS IT ONCE WAS.
AND OUR PEOPLE WITH IT.
WHAT WAS IS THE DARK PATH BEHIND US, MY FRIEND.
LET US INSTEAD ENJOY THE WARM GLOW OF WHAT IS.

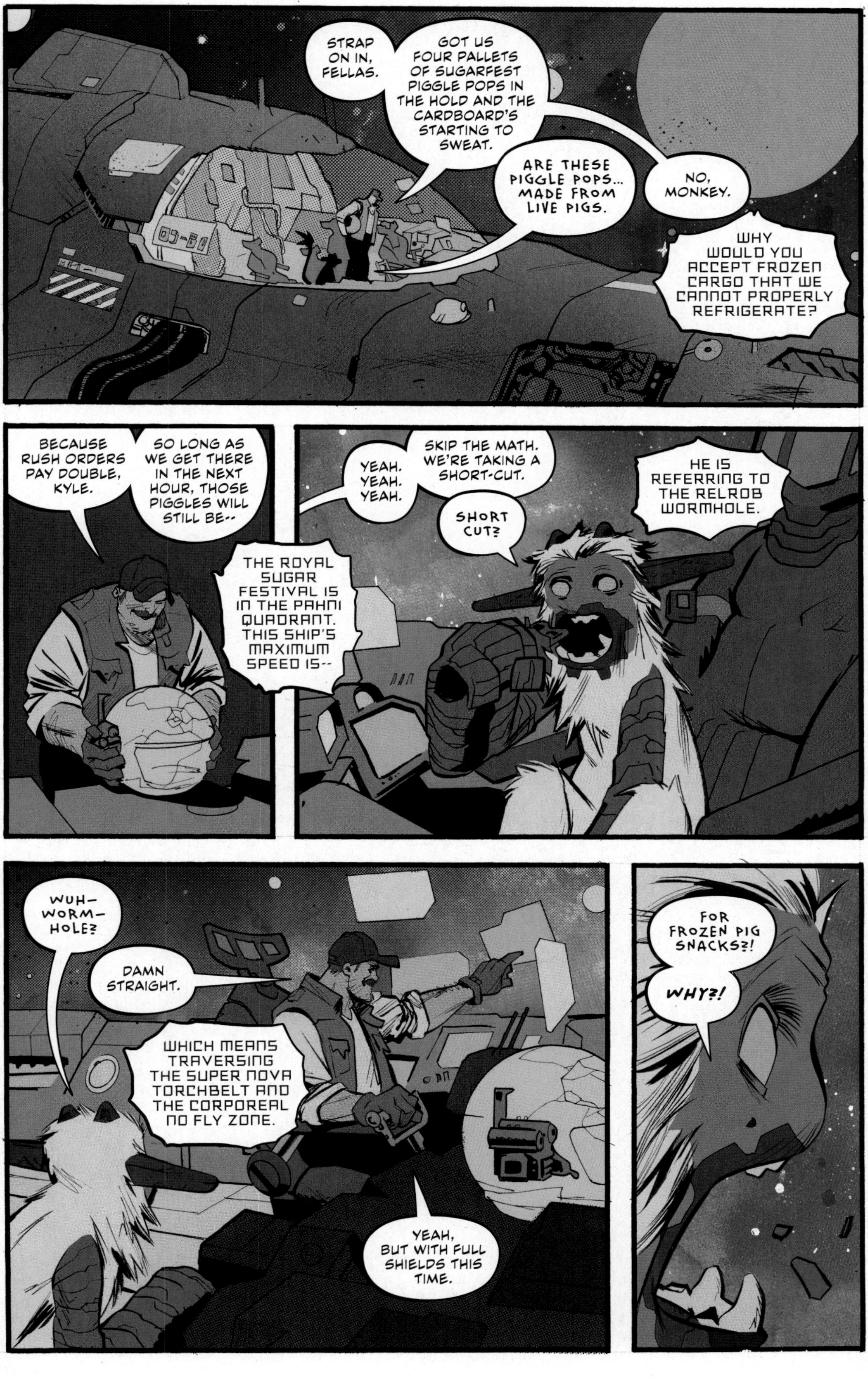

STRAP ON IN, FELLAS.
GOT US FOUR PALLETS OF SUGARFEST PIGGLE POPS IN THE HOLD AND THE CARDBOARD'S STARTING TO SWEAT.
ARE THESE PIGGLE POPS... MADE FROM LIVE PIGS.
NO, MONKEY.
WHY WOULD YOU ACCEPT FROZEN CARGO THAT WE CANNOT PROPERLY REFRIGERATE?
BECAUSE RUSH ORDERS PAY DOUBLE, KYLE.
SO LONG AS WE GET THERE IN THE NEXT HOUR, THOSE PIGGLES WILL STILL BE--
THE ROYAL SUGAR FESTIVAL IS IN THE PAHNI QUADRANT. THIS SHIP'S MAXIMUM SPEED IS--
YEAH. YEAH. YEAH.
SKIP THE MATH. WE'RE TAKING A SHORT-CUT.
SHORT CUT?
HE IS REFERRING TO THE RELROB WORMHOLE.
WUH-WORM-HOLE?
DAMN STRAIGHT.
WHICH MEANS TRAVERSING THE SUPER NOVA TORCHBELT AND THE CORPOREAL NO FLY ZONE.
YEAH, BUT WITH FULL SHIELDS THIS TIME.
FOR FROZEN PIG SNACKS?!
WHY?!

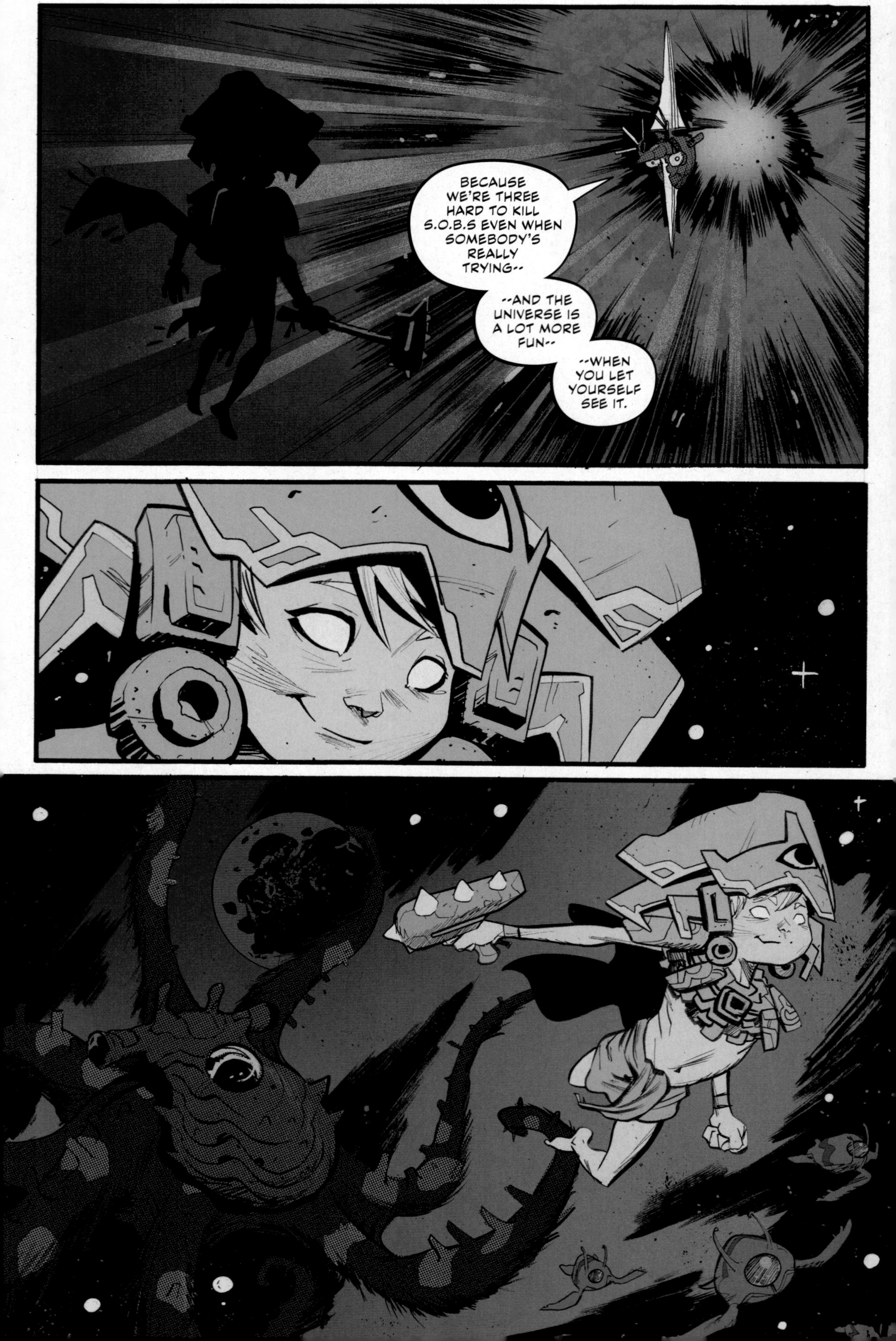
BECAUSE WE'RE THREE HARD TO KILL S.O.B.S EVEN WHEN SOMEBODY'S REALLY TRYING--
--AND THE UNIVERSE IS A LOT MORE FUN--
--WHEN YOU LET YOURSELF SEE IT.

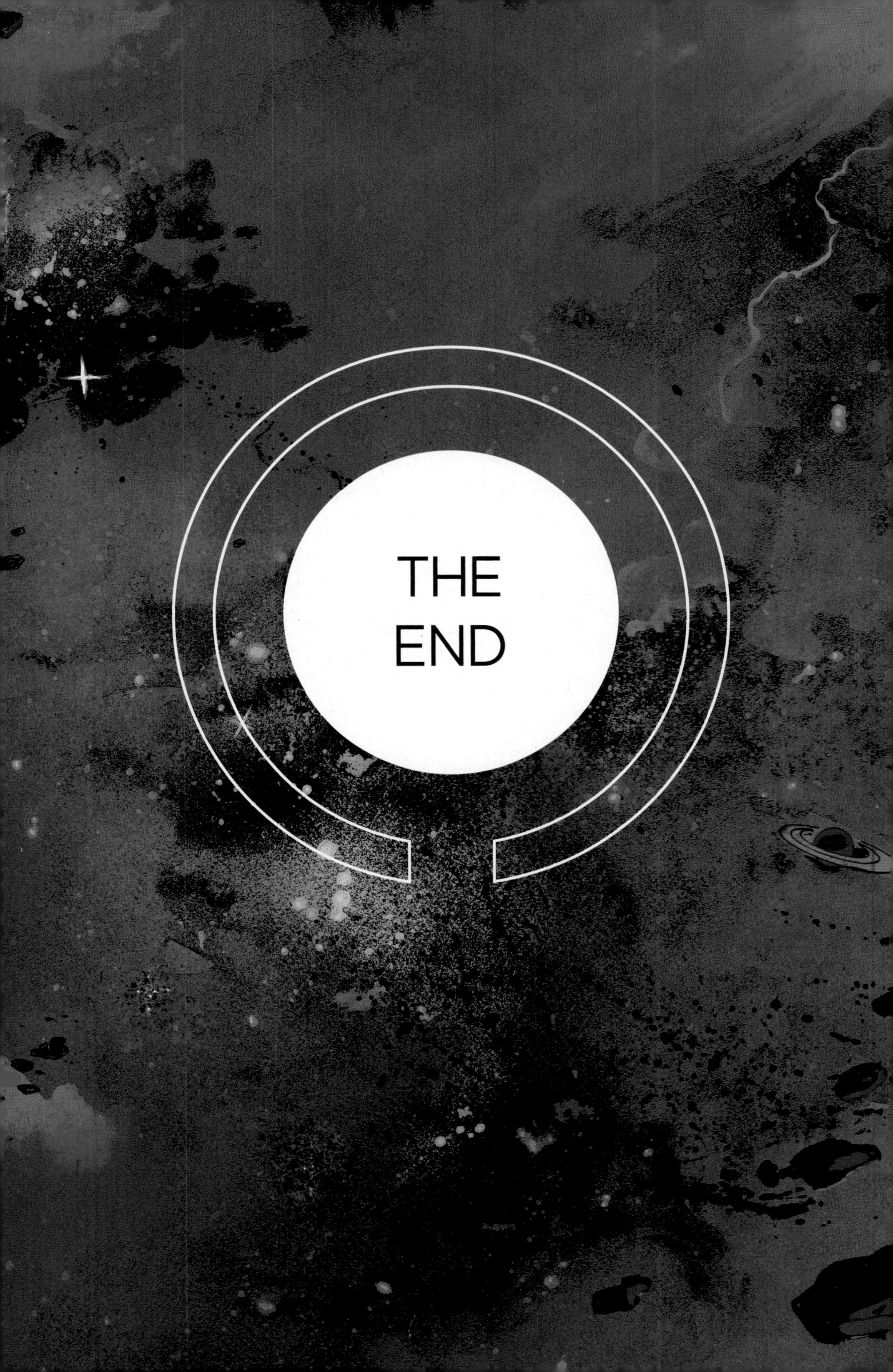
THE
END